John Campbell was born in 1936 in Belfast's York Street area. He worked at Belfast's docks until 1985. Now retired, he is still active in Trade Union activity for the Transport & General Workers' Union. He has published four collections of poetry: *Saturday Night in York Street* (1982), *An Oul Jobbin' Poet* (1989) and *Memories of York Street* (1991) and *The Rose and the Blade: New & Selected Poems 1957-1997* (1997). *Corner Kingdom* was published in 1999. A miscellany of his various writing, *Once There Was a Community Here*, appeared in 2001.

THE DISINHERITED

THE DISINHERITED

JOHN CAMPBELL

To broth Ross. Belfast Nov. '06

May Thanks for you kind words and encouragem

Best Wishes

Brother Campbell

LAGAN PRESS
BELFAST
2006

Published by
Lagan Press
1A Bryson Street
Belfast BT5 4ES
e-mail: lagan-press@e-books.org.uk
web: lagan-press.org.uk

ISBN: 1 904652 32 8

Author: Campbell, John
Title: The Disinherited
2006

Set in Palatino
Printed by J.H. Haynes & Co. Ltd., Sparkford

To the Spud Men

Bucko: who got me my very first check*
Davy: who trained me to carry a bag.
Joe: who encouraged a boy to talk back.
Hughie: who taught me to smuggle out swag.

John Nicholson's input was morally strong.
Old Whitey encouraged each poetic draft.
John Gilchrist: who often would burst into song.
Alec: whose clowning made certain we laughed.

Some are still living, whilst others are dead.
The ones that remain have been scattered.
The lessons they taught me remain in my head.
They said honour and principle mattered.

To each of these spud men I owe a great debt.
Some used their muscles, others their brain.
They carried a boy whilst his ears were still wet.
I'll never, in my life, see their likes again.

*job token

Acknowledgements

For many years Denis Smyth, a local historian and author, has encouraged me to write about the people of the Belfast dockside community from where we both came. He believed the story of the red-button section should be told and furnished me with some facts and figures for which I am very grateful.

While I began to think of this book as a project, I got in touch with Mr J.B. McCartney, who was a Queen's University lecturer on Industrial Law at the time of the dispute. He was more than willing to supply me with valuable information. After many telephone conversations, we arranged to meet in the Senior Common Room of Queen's with some other principle players, one being the much-loved Jackie Myers, a member of the Transport & General Workers' Union. For various reasons, the meeting never occurred and both men are now dead as are many of the first and second preference men and outsiders who gave me their side of the story.

After the publication of my first book of verse, *Saturday Night in York Street*, in 1982, I was contacted by a full-time officer of the T&G called Andy Holmes. He invited me to his home and gave me a taped interview of his first-hand knowledge of that tempestuous time on Belfast Docks. Andy was a dyed-in-the-wool socialist who fought hard for the members he represented, and remained involved with trade unionism until he died. George McKinley, a full-time T&G officer now retired, proved to be a good friend, answering questions and explaining the trade union procedures of the era concerned.

I would also like to thank my wife Barbara who takes care of the present and all its problems whilst I remain locked in the past and oblivious to anything else.

Although eighty-six years old, and registered blind, my old friend John Nicholson listened intently as I read the first draft of the story to him. His sharp mind and perceptive memory was invaluable as I worked my way to the finished article. Sadly, John died on 28th May 2006. His last input was to approve the dedication to the spud men. He and I had 'bit parts' in the real drama, as we were both employed on the Cross Channel section of the docks, as outsiders before, during and after this very stormy period. I watched it unfold, never dreaming that half-a-century later I would write a fictionalised account of these events.

To others who also helped but aren't mentioned, please accept my deepest gratitude.

John Campbell
June 2006

Foreword

In the previous novel called *Corner Kingdom*, teenager Jim Harvey is thrown into the slave auction atmosphere of Belfast Docks in the early 1950s, when he seeks work there after the sudden death of his father. On his first day, he is accidentally selected for a cement boat. The ganger is about to discharge him when the lad is befriended by an ex-World War II veteran called Billy Kelly who takes the boy under his wing. The reason for Kelly's interest in the boy's welfare is explained later in the story. The work is physically hard and dangerous and Jim's amateur boxing training helps him survive the first day, during which he witnesses a brutal attack on a winchman by Kelly.

At the end of the day's work, they visit a notorious public house where the young lad is molested sexually by a woman plying the oldest profession. He is later knocked down by the winchman, who is in turn brutally assaulted by Kelly. His first day on the quay ends with him being carried home drunk on Kelly's shoulder and deposited on the kitchen sofa whilst his weeping mother fears for his future.

His uncle Henry who commands a squad of potato carriers, all of whom are non-union family members, forces him from his bed the next morning. He and another uncle frogmarch Jim to the cement boat. Despite his heavy hangover he is able to finish the job. The laid-back Kelly continues to protect him, as the surly winchman waits his chance to take revenge.

As the days pass Jim learns of the pecking order on the quay and continues to get work because of his Uncle Henry's influence and his own willingness and ability. Kelly is a first-preference man, who has been stripped of his blue button for striking a ganger. His privileges will be returned if he apologises to the foreman concerned. This he is unwilling to do, much to the embarrassment of his father who is a founding member of the Dockers' union and a much loved and respected member of the branch committee.

The branch committee run their section of Belfast Docks with an iron fist. The blue-button men whom they represent are the sole arbiters of the rules and regulations. They have first preference on all work and negotiate local terms and conditions with the docks employers who are constrained by the closed shop approach, but can do nothing about it. The second group of workers are the red-button men who are employed after the first preference men. This section was set up in 1939 when the coming war created more sea traffic than the first preference section could handle. They reluctantly accepted the 250 extra men who were not subsumed into the Dockers' branch. They were members of the Transport and General Workers' Union, but had none of the privileges afforded to the first preference.

The closed shop syndrome enabled the Dockers' branch to recruit new first preference members from outside. These new intakes would be family members of the Dockers, and only those with blood links were accepted. When the branch opened for membership in 1948, most of the successful applicants were ex-service men. The intake included a reluctant Billy Kelly who was coaxed to leave the regiment of the Royal Ulster Rifles. He had achieved the rank of Warrant Officer and had planned to remain in the regiment, but bowed to his father's wishes to become a docker.

The only red-button men considered for the blue-button section were brothers, sons or nephews of first preference men. The non-family members of this section fumed at the perceived injustice and some threatened legal action to overturn the edict. Many others, including Jim's uncle Henry were against such moves, knowing the union branch was all-powerful and unforgiving.

Kelly continues to watch over the youngster and Jim survives the initial drawbacks to become a member of the third and unofficial group of workers. These are the casuals. They are non-union men who flood the quay to take whatever work was left when the other two sections were employed.

The casuals accept the pecking order without rancour and also the abuse and ridicule that came from some of the registered Dockers and red-button men who see them as scavengers. Many are highly skilled dockworkers who only survive because of their outstanding ability. The gangers are under no obligation to hire them and don't unless they are more than capable.

A further complication is the fact that men in permanent jobs holding trade union membership could attend the schooling pen on Saturdays and holiday periods and demand jobs in front of the time served casuals. This often caused friction in the local bars and added to the problems of the publicans who tried to keep the warring factions apart.

Young Harvey graduates to the potato gang run by his Uncle Henry and much to his mother's consternation, begins to drink heavily. Although technically underage, the barmen who serve him feel if he is old enough to order a drink, he is old enough to get what he asked for. He is occasionally sent back to the schooling pen by his uncle to learn to handle all kinds of cargo. The money he earns is split equally between the potato gang. Henry pays him a set wage which is way below the money his hard work earns. His showdown with his uncle leaves him in no doubt as to who is the boss.

Meanwhile, Kelly's troubled existence causes problems with his father. Kelly hates the inequality of the system and regrets leaving the army. His wartime experiences cause unpredictable and violent mood changes that bring him to the attention of the district's Head Constable, a formidable Scotsman who keeps a tight rein on the unruly elements that live on his patch. He also meets a young girl called Minnie, a tobacco factory employee, who is immediately attracted to him. This causes problems as Minnie's father is a first preference docker and a friend of the ganger Kelly assaulted.

The wayward docker has other problems, including a deserted wife and son somewhere in England. Meanwhile a hard man from the east of the city is making life hard for the casuals and Kelly and they eventually clash in a brutal fight that erupts in Pat's Bar and continues into the street.

Another intake of first preference men in 1955 causes much resentment and the reds decide to go for legal advice. This throws them into violent confrontation with the leadership of the Dockers' Branch, causing an explosive situation that fragments on the entire dockside population. It also causes friction among the full-time officers of the T&GWU in Belfast.

Kelly's problems are further complicated when it turns out that the last surviving member of his wartime platoon is the leader of the red-button revolt. He is torn between his loyalty to his father and the man with whom he shared many dangerous wartime missions behind enemy lines.

The Disinherited is a fictionalised account of that power struggle—on the docks, in the streets and pubs of Sailortown, right through to the grander arenas of Stormont and the Northern Irish High Court—which changed forever the face of the cross-channel section of Belfast Dock.

John Campbell
November 2005

One

JIM HARVEY DIDN'T KNOW WHAT HE heard first: his mother's long, horrified scream or the loud mewling of the cat. He opened his eyes quickly and studied his surroundings. His concentration was broken as he saw a shiny black object perched on the bridge of his nose. Feelers from its head brushed across his eyelids as its many legs continued to walk slowly, tentatively, up his face. With a terrified shout he tried to raise his arm to brush the large insect away. He found he couldn't move arm, hand or body. His mother stopped screaming and rushed to where he lay on the kitchen floor and began brushing away with her bare hands the insects that almost covered his body.

His muddled brain struggled to adjust to the situation as his mother also stamped on the cockroaches that covered the kitchen floor like a glistening black moving carpet. The cat's yammering continued at a loud monotonous tone, like a gramophone record being played at too fast a speed. He could hear it scratching frantically, and imagined its razor-sharp claws cutting slivers of wood from the backyard door.

He tried to speak, but could only croak in a cracked but desperate drink-sodden voice: "Let the cat in, ma! Let the cat in!"

He tried again to rise from the floor and managed with a superhuman effort to raise himself onto one elbow. He forced his arm to move and his hand lifted one of his heavy working boots from beneath the settee. He shook out the insects he knew would be nestling in it. Grabbing the toe of the boot, he lashed out at the cockroaches scurrying in every direction.

Grinning gratefully, he watched the cat spring through the open door to immediately attack the insects. He heard the crack of their shells as the cat impaled them on its claws and tore them apart with its teeth. With another effort that almost caused him to fall down again, he rose to his knees and stretched his arm to crush with the heel of the boot those that were still within his reach. His mother pulled her nightdress tightly around her legs, lifted the coal shovel and engaged in the mass slaughter. The cat continued with great enthusiasm: leaping, stretching, and bounding into the air with the grace and finesse of a ballet dancer; its claws outstretched and its mouth full of wriggling insects.

A few moments later only the dead remained as the others managed to scurry through the numerous openings in the skirting board and under the tiled fireplace or beneath the door of the coal hole.

His mother sat heavily down on her rocking chair, as Jim heaved himself to his feet and rubbed his aching head.

"Bloody clocks. I hate them," he fumed, brushing his shirt and trousers with his hands before running them through his long lank brown hair.

"I almost fainted when I turned on the light and saw yew lyin' there on the floor. They were on yer face an' in yer hair. Ya shoulda went till bed when I tole yew to. An' what happened till Tibs? How did he git locked in the yard? Shure them things cuda got down yer throat and choked ya," she said, her voice breaking into a sob.

She rose and reached for the floor brush and began to brush the dead cockroaches onto the shovel. Some were smashed into pulp, the white creamy innards meshed with the hard shiny shell that cracked when they were stepped on, or crushed. Others were on their backs still alive, but helpless, with their many legs and feelers clawing frantically in the last throes of life. Tibs lay down in front of the softly glowing Sofona fire that was now ready for another shovelful of coal. The fire brightened and spluttered and flamed as Mrs. Harvey threw the shovel's contents onto the glowing ashes. Tibs licked his lips and proceeded to curl up before closing his eyes with a satisfied purr.

"How did the cat git locked out? I made sure he was in the house when I saw ye were in no state till get yerself till bed."

"I went out till the toilet about midnight. He musta followed me an' I closed the dour on him," Jim replied sheepishly. He knew she was growing concerned about his drinking and sought to reassure her.

"I'll go till bed in the future, ma," he shuddered as he remembered the loathsome creature perched on his nose. "I threw DDT all over the place and spread it aroun' the hearth."

His mother sniffed with the air of an old campaigner. "Clocks are immune till that stuff. There must be millions of thim behin' that grate. Yer da always blamed it on the blitz. He said the boms that hit the Street in nineteen forty one caused cracks in the cement foundations below the houses and allowed the creepy crawlies till come up from the mud banks below. Myself, I blame that bakery next door. But no matter: they're a fixture in the house an' we'll have till learn till live with them."

"Like the mice," added Jim sombrely, looking around him for his socks.

Mrs. Harvey rose and walked into the scullery. "Aye," she agreed with an exaggerated shiver as she lifted the frying pan, trying not to look at the tiny footprints embedded in the thick coating of lard. She lit the gas and tramped on the solitary cockroach that fell to the floor as it scurried from beneath the flaming gas ring. When the lard began to bubble under the heat she lifted the pan and emptied its contents down the sink. Taking a dishcloth, she wiped the pan clean and put it below the hot running water that spluttered from the gas geyser above the sink.

"Do ye want a wee fry till warm ye up?"

Jim groaned. His throat was dry and all he wanted was some liquid to pour down it. He also knew he needed something substantial to get him through the day.

"Aye, ma. I'm with Uncle Henry the day. He says he'll need me for the rest of the week." He took the card table from behind the sofa and assembled it in front of the fire. His mother grimaced at the mention of her brother's name.

He was finishing his breakfast when he heard someone on the stairs and banging each step on the way down.

"Lizzie's comin', ma!"

The door handle rattled and his sister walked into the bright light.

"No need till wreck the place," he laughed. "The war's over. Me an' mi ma has the place cleared."

Lizzie walked warily into the room staring intently at the floor, holding the hem of her nightdress up around her knees, as she navigated the shiny orange-coloured oilcloth towards the scullery. She pulled the curtain behind her and checked the geyser.

A heavy battering on the front door made Jim shiver. It could only be Uncle Henry at this time of the morning, and that meant a change of plans, and that made him uneasy. He rose wearily and opened the door. Henry barged in past him as if he were invisible and walked straight into the scullery, doing a quick about-turn at Lizzie's indignant scream. He sat heavily on the settee and bellowed, "Bring us in a cuppa tea, Aggie."

He turned his attention to his nephew.

"'Uncle' has a beg-boat this mornin'. Instead a comin' wi me, ye kin stan' that. He'll give ye a lie on, if there's nat too many second preference there." He put down the untouched tea and started for the door. "Don't be late," he shouted over his shoulder.

Jim found his voice. "I've niver worked at a beg boat before."

"Weren't ye at the cement? If yew kin work there, yill be alright," answered Henry. The front door slammed and he was gone. Lizzie popped her indignant face around the curtain. "Why do ye let that big shite talk till ye like that?"

"He's the boss," said Jim lamely.

Lizzie ignored her mother's sharp gasp of shock at her language.

"I've gat bosses in Gallahers an' well dare any of thim speak to me like that. Do yew know what his problem is? He thinks he's King of the castle, an' the rest of yis are his slaves. Yis wanta wise up," she added almost sadly as she returned to the scullery. She popped her head out again a few seconds later.

"I bet he doesn't talk till Uncle Sam like that. He'd lutter him," she added triumphantly.

"Henry musta cum back from Liverpool yesterday," said her mother.

"Aye. Wonder what caused him till cum back early?" Jim added thoughtfully

His mother began to sob.

"Jim, I don't want yew on the Docks. I toul yew a hunnert times, there's too much drinkin' an' fightin' an' womanisin'. I know the money's good when ye kin get it. But there's too much time for drinkin' on strap when there is no work. I'd rather yew got a job in the mill or even Gallahers. There wudn't be as much money, but yid be workin' wi civilised people who don't think it's part of life to git drunk every night. If yer da had lived, he wud have had yew in the shipyard serving an apprenticeship. Yid have niver been mixed up wid Henry."

She fumbled with her handkerchief and sobbed into it. Lizzie came from the scullery and cuddled her affectionately. The mention of her father had brought tears to her eyes. She looked sternly at her only brother, a mixture of love and hate in her eyes.

"Yer breakin' her heart. I hope yew know that," she said softly but bitterly.

Jim rose without answering. He walked into the scullery and pulled the curtain behind him. Switching on the geyser, he took off his shirt and Simmit and scrubbed his face and body vigorously, concentrating on the area of his face where he could still see the shiny black cockroach perched on the end of his nose. He attacked the spot with a shudder before splashing it with cold water from the tap. Dressing quickly, he lifted his cap and coat from behind the kitchen door. He looked briefly at his mother and sister huddled together on the settee, before leaving.

He hadn't expected Henry back from Liverpool so quickly. He'd been happy working in the Spencer Dock with the Potato Squad. He was learning quickly how to build the sacks of potatoes into orderly tiers. A layer as thick as parchment had, as Henry predicted, replaced the torment of broken skin on his back.

He trudged wearily down Earl Street and into Garmoyle

Street. Jumping onto a horse-drawn four-wheeled cart that was heading towards the schooling pen, he looked down absently at the square setts moving below him. The carter nodded civilly at him when he dropped him off at Sinclair Seaman's church. Men were walking in the direction of the open-air schooling pen at the bottom of Great George's Street, and he followed. He stopped with Bucky the newspaper seller and asked for a *Daily Mirror*. Bucky eyed him appraisingly as he reached him the daily and threw the coins into a satchel.

"Still here an' in one piece. Yer doin' well kid."

Jim knew he was being complimented. He smiled at the grey-haired paper seller who grinned in return.

"Long way till go yit, Bucky," he said before moving in the direction of Uncle's line-up.

He stood self-consciously in the outer circle, trying hard not to look at the pinch-faced men beside him. He lowered his eyes to the cobbles as the ganger known as Uncle stared expressionlessly into the sea of faces before him. Hearing his name being called, he raised his eyes and saw Reilly waving to him. The little trucker moved through the crowd.

"Thought yew were dug in at the spuds?"

"Naw. Henry paid me off. Said there wasn't enuff werk for all of us," Jim lied.

"Yah," replied Reilly sympathetically. "I hope yew know what yer lettin' yerself in for. The cement's ruff, but this is a murder picture."

"What is it?" asked Jim nervously, feeling the pangs of fear rise in his stomach.

"Begs as dead as Maggie Wilson's first husband an' jist as awkward. Each one weighs two hundredweight and they're filled wid chemical powder that wud strip the paint off a hen-house. If yew git a check, stick to me. I don't like the luk of any of these hallions," he continued in a voice of doom that almost caused the youth to leave the school.

The harbour office clock interrupted his words as it chimed eight times. Uncle fixed his eyes on the men around him. He nodded silently to two first-preference men.

"Winch, Bobby; you, bullrope, Cedric."

The men watched as the only other first-preference man made off to another school.

"Houlsmen," said Uncle tonelessly, "I want six houlsmen."

Jim watched as a second-preference man strode purposefully forward and put his hand out. The crowd stiffened as Uncle ignored him and reached around him to put the check in the hand of a surprised non-union man.

The other second-preference men growled angrily as the ganger continued to school around them. The man who'd stepped forward tried to intercept a check and was pushed roughly aside by the grim-faced ganger.

"Fuck off," he snarled, "and take the rest of them ungrateful mouthpieces wid you."

"Yew can't do that," shouted another man as he moved forward.

Uncle stopped in mid-stride. He glared contemptuously at the second-preference button in the man's lapel.

"I kin do whatever the fuck I want! Nigh go an' tell that till yer friends in the *Belfast Telegraph*. Tell thim I don't have any werk for slabbers and informers. Maybe they'll give yew a job sellin' papers. I hope they do 'cause yiv got yer last fuckin' job on the quay as far as I'm concerned." His voice rose. "Nigh, fuck off, or I'll gie ye a lutter in the gub! I've gat a boat till school."

The two men stepped back, ashen-faced, as Uncle selected the remaining holdsmen. They could only watch as he continued to give checks to grinning non-union men.

"That's it," he growled, handing the last check to Jim Harvey. "Reilly. Snodden, Goodall—git the trucks and gear from the store in Nelson Street and git down there as quick as yis can. Don't fergit the can-hooks," he added before jumping into the back seat of the stevedore's car.

All over the pen the same thing was happening. Angry red-button men converged on a first-preference committeeman and almost bowled him over.

"What's happenin', Dickie?" cried one man in his early sixties. "What have we done?"

The union representative turned haughtily away.

"Yis'll havta take it up wie the branch," Jim heard him say before Reilly quickly grabbed his arm.

"C'mon kid. Let thim fight it out. We've work till do."

They had crossed over Garmoyle Street and were walking towards the stevedore's yard when Jim broke the silence.

"What happened back there?" he muttered to Reilly. "Shure the reds always git in fronta us."

The other men laughed as Reilly rubbed his hands together and exploded into giggles of delight.

"Nat anymore kid," he chortled. "Them guys is history, an' none of us is gonna weep at their departure." He broke off to get between the shafts of a truck with ropes and canvas sheets tied to its base.

Jim continued with the persistence of a child badgering a grown-up, as they moved from the store into Nelson Street.

"Does that mean we'll git jobs in fronta thim?"

Reilly continued to chuckle.

"Some of them daft bastards were stupid enuff till write till the head man in the transport union till complain about the new intake a blues. The lame an' the blind 'ill git jobs in fronta them nigh. They're finished on the quay. Beaten dockets, the lot of them."

The lad took a nervous breath.

"Does that include Uncle Henry?" he asked quietly.

Reilly heard the question above the racket made by the three trucks as he and his companions pulled them across the square-setts in Dock Street. He stopped laughing.

"Aye," he said without any joy in his voice.

Uncle addressed the men as they arrived at the boat to be unloaded. The sailors had already stripped the hatch covers and hatch boards.

"Some of yis are men who I've niver schooled before, an' yis probably wudn't a gat a job if them bastards hadn't gat above themselves an forgot who's good till them. The *Belfast Telegraph* 'ill nat give a fuck if they can't feed their childer next week, but that's nat my problem. My problem is gittin' this boat emptied as quickly as possible. Some of yis 'ill be sorry yis stepped forward for a check before this is over an' it'll probably be the hardest dough yis have ever earned, but if yis pull me out, yis 'ill be in my permanent gang from nigh on. Nigh, I want youse experienced men till split up and take any greenhorns under yer wing. The derrick's topped an' we're ready till start . By the way, the cargo has a chemical name that's unpronounceable. We call it the rosy snatter boat. Yis 'ill find out why in an hour or two. Nigh git till it an' make me proud of yis."

He was somewhat perplexed when he saw most of his regular holdsmen were absent. The second-preference men had followed him for many years. Now he'd left them in the schooling pen. He glared at the two first-preference men.

"Git aboard an' git the winch running, Bobby."

He lifted a clamp from one of the trucks and threw it on the steel deck where it bounced a few times before resting at the feet of the bullrope man.

"Secure that onto the hatch coamin', Cedric. Git one a the deck hands till give ye a fid or a marlin spike till tighten it so it can take the strain. I don't want it flyin' free and takin' the head off a houlsman. Check out them guy ropes and make sure the men work inta the shore side till we git a list on her that'll make the heaves hit the quay faster."

Both nodded mute obedience.

For a moment Uncle felt a pang of guilt. He missed Bacon Neck, his regular winchdriver. This was the first time he'd left him in over fifteen years. He wasn't even aware if Bacon Neck was in on the conspiracy, but he'd been told to school only first preference and non-preference, and obeyed the order. He looked over the rest of the men.

"Anybody who kin sling git down intil the bowels. An' I said *sling*, not *sing*! The rest of yis git mated and git them trucks movin'."

He thrust his hands into his navy blue duffel coat and went aboard the ship.

"Hey Steerman, where's the galley? I could do wid a cupa coffee. I'd love it if ya laced it wid a wee drap a rum."

Reilly stuck close to Jim Harvey, and searched the gang for a man to make up the trio and complete the shore team. He introduced Jim to a heavy-set man with a red face and middle-aged spread.

"This is Billy McConkey; he's gonna mate wid us."

The look on his face said he wasn't entirely overjoyed with the choice.

The ship was low in the water and the shore gang was able to watch from the edge of the quay as the six men in the ship's hold began to wrestle the ungainly sacks into the roped slings.

Reilly briefed Jim in a low rasping voice: "They're two hunnertweight bags kid. They'll sling six till a rope. Yew know the score: same as the cement boat. Yew an' Billy 'ill steady the heave an' I'll make sure it's far enuff up the truck. Let me decide when till lower. Okay?"

They nodded in silent agreement.

The first heave was hoisted about ten feet into the air and promptly fell out of the rope sling causing the men below it to run for cover. Uncle, who'd been watching from the bridge of the ship, ran out onto the deck.

"Tighten that bight wid the jammer an' make sure the heave's secure before yew hook on!"

One of the other set of slingers grabbed the lowered hook and threw off the empty sling. He pulled it to his mate who hooked the end of the sling holding their heave onto it. Under Uncle's eye he lifted a short wooden club that resembled a baseball bat. When the winch driver took the strain on the sling, the holdsman hit the rope sling two solid thumps, tightening the grip of the rope around the bags, lessening the chance of the sacks falling out. The winch man dragged it to the centre of the hatch and in the process knocked over another heave. Uncle squealed in frustration and the men who had built the heave scowled as they stooped to rebuild it.

Reilly tucked a small black stone into the corner of his mouth and moved forward with the truck.

"Don't fergit. Only hook off when I say. Git it right on the first swing an' it'll be OK," he muttered through dried lips.

They watched as the heave swung towards them. Six bags,

in a three-two-one formation, hovered over the truck. Jim strained to keep his side in line with the base of the truck. Reilly grabbed hold of the front of it and screamed, "Lower!"

The heave landed with a thud. Jim hooked off as Billy grabbed the bight and tucked the end of the rope between the bags. Reilly lifted the shafts.

"Nigh!"

The men at each side of the truck grabbed hold of a sack corner and pulled with all their might. The truck lurched forward and into the shed as another rolled into its place.

The ground was level and the truck glided swiftly along the concrete.

"Head toward Ballyclare!" yelled Reilly.

Jim lifted his head in puzzlement.

"What directions that?"

"Ballyclare Johnston. That fella stannin' at the back at the shed. That's where the pile 'ill start."

Reaching the man, the trucker spun the truck and the two men at the back quickly threw off the rope and grabbed at the ends of the bag on the top.

"Don't try till lift it boy! Roll it," growled his companion curtly. "It's too heavy till lift from the top."

Jim grabbed the back of the top bag and pulled it forward. They lifted it cleanly and dropped it to the floor at Ballyclare's feet.

"Five high boys," he shouted. "An' try an' keep the rows straight. I don't want it lukin' like a dog's hind leg."

He was a dapper little man wearing a cloth cap and a suit. He had a small moustache, reminding Jim of his Uncle Henry. A notebook protruded from his jacket pocket and a pencil rested behind his right ear. They lifted the second bag and placed it on top of the first.

"Roll!" grunted Billy.

Jim obeyed. The fifth bag was a little awkward as Jim's end went up before Billy's. The last bag thudded to the floor and Reilly was off and away. The second truck came into view with its heave partly hanging off. Some few feet later, despite the efforts of the truck's crew, the heave rolled off and overturned the truck in the process. Reilly grimaced. It was going to be worse than he thought.

Henry entered the front door of the Unionist Hall in North Thomas Street. Two men stood at the bottom of the stairs, checking the credentials of those who entered.

"They're all in the billiard room, Henry."

Henry looked squarely at the man who was wearing a suit and tie.

"What's this all about, Tommy?"

"Yill git the message up there. We're waitin' on a union man till come an' talk till us."

Henry knew more than he was admitting to. He had cut short his trip to Liverpool after receiving a call from the stevedore he worked for. He was the only preference man of any description in the potato squad he was in charge of and had left the rest of the men who were casuals to continue working whilst he attended the hastily called meeting.

The room was packed with second-preference men. Some sat on the billiard tables whilst others stood in groups. The air was thick with smoke and anger.

A number of men sat around a table under one of the many large windows that looked out onto York Street. Henry pursed his lips.

"The secret seven," he muttered under his breath, loud enough for one man to hear.

"Nat secret anymore," he snarled indignantly. "That's why we're all out on our arses."

He walked away shaking his head.

"We're finished," he added lamely.

Henry studied the men seated around the table. He knew all of them. Five were checkers and two were constant men at the Heysham boat. All were employed on an everyday basis and didn't go to the schooling pen. Each man had a worried look on his features and they were talking nervously amongst themselves. He found a chair close to the coal fire and sat down to await the arrival of the union representative.

One of the men Henry had passed at the door entered the room and rushed to the men at the table. The man at the centre of the table rose and waved for attention and silence. Henry knew him as Sammy Wilson.

"The union rep's at the bottom of the stairs. We're movin' among yis, because we don't want thim to know we've bin workin' as a committee. Regardless of what he says we're gonna proceed wid the legal case." He paused briefly. "If we kin find two men willin' till be named in a test case."

They dispersed from the table and joined the crowd when a shout from the doorway told them the union man was entering the room.

He was well-dressed with a thin and angular body that stooped slightly at the waist giving him the look of a man who suffered back pain. He wore a cloth cap and a blue striped suit with a white shirt and a dark tie. No one stepped forward to greet him and he stood for a moment before starting to speak in a nervous voice.

"Can't hear ye!" shouted a man from the back of the room.

"Can't see ye!" yelled another.

The union man looked around in a moment of baffled silence before climbing onto a seat beneath a window. He observed the sea of hostile faces and studied them for a moment or two as if uncertain of what to say. He cleared his throat.

"My name is Todd Hamill, Brother Hamill. I'm the full-time district official for workers at Rank's flour mill."

"What are ya doin' here then?" came a sarcastic voice from the back.

He grinned nervously.

"That's a good question. Apparently most of you men carry Miller's Branch union cards. That means I represent you. I've been sent here by the union to hear your grievance, although I'm not quite sure why, as you don't work in the milling trade."

"Maybe I can explain that, Brother," came a voice from the rear of the hall.

Henry craned his neck and gulped when he saw William Shaw, the full-time representative of the first-preference men. Six heavily built men pushed a path through the crowd until he was in the centre of the room. They formed a protective circle around him as he stood on a chair and then climbed onto the table vacated by the secret seven. His fleshy face was expressionless, but the anger in his eyes was raw and unmistakable. He looked over at his colleague standing forlornly on the chair.

"I'll tell yew who yer talkin' to, Brother; yer talkin' to a mob of ungrateful, yella livered bastards who haven't the balls to bring their argument to where it belongs."

He eyed the men in front of him with undisguised scorn.

"Who the fuck do yew think yis are? Yis are nat Dockers. I'm a Docker."

He pointed at the men surrounding him.

"They're Dockers. Youse guys are just the back up line brought in by the stevedores to make sure they don't have till pay mooring rates if a boat lies overnight. Yis aren't Dockers," he thundered, "an' yis niver will be! Nat while my arse looks down!"

Henry gazed at the ashen-faced crowd. Not a man had heckled or spoken during the heated outburst. They were undecided, unable to function without a cue from those leaders who had momentarily deserted them.

Shaw continued, as the other representative stood on his chair looking bewildered, yet relieved that the spotlight had been taken off him.

"Dockers and their families have been working this port since the days of sail and before. When there wasn't any sea-going freight worth talking about we didn't lave and go till other jobs. We stuck it out. My grandfather was killed by a heave of timber when my father was just thirteen years old. Our family wuda perished if the dockers hadn't tuk my da outa school an' give him a first-preference button. It allowed him till go on the quay and earn money to keep the rest of his family outa the poor house. My family have lived in Belfast for over a century. Most of yew don't even come from Belfast. As second-preference men, yis had jobs. Good jobs. Better paid jobs than the men who work in Rank's Mill or the shipyard or anywhere else. But that's nat enuff. Yis want till be Dockers. Then yer sons 'ill want ta be Dockers, and then the very families that kept the tradition alive will be forced out. That won't happen. Thanks to the principles of the closed shop, we don't havta bring in anybody we don't want ta, or work wid anybody we don't respect."

He paused for breath, and looked across at Hamill.

"This problem arose a few months ago when we opened the books and made up over a hundred new first-preference members. Naturally, we turned to members of our own families, for after all it was our own older family members who had left the deficit, either by death or ill health." He turned his anger to the silent audience.

"Yew were annoyed. Did yis come till me? No! Yis abandoned union procedure, formed the so-called secret seven and launched a fightin' fund to git the law to take yer case. We know all about it. An' we know every one of the seven. Did yew really believe yew cud operate in secret, Wilson?" he said looking at the medium-sized man wearing a cloth cap and a threadbare jacket over a tartan shirt, who had earlier addressed the crowd.

Wilson ignored the taunt.

"What's gonna happen nigh?" he asked with an air of resignation. "The case is lined up to be heard as soon as possible."

"We know that as well," snarled Shaw. "Yer letter till the secretary of the union was handed to me to sort out. What did yis think he cud do? We control the Dockers' union. Nat him or anyone else. So yer letter was a waste of time."

He looked at the crowd below him. "As fer the court case: yis have wasted yer money. Yis 'ill niver win." He raised his arms and pointed at the listeners. "Yer leaders have mislead yis, boys. Yis are finished on the quay. There's no more second preference. Yis bit the han' that fed yis and from now on yis 'll hav'ta take yer chances wid the Arabs who'd give their eye teeth for the privileges youse have just threw away."

"Yew can't just throw us outa werk," shouted a man at the front of the crowd.

"He just did, Granda," grinned one of Shaw's entourage,

35

before shoving the slightly-built man. The crowd were silent as he fell to the floor of the billiard room.

"I'd advise yis till talk till yer man here about a job in Rank's, but I don't think he'll have any time for troublemakers either."

His voice rose as his pent up anger finally exploded.

"Yis are finished on the quay! Nigh get ta fuck outa my way—I've men ta represent!"

Wilson stepped forward and confronted Shaw. His face was expressionless. "This will be settled by the law. I don't see why yew shud have a monopoly on Dockwork. Or why yew shud be able to make such decisions without consultin' us." He looked at the strained faces listening intently to his every word and continued angrily, "Mebbe we shud consider amalgamatin' with the Arabs and formin' a union branch of our own. The stevedores wudn't mind a bit of competition; in fact they might encourage it."

"Some of us have worked on the quay for as long as you or anybody else," snarled a small man with a broken nose and a cauliflower ear. He angrily pulled a buff-coloured employment book from the inside pocket of his jacket. "I'm tole this paybook issued by the Docks agency constitutes a contractual obligation," he added.

Shaw could barely suppress his rage. He hadn't expected anyone to challenge him, and Wilson's audacity had unsettled him. He grabbed the man's paybook and ripped it from his hands. As the other man struggled, Shaw slapped him dismissively across the face. He handed the wage book to a swarthy red-faced man at his side.

"No book, no work. See yis in court," he snarled contemptuously, brushing his way past Wilson.

His fury and the closing in of his entourage to protect him caused him to fail to see the man close to the exit hastily pushing a notebook into the pocket of a donkey jacket that was much too large for his narrow shoulders. A closer inspection would have showed highly-polished shoes and heavy tweed trousers. Under the donkey jacket, hidden by a long woollen scarf, were a striped shirt and a monogrammed tie. The man, who was clearly not a Dockworker, pushed his soft white hands into the pockets of the borrowed donkey jacket and moved quietly out of the door after the union representative. The representative for the flour mills slowly climbed from the chair he was standing on and breathed a deep sigh of relief.

"Best news I've heard since Hitler shot himself," laughed Sam Harvey.

Henry scowled at his hilarity.

"Mightn't be that good for yews. If I lose control of the spud gang, yews guys might be out on yer ears as well."

Sam refused to be dismayed.

"Naw," he said. "We know the job backwards, an they'll nat git rid a yew. Yew weren't in the set-up, an' ye niver paid a penny till the fund, an' besides yev gat an inside track wid Collins who yew saved from goin' till jail. He'll houl on till yew, 'cause yew know where the bodies are buried, an' yew'll houl until us, cos we're the only ones who'll work for the wages yew give us."

Henry's face reddened visibly, as he pushed his cap to the back of his head in exasperation.

"Don't be startin' that oul nonsense! Yis git paid what yer worth!"

"Aye, an' yew git the same pay for swannin' off till Liverpool for a coupla weeks till meet yer fancy women or whoever yew take the boat till see over there. What's fair about that?" snarled Sam, his face a mask of hatred. "What do yew say, boy?" he added, looking in the direction of his younger brother Jack who was leaning against a checker's desk in the Chapel Shed.

Jack scratched the bristle of hair on his bullet-shaped head. "Why did yew not pay intil the fund for the cause, Henry?" he asked, ignoring Sam's heated question.

Henry sniffed. "I don't want till be a first-preference man. I'm happy where I am, an', as yew've maybe noticed, the only childer I heve is yew an' yer brother an' them other sleekit lazy bastards I fight every day of the week to keep in a job."

"Yew don't do it for nuthin'," countered Sam.

"There's a lorry in: away and give the driver a han' till unload it. I'm goin' til Pat's for a cure," Henry scowled.

Sam was about to continue, but Jack took his older brother's arm and led him down the shed to where the driver and his helper were taking the heel rope and cover from a lorry filled with sacks of potatoes. Henry moved in the direction of the bar at the other side of the road. As a second-preference man, he was not too worried about the current situation.

He knew a list of the names that had contributed towards the cost of a court case was in the hands of the dock committee. Probably delivered by a docker's relative who was a second-preference man with hopes of joining the elite first preference. He equally knew his name was one of the very few not included.

"Givus me usual, Seamus," he growled to the barman, as he pushed his way through a crowd of angry red-button men. He shied away from a group who approached him.

"I wanta know fuck all about it," he yelled at the top of his voice. "Yis brought it on yerselves, an' Wilson has hardened the issue by threatenin' till start his own union branch. Git away an' lave me alone."

The men moved off sullenly.

Sitting down at a vacant table close to the fire, Henry began to drum his fingers on the table top before lifting the half glass of Guinness and pouring some of it into a measure of Bushmills whiskey. Holding his nose with the first finger and thumb of one hand, he lifted the mixture with the other and poured it down his throat. He could have done with another, but finished the remainder of the Guinness and rose from the table. This was going to be a long eventful day and he knew he needed to keep his wits about him.

Jim Harvey grimaced as he helped an exhausted Reilly pull the hand truck along Nelson Street towards the stevedore's store. Reilly's head was down and he was moving on instinct alone. Both men were covered from head to toe in the white chemical residue. Their noses were red and runny and their eyes were stinging with the dust that lined their tired and gaunt features.

"I think I'll take my ma's advice an' git a job somewhere else," Jim whispered to Reilly. The little trucker didn't answer, but nodded his head vigorously. He licked his dry lips and rolled his eyes from side to side. His chest was heaving and every now and again he would cough, bringing up a mouthful of thick black phlegm that he spat unceremoniously onto the street. The young lad realised again that only his boxing training had prevented him from collapsing before the cargo had been taken from the hold. The third member of the trio was still sitting in the shed, unable to rise. He had lost interest halfway through the proceedings and rather than have Jim's strength depleted carrying him, Reilly exchanged places with him and went behind the truck with Harvey. McConkey went between the shafts and they were able to keep going until the final bag was thrown to the shed floor.

Uncle had come ashore to tell them the tonnage and their money.

"Yis are on twenty-nine shillin's an' eleven pence. Nat bad for a job that usually takes three ires. Nat my fault it tuk youse clowns nearly five. Some of yes have a lat till learn, an' yis 'ill havta buck-up if yis want till follow me."

Jim linked Reilly down Trafalgar Street, after leaving the truck in the stevedore's yard. They entered The Bowling Green, brushing off what chemicals they could from their clothing, and sat down wearily. Reilly was still unable to speak. He motioned with his hands. Jim assumed he wanted a pint.

"A pint a Guinness an' a pint a shandy, Barney," he croaked courteously through the dryness of his throat.

He carried the foaming glasses back to the table and both sat eyeing the drinks in stupefied silence. Licking his lips with childlike anticipation Jim was about to taste his when he saw Reilly's beseeching look. He lifted the glass of black liquid and steered it with shaking hands to Reilly's open mouth. The man's eyes glowed with sheer gratitude as he gulped at the porter. A few other drinkers witnessed the act of kindness.

One snorted: "Reilly, yer getting too oul for that kind of work," as he puffed strenuously at a briar pipe, sending dense black smoke to the ceiling.

Reilly nodded in silent consent and leaned his head gratefully against the wall of the bar and closed his eyes.

Jim felt somewhat concerned. He knew it was his strength that had carried them through when the other man in the team gave up the ghost. He also knew Reilly's act in coming out of the shafts to work behind the truck had saved all three of them from being sacked. He supped at his shandy reflectively and thought about the events of the morning.

"Did yew hear about the gangers leavin' the reds?" he said to the pipe smoker.

"Aye—it's all over the place. They held a meetin' in the Unionist Hall and Shaw and some of his cronies gatecrashed it. Shaw tuk Mackey's paybook, an' hit him a slap on the gub for being insolent. The others are shit scared they'll lose theirs as well."

"Kin they do that?" asked Jim

"They kin do what they like, kid." The pipe smoker started to laugh. "The likes a yew needn't worry. That removes the red-button men an' laves guys like you technically getting whatever work the blues can't do or don't want. So yis are on the pig's back."

"Uncle said the reds wrote a letter till the *Telegraph*. I get it every night from the wee man at Gallaher's gate an' I niver saw any such letter," Harvey said.

The other man laughed. "Uncle can't read or write, so what wud he know! He heard there wus a letter an' probably said the first thing that cum intil his head, an' that's how rumours start. I believe there was a petition sent to the top man of the union, an' that's wat put the cat among the pigeons, as they say."

Reilly was snoring soundly as Jim ordered another shandy. The barman smiled knowingly.

"Bet yew didn't even taste the first one goin' down."

"Yer dead right," smiled Harvey. "It's like pourin' coul water inta the radiator of a hot car engine. It evaporates intil steam when it hits yer belly."

"Aye," laughed the barman, "it takes about six ta git the benefit."

His tone changed as he looked at Jim's haggard features.

"Why don't ye go on home after that one, son. Yew luk about done-in. Don't worry about Reilly: he'll sleep a while an' then he'll git up an' go home."

The lad nodded and finished the drink. He cast a quick look at Reilly before walking out into Trafalgar Street and down Little York Street. His arms and legs were weary and strained and his face was burning. He smiled tightly.

"At least it'll sanitise the bug bites," he murmured to himself as he opened the kitchen door.

His mother immediately leapt from the settee.

"Ack son, yer at the oul C&A boat," she wailed.

Jim tried to smile but the chemicals had set his face like a mask and he only managed to grimace.

"No, ma," he replied, "The C&A is a department store in Royal Avenue. I was at the ICI boat an' I hope I niver havta be at it again. If there's such a place as Hell, that's what it must be like."

He spread the sheets of the *Belfast Telegraph* over the sofa, before going to the yard door and kicking off his boots. His mother rushed to get him his supper.

"An' ye know the laugh of it?" Jim added bitterly, "I gat twenty-nine shillin's and eleven pence an' it has to be split five ways."

His mother grimaced.

"But shure yill be gittin' paid for a day's work at the spuds as well, won't ye?"

"Aye, but I'd a gat a few bob in tips an' I'll miss out on that." He knelt down and slapped his cap against the hearth causing the chemical dust to whiten the tiles. Rising, he did a quick impromptu dance that caused more powder to fall from his jeans.

"Maybe that'll kill a few a them bugs durin' the night," he laughed dryly.

After supper and two bottles of cold milk, he went out into the yard and undressed. His mother attached a hose to the kitchen tap and he walked to the outhouse that was out of view of the kitchen and scullery windows. He undressed to his Simmit and underpants, and played the water on his shirt and jeans. He scrubbed both articles with a yard brush before

41

hanging them up to dry. He then stripped naked and washed himself down, shivering as the cold water cascaded through his hair and over his body. The dust turned to a soapy substance and he persevered until all the suds were off his body. He took a towel and fresh underclothes from the wash rail beside him. Walking back into the kitchen he reached up and pulled a clean pair of jeans from a set of pulleys on the ceiling.

He switched on the wireless.

"I'm gonna lie down fer awhile, ma," he called as the strains of a popular song began to waft from the radio. "Whatever ye do, don't let me sleep down here."

"Aye, son," replied his mother grimly as she picked up her knitting. She was so glad to see him home and sober. She suppressed a sob, knowing tomorrow would be the same. She wished with all her might that his father had not died suddenly, leaving him at the mercy of people who would use him until he became like them. The needles continued to click as she gazed unseeingly into the fire.

Hurried footsteps in the hall heralded the arrival of her daughter Lizzie. As she entered the room and hung her coat on the back of the kitchen door, she glared at her brother spread out on the settee.

"I suppose that lazy git has lay there all day, or else he's bin out an' gat drunk again. Ack, ma," Lizzie cried, "when is he iver gonna catch himself on? I'm jist about sicka it."

She stormed into the scullery and lifted her supper from the top of a simmering pot.

Shaw sauntered confidently into the late afternoon meeting in a stevedore's office in Dock Street. The group that ran the cross channel section of labour on Belfast's dock had hastily convened the meeting. Opening the door to the main office he was met by a female secretary who ushered him to an ante room. The stevedores sat around a large and brightly polished mahogany table. A tall man with curly brown hair and a thin straggly moustache rose to greet him.

"What the fuck's goin' on?"

Shaw ignored the question and smiled with the air of a man who knew all the answers as he opened a thin brown briefcase and placed papers on the table.

"Let me fill yew in on today's developments, gentlemen," he continued, taking a seat and pulling a pair of spectacles from the top pocket of his tweed jacket. "Today we cleared the quay of a nest of parasites who for too long have been gumming up the werks of progress and causing instability in the Dock force."

He looked pointedly over his glasses at the listening men.

"Did any of yew lose any werk or any time? Did any of yer shipping fail to be discharged or loaded within the allocated time?" He looked at his papers. "Nat according to my reports. So what's yer problem? I'm quite sure yer nat interested in the welfare of two or three hunnert second-preference idlers. No: yew are more interested in the amount of time it takes to git the shipping away from the wall of the quay.

"The removal of the reds has nat damaged our capability of doin' yer biddin', so I wud ast ye to leave the dock work in our han's an' yew git on wid bringin' the boats an' their tonnage till us. We'll do the needful. Youse 'ill git yer profits an' we'll have rid of a mob of ungrateful conspirators."

"Can yew guarantee us an experienced labour force without the reds?" asked Collins from the top of the table.

Shaw grinned.

"There'll be no change in the size of the labour force. After a day or two the reds 'ill be back lukin' for werk, but they'll be back on our terms."

"What terms?" enquired Collins as the other stevedores listened intently.

"They'll be schooled along wid the Arabs," continued Shaw. "No second-preference privileges, no terms an' conditions, no rights, no holiday pay, an' best of all, no aspirations for a first-preference button."

"Wouldn't that be illegal?" came a soft-voiced question from a man wearing a smart blazer with a crest on it. His grey hair was parted in the middle and his face was thin and thoughtful.

Shaw's tone hardened.

"The reds were formed in 1939 to help wid the war effort. We accepted them on that condition. Someone had ta slap them down. They are takin' a court case which we're advised they'll lose. As the mother union, we believe they broke the terms and conditions of their employment when they sought legal advice, rather than consulting wid the branch re the intake of new blood. A matter that technically doesn't concern them. They were niver promised anything other than second choice. We feel comfortable withdrawin' that. They are nat in the dockers' union. Therefore they have no legal rights or redress."

His voice took on a menacing tone.

"We operate hand in glove with yerselves an' I'd hate to see that well tried and long standing arrangement fall over some useless labour that will be back on their knees beggin' for work without any preconditions."

He paused and looked directly at Collins with the whisper of a smile on his face.

"I'm well aware some of yew have obligations and debts of some description to certain of the red-button men. Some may even have blood links. If yew want to continue hiring those men on a day-to-day basis, we'll turn a blind eye, as long as they continue to pay their union dues."

"What about the ringleaders?" asked Collins.

Shaw smiled.

"We're a forgiving lot. We wudn't discriminate agin anyone. They'll be taken back as well under the same aforementioned conditions. But some of them may have to suffer for the trouble they've caused." His eyes hardened. "Every war has its casualties, gentlemen."

Collins rose and shook his hand.

"I'm speakin' for all of us. We won't interfere in what seems to be primarily an internal union matter, just as long as you keep the wheels of industry turnin'."

"It's in the beg," grinned Shaw as he picked up his papers and left the room.

The stevedore waited until he heard the door close. He looked at the men around the table.

"We've no other choice than to go along with it. If we object strenuously, he'll pull out the labour; contact the Dockers in other ports and we'll be strike bound with ships lying against harbour walls and port payments growing with each day."

"What about the Irish Transport Dockers?" asked another man wearing a soft trilby hat and a corduroy jacket. His clipped tones identified him as English.

Collins pursed his lips.

"Not a chance," he muttered. "They're not above a bit of work poaching, but on a big issue like this, they'd back the Blues to the hilt."

The Englishman growled with exasperation.

"Typical Irish situation. Two of everything. Customs, police forces, rules and regulations, dock unions."

Collins smiled again.

"That's the way we like it, Fergus. We pay the lowest working rates in the British Isles and that's how we do it. We play the two unions off against each other, rates wise. That way we can pare the stevedoring charges down to the knuckle. Don't knock it. It works in our favour. Anyway, I vote we leave them to it. It'll be a storm in a teacup as far as I'm concerned. All in favour," he concluded in a voice that already knew the answer. "Meeting over," he said as a show of hands carried his proposal.

Shaw, standing outside the room door, heard every word. He tiptoed out to the main office and nodded courteously to the secretary.

"Are yew finished already sir?" she asked, rising to her feet.

"Yew cud say it's all signed sealed and delivered, Missus," he replied gallantly, as he left the building and made his way into York Street, where he waited for a trolley bus to take him back to the union rooms. He knew those whom he represented would be well pleased with the day's work. The gangers had more than relished the orders given to them the previous week. The reds had got an unpleasant surprise. Tomorrow they were going to get an even bigger one.

He stood back as a red trolley bus marked CITY CENTRE screeched to a stop outside the Sportsman's Arms. He had decided not to bring his car as it was well known and could have been vandalised whilst he was in the stevedore's office. He was a man who left nothing to chance. Clambering quickly onto the double-decker, he paid the conductor and sat down close to the door, still unable or unwilling to remove the smirk of self-satisfaction from his face.

Jim Harvey awoke to the delicious smell of bread being toasted. He looked at his feet and saw the familiar and welcome sight of Tibs, the ebony-coloured cat, languishing on the sofa. He stretched and groaned as he looked at the clock in the centre of the mantelpiece.

"Is it only eight a clock?"

"Yill nat sleep the night," answered his mother as she held the piece of bread attached to a long stemmed toasting fork close to the flame of the fire. "Do yew wanta drap a tea and a bita toast?" she asked as he struggled to sit upright.

The cat leapt from the settee and moved to the back door where he began crying.

"Yew may let him out for awhile," said his mother.

Jim rose and opened the door.

He turned on the cold water and dashed it against his face. His hands ached with constantly gripping the heavy sacks and he noticed small spots, like burns, on the back of his left hand. He washed them under the cold water and then threw more water over his face and head. Lifting a comb, he ran it through his hair as he walked back into the living room.

"I'm goin' out fer an ire or two, ma," he said haltingly.

A frown appeared on her face and he quickly continued, "But I'm nat goin' till the pub. I'm goin' up till the corner till git a breath a air. My lungs feel like they're ready till bust."

"Wait till ye git a wee cuppa tea. An' hap yerself up! It's coul out there the night."

He nodded obediently.

"Where's Lizzie?" he asked as his mother handed him the tea.

"Hor an' them other ones is away till Nelson Street till see a fortune teller till git their cups read. She'll nat be back till about ten."

He grinned in spite of his aches and pains.

"S'pose we'll git it all whin she comes in." He rolled his eyes. "Like there's a big rich man who is gonna marry her and buy her a big house an' give her all her orders."

He was glad to hear his mother laughing as he continued. "An' she's gonna have five childer, an they're all gonna be doctors and professors an' businessmen, an' they'll niver be allowed till come down York Street in case they get corrupted an' turn intil no good alkahalics."

"Mebbe she'll let us go up the Malone Road till visit thim nigh an' agin," laughed his mother.

He rose and put on his overcoat; glad he'd brightened her mood. He turned in the open doorway.

"Don't worry, mum," he said softly. "I'll be back in about an ire." He closed the room door tightly and walked down the hall and into the night.

He moved towards the bright lights of Crookes' chip shop. A few of the local men were grouped at the corner of Earl Street and Nelson Street. Unsurprisingly, the topic of conversation was the events of the day. He was about to return home when he saw his uncle Henry weave unsteadily down Earl Street. He watched as he stopped outside the chip shop and began searching his pockets. Jim approached him.

"Are ye alright, Uncle Henry?"

Henry raised his head and looked at him with glazed eyes.

"Away in there an' git me a two fish supper an' a fish. I'll give ye the dough later," he scowled.

Jim nodded in servile agreement.

"Bring thim round till my house," called his uncle as he moved unsteadily towards his home. The men at the corner watched in silence as he wove his way past Quinn's Place, and laughed uproariously when he stopped at Billy Turner's grocery store and held onto the lamp standard outside the front door. Henry took a deep exaggerated breath before striding purposefully down North Thomas Street.

Stopping at the entrance to Croskery's bakery, he leaned heavily against the reassuring wall until he felt strong enough to battle the few remaining yards to his house. He moved as if his legs were about to fold and swung his arms backwards and forwards as if he were swimming. Reaching the front door, he staggered up the hall and burst into the kitchen where he fell on his mouth and nose.

The room was filled with the women of the family who watched in disgust as he rolled onto his back and began snoring loudly. His mother continued clicking her knitting needles with a look on her face that forbade any comment on the behaviour of her favourite son.

"Men do things like that," she sniffed philosophically, "It's in their blood. Yew can't blame him. His da before him was a drunken oul git, an' his father before him. Like father like son."

The youngest daughter scowled as the others held their tongue. Jim burst into the room with the fish and chips, which his grandmother quickly took from him.

"Git some plates from the cupboard," she ordered, "an' we'll enjoy a late night supper."

"That was three shillin's, Granny," said Jim, almost apologetically. "Henry said he wud give me the money ... "

His granny cut him short.

"Aye, so he will, son, so he will," she answered dismissively, turning him towards the door. "Have yis gat them plates out yet? Hurry up or the bloody things 'ill be coul."

The women ignored the snoring Henry and enjoyed the unexpected treat as Jim walked wearily out of the house.

He decided to take a stroll along York Street, towards the railway station, and breathed deeply to clear the chemical residues from his lungs. There was little traffic. A steady stream of people passed, and smatterings of foreign languages reached his ears as seamen in groups or pairs made their way back to their ships.

He stopped at the bank at Earl Street corner and looked across at the massive cigarette factory where his sister Lizzie worked. The lights were still on as the night shift continued to turn out the famous brands that went all over the world. He leaned back against the wall of the bank and enjoyed being alone and able to think. The nightmare of the cockroaches was fading, and he knew it was something he would have to live with: sharing his home with creatures and insects that wandered about at will when the lights were out and the house was quiet. Thankfully the bedrooms were reasonably immune from them. Mice were the problem there. Tibs slept at the foot of his bed to protect him from the little furry creatures during the night.

"Wee Harvey?"

The concerned voice broke into his reverie. He turned and saw two men approaching him. He knew them by sight and smiled at the one who called his name.

"Did ye hear about oul Reilly?"

Jim laughed mirthlessly.

"Aye, Matt. Him an' me gat mangled at the rosy snatter boat. He'll hardly be out the marra, although I wudn't put it past him."

Matt continued grimly, "Aye, they said he came in with yew."

"What happened?" laughed Jim. "Did he knock a table a drink over on his way out?"

Matt put an arm around the lad's shoulder.

"He's dead, kid. There's no easy way a tellin' ye. He's kaput. Gone to the big schoolin' pen in the sky."

"He wus alright when I left him," cried Jim defensively. He thought for a second. "He wus sleepin, but that wus because he wus knackered. He hadda cum outa the truck till help me ... " His voice was rising in panic.

"It's nat yore fault, son," said Matt reassuringly. "His time had cum. Oul Barney says he sent yew home and let Reilly sleep. He tried to wake him an hour ago an' cudn't. Doctor Calder came over from his surgery an' pronounced him dead. The cops came an' tuk his body away."

"The cops?" echoed Jim nervously.

"Aye, but it's just routine. There'll be a coroner's report seeing as he died sudden."

"Sure yew cudn't die in a better place than a pub serving good drink, an' pleasant company all around ye," laughed Matt's mate, trying to lighten the situation.

Jim turned abruptly and walked away. His mind was in turmoil. He saw Reilly's anguished and perspiring face on the other side of the two hundred weight bag as he struggled manfully to keep up with the youngster. He realised how much the ordeal had taken out of him and knew he should have shown more concern for the old and plucky trucker. Reaching his home he burst into the bright light of the kitchen.

"Reilly's dead!" he blurted out to his mother.

She gasped loudly and clasped her hands together. She said nothing, but gazed at her son with a frightened look in her eyes. His face was drained of colour as he turned on the radio and slumped into his chair. His mother produced a skein of wool, and he absently held out his arms and watched as she carefully looped it over his wrists. He stretched them outwards, tightening the wool, as she proceeded to roll the strand into a ball until the last strand fell from his arms. He listened to the radio and the click of the needles, until the national anthem sounded the end of transmission.

"I'm away till bed, ma," he said through childish tears.

He almost collided with his Uncle Henry who glared at his pallid features.

"What's up with yew?" he scowled.

He softened a little when Jim blurted out the reason for his grief.

"That's the way it goes kid. Men like Reilly shudn't be stannin' jobs like the Rosies. It's hard enuff for fit and able men. Shure he must be nearly seventy years old," he continued, as Jim looked at him with surprise. "On top a that, he's had a dodgy ticker fer years."

His voice changed to a businesslike tone.

"Git yerself till the corner the marra. Uncle was fulla praise fer ye. Yer makin' a name fer yerself." He made no mention of meeting Jim earlier in the evening. Jim was tempted to ask for his three shillings, but reneged. He watched his uncle until he was out of the hall and into the street. He nodded at his grim-faced mother and pursing his lips, called the cat to him. Its tail arched as it leapt from the settee to the floor and rubbed itself against his leg. He smiled tightly.

"That was some day, eh ma?" he muttered, before closing the door and climbing the stairs.

Helen Wilson watched her husband as he picked over his breakfast in the manner of a man with something on his mind. She looked at his sparse form and unshaven face.

"What's biting ye, Sammy? Ye haven't bin yerself these recent weeks. Anything wrong at work?"

He lifted his head and spoke without looking at her.

"Men's business. Let that be an end till it."

She took the dismissal without rancour as she rose from her chair and walked to the foot of the stairs.

"Right, c'mon," she yelled at the top of her voice. "It's time youse hallions were up fer school!"

Returning to her seat, she leaned on the back of it and looked at her husband. He rose from his half-eaten breakfast and went to the kitchen where he soaped his face for a shave. She knew the subject was closed and the conversation over.

Wilson felt his wife's eyes on him as he carefully guided the open razor around his sunken cheeks. He rinsed his face with cold water and combed his thinning brown hair. Lifting a threadbare cream coloured collarless shirt, he stuffed the tails down his trousers. A clean collar hung on a pulley rail and he put it around his neck and looped a dark shiny tie around the collar. As he put on his jacket and cap, Helen continued to look at his tense features.

She remembered the last time she had seen him in such a frame of mind: they had been married during the first year of his demob and he had suffered terribly from dreams and nightmares that had left him sweat-soaked and weeping. She had nursed him patiently through these occurrences, until they stopped. She instinctively knew something was wrong and hoped he would tell her.

A slow reluctant tread on the stairs warned her that one of her brood was up. As she went into the scullery and poured a kettle of hot water into the sink, she heard the front door close as her husband left without a word. The deep frown returned to her features.

He felt the iciness as soon as he entered the small hut that

51

served as a rest room inside the Mersey boat transit shed. He sat self-consciously on a chair he had occupied every morning for the last ten years. Other chairs, generally filled by his red-button colleagues, were empty. He looked into the openly hostile faces of men he had shared laughs, stories and food with over all those years.

"Didn't think yew'd have had the nerve till show yerself here," scowled one beefy man with a bald head and protruding teeth. "Yer other mates have bailed out. They're away till the corner where they may or may not git a turn." He stared unrelentingly into Wilson's face. "If yew hurry, yew might git a job. If yew don't, don't hurry back here. Yer nat welcome or wanted. We're waiting on some of the new men. They're pleased till take yer place. Nigh, wud yew git a move on. We're particular who we're seen socialising with."

Wilson rose slowly and went for his coat behind the door. He looked around the room he had spent a lot of time in since he'd come out of the army. He observed without any hatred or malice the anger on the faces of the men he'd come to regard as friends. Their eyes were full of contempt and he felt like a dog that had bitten the hand of those who fed him. Opening the door, he left without a word. Looking at his watch, he quickened his step as he walked to the schooling pen. He didn't want to go home and face his wife.

Striding through the harbour gates, he passed groups of surly tight-faced men, most of whom declined to speak to him as the gangers were watching every move. He saw the smallest group around Ned Semple and joined the school. The ganger surveyed his arrival with a sarcastic grin that left the red-button man in no doubt as to where his sympathy lay. When he spoke, Wilson knew it was for his benefit and others like him.

"This is a sleeper boat I'm schoolin'. Three hunnert ton a railway sleepers an' I want thim outa her the day, nat next week. So I want men who know what they're doin'. These planks are fulla creosote, so yis 'ill haveta rub some olive oil on yer gubs an' hans or it'll burn the skin aff ye. But I haveta say only the big girls do that. The rale men don't need to. Anybody nat happy kin go."

A few men made hurried exits. Wilson stayed. He knew he wouldn't get a look in at a handy cargo. He had a penance to serve and it was about to start.

Ned took the only blue button in the school.

"Winch, Billy," he scowled tonelessly. He looked pensively at a tall thin man wearing a red and black striped cap. "You, Davy. Bull-rope."

Davy was a non-union man and Ned waited for a reaction. A smug tight smile crossed his baleful features, as there was none. He squared his feet and looked across the pen at the other groups: all was going smoothly. "Houlsmen," he continued. He studied the faces in front of him for a few seconds and then quickly called five men by name. His eyes locked with Wilson's. "You," he said with a grim smile. He schooled the rest of the men quickly, and moved to his car. "Open berth, Pollock. Shore men. Don't fergit the trucks and the gear. They're in the store."

He beckoned to the winch driver who climbed into the passenger seat.

"That bastard Wilson had the gall till stan' me after all the trouble him and them other glipes have caused. He is a checker, isn't he?" he enquired of the man beside him.

"Aye," replied Billy. Ned grinned at the road in front of him. "We'll see how long his nice soft han's houl out. Then I'll take great pleasure in sackin' the bastard."

Billy nodded whilst looking straight in front of him. He didn't want to register his true feelings. Like many other first-preference men he was appalled at the treatment being handed out to the second-preference men. He believed they were entitled to better conditions. He had soldiered with Wilson in the Rifles in quite a few theatres of war during the recent conflict, and had a great regard for the man's intelligence and integrity.

"See them paybooks on the seat?"

Ned's grating voice interrupted his thoughts.

"Yis," he replied obediently.

"Put thim in the glove compartment. They'll soon be history, like the bastards who own them," Ned added with relish.

He was on the bridge of the sleeper boat when the men arrived. He saw Wilson hesitating on the edge of the quay.

"Houl, Wilson. Yew were schooled fer the houl: so don't be lukin' fer a handy turn ashore," he snarled. "Team up wid somebody who knows what they're doin," he added as he moved to a guy rope and adjusted the drift of the single derrick winch.

The hatch was open and the men could smell the fumes of the creosote as it rose from the cargo. It stung their faces and seared their throats and nostrils. Most of them scorned the olive oil and moved quickly into the close confines of the hold.

Wilson saw the other four men pairing.

He felt a stab of panic when he realised the only one left was a red-button man like himself; a checker from the Glasgow shed. He knew also that Ned was watching his every move. The other holdsmen, who were regular outsiders, watched with unconcealed contempt as the two men struggled to build a heave.

"Hav yis nat a timber hook?" squealed Ned. "Yew need a fuckin' hook till break them planks apart. This is nat a paper an' pencil job. There's no pickin' an' choosin' here. If yis can't do it, git ta fuck outa it."

The two men ignored the verbal abuse as they tried unsuccessfully to prise out the first sleeper. Ned walked to the shore side of the ship.

"Sammy, givus yer hook. Yew don't need it."

He snatched the long stemmed cargo hook from the shore man and threw it into the hatch.

"Try this," he snarled. The hook bounced a few inches from Wilson's feet. He lifted it and dug it viciously into the side of a plank. During the ganger's tirade, he'd been watching the other men and quickly grasped the method they were using. Once the first stick was prised from its tight bed the rest was relatively easy.

He spoke to his bewildered partner at the other end of the eight-foot-long plank.

"Lift that heel-stick," he whispered, pointing to the three-foot-long piece of four-by-four timber close to their feet. "When

I pick up two sleepers, yew put that heel-stick in below them. Don't touch the sleepers till I tell ye."

He sunk the hook into one plank and lifted it between his legs. Holding it with one hand he then lifted the second plank using the same method. His colleague dropped the heel-stick beneath them, slanting it to fit the space Wilson had created.

"We'll lift the four sleepers on either side an' that'll git us a heave," Wilson gasped. "But we'll havta move fast till keep up wid these other guys. They're experts." The other man rolled his eyes and mumbled what seemed like a prayer.

Billy looked over the winch at the struggling men, and knew he had to help them. He purposely misjudged lifting the first heave and knocked down a second, thus giving the two red-button men a little extra breathing space. Luckily, Ned was in the galley having a coffee; otherwise Billy too would have felt the raw edge of the ganger's tongue. He continued with this ploy until the ganger returned. The holdsmen glared angrily at him as heave after heave was rebuilt. Wilson's heave remained untouched and he flashed a brief smile of gratitude at his former comrade in arms.

"Us next," he grunted to his companion as he walked out to the centre of the hatch and waited until the nipper chain attached to the hook was within reach.

He grabbed it and pulled it in the direction of the heave.

"Git till the other side of the heave, Mick," he shouted above the roar of the winch's engine.

Gathering the slack of the heavy chain sling in one hand he hurled the end with the open-mouthed hook under the heave. His companion pulled it across the top of the timber and secured the hook in the centre of the heave. Wilson signalled for the driver to lift. The heave was dragged to the centre of the hatch and raised skyward as Ned watched impassively.

Wilson called Mick to him.

"There's a pattern to this. They lift the stick layer by layer. Now we've opened the floor that's the hard work done for this layer. Put the heel stick down there and we'll build another nine onto it."

His mate nodded obediently and with a little effort the heave was built. They heard the sarcastic voice of the ganger,

"Don't luk nigh, Wilson, but the hook's hangin'."

He ran to the centre of the hatch and grabbed the winch hook. His breath was short and his heart was pounding in his chest.

"We'll havta speed up, if we wanta git a blow," he muttered. Mick nodded grimly. Before the heave moved they were throwing sleepers onto the heel stick. As the morning wore on they became more confident despite the ganger's unmasked snarl: "We're wurkin' through the male ire."

Wilson's right hand was developing huge blisters in the areas where the hand-hook cut into it. His clothes were soaking with sweat that oozed freely from every part of his body and his face burnt with the creosote. He saw his friend had the same problem. He summoned what strength he had and stuck the hook bitterly into the edge of the sleeper, clenching his teeth as the pain shot through his fingers.

Ned watched with grim satisfaction as their movements became slower.

"Don't give thim any quarter," he snarled savagely to the winch man. "Yer in charge. I'm away for my dinner."

Billy nodded curtly.

As soon as the ganger turned into the alleyway leading to the galley, he purposely dragged the heave on the end of the winch into the centre of the hatch. It collided with two others. He slackened the winch wire and the hook slipped from the sling. The heave in transit spewed out over the deck: he winked guardedly at Wilson's almost prayerful glance of gratitude. The hold-up was enough to give them their second wind. When the hook arrived for their heave, he hoisted up the trousers that were sticking to the sweat on his legs and walked defiantly towards it.

An hour later saw the last heave out. Both men watched as it swung from the centre of the hatch towards the shore.

"That's me finished," choked Mick. "I'll niver be back."

Wilson got his buff coloured paybook from the ganger. He washed his face at a nearby water tap and dried it with the tail of his shirt, before making his way slowly to the shed where they were paid each Thursday. He wondered wearily what further surprises were ahead of him.

Entering the shed on the Clarendon Dock he was besieged by a crowd of angry second-preference men.

"They tuk our fuckin' paybooks," screeched a man on the brink of hysteria. "Kin they do that? They can't do that," he continued, answering his own question. "What are we gonna do? How'm I gonna tell my wife I've gat no job?"

Wilson tried to speak calmly despite the rising panic in his voice.

"Yew hav a job. Yiv lost yer preference, till we git this sorted. But yill still gat a job."

"What at?" screamed the man. "I've a club fut. I can't do anythin' other than use the pencil, an' the new intake has filled all the checkers' posts. I can't work anywhere else. Where am I gonna git a job?"

"This is an illegal act an' we're gonna fight it tooth an' nail," shouted Wilson.

"Have yew gat yer two mugs to take the test case yet?" called an ashen-faced man.

Wilson couldn't meet the hostile glance.

"No. Nat yet, but it's only a mattera time," he yelled, trying to make himself heard above the angry voices.

He noted with some dismay, a few men who had aided and abetted him to collect the legal fees were now remaining silent. He dropped his head as the men dispersed, angrily refusing to listen to him. With a shrug of resignation, he walked to the queue and waited in the line until he reached the payout window.

The man wearing a white shirt with rolled up sleeves didn't look at him, but extended a hand.

"Paybook," he said.

Wilson reached the book through the opening. The clerk opened it and took out a page. He checked the number and reached out a pay packet, before tossing the book into a drawer.

"Next!" he shouted.

Wilson found himself shouldered to the side. The pent-up anger burst within him. He pushed forward and shoved the man who had taken his place away from the window. His cap flew off as he forced his head into the opening.

"That book is my property an' I want it back!" he screamed, grabbing the clerk by his shirt front and pulling him forward so that his nose was inches away from the clerk's frightened face. "It's mine an' I want it nigh!" he repeated savagely. The blood from his blistered hands smeared the front of the payout clerk's shirt.

"I've bin ordered till gather all the second-preference books in. I'm jist obeyin' orders," squealed the cashier, as Wilson tried to pull him through the aperture.

A harbour policeman raced forward and dragged Wilson away.

The clerk thrust his frightened face out of the window.

"I want that bastard charged with assault!" he screamed.

The constable relaxed his grip.

"Okay. Name an' address. Yew can't take the law intil yer own han's."

Wilson shook himself free, with a speed that surprised the constable.

"My name's Sammy Wilson and I'm a member of the secret seven," he shouted.

"What sorta an address is that?" retorted the constable. The question was drowned in the roar of approval by the crowd in the pay line. He looked to the rest of the men.

"Behave yerselves or I'll havta escort yis off harbour property," he said curtly.

Wilson gazed at the strained, frightened and angry faces that looked to him for hope and felt a certain responsibility for the situation.

"Do what he says, lads. We'll fight this in a legal way, an' maybe start a union branch of our own when we git till court."

He realised he had now identified himself as one of the more militant members of the seven. He knew life would get harder, and didn't relish the thought. He left the shed and walked towards the swinging bridge that had opened to allow the flour boat to steam towards its berth in the basin.

"I figgered I'd done all the fightin' I wus gonna do when the war ended," he muttered to no one in particular, as he waited for the bridge to swing back into place.

He opened his pay packet and checked the amount. He owed Paddy a pound, but decided against paying it until later. The bar would be packed, and the atmosphere would be distinctly hostile.

Two

PADDY FELT THE SAME SENTIMENTS AS he looked around his pub whilst pulling a pint. The bar was crowded, but there was little or no noise and an ominous chill hung on the air. He'd heard the story of hostility at the cross channel docks and was anxiously watching the clientele for any sign of disorder. A smile softened his features when he saw Jim Harvey walking through the open door.

"What kin I git yew, wee Harvey?" he called cheerfully.

"Givus a bottle a stout, Pat."

The barman reached down and lifted a bottle from beneath the counter. He placed the neck into a device that quickly removed the cork.

"Sorry to hear about Reilly," the barman said softly. "Don't be blamin' yerself too much. That's the way he'd a wanted till go."

Jim nodded glumly.

"Where were ye the day?" asked the big man cheerfully. "I heard there wus so much work, they put a woman over the hatch at the bran boat."

Jim laughed despite himself.

"I gat a turn at the carbide boat. Handy enough," he finished with the air of an old campaigner.

Paddy poured the stout into a bottle.

"Keep on the way yer goin' an' yill be able ta put in for a blue button," he laughed.

"I stud the carbide boat an' gat left," growled a middle-aged man wearing a suit that had seen better days over a striped collarless shirt. His gaunt face was unshaven. Jim recognised him to be a second-preference man, and said nothing.

Paddy pursed his lips.

"Ack sumthin' 'ill turn up tamarra, Dinky."

"I don't blame the blues," muttered Dinky. "I blame Wilson an' them other poxy bastards who organised that bloody campaign till git first preference," he continued more to himself than anyone else. Paddy moved on to another customer and Jim took a swig from his glass.

He felt a little apprehensive when he saw his Uncles Sam and Jack come in by the Fleet Street door. They made directly towards him.

"Well boy, how much did yew make us taday?" laughed Sam.

"Thirty bob," answered the lad self-consciously.

Sam narrowed his eyes and glanced at his brother Jack who was trying to catch Paddy's attention.

"We'll need ta make sure that big shite marked it in fer all of us."

He turned his mocking grin to the man beside Jim.

"Well Dinky," he laughed sardonically. "Did ye nat git a turn the day?"

The red-button man looked into his pint glass.

"Naw," he muttered guardedly.

"Ack that's a shame," continued Sam in a tone that was mocking and brutal. He pursed his lips and narrowed his eyes. This time there was a mixture of hatred and satisfaction as he spoke through clenched teeth. "D'ye remember the last time yew didn't git a check?"

Dinky didn't answer, and Sam continued relentlessly, "Well, if yew don't ... I do! Yew came down till a beg boat I wus workin' at an' tuk my job. Yew probably earned more in that week than I had got for a fortnight, but yew still came an' tuk the bread outa my mouth an' the mouths of my wife and ten childer."

Paddy spoke sternly from the barrels from which he was drawing a pint.

"Sam, I don't want any trouble."

Sam lifted his glass, his gaze fixed firmly on Dinky who remained silent.

"No problem, Paddy. I'm finished. Just wanted till git my dig in. As the man says, wee apples grow big an' every dog has its day. The shoe's on the other fut nigh an' bastards like him deserve all they git," he added remorselessly.

He couldn't resist a parting shot at the other red-button men scattered around the bar.

"An' that goes for the rest of yis," he finished triumphantly, before taking a drink from his glass.

Sam who was known as a formidable street fighter defiantly eyeballed the men at each table and most of them averted their eyes.

Dinky looked sideways at him and asked the question on all their lips.

"Does that include yer brother Henry?"

"Him especially," snarled Sam.

Jack waited until the anger had left Sam's face before speaking in a low measured tone.

"They're nat all bad, Sam. Some of thim don't deserve this."

Sam didn't answer, but continued to stare at Dinky with contempt.

"I wudn't feed bastards like him. He helped to start the whole thing. Is it any wonder he didn't git a job? An' that bastard Wilson's runnin' about slabberin' about startin' a new union branch. That's like wavin' a red flag at a bull. The blues 'ill crucify him an' anybody that listens till his hare-brained schemes."

He lifted his drink angrily, and the eerie silence caused Paddy to shiver.

At that moment the phone rang in the stevedore's office just around the corner from the bar.

"Call for yew, Mr. Collins. Mr. Shaw on the line."

The stevedore took the phone from his secretary.

"Collins," he said and waited.

Shaw's voice came soft and reassuring.

"Day one an' it luks like the war's over. We tuk their paybooks today. There wusn't much resistance, so technically, they're history."

Collins felt a little more confident. "What about the court case?"

"Luks like it's gonna fall through. The secret seven can't git any mugs to sit in the hot seat, an' they're too smart or too shit-scared to do it themselves. Hittin' 'em fast an' hittin' 'em hard seems to have nipped it in the bud. The ringleaders were given jobs in some instances; this didn't cement any solidarity among those who were left in the pen. An' jist to add further confusion in the ranks, we left some of the seven to give them feelings of insecurity."

Collins was impressed.

"So yew reckon it's over?"

"Aye. They're a broken stick. The leadership has folded. Things 'ill be back till normal in a few days nigh they know what side their bread's buttered on."

Collins couldn't resist a parting jibe.

"Weren't yew in Russia recently?" he asked.

"Yis," replied Shaw proudly. "Spent a month there last year studying Soviet sociology."

"Who were yer tutors? The KGB?" asked Collins dryly, before putting the phone down.

He turned to his secretary.

"Call the gentlemen who attended the meeting yesterday. Tell them there's no cause for concern."

The woman nodded agreement.

"Should I include Mr. Shaw?"

Her boss looked at her sharply.

"I said gentlemen," he hissed, before closing the door and retreating to his inner office.

Paddy continued to watch closely as his customers glared at each other. He noticed the bar was devoid of the smattering of first-preference men who generally called in for a drink on payday. He was glad when Sam Harvey and his brother left, but shook his head in exasperation when Henry Harvey walked in the front door a few minutes later.

"Git me me usual," he told Jim Harvey who was about to leave. Jim groaned inwardly and searched his pockets for the money before ordering. Paddy looked sympathetically at the youngster as he took the coins and set up the whiskey.

Henry stood for a moment in the centre of the bar as he glared from table to table.

"Where's that bastard Wilson?" he shouted, "He has a lat till answer for."

"He's gone till groun' like the rest a thim," answered a thinly-built man with a cigarette dangling from his lips.

"Yis shud tar an' feather all of thim fer what they done till us," said Henry.

"Wilson says the blues are outa order," snarled one man defiantly. "If men like yew had supported the cause it wudn't a tuk us so long till git the necessary dough an' we might nat a gat rumbled."

Henry laughed scornfully.

"Yis were rumbled the day yis started it. Did it niver enter yer stupid heads that a red-button man from a family of blues wudn't pass on details of yer stupid little operation till their da or brothers?"

He turned his back and returned to his drink at the bar.

"Mebbe it wus yew tole yer oul mate Collins. Everybody knows yew lick his arse till keep yer family at the spuds."

Jim gasped at the speed of Henry's reaction as he dashed in among the men. Knocking tables and chairs in all directions and drinks crashing to the floor, he roughly grabbed hold of the man who had shouted across the bar room. Jerking him upright, Henry hit him with a wide looping open-handed slap that sent him tumbling, senseless, to the floor. He glared at the rest of them for a few seconds before speaking in a harsh breathless voice.

"Henry Harvey may be a latta things: aye, mebbe even an arse licker. But nobody kin call me an informer. I draw the fuckin' line at that. If yer lukin' fer who sold ye out, don't be lukin' at me."

He walked to the bar and downed the whiskey in one go.

"Same again, Paddy. Sorry about the mess, but I ain't no informer. There's a limit till what a man will take."

Paddy nodded his head in agreement; glad the physical argument had been brief. A quick appraisal showed a few tumblers smashed. The injured man had been lifted back onto his chair and was rubbing his cheek.

"Yew said the wrong thing," chided his mate. "It's common knowledge that Henry went till jail because he wudn't squeal on the rale culprit. "

"Ack," muttered the injured man lamely, "It wus outa me before I realised it."

At that moment the front door opened and Ned Semple walked in with three of his henchmen. He grinned sarcastically around the bar.

"Yew mightn't have as many of them in next Thursday, Paddy; nigh that they have to work fer a livin'."

He glanced briefly at Henry and the grin disappeared. He'd been forcefully told he was exempt from any pressure. Henry pointedly ignored him. He paid for the drink and again apologised. He was about to launch into another outburst when the barman stopped him.

"It's OK, Henry. I know what's happenin' an' it has put yis all under pressure." He smiled broadly at the big man. "We all know yer nat an informer," he added softly, as though he was speaking to a child. Jim watched with amazement as Henry's eyes filled with tears.

Paddy turned to the barrels and automatically considered the knock-on problem. The decision to pull the paybooks meant the money he had lent without interest, and the bill for drink on tick, would be a lot slower coming in, if it came in at all. He'd already noticed quite a few of his Thursday evening patrons were conspicuous by their absence.

Helen Wilson managed not to gasp aloud when her husband limped into the kitchen of their home in Spencer Street. His face was bright red and he was bent over like an old man. She fought to control the fear in her voice.

"I wusn't expectin' yew for an ire or two. Don't yew generally call inta the Sportsman's on payday?"

He walked straight to the scullery and began taking off his coat and shirt. She noticed the blood on his palms and went to help him.

"I'm OK," he snapped, causing her to step back.

He ran cold water into the sink and bathed his hands. She went to her rocking chair and resumed her knitting. Some minutes later he emerged stripped to the waist with the towel thrown around his shoulders.

"I threw the shirt an' simmit in the wash. They're stinkin' wid sweat," he growled.

She put down the knitting, determined to know what was going on.

"An' what are yew doin' sweatin'? Yew'r a pencil man. Sweatin's fer the tonnage men an' the Arabs," she said indignantly.

"Nat any more," he sighed.

He looked at his burnt features in the kitchen mirror and grimaced as he lowered his body onto the sofa. Helen felt a twinge of panic as he looked squarely into her face.

"They've tuk away our paybooks. We're surplus till requirements, love," he said slowly and softly.

"Is this till do wie that money collectin'? I toul yew till have nathin' till do wie that. Is that why yew didn't go till Paddy's?" Her voice rose with apprehension. "Have they nat paid yew?"

He took the pay packet from his pocket and reached it to her.

"Nigh, be quiet an' I'll tell yew all about it," he said, reaching out to her.

She looked at his blistered hands, then at his raw features and lastly at the defeat in his eyes. Leaning forward she hugged him tightly.

"Don't let them bastards bate ye, love."

He didn't speak as he stared straight ahead of him at the photograph of his four young children in their school uniforms, smiling out at him.

As he held tightly to his wife, his eyes wandered around the sitting room of the house they had lived in since they were married. The home he returned to religiously every night of the week. Only on a Thursday would he be that few hours late when he called in to pay Paddy for the two half pints of Guinness he had each night. He drank alone, refusing to get into company that would see him spending too much or staying out too late.

The war had made him realise how fragile life was and too precious to spend with people other than those you loved and who loved you. From the Dunkirk retreat to the Normandy beaches, he had experienced what man could do to man. The everyday ritual of life-taking behind enemy lines had been his job, but it was not a job he relished. He longed for the war to end and dreamed of a mundane life.

When hostilities ended he'd applied for a red button and became a checker. After a few months the steam ship company he worked for hired him on a regular basis. He was found to be trustworthy in an industry where men thought it part of the procedure to steal and pilfer, and drink during working hours. He went directly to his place of work and didn't suffer the indignity of the daily visit to the schooling pen.

Melting gratefully into his surroundings, he loved the quietness and regularity of his work. The creation of one hundred new first-preference men had put that calmness and order at risk. Many of the second-preference men had applied to be made up and all were disappointed when only those related to first preference were selected. To add insult, family members, employed in other industries, were chosen. Many of these were time served tradesmen.

The red-button men railed at the injustice. They secretly gathered funds to fight what they called an unlawful intrusion into their workforce. The fund went undetected, or was ignored for months, before it was made public by angry first-preference men who set about taking their revenge, after a letter sent to the regional secretary of the union concerned was passed to Shaw.

He explained all this to Helen quietly and without anger. Looking at him through tears she realised why the men had regarded him as a leader. She gazed at him with pride but viewed the coming days nervously.

"Will yew git the two men to go forward for the trial case? Is it nat too late, nigh the damage is done?" she asked.

"The case is already in the court system."

"So yew've got the two men?" she said, relieved.

"No," he answered quietly. "We've got one."

"Well, that's a start," she replied brightly. "Who is he?"

Her brief moment of joy was shattered when he replied, quietly and without emotion, "Me. Our solicitor said the name cud be changed in the event of other volunteers."

She stared into the fire as he tried to ease her anxiety.

"Does that mean the case won't go without the other man?"

"No," he said. "They kin go with one complainant, although two wuda bin better ... "

"So yer in it," she concluded, with an air of resignation, with just a hint of pride.

He nodded dumbly.

"Up till my bloody neck."

For a split second, Henry hesitated outside the Stalingrad bar, before entering by the Dock Street door. The noise was almost unbearable as was the smoke that hung around the bar like a thick curtain of fog. He was about to order when he felt a hand on his backside, and smelt the heavy waft of perfume that accompanied it. He turned and looked into the tired but enthusiastic features of the Duchess.

"What about yew an' me in the backroom, big fella. Yer so sexy lukin' I wud do it fur nuthin, but yew know there's overheads an' what have ye. I'll settle fer half of my usual asking price."

Despite the anger in him, he was soft spoken and civil as he gently took her hand away from his backside, as it was dangerously close to his wallet.

"Nat at the minute girl," he replied, looking her up and down approvingly. He clicked his teeth appreciatively. "But that's a good offer. I'll maybe take yew up on it some other time."

"The offer closes tonight. There's a Clan boat berthing at the Pollock the marra, an' I need to rest up," she said dismissively, before moving haughtily away.

Henry half smiled as he watched her retreating figure. A moth-eaten and bedraggled fur coat hung loosely to help hide a dumpy middle-aged figure. She looked more like someone's favourite granny than a piece of merchandise soon to be fought over by the sex-hungry seamen on the incoming Clan boat.

"Givus my usual, Thanny," he called to the white-aproned barman above the noise of the Dockers and casuals celebrating payday. He searched in his pocket and lit a Woodbine, pulling deeply on the cigarette as he glanced at the men around him. He was annoyed at losing his temper in Paddy's Bar. The explosion on the quay had caused quite a bit of friction and he knew it was far from over. The militant reds had nothing to lose now, but they were in a tiny minority. Most of the men thought like him: they just wanted to go to the jobs of their choice.

The bartender washing glasses at the sink seemed to read his mind.

"This trouble affecting yew, Henry?"

"Naw," growled Henry, "our werk's too physical: too dirty, and the ires are too long for the blues to be interested. But this new intake has raised quite a few problems fer red-button men up the coast where the handy jobs are. That's what caused the trouble."

"Kin they do anything about it?"

Henry frowned.

"Nuthin'—except mebbe dig a bigger hole fer themselves. But then," he paused, "Wilson's a principled man, an' yew know how men of principle kin fuck up everything for everybody else as well as themselves. There's bad days comin'," he added darkly as he poured half of his stout into his whiskey and took a mouthful.

He grinned as the Duchess escorted a very drunk railway worker out of the door, taking some silver coins from his jacket pocket as they left.

Jim crossed the road into Henry Street and walked up the narrow confines of Southwell Street, stopping at number sixteen. He knocked hesitantly and waited until the door opened. A petite elderly woman with grey hair tied tightly in a bun at the back of her head motioned him up the long dark hall. He took off his cap and walked across the small living room to a woman sitting with her head bowed on a wine coloured sofa that was faded with age. He assumed she was Mrs. Reilly. Two women sat on either side of her, clutching her arms as if to give her spiritual aid and comfort.

"Mrs. Reilly," he began haltingly.

The woman on her left interrupted him harshly.

"Nat Missus," she hissed, "Miss. There is no Mrs. Reilly. Sally's his only child," she added primly.

He realised when the woman lifted her head that she was too young to be the widow. His face burned with embarrassment. He was the only male in the room and the small scullery was filled with women making refreshments. Sally lifted her head and smiled at him. Her pretty face was tear-streaked and despondent.

"I'm terrible sorry," he stammered.

"That's alright," smiled the woman being comforted. She nodded at the empty space at the window looking into the narrow street. "The body's not home yet. The police say they'll haveta do an autopsy on him to find out how he died."

"I know wut killed 'im," scowled a heavy-set woman wearing a black embroidered shawl. Her face was sharp and her dark eyes were filled with anger. "Hard bloody work! That's wut killed 'im. The same as wat killed my Willie John ten years ago."

"I wus with 'im at the boat ... " stammered Jim. "I left him in the Bowling Green ... The barman said he wud be alright." His voice became a sob. "If I'd a knowed he was sick I'd a gat him home ... "

The woman in the shawl smiled cynically at his innocence.

"Nat yore fault, son. His time had cum. Just like my Willie John. Driven inta the soft groun' by hard graft."

Reilly's daughter smiled tiredly at him.

"That's true. Don't go blamin' yourself. He was killed by the filth he breathed in every time he worked at one of those chemical cargoes. Exposure to harmful substances over a long period of time is what kills most of the men around here. My father's death was just a matter a time. Who knows what you are inhaling? Who knows what the fumes are doing to your lungs and other vital organs?"

"Aye," interrupted the woman in the shawl, "an' who cares? Them bastardin' foremen don't give a shite as long as they git the boats emptied. Nat much chance a them being affected. They were either in the pub or in the galley drinkin' coffee, accordin' till my Willie John."

Jim edged for the door.

"I jist cum till pay my respects. I worked wid yer father a few times, an' he wus a good man."

He reached out awkwardly and closed his large hand around her slim wrist.

"I'm sorry fer yer troubles," he muttered lamely, and turned for the door. The same woman who let him in followed him. He opened it to let himself out into the street and she closed it behind him without a word.

Putting his cap on, he started for home. He was tired and scared by the words of the two women. He wondered what tomorrow would bring as he walked past Mawhinney's shoe shop. He stopped at the Bowling Green, and decided to go in. The white-haired owner came over as soon as he saw him enter.

"Young fella, the peelers in York Street barrack want till talk till yew." He smiled sympathetically at the look of panic that crossed Jim's features. "Don't worry," he continued with a friendly smile, as he set him up a bottle of stout. "It's jist a matter a routine. They want till know Reilly's whereabouts for the period before he kim intil the bar. I toul thim I didn't know were yew lived but that I'd contact yew." Jim nodded dumbly as he continued, "It was when Jonty Burke went till use the wall telephone. He sat down beside Reilly an' noticed he wusn't breathin'. I sent fer Doctor Calder."

"I know," muttered the lad, feeling a chill running up his spine as he looked at the corner where he'd last seen Reilly. He put a florin on the counter to pay for the drink. The owner waved it away.

"It's on me," he said with a kindly smile.

Jim finished the bottle and walked back to the police station, at Little Georges' Street. He strode up the stone steps and opened the door. A constable seated at a coal fire looked up as he approached the counter. His tunic was unbuttoned, as was his shirt collar.

"I wus tole yew wanted till see me about the sudden death of Mr. Reilly," Jim stammered.

The constable walked to a large ledger book and flipped the pages. He took a pair of spectacles from his tunic pocket and studied the handwritten entries.

Jim watched his lips move soundlessly as he read the pages.

"An' who are yew?" asked the officer, absently buttoning his tunic.

"I'm Jim Harvey, sor. I wus wurkin' wid Mr. Reilly that day. When we finished we called intil the Bowlin' Green ... "

The constable sensed his concern.

"That's alright, son. There's an entry here says the old guy died from natural causes. He wus seventy three on his last birthday. A bit oul till be doin' that kind a work, eh?"

He saw the surprised look on Jim's face and grinned.

"Did yew nat know he wus that oul?"

Jim shook his head dumbly.

He reached for a pen and dipped it into an inkwell. Jim heard the nib scratching as he wrote a few lines in the book.

He looked up, surprised to see the boy still there.

"I've entered in the occurrence book that yew called in, son. Nigh go on home an' git it outa yer mind. The oul man wuda died no matter who was wid him."

Jim turned and walked into the street as the officer returned to his seat by the fire.

Lizzie looked up from her book as he entered the kitchen. Her voice was soft and concerned.

"Big Henry wus in lukin' yew twenty minits ago. Yev till

report till the corner as usual tamarra," she said, before returning to the pages of her book.

Music wafted through the house as he sat down thankfully glad to be back in the comfort of home. He saw the sad eyed Miss Reilly clutching her handkerchief and staring into space, before sleep engulfed him.

The next morning Jim moved slowly along Corporation Street and cut through the gate at Hamilton's Engineering Works. There were small clusters of men before and behind him, all going in the same direction. He felt stiff from the exertions of the tonnage boats, but along with that was a fast growing confidence that he was mastering the art of dock work. He turned into the schooling pen and saw it was five minutes to eight according to the harbour office clock.

There was something amiss but he couldn't immediately put his finger on it. He looked purposefully around the large area that was covered by men from one end to the other. Suddenly it hit him. The silence was deafening although there were almost two thousand men assembled in the immediate area. It was eerie, and frightening. He moved towards Ned's school. Henry hadn't specified where to go, so he made the decision himself.

He positioned himself within range of Ned's gaze and waited. The ganger's face was uncharacteristically tense as he waited for the clock to chime. At the first peal, Jim felt the school tighten. Suddenly an arm went around his neck and he was thrown roughly to his knees. He hit the square setts with the palms of his hands and bounced back to his feet. His eyes were wide and alert and ready for trouble. Another man was pushed roughly into his path knocking him down again. He landed heavily on his side, with the wind knocked out of him. He heard the ganger snarling loudly, and swung himself to the left to evade a heavy steel toed boot aimed at his ribs.

"Get the fuck back, ye parcel a bastards," screamed Ned.

Jim rose, guarding his head with his open hands. He saw second-preference men wrestling with the ganger who was roaring obscenities and holding tightly to the job checks. Others were physically assaulting the startled non-union men beside them. Jim was grabbed roughly by the shirtfront, and saw a huge fist moving in the direction of his head. He didn't look at the face of the man who was snarling hysterically at him. He ducked to avoid the punch and let go with a short sharp right jab. It hit his assailant just below the heart and he fell to the cobbles. Casting a quick eye behind him he saw men fighting the length and breadth of the compound.

The man he had knocked down rose to grapple with him. Slightly built, his face was contorted by hatred, but his eyes were frightened.

"Dirty fuckin' parasite!" he screamed, as he again went for the lad's exposed throat.

Jim held him in a boxing clinch and looked over the man's shoulder. Ned was pinned against the shed wall. Two men were holding him and one was trying to prise the job checks from his closed hands.

He felt a stinging in his shins and realised his attacker was kicking him whilst incessantly snarling insults in his ear. He tried to reason with the small red-button man whom he'd worked with only a few weeks earlier.

"Johnny," he yelled, to make himself heard above the screaming and shouting, "I don't want till fight wid yew."

A punch from behind sent him to his knees.

He rose groggily to face his new attacker. A wild-eyed man, his face full of anger, charged at him. Jim dropped into a fighting crouch and hit the oncoming attacker twice to the soft belly with a hard left and right that knocked the wind out of him, and sent him to his knees. The lad turned a full circle and saw Ned on the ground with at least three men on top of him. There were pockets of men fighting all over the schooling pen. He saw Uncle slugging it out with another group of red-button men as blue-button Dockers raced from the other end of the schooling pen to rescue the gangers. He ran to help Ned and pulled a squirming, screaming attacker off his back. He was pushed aside as a squad of blues came to the ganger's rescue. Feeling out of his depth, he found a gap and ran through it to the outer perimeter where men were watching the proceedings with disgust and contempt in their eyes.

Wilson was moving frantically through the fighting men.

"No call for this!" he was shouting as loudly as he could. "This is a legal matter."

A heavily built first-preference man struck him viciously from behind and his voice was silenced as he crashed to the ground. Jim noticed a man beside him, clad in a donkey jacket that was much too big for him. He was writing furiously in a small notebook, but put it away and ran to where Wilson lay on the cobbles.

Jim's eyes were drawn to his footwear. They were shiny expensive-looking shoes, and the trousers above them tweed with sharp creases down the front.

"Not suitable attire for a beg boat," thought the lad absently. "Probably a stevedore," he concluded.

A contingent of burly harbour police officers sprinted from the nearby barracks and were using batons to restore order. He saw Wilson, still lying on his back, being assisted to his feet by the man with the large donkey jacket and shiny shoes. Moments later both he and the injured man were taken into a landrover.

Order was restored and a chief inspector climbed on to the bonnet of the police vehicle to address the mob.

"Yew are on harbour property and I will not tolerate behaviour such as I've seen this morning. Those of yew who want work, form up as you usually do. Those of yew who want to create mayhem, please leave the compound. Any more disgraceful behaviour and the perpetrators will be taken across to the harbour courthouse and locked up until a date is set to try them for assault and disorderly behaviour. My constables have been ordered to arrest anyone who tries to take the law into their own hands." He eyed the crowd sternly. "Some of yew will be receiving summonses anyway for your disgraceful behaviour," he added menacingly.

Both gangers were on their feet, surrounded by furious first-preference men, and staring defiantly at those who had attacked them. Ned's voice trembled with anger as he glared at the men.

"Whoever's here for wurk an' nat fisticuffs, put yer han' up."

Jim raised his hand tentatively as did others. Ned glared around the depleted school, his black eyes bitter and angry. He had already schooled two blues for the deck, and two for back-jagging.

A harbour policeman watched as he picked the rest of his men. Harvey got the fourth check and knew it was a job in the hold. He smiled when he saw Billy Kelly step forward and automatically moved towards him. They waited for instructions. Ned gave them as he handed out the last job token.

"China clay. She's berthed at the old Dufferin, an' I want outa her the day."

He looked bitterly at the men he had left.

"Youse bastards who jumped me will be only wastin' yer time if yis stan'me again. Yis are done for. Kaput! Yis might as well be dead," he added as he turned on his heels and stormed to his car.

"Mosey on," muttered Kelly, "I'll catch up wid yew."

Jim clambered over the ship's rail and stood on the cargo of hundredweight sacks that filled the hold to the hatch coamings. He watched as the shore men threw slings and canvas sheets into the centre of the hold. The deck man set about preparing the derrick and the guy ropes. His mate attached a clamp to the lip of the hatch top. The lad was relieved when he saw Kelly beside him.

The holdsmen ran their eyes over the cargo, looking for the best place to build a heave. Jim looked at his friend.

"Yew an' me's about the youngest here, Billy. Will we make the first sink?"

Kelly grinned at his insolence.

"Don't let any a them oul han's hear yew sayin' things like that, or they'll toss yew inta the drink."

Jim's newfound confidence evaporated quickly as Kelly studied the bags.

"Over here," he said, pointing to the waterside of the hatch.

Jim nodded mutely and followed him, embarrassed at undermining men because they were older than him. He moved boldly and confidently, wanting to show he knew his way around a cargo.

Kelly spread the rope sling and Jim dutifully laid the canvas sheet on top of it. His companion produced a small hand hook and hid it in the palm of his hand. He ran his forefinger along the top of the steel shank, thus concealing it from everything but a close view. He winked at Jim.

"Man's best friend," he grinned, nodding at the hook.

He stooped and dug it into the side of the hessian bag, quickly twisting it in a follow-up movement. He shook the sack and jerked its other end clear.

"Right kid."

Jim dug his hands into the bag and both men threw it onto the rope. Within seconds twenty sacks were in the sling, and the heave was ready to be slung ashore.

The winch stopped running and the men peered upwards as the heave swung lazily above them.

"Everybody ashore!" yelled the man on the bull rope, before disappearing from view. The holdsmen looked questioningly at each other.

"Sumpthin's wrong, 'cause it's too early fer a tea break," muttered one.

Clambering onto the jetty, they saw the shore gang being addressed by a squad of first-preference dockers.

"Go on home," yelled one stocky figure. Well dressed with yellow boots and blue denim jeans, he had a shock of red hair and a ruddy complexion that was usually wreathed in a smile. Jim knew him only by his nickname, Tasty.

"We've called a meeting in the Assembly Hall. So yill have no winch or bull rope man: or back-jaggers fer that matter. The rest a the quay closed down for the day, so beat it." He finished in a tone that was threatening, but not unsociable.

"I kin drive the winch," said one man, almost politely. "Kin we nat go on without yis?"

The look of benevolence on Tasty's face vanished to be replaced with a hate-filled snarl.

"The man who puts a han' on that winch lever personally gets a kick in the balls from me. Nigh go on home, Peter, before we put yew on the blacklist with them other bastards who tried till kill our colleagues."

They moved off leaving the disconsolate men wondering what their next move would be.

"Let's go," said Kelly, "Nuthin' do be done here."

"Why are yew nat goin' till the meeting?" asked Jim.

Kelly grinned philosopically.

"They see me as one of youse. I've no rights either," he replied.

They walked slowly down the Pollock Road and watched as men from other ships moved to the exit from the Docks. The numbers had swelled considerably when they reached the harbour gate at Garmoyle Street. Many of them drifted into the little café next to Cullen's Bar. The owner couldn't believe his luck. He ran to the foot of the stairs.

"Git up ta hell a that, Maggie!" he shouted, "There's a horde a hungry men down here lukin fer sausage baps an' egg sodas!"

Tasty looked around the large hall packed with his work colleagues. He nodded confidently at Shaw seated at the front and flanked by branch committee men. He tapped the microphone in front of him a few times to test its volume before he spoke.

"First of all I want yew to look at the man beside yew. If yew don't know him check his lapel badge. If he hasn't one, git a steward to check him out. We don't want any interlopers interferin' in what is a branch matter—especially nosy newspaper reporters."

He waited a moment or two until the men established each other's bona-fides before continuing.

"I want to thank yew for yer backing. Yew all know the circumstances that led to the unforgivable scenes of violence by gangsters masquerading as werkers in our schoolin' pen this mornin'. I say *our* schoolin' pen," he said sharply and emphatically.

He paused for a moment, anticipating the roar of approval which swelled to ear-bursting proportions behind his words.

"Our colleagues have been attacked in a most cowardly way as they went about the job of selecting people for werk. I'm glad to say they were nat diverted from that purpose by the gangsterism that has infiltrated the honest and decent men of the second-preference branch.

"They question the actions of Brother Shaw in taking away their paybooks. When it was done individually they niver complained. When they were fined for being drunk at work or failing to turn up for work or otherwise bringing the branch into disrepute, they accepted the punishment as part of the responsibility of the job.

"I want to tell yew nigh, this meeting was called to let yew know the branch committee will vote unanimously to back Brother Shaw's decision; an' we would want a show of han's from yew men to ratify that decision, when it is taken."

The hands shot swiftly into the air.

"We want yewr consent and approval. Have we got it?"

He finished with a triumphant roar as he turned his head and put a hand to his ear. The almost deafening howl of acceptance saw him smiling down at Shaw who nodded in return.

"Right," continued Tasty, "I'm sure the stevedores will forgive us this first strike action since the day of the Docker's sixpence. Brother Shaw will be contacting them to tell them we'll all be at our posts the marra, doin' what we do better'n anybody else."

The body of the floor rose to give him a standing ovation. A section of the men around Shaw surged forward, placed him on their shoulders, and carried him from the building.

The atmosphere in the Goodall home at lunchtime was strained. The father, a first-preference man for over thirty years, had just returned from the meeting in the Assembly Hall with his two eldest sons, both of whom wore the same blue button. Charlie Goodall looked sternly at his other two sons already seated at the dining room table. He threw his cap on the sofa and growled a greeting to his wife.

Mrs. Goodall gazed with concern at both sets of sons who pointedly ignored each other. She made to speak but the father narrowed his eyes in her direction.

"Git me some tea an' a bita toast, Lily, an' keep outa this," he ordered.

The woman walked to the scullery, glancing behind her as she went. The father turned his attention to his youngest sons and addressed the one closest to him.

"Yis are gonna be alright, Gilbert. Tasty says it's jist a matter a time before the books open again an' yis 'ill be brought in."

Gilbert couldn't conceal his simmering anger.

"An' what happens in the meantime till me an' John? None a the reds wanta wurk wid us 'cause they think we're informers, an' the gangers don't wanta give us a job cos they think our names is on the petition, an' the Arabs don't trust us cause our da's an ex-committee man!"

One of his older brothers intervened.

"Yis 'ill jist havta put up wid it till it's sorted. We have till lower the boom on these guys. It'll blow over soon enough. An' yis needn't worry about wurkin' wid fella reds. When we're finished ... "

Gilbert wasn't convinced.

"It's alright yew talking nigh. Yew'd feel the same as me if yew were the youngest son. Yis are all certain this is gonna blow over. It isn't! I've heard thim talkin'. They've bin collectin' fer weeks, an' are determined till see it through till the bitter end."

His father raised his head sharply, his thin face enveloped in a scowl.

"Yew didn't contribute, did yew?" he asked harshly.

Gilbert didn't answer. The old man's eyes were pained as they swung in the direction of the second youngest brother.

"What about yew, John?"

John placed his fork on the table and didn't meet his father's hostile glare.

"We had to, fer the first coupla weeks, or they'd a sent us till Coventry. They wanted full solidarity. Besides we were a bit miffed that we'd bin passed over in the last selection."

Mrs. Goodall brought in the tea and toast as the men glowered at each other across the table. Her husband ignored her.

"So yer names is on the list then?" he continued.

"Yis," yelled John, desperately and harshly.

His father's open hand slapped him viciously.

"Don't yew dare raise yer voice to me at the dinner table or anywhere else. There's men on the committee have no time fer me, an' yew've given them the opportunity till git back at me, yew silly bastards."

He rose abruptly and pushed the tea and toast to the floor.

"I'm away till the pub," he snarled, slamming the door as he left the room.

"How cud youse two be so stupid!" shouted the eldest son, rising from the table in anger. "Yis have put Da at the mercy of them bastards on the branch committee who hate him from the time he opposed Shaw's selection as secretary."

John rolled his eyes sarcastically.

"He already tole us that," he muttered. "What wud yew a done if yew were in our place?"

"I wudn't a bin stupid enuff till put my name on a sheet, or contribute to a cause I knew was bound till git me inta trouble," snarled his older brother. "But then what do yew expect from a red-button man?" he continued, sarcastically. "Yis are as thick as two short planks."

The table shuddered as the four men rose to face each other.

"That's enuff!" screamed Mrs. Goodall, walking between the men as they squared up to each other. "This thing has ripped apart families all over the town. I wus in Bela Wilson's yesterday gittin' the messages, and Jennie Ritchie tole me her husband an' their two sons haven't spoke till each other since this thing began. I don't want that till happen here. In future I want yis till leave it where it belongs—on the quay."

She looked at her two eldest sons.

"Yer da worked hard till git youse the security of Dockers buttons." Her tear-stained face turned to the youngest men.

"It's nat his fault this row has broken out before he cud git youse two in." She turned again to her eldest sons, her tired eyes blazing angrily. "Them two are stuck in the middle. Takin' insults from them that don't like yer da, and their red-button colleagues who don't trust thim. They're gittin' enuff grief without yews, their own flesh an' blood, addin' till it. Nigh eat yer lunch. It'll all cum to a head sooner or later. But I don't want another wurd about it in this house."

He sons didn't reply, but continued to glare at each other as she stooped to mop up the spilt tea that had left a dark stain on the carpet. She shuddered as it reminded her of blood.

Collins was livid as he tried without success to contact Shaw who wasn't answering his office phone. The other stevedores had been inundating him with angry calls regarding the termination of labour. He saw Ned, his ganger, through the office window and called to him when he entered the outer office. The big ganger shuffled into the room and took off his cap.

Collins put the phone down.

"What the fuck happened there this mornin'?"

Ned sat down heavily on a soft chair that groaned under the impact of his weight. He crossed his legs and placed his cap on his knee.

"Lightnin' strike. They called it to show their solidarity with Shaw. They'll be back tamarra," he added matter-of-factly.

The stevedore exploded.

"Niver mind the marra! What about the expenses that will occur because the boat yew schooled the morning will have to lie over until tomorrow?The other stevedores are in the same position an' have bin eatin' the arse off me all mornin'."

Ned shrugged his shoulders.

"I havta do what the committee tells me."

"But I pay your wages," insisted Collins.

"I wudn't have any wages if the committee blackballed me for failing to honour strike commitments."

"But yew work for me," stressed Collins.

Ned was unperturbed.

"I wudn't be working for anyone if I lost my button, an' I'd lose it if I didn't follow the procedure endorsed by the branch committee."

"But the branch committee hasn't met as far as I know," protested Collins.

"When they do meet they'll vote the stoppage as legal," replied the ganger.

Collins abandoned the argument, not wanting to admit the Dockers held the winning hand. He tried another approach.

"How do yew see it pannin' out?"

Ned rolled his paunchy body to one side and fished a packet of *Park Drive* cigarettes from his overcoat pocket. He looked squarely at the stevedore.

"It might git a bit dirty in the clinches," he said, lighting the cigarette, and blowing smoke to the ceiling. "The guy arrested wid Wilson this mornin' is a lawyer of some description. He give his address as the legal department at Queen's University. Apparently he's been in the schoolin' pen incognito, more than once, observing the fall-out between us and the reds."

"Was he prosecuted?" asked Collins anxiously.

"Naw. They drew back sharpish, when they heard who he was. They didn't prosecute Wilson either. The reds gathered outside their tuppence-ha'penny courthouse and threatened till wreck it if he wasn't released."

Collins swore vehemently as Ned took a deep draw from his cigarette.

"There's worse till come," he said tersely, "The Bulkies didn't release Wilson because of the threat from the crowd. One of our men spoke in his defence."

Collins narrowed his eyes.

"What do you mean? Our men?"

"The detective who interviewed me re the assault on myself said Wilson had been released on the word of a blue-button man, who swore he was only trying to stop the fightin'."

He heaved a sigh and stubbed out the cigarette.

"The detective also tuk great delight in tellin' me the blue-button man tole the guy from Queen's he supported the argument the reds are puttin' up. That's one of the reasons we called the stoppage. We need to put pressure on this guy. He cud fuck everything up."

Collins was aghast.

"What are we gonna do?"

Ned grinned unpleasantly.

"Relax," he advised. "I'm arrangin' ta met Shaw later on. He'll put the heavy han' on this guy. He'll listen till good advice or he'll be out on his arse."

Collins wasn't so sure.

"You don't know who he is. The detective wouldn't say, you said ... "

Ned interrupted with a smug smile.

"That's right, but one of our lads has a sister who's married till a Harbour cop who wants till be a first-preference man. He givus the name."

"Who is he?" asked Collins.

Ned pulled out another cigarette and tapped the end of it on his thumbnail, before putting it in his mouth.

"A headcase called Kelly. He's halfway out the door already. He's bin suspended for hittin' the ganger at the Heysham boat, an' won't apologise fer his behaviour. He's bin wurkin' as an Arab ever since."

Collins pursed his lips thoughtfully.

"I know this guy. He won't be a pushover."

Ned played with his cigarette.

"Yer right there. As a fightin' man he has no equal on the quay. A spell as an officer during the war gave him principles he hasn't bin able till shake off. However he loves his da, an' his da's a red hot committeeman, the longest servin' member on it. He's completely devoted to the union and its operation to wipe out the reds. Let's see where Kelly's real loyalties lie—with outsiders or flesh an' blood."

Collins took a *Gold Flake* cigarette from a silver box on his desk top. He lit it with a silver plated lighter and blew the smoke to the ceiling with a gasp of relief.

"I feel better already," he grinned.

Kelly finished his whiskey with a flourish and looked at the pub clock.

"Time I wasn't here," he grinned at Jim. "I'm goin' fer a fish supper, then home."

Jim drank the remainder of his pint shandy.

"Think I'll head too," he said, rising from the table.

They'd been been in the Bunch of Grapes since seven o'clock. Jim had walked the length of his street to get a couple of shandies and was surprised to see Kelly sitting at the bar.

"I thought yew were goin' till see Minnie the night?"

Kelly grimaced.

"So did I, but her da thought different. She's bin forbidden till associate with me," he finished sadly, but with a humorous glint in his eye. "Her da says I'm a bad influence."

He looked at the whiskey glass as he swirled its contents.

"Me own da agrees wid 'im."

Jim had no answer and ordered a drink for both of them. There wasn't much talk. It seemed as if the Docker had a lot on his mind. The lad drank his shandy and kept quiet, until the moment when Kelly decided to leave. They walked out into the darkness towards the brightly-lit window of Crook's chip shop. The Friday night crowd milled around the open door or stood in the long queue to be served.

"Hing on an' I'll git ye a fish," said Kelly as they shouldered their way into the shop. The line proceeded slowly and still there was no talk from Kelly. Jim knew he was fond of Minnie and was saddened at her father's decision. He also knew her father was a docker and thought it was another way to put pressure on the wayward first-preference man to bring him back into line.

Four men noisily entered the chip shop and moved to the top of the queue, interrupting his thoughts on the matter. They demanded immediate service. The woman wrapping the fish and chips in sheets of newspaper pointed to the end of the queue. Jim couldn't hear what she was saying over the noise of the crowd. The men refused to obey her order and began shouting in loud harsh voices.

"Bloody foreigners, always actin' stupid an' jumpin' the queue," sniffed a woman beside them.

Kelly's face darkened.

"Germans," he hissed through clenched teeth. He took off his cap. "Hold this," he muttered to Jim as he moved to the front of the queue.

"Need any help, Missus?" he asked.

"They won't go till the back of the queue," she answered.

Kelly smiled at the tallest and largest one.

"Entschuldigung, mein Herr, würden sie bitte Schlange stehen?"

The man looked surprised.

"Fuck off," he said in perfect English.

Two seconds later he was lying unconscious on the floor of the chip shop: felled by a punch from Kelly that hit him on the side of the jaw.

Jim was mesmerised by the action and watched as the man seemed to flounder before falling in a senseless heap, like a life-sized puppet whose strings had been suddenly cut. Another German leapt at Kelly who calmly ducked under his body and threw him across the room. He landed among a group of women who proceeded to kick him savagely. The local patrons of the supper saloon cheered as Kelly faced the startled foreigners with his fists clenched.

"Nächst?" Who's next?"

No one spoke. They looked to their fallen comrades and the crowd moved back to allow them to be carried them from the scene.

Kelly went back to his position in the queue and took his cap from Harvey.

"German bastards. Yew'd think they won the war," he scowled to no one in particular.

His face was a mask of hatred and the look in his eyes frightened his young companion.

After being served, they moved to the door. Kelly had returned to his usual relaxed self.

"Go yew out first, Jim. See if any of the Krauts are still around," he whispered.

Jim nodded vigorously and walked from the bright lights of the supper saloon to the darkness of the street. He looked first up Earl Street and then along Nelson Street. He saw the Germans at the corner of Quinn's Place. They were arguing bitterly among themselves. Kelly came out behind him and watched the scene for a few moments. He walked towards a crowd of men standing at the corner opposite the chip shop.

He spoke to the men who quickly followed when he moved in the direction of the German sailors. They watched warily as Kelly approached them with at least ten of the corner boys behind them. Jim joined them. Kelly addressed the man he had knocked to the floor. He spoke in English, but very slowly.

"Mebbe yer nat the best man in yer group. Point out who is and him an' I'll go down the wee lane there behin' us, an' see if we kin work out an honourable settlement. Win, lose or draw none of the rest of ye will be harmed." The German listened and nodded understanding.

"Big isn't always best," he acknowledged, ruefully rubbing his jaw.

He spoke to the other men in German. A thick set medium-sized sailor about thirty years old stepped forward. He was about the same height as Kelly. He was bald with a deeply tanned face. He showed white teeth as he grinned at the docker.

"Karl is ex-SS Waffen. He has no English," replied the spokesman. "He says he killed many of your countrymen during the recent war and will delight in showing you how he did it. But he'll only fight if you promise it will be one to one."

Kelly nodded curtly and was about to walk down the entry when the screeching of car brakes stopped him. The headlamps of the police car bathed them in a white light as Head McKinstry jumped from the still moving vehicle. Three other constables moved quickly behind him as he forced his way through the gathering crowd.

Straightening his cap, he placed his blackthorn stick beneath his armpit.

"Nigh, Kelly. What's goin' on?" he said sternly, looking with contempt at the strangers. "Is this rabble causin' a breach of the peace?"

"Naw, Head," said Kelly, "we were just exchangin' pleasantries. They're Krauts who still see themselves as the master race."

He was intent on returning the defiant stare of the sailor called Karl, the only one who didn't look frightened. He was sorry the police had arrived. Karl was someone he would have liked to work out his frustrations on.

McKinstry scowled.

"Did yew nat kill enough a them pore divils during the war?" he snorted under his breath as he moved towards the group of foreigners. "Who's the spokesman?" he snarled. The tall man put up his hand; his face was tense as he looked at the growing crowd and the large Webley revolver on McKinstry's belt.

"Do yew understand English?" asked the policeman.

"Yes," replied the German.

"Do yew understand fuckinsie off? If so, fuckinsie off till yer ship wherever it is. If I catch yew in this area again, I'll throw yew in jail." He stuck his face into that of the German. "Understanda?" he snarled, as he signalled two constables. "Escort them till the harbour gates." They nodded as the crowd opened to allow them to walk along Nelson Street. Kelly met with Karl's tight grin he looked at the ex-SS man.

"Hope we meet again, Karl. *Hoffentlich werden wir uns nochmal treffen?*" he said gently.

Karl didn't answer, but nodded.

McKinstry watched until they disappeared into Dock Street. He looked at Kelly.

"Were they at the old master race tricks again?" he asked, as he returned to the car.

Kelly nodded. The Head constable leaned over and whispered in his ear.

"Sorry I interrupted."

McKinstry climbed into the passenger seat and rolled down the window to scowl at the bystanders.

"Move on nigh. Yis don't need me til tell yis, three's a crowd and such an assembly unless lawfully convened is an arrestable offence." The men moved dutifully on and the driver accelerated in the direction of the officers who escorted the sailors out of the area.

"Didn't know yew cud speak German," Jim said as the

crowd returned to the corner, and they continued down Earl Street. Kelly grinned without answering. "Are yew goin' till the corner tamarra?" asked the boy as they parted company.

"Naw. I'm havin a lie-in. Then up till Peter's Hill for a good bath till git all the dock shit off me," his companion replied.

Jim nodded.

"I cud do wid a lie-in meself, but if I did Henry wud be up our stairs like a bloody tank an' haul me outa my bed," he muttered as he turned and walked up the dark hall.

His sister Lizzie came to the front door and saw Kelly's receding figure. She ran back to the kitchen.

"He's bin with that head-the-ball Kelly again, ma," she shouted, "He's niver gonna lern sense runnin' aroun' wid that nutcase."

Mrs. Harvey looked up from her knitting.

"Kelly's nat as daft as he lets on to be, and he's luked after yer brother more than once. That's more than most of his relatives wud do, although they promised miracles at yer da's funeral," she answered bitterly. Putting the knitting to the side, she rose from her chair. "Yer Uncle Henry's jist away. He says yiv till go till the corner tamarra and stan' Ned Semple. He's re-schoolin' the boat yis were at taday. He says yew haven't till be late, an' don't git involved in any fightin', if there is any," she added fearfully.

Jim sat down on the settee and looked over at his mother. "Kelly bought me a fish," he said, adding in an earnest voice, as Lizzie took the package into the scullery, "I only drank a few shandies the day, ma. I wudn't a drunk any but Kelly says we need to replace the liquid in our bodies that is dehydrated by the hard wurk."

She looked at his earnest face and grinned warmly in spite of her misgivings.

"That's a big wurd fer a York Street man," she teased softly. "What does it mane?"

"It manes yer as dry as a bone when yew finish an' it takes about six or seven pints till git yer liquid levels back till normal," shouted his sister from the scullery, "Talk about drinkin the profits," she added sarcastically.

She entered the room and set a plate containing the fish on the card table with a thump.

"Did yis ever think a replacing yer liquid deficiency with a chape commodity called water?" she continued. "Naw," she said, answering herself in a manly gruff voice. "Big tuff Dockers don't drink water or lemonade or anything that hasn't the kick of a mule."

"I wus drinkin' shandies," he protested through a mouthful of food.

"Aye," she continued laughing, "Keep that up and some a them big dockers 'ill be feelin' yer arse."

Her mother's angry scowl cut the laughter short.

"That's enuff, Lizzie Harvey. I don't wanta hear talk like that in this house. Yer father wud skin yew alive if he was to hear yew comin' off wid such vulgarities." She returned to her knitting. Jim grinned at his sister's irreverence and concentrated on the music floating from the radio.

Kelly entered a silent home. The atmosphere hadn't changed since he'd been suspended. When he walked into the brightly-lit kitchen, his father looked up from the newspaper, spat unerringly into the fire and returned his eyes to the paper. Billy walked into the scullery and put the fish supper onto a plate.

An hour later he was washed and dressed and going out of the kitchen door when his father spoke.

"Stay away from Minnie Renwick," he said sternly, his pipe still clenched between his teeth. "Her da doesn't want yew about her. Says he wants better fer his only chile than a drunken brawler with no respect fer the button he wears or the men who made it possible fer him to git a good job he obviously doesn't want. Heed what I say," he finished harshly.

The fire sizzled as he dropped the paper and spat directly into the flames. His son didn't answer as he left the kitchen and walked into the dark narrow street.

The White Lion was only a few hundred yards from his doorway. He stood at the lounge door and hesitated, knowing Minnie would be in there with her work mates from Gallaher's tobacco factory. It was Friday night and they met for the singsong. He turned instead into the bar. Thick smoke greeted him as he walked to the counter. "A pint an' a Bush, Jackie," he called, raising his voice to make himself heard over the unbelievable volume of noise that came from the patrons and a black and white television that was playing heedlessly above the bar door that led to York Street.

He looked slowly around the clientele as the barman set his order in front of him.

"Any wurd as to when Reilly's gittin' buried? My da was reading the *Tele* so I didn't git lukin'."

"No wurd yet, Billy. It jist says interment notice later. I believe his daughter's breakin' her heart."

"Aye," replied Kelly, "He wus very prouda her makin' a good life fer herself in England."

He saw two young, newly initiated first-preference men sitting at a table close to the door. He knew they were watching him, and wasn't surprised when they left their table to join him. They were more than slightly drunk. The taller one was over six feet four inches. He was thinly built with long black curly hair that protruded from under his eight-piece cap. He gave Kelly a friendly smile.

"Yew're one a us," he grinned. "Do yew want a join us? We were checkin' at the Heysham and haven't bin home yit."

Kelly could see the man wanted to be friendly and replied cordially, "Yis are nat local boys. Where in the city are yis from?"

"I'm Ernie from Sandy Row," said the tall one, "Tommy's from the Whitewell Road. We're new starts on the quay. I wus workin' as a fitter in the Ulster Transport Authority, an' Tommy here was a merchant seaman. We gat chosen for first preference in the last selection committee." He winked at Kelly and grinned knowingly. "Money from America."

Kelly found he couldn't disagree with their sentiments, but thought he would warn them of the recent events.

"I wudn't hing aroun' these local bars too long. There's some men wudn't take too kindly till seeing them first preference badges in the lapels of youngsters."

Ernie nodded knowingly.

"Do yew mane the reds?" he asked quietly.

Kelly shook his head.

"Nat the reds. They'll be keepin' their noses clean in the hope that this thing'll blow over. But there's other men aroun' here who've spent their lives on the quay as outsiders who won't appreciate seeing some of the new edition in their local."

"Aye," said Ernie seriously. "I know what yew mane. C'mon, Tommy. We'll drink up an' go somewhere closer till home where we're recognised."

Tommy looked at his companion and snarled, "I'm nat goin' anywhere. I kin take care of myself. I gat this button legally an' I'm proud of it."

Kelly grinned at his self-confidence.

"Good man," he laughed, giving the docker a friendly tap on the shoulder. He knew he wouldn't be able to get rid of them so he finished his drink and excused himself. "Goin' till meet the girlfrien'," he grinned. "See yis aroun'." He narrowed his eyes at the taller man. "Be careful," he whispered, before disappearing out of the bar door and striding the stairs to the lounge.

They returned to their seats. Before he sat down Tommy pulled out a wad of notes.

"What's yer pleasure, Ernie, same again?"

His companion nodded drunkenly as Tommy pushed his way to the bar.

Kelly entered the lounge and stood in the shadow of the door until a frail woman with spectacles as large as her face wailed a sad lament about forbidden love. He could see Minnie through the haze of smoke and knew the theme of the two star-crossed lovers in the lyric wasn't far from their own story.

We kiss in the shadow,
we hide from the moon.
Our meetings are few,
and over too soon.

Her head was in her hands and she stared listlessly at her untouched drink. When the song finished, he strode quietly to the bar and ordered a Black Bush. One of Minnie's girlfriends saw him, and her eyes lit up. Kelly watched slightly amused as she drew the attention of her other friends around the table.

Minnie became aware of the fuss. She looked up and saw him standing at the bar, one foot on the rail and one hand on his drink. He was gazing straight at her.

"He's gorgeous, Minnie," squealed one of her friends.

"Give over," snorted another girl, fixing the speaker with a withering look. Minnie returned her glance to the table as Kelly toyed with his glass.

The chairman's voice crackled over the microphone.

"Right nigh, ladies an' gentlemen. Settle down. We've had our little break. I think it's time we called our Minnie, brought to yew direct from Gallaher's tabacca factory, for one of her specials."

Minnie grabbed her handkerchief and started to cry whilst shaking her head vigorously from side to side.

"She doesn't want till sing. She's nat herself the night," shouted one of her friends at the table.

"Ack, is she nat?" called the chairman in a mocking tone. "Well, tell us who she is, if she's nat herself? Mebbe she needs a bita coaxin'?" The audience responded by clapping loudly. "C'mon wee Minnie: givus the one yew got six months for."

The crowd roared at the often-repeated joke. It caused Minnie to smile through her tears. Putting down her handkerchief, she rose and hurried to the rostrum. She whispered into the accordionist's ear before going to the microphone. She waited until he played the introduction, swinging the hand held mike gently from side to side and staring into space. As the accordionist emphasised where she was to join him with an exaggerated flourish on the keyboard, Minnie lowered her gaze to the floor and began singing.

Once I had a secret love
that lived within the heart of me

All too soon my secret love
became impatient to be free.

At that moment the lounge doors burst open and McKinstry entered, waving his blackthorn above his head. Four constables charged in behind him and stood at the door until he reached the centre of the room. The music stopped abruptly and Minnie fled to her table in tears.

"I'm all cut," she sobbed to her companions who tried to comfort her.

The head constable positioned himself in the centre of the room and looked around the drinkers. He waited until he had everyone's undivided attention before turning his head slightly to address the chairman.

"Sorry, Moe," he whispered. He turned to the drinkers. "Ten minutes ago, a serious assault on two young men took place in the male toilets downstairs. It was a particularly brutal and vicious attack carried out by some person or persons that has left these two young men with smashed faces and possibly broken bones.

"My officers are going to come among the males and check for bloodstains on clothes or footwear, or bruised knuckles. For I have to tell yew that toilet is like an abattoir down there."

"Do yew know who they are?" cried a woman in a frightened voice. "My Johnny was down there wid a couple a his mates."

McKinstry signalled one officer to remain at the door and the others to check out the drinkers. He gazed at the woman.

"It's nobody local," he replied. "We know who they are, an' they're nat from this area. An ambulance is on its way from the Mater. In the meantime, I'm sorry fer spoilin' yer night, but nobody leaves here till we check it out. The two men were headin' fer a bus, an' visited the toilets before they departed. Another man who went out a few minutes later found them. This was no amateur job. This was done by someone who knew how to inflict punishment."

His eyes locked at that moment with Billy Kelly, who was returning his glance, when a constable grabbed his hands and examined them for bruising. After turning them over, he looked closely at his clothes and shoes before moving away to examine another man. McKinstry stopped him with a roar.

"Check his pockets for gloves!"

The constable obeyed and shook his head, as nothing was revealed.

McKinstry smiled tightly. He walked across the room and stopped at Kelly.

"Haven't seen anyone as badly beaten since yew sent that lorry driver to hospital stretched out on the back of his own lorry. Still yer in the clear on this one," he smiled sardonically. "Whoever did it was probably wearin' gloves, to save knuckle bruisin' an' dumped 'em. Yew lern strokes like that in the army, don't yew?"

Kelly grinned tightly, ignoring the reference to the gloves.

"That lorry driver was deservin' of all the attention he gat, Head."

"I know," retorted the head constable, "If it hadda bin any other way, yew'd a bin languishin' in the Crum nigh."

Both men stood in silence as the police officers made their way slowly through the drinkers.

Kelly felt Minnie's eyes on him and walked to the table where her girlfriends were comforting her. She looked at him with fear-filled eyes. As he sat down she threw her arms around his neck impulsively.

"Thank God it wasn't yew, Billy," she sobbed.

Her body was shaking as she buried her head in his chest. Another girl stood behind him holding Minnie's hand. He watched as McKinstry returned to the centre of the room.

"We're leavin' nigh. If anyone has any information, pass it onto us at York Street Station. This was a particularly brutal attack, an' we want the people who carried it out," he said as he ordered his men to leave the lounge.

"Well, folks, after that unwelcome interruption from McKinstry an' his stormtroopers. I think we'll have Minnie back for an encore," called the chairman.

Minnie buried her head further into the folds of Kelly's

tweed jacket, and cried all the harder. The chairman saw her friends wave their hands and turned again to the mike.

"It seems Minnie has better things to do," he laughed, winking broadly at Kelly. "So without any further ado we'll have Agnes Rhodes fer the number she made famous during her recent tour of the Sailortown pubs. C'mon nigh, Aggie!" he roared. "It's nat like yew till be shy."

Kelly whispered in Minnie's ear.

"I'm goin' till the Sportsman's. Meet me there in the wee loose box. Paddy'll make sure we're left alone."

She looked at him with panic in her red-rimmed eyes.

"I dursn't, Billy. Yew know what me da said."

He looked at her.

"I'm nat after yer da," he replied with a soft mocking smile.

She turned from him, embarrassed at her public show of affection. Kelly rose and looked at the anxious faces of her girlfriends.

"Goodnight," he said tersely, taking his leave quickly during a break in the singing.

He turned at the bottom of the stairs and walked into the bar.

"What happened?" he said to the barman.

"Them two kids yew were talkin' till gat a terrible beatin', Billy," he replied. "Niver seen anythin' like it. Blood all over the place. One had his head stuck down a toilet bowl." He shuddered at the thought. "The big guy's face was smashed against an oul steel radiator. The blood was still gushin' from his mouth when they foun' him. McKinstry's away till the Mater to see if they kin give him any info."

"I warned them till go home, because of the problems on the quay," Kelly muttered as he sipped his drink.

"It wasn't long after yew went till the lounge when they got up till leave," replied the barman. "They were drunk an' throwin' money around like it was waste paper. One turned his tumbler upside down on the bar before he went out. Somebody musta spotted it an' followed them intil the piss house. They wudn't a bin able till defend themselves."

"Like mi da used till say," replied Kelly softly, "When boys

96

have money, they think they're men. When the money's gone, they're boys again."

"Aye. We know that well enuff in this game," replied the barman, moving off to pull a pint of single from the barrels at the other end of the bar. He continued to talk.

"The cops asked if there were any strangers in besides them boys. I tole them there wasn't 'cept fer a handfula sailors who left shortly after the fracas. Probably didn't want till git inta any trouble in a foreign port."

Kelly nodded a mute agreement and left.

Three

PADDY GREETED HIM IN HIS USUAL flamboyant way. He was relieved to find the snug empty. He spoke quietly to the pub owner who proceeded to put up a sign.

"There yew go! Yer havin' a private party, an' no one will interrupt when they see that sign."

Kelly looked around the body of the public house before he entered the little room. He saw Wilson sitting on his stool in his usual position: one hand rested lightly on a half-finished glass of Guinness, the other propping up the side of his head. He returned Kelly's wave with a guarded nod.

The clip of high heels sent him to the door. Minnie entered with her head down, wearing a pink scarf over her hair and a long mauve coloured coat that stretched to her ankles. He opened the lounge door and she squeezed past him. He looked into her wide eyes as she sat down.

"What's it to be?" he grinned.

She laid her handbag on the table.

"Billy, is there no bottom in yew? I tole yew the other night me da doesn't want me till go near yew!" she cried.

He leaned over the table and looked closely into her strained features.

"Let me hear yew say yew don't want me near ya, an' I'll be out that dour like a shot."

She fidgeted with the clasp of her handbag, keeping her eyes away from his.

"Billy, he's me da. I havta live wid him. He says only hoors run with married men."

98

"I'm nat married," he stated flatly.

She rose from the table in anger.

"But ye are Billy. Ye are. No matter if yer wife an' son's in Timbuctoo, they're yewr responsibility, an' will be until ye git a divorce, if she'll give yew one, or better still if yew want one. My da says yer a waster wid no future. I've heard yer thinkin' a joinin' the army again. Where wud that leave me?"

Kelly sipped at his drink.

"We could meet widout yewr da knowin'. Isn't he still on the Clyde boat cattle run? How wud he know if he's on the water most of the time?"

"There's plenty wud take pleasure in tellin' him, an' I'd git the legs scalped off me," she replied, fixing him with a petulant stare.

Kelly looked intently at her across the table.

"He's only usin' yew. Yer an unpaid housekeeper lukin' after his home whilst he sails back an' forward till Scotland." A cruel glint came into his eyes. "Some day he might bring an oul girl home from Scotland an' set up house wid her an' what'll yew do then? Yew know two wimmin can't live in the same house together."

His tone was mocking, and caused Minnie to reach for her handbag and move to the lounge door.

"My da wud niver do such a thing. Like yer own father he's a man a principle. Nat like yew. A drunken fightin' disrespectful ungrateful pup outa Hell. I'm sorry I ever set eyes on yew," she sobbed as she rushed out into York Street.

He sat stonily silent as the clip of her heels faded. Lifting his drink, he took the sign from the door, and looked with a wistful grin at the occupants of the bar who'd heard every word. He reached Paddy the cardboard sign.

"The party's over. Givus a pint an' a Bush."

Paddy turned mutely and dished up the order without any of his usual platitudes.

Kelly walked slowly up the bar to where Wilson sat with his head in his hand and a faraway look in his eyes. The angry redness from the creosote in the sleepers had not left his features. Kelly grinned.

"Yew luk like yiv bin boiled in oil."

"Aye, Staff, an' it felt like it."

Kelly smiled.

"The war's over, as yew niver tire tellin' me."

"Sorry. I wus daydreamin'," smiled his companion. He took a sip from his drink. "It might be over in Europe an' elsewhere, but I think it's startin' up again here: an' this time yew an' me's on different sides," he added with a cynical laugh.

Kelly looked at him with affection.

"Yew know that's nat true."

"Billy, yev gatta luk after yerself," warned Wilson sincerely. "Stay away from me an' the rest. No good us winnin' our argument if men like yew become sacrificial cows."

Kelly didn't answer and nodded tersely at Paddy.

"Give him his pleasure," he said quietly.

"Jist a half pint, Paddy," smiled Wilson. "I've gat till keep me powder dry an' me brain from addling."

Paddy set up the drink and returned with the change. He ran his fingers through his sand coloured hair as he looked at Wilson.

"Do yew see any quick end till this dispute?"

Wilson thought a moment.

"Naw," he replied softly. "This is a fight till the death, with only one winner."

"But more than one loser," muttered the barman. "My takin's have dropped like a stone these last coupla days. Nigh, I'm nat too worried if it's in the short term," he added hopefully.

Wilson took a tentative sup from his glass.

"Paddy, there's men I think yill niver see again. They won't be back till the dock. They wudn't be able fer that hard physical wurk." He shuddered. "Neither am I, fer that matter. We're too oul an' too soft." He looked at the barman. "I suppose a lotta them owe ye?"

"I'm nat worried about that," stated Paddy. "I'm worried that they won't come in. Will yew tell them ta keep comin' in?" he said with a hint of desperation in his voice. "They kin pay me when this blows over. I jist don't wanta lose their custom."

Wilson smiled.

"I'll pass it on."

Paddy flashed him a grateful grin.

"How's the legal end comin'?" whispered Kelly when the barman departed.

Wilson drew a deep breath.

"I've till go to the law department in Queen's University tamarra till see the man who's been sneakin' ontil the quay this last couple a weeks observin' the procedure. The one yew met in the harbour peeler's office. We're gonna draw up a battle plan."

"Fair play till yis." He shook his head resignedly. "Yis have a hard battle in fronta yis. My da's still nat talkin' till me over the issue. He's every bit as bad as the rest of them. Jist won't listen. If yis git as far as the courts, maybe the fellas wid the wigs 'ill turn a pin in their noses."

Wilson looked around the bar.

"Haven't seen too many of thim in here the last two days. Even big Ned's been conspicuous by his absence. But they're nat all bad," he said reflectively, "Bradley was on the winch at the sleeper boat. Ned put me an' Mick McKnight in the houl. We hadn't a clue what till do. But yer man knocked over two or three heaves every nigh an' again till give us breathin' space to figger out how to sling the sticks. He saved our bacon."

Kelly nodded.

"He soldiered wid us fer a while in Burma, didn't he?"

"Aye, he went well above the call of friendship. Ned wud a sacked him and reported him till the committee if he'd a caught it on." His ruddy features broke into a seldom seen grin. "But mosta the time he was down in the galley stuffin' his ugly face." His voice changed in tone. "Wasn't that awful news about oul Reilly?"

"Wee Harvey wus wid him," replied Kelly ruefully. "He'd a bin alright if he'd stayed in the shafts, but the guy behin' the truck wid Harvey was a knacker an' the wee buck wus gettin' murdered. They were also slowin' down. Reilly changed places an' went behin' the truck wid Jim. He was much too oul till be wrestling wid two hunnert weight bags. Nigh he's outa it."

Wilson studied his companion for a moment before speaking.

"Harvey's name is on the list I sent to the guy at Queen's. He's part of a hard rump that gets wurk in front of our people, yet they don't pay any money to the union."

"But yew know they can't git intil the union. Any union," protested Kelly.

"They can if they take a job in Corry's timber yard or Rank's flour mill," answered Wilson softly.

"Yeah but they'd need to be wurkin' away from the quay fer at least six weeks ... " began Kelly. His voice trailed off and he smiled at the logic of Wilson's thinking. "If yew kin git them off the quay for that period of time yis might git back inta the drivin' seat."

Wilson nodded.

"Our friend in the legal department thought that one up. He's gonna send a copy of my letter till the head office in London an' state that non-union workers are gettin' jobs in front of people who pay their society every week. He reckons we kin at least force them to defend their members. Only casuals wid paid up cards will be selected. That means the Arabs will have to take employment off the quay for the period yew stated or they won't be schooled. Some of them might like the jobs and stay in them: others might just drift away."

Kelly didn't answer. He knew the reds were fighting for survival. He didn't want to be the one to tell Wilson that the representatives of the blue-button men had turned their faces against reinstating the reds, and would use whatever labour they needed to man the shipping. This would be done with the backing of the stevedores under the threat of moving all their work to the Irish Transport Dockers. Whether or not they would accept this work whilst their cross-channel colleagues were in dispute was a moot point.

"What about the secret seven?" asked Kelly with a slight sardonic grin.

"We keep in touch," answered Wilson, "I'm the only one lives on this side a town. Incidentally, thanks fer speakin' up fer me to the bulkies. But be careful. Yer makin' enemies."

Kelly's gaze frosted over.

"We've made enemies before, an' dealt with them."

Wilson nodded, before replying with a worried tone in his voice, "Yer right, but this is a different situation. We can't sort this one by cuttin' throats an' breakin' necks."

Kelly didn't answer. He sipped reflectively at his whiskey.

Wilson didn't like the look in his eyes, and was relieved when whatever he was thinking disappeared, as he called loudly for another drink. He rose from his stool.

"Billy, I'm away. Promised the wife I'd git home early. She worries if I'm behin' schedule. We're takin' the kids till the Duncairn tonight ta see a John Wayne picture."

Kelly grinned.

"Is he winnin' the war singlehanded again?"

"Doesn't he always? But the kids love him," laughed the red-button man. His voice changed to a sombre tone as he rose from the stool. "I suppose yill be goin' till Reilly's funeral?"

Kelly nodded, and watched over the top of his glass as Wilson left by the back door.

"A wild dacent man that," said Paddy, as he lifted his empty glass. "Yew cud set a clock by him. Two halfs an'sits over them. His head in his hand an' his wee brain goin' a mile a minute."

Kelly didn't answer. He turned and took a long, studied look at the occupants of the bar. He wondered how long it would be before the news of his lengthy conversation with Wilson would get to the dock committee.

He finished his drink and walked slowly into York Street. He looked at the Railway clock, and checked his wristwatch. He thought of the earlier conversation with Minnie and decided he needed to apologise to her. He turned and began to walk swiftly in the direction of Henry Street.

Minnie knew it was him before she opened the door. She'd been waiting since leaving the bar. She knew he knew the tearful scene was nothing more than an act. She loved her father dearly, but her heart told her she loved the wayward docker more, and didn't want to lose him.

Opening the door she wasn't surprised when he walked up the hall and into the kitchen without a word. She followed and stood with her hands on her hips as he settled down on the settee.

"We've till half-six the marra night before yer da docks at the Clarendon," he said with a mischievous grin.

"Didn't yew take in one wurd I said in the pub?"

"Ack sure yew were a wee bit distressed, so I forgive yew fer callin' me names."

"Billy Kelly!" Minnie yelled, smiling despite herself. "There's just no fathomin' yew."

He grabbed her outstretched arm and pulled her down beside him. She didn't struggle. She was where she wanted to be: wrapped in his strong arms. She gazed fleetingly into his open eyes as his face came closer.

"Billy Kelly, don't yew dare ... " she managed to say before his lips closed over hers.

Henry Harvey skidded up his sister-in-law's hall and collided with a half-moon hall table holding a large multi-coloured vase of flowers.

At that precise moment Mrs. Harvey rose from her chair with a scream.

"He's smashed my vase!"

The kitchen door crashed open with a thud that sent it flying back. Henry fell against the door jamb and looked at his brother's widow. His eyes were glassy and his breath was coming in laboured gulps.

Mrs. Harvey threw down her knitting.

"Every time yew cum up that hall drunk, my heart's in my mouth just waitin' till hear that vase smashin' till the floor. It's the last thing yer brother bought me before he died, an' I don't want yew breakin' it on one of yer drunken rampages. Jim's away till bed," she finished angrily.

Regaining his composure and his breath, Henry half-closed his eyes in sullen contempt.

"Tell him nat till be goin' till the corner tamarra. Tell him till go to the Chapel Shed. I'll pay him outa my own pocket. Tell him they're ontil him an' the rest and they're after thim," he added darkly before turning on his heels and lurching into the hall. The woman held her breath until she heard the front door slam with a bang that woke a puzzled and frightened Jim from a deep and heartfelt sleep. He sat bolt upright in bed for a few seconds before falling back onto his pillow.

His mother went to her vase and gently put it into its original position. She rearranged each flower carefully before returning to her knitting. Lizzie, who hadn't said a word, looked up from her book.

"Yew shud put a lock on that door before he smashes yer vase till smithereens."

"Wouldn't do any good," sniffed her mother, clicking her knitting needles. "That big gob-shite wud just charge through it."

Frosty sunlight streamed through the window of the third floor room in Transport House as the chairman of the Dockers' branch called the committee meeting to order. He nodded approval at the immediate decorum.

"If yill pay attention, brethren. Firstly, I'll havta apologise fer takin' yis away from yer warm work for an ire or so. This extraordinary meeting has bin called because of the ongoing problems caused by the second-preference men questioning our right to employ our own kith and kin. As a sovereign branch, we reserve that right an' will nat be tole what till do by a gang of cowboys.

"As yew further know a letter was sent till the secretary of this union re that very issue. There wus also a stong rumour that the same letter had been printed in the *Tele*, but that isn't true. Them journalists have always been anti-trade union, except when it suits themselves. Don't be surprised if some of 'em them are skulkin' about the quay, lukin' fer a story till twist till suit themselves. If they approach yew, give them a kick up the arse an' send them on their way. This is a sovereign branch that will make its own decisions. We won't be put under pressure from anyone, no matter how many letters are sent. If the powers that be in administration don't like our way of doin' business, then we'll simply break away and form our own union. The miners kin git along on their own. I don't see why we couldn't."

This brought a resounding cheer from the committeemen.

"I have passed this on to those who count an' they understand. Unlike the other branches, we are unique in that we hire whoever we want to. We are enthusiastic about the closed shop and will operate at all times under those principles. Can I have yer vote on that, before we go any further?"

He looked at the outstretched right arms.

"Carried unanimously," he said. "A letter to that effect will be despatched to the Regional secretary. Next on the agenda is the procedure to follow regarding the proposed disbandment of the red-button section." He held his hand up. "I don't want any of yis wid sons in that section to worry. We'll bring most of 'em in on the next intake. In the meantime, the gangers 'ill be told to hire 'em as if they were first preference."

He smiled broadly at the hum of approval.

"We know some of thim were forced till pay intil the scheme by members of the secret seven. That won't be held agin them. We ask only one thing in return. That they call in an' see me an' tell me, and, through me, the branch, everything them nefarious bastards are planning. An' there's a few a youse committeemen who have relatives and friends who are Arabs. They'll be protected as well, under the same conditions. So any information gathered will be confidential.

"Wilson was slabberin' about formin' a new branch. This has caused a ripple a fear among those in this buildin' who shud know better. The employers sniffed at it, but I've tole them there's no way we'll tolerate that notion, an' informed them there'll be trouble if they give succour to that notion. That's why I want those reds who are sympathetic to us to keep their ears to the groun'. We need to know where these bastards are gonna shite before they take their trousers down."

He turned his attention to the secretary of the branch.

"Any correspondence, Ronnie?"

The secretary put down his pen and opened the first envelope.

"This is a letter from Wilson. It's a duplicate of the one he sent to the Regional secretary." He started to laugh. "It begins: 'Dear Sir, I would beg yore indulgence on a matter' ... "

He got no further. The chairman snatched it from his hand. "What about it?" he said to the members.

A tall spindly man wearing a tweed cloth cap and a collar and tie beneath a navy duffel coat took a pipe from his mouth and said sarcastically, "I propose it's marked 'read'."

The chairman tossed the letter unceremoniously into a wastepaper basket placed strategically at his feet. The secretary looked apologetically at him.

"The next three are anonymous letters attacking our decision to bring in men from outside the dock labour group, when we opened the books."

The chairman swept all into the wastepaper basket.

"We haven't time till read letters from bastards too yella till sign their names," he snarled.

He took a cigarette butt from behind his ear and lit it.

"Nigh to a more serious matter," he continued. "Two of our recent young members were brutally attacked last night in the White Lion. Both are in the Mater Hospital an' will be there for a while. The police were on the scene but no one was made accountable, although a few likely suspects were in the bar. I want a proposal from the floor that a letter be sent to Head McKinstry of the RUC telling him that we want the matter fully investigated, with no cover-ups."

He looked at an elderly man two rows back.

"Brother Kelly, I'm sorry ta say yewr son is still givin' us heartache. He was one of the suspects in the bar at the time of the attacks. Despite the hand of friendship being reached till him on account of yerself an' yer sterlin' service till this branch, he continues to embarrass us by mingling with the reds an' on some occasions arguin' their case. He was seen last night in the company of Wilson whose letter to the union started all this."

The old man rose shakily to his feet. He grabbed hold of the back of the chair in front of him.

"Mr. Chairman. I don't have a son. There's a man lives in my home, but we don't speak or in any other way communicate. I deeply regret bringing him out of the army to become a dock labourer for he has caused me nothin' but embarrassment since the day he landed on the quay. He's full of stupid notions about equality an' nonsense like that, with little thought of gratitude. As I said Mr. Chairman, I have no son."

He stopped for a moment and looked slowly around the men in the room.

"But I have brothers, Mr. Chairman. Brothers who have stud by me jist as I've stud by them. First, again' the stevedores who tried to destroy us with their threats and skulduggery, an' their attacks on the closed shop that allows us to create our own destiny. Secondly, against those who think they kin threaten us with the law to git their way. A way that would ruin everything we have worked fer over all these years. The two lads beaten up last night are martyrs to that cause. They should wear their cuts like medals an' their stitches like campaign ribbons. They're nat the first to suffer for principle and conviction, an' they won't be the last. But we've gat a few tough guys of our own who'll deal out appropriate retribution if we git the right information as till who carried out this cowardly attack. An' if my son is foun' till be a guilty party on that count ... then so be it. I say when we do hit back then we hit back harder then we've bin hit. It's the only way."

He looked again around the hushed room.

"Mr. Chairman, in the matter of the suspended Brother Kelly, I propose his name be struck from the books of this union branch. As I stated, I have no son; only brothers whom I hold dear, in a family I'm proud till be a part of."

He sat down to a burst of applause led by the chairman.

"We need a seconder for the proposal to go through," said the chairman.

No one moved. He looked at the old man's defiant glare.

"Yewr sentiments have been noted an' appreciated. However, we hate to lose or punish one of our own with dismissal, despite the provocation. As yew can see there is no seconder so the proposal falls. Mebbe between this emergency meetin' and the next regular meetin', Brother Kelly junior will have seen where his true loyalties shud lie.

"As yew know the reds have enlisted legal help. Their claim that our gangers take non-union men before them is an embarrassment to the other branches of this union and could possibly lose us some support from our fellow trade unionists. I would hereby propose that two weeks from now, anyone without a valid union card will not receive a job on the quay."

"But won't this play into their hands?" gasped the secretary. The chairman frowned.

"Yeah, it's a bit of a setback, but we kin turn it to our advantage by supplying cards of convience to those outsiders the stevedores want to retain on a casual basis. That'll keep 'em happy. The others kin git a turn fer a few weeks somewhere legit. Most of the firms are closed shops anyway, so they'll havta join as soon as they git the job. Then they'll return to the quay. As fer playin' intil their han's. On the contrary. If they've all gat cards then we kin hire who we like. We'll use the reds till the Arabs return. If they don't return we'll continue to use the reds, but on our terms. We've jist gat till keep our nerve fer a few weeks."

He gazed at his colleagues with a smug, satisfied smile.

"Any further business for the good an' welfare of this branch, Mr. Secretary? If not, I declare this emergency meeting for February 1960 closed. Members will receive details of the next regular meeting through the post. I know I don't have to remind yew that all discussions here today are private and confidential and shud nat be discussed outside this room. Only one thing needs to be made public. Spread the news. A fortnight from today: No union card, no job! That's the only warnin' they're gittin'."

"Wilson will see that as a victory, an' mebbe forego the court case. Branch declared closed," he added, rising to his feet and walking to Kelly.

"Yer a true brother," he said warmly, shaking the old man's hand. "But we couldn't let yew be the one to lower the boom on yer only son." He turned away quickly as the old man's eyes filled with tears.

He left and walked downstairs to an office on the administration floor and spoke to the female secretary who looked up at his entrance.

"Tell yer boss to expect a surge in union membership in the

next few weeks," he said with a broad grin before closing the door and heading for the building's car park.

As he drove from his private parking space, he pulled a cigarette from a twenty pack of Gallaher's *Blues*, placed one end in his mouth and lit the other with a silver monogrammed lighter. Seeing a break in the traffic he changed gear and gunned the powerful Rover car into the traffic lane in the direction of his bungalow in Ballygawley on the county Down coast.

Wilson got off the trolley bus at the stop before Queen's University. He turned into University Square and walked down the tree-lined avenue until he came to a house with the number he was seeking. He climbed up the steps and into the hall. The houses were massive compared to those in Sailortown. They had been turned into offices when the ever-expanding university bought them.

He took his cap off and knocked on a door with a small gold plate bearing the words GENERAL OFFICE. An amused young woman opened it.

"Can I help you?" she asked as Wilson crushed his cap nervously.

"I've to see Mr. McCartan. He gave me this address and said he'd be waitin' fer me."

The woman smiled and pointed to the wide staircase.

"Yes, he's expecting you. His room is second on the left, on the first floor."

Wilson muttered a shy 'thank you' and made his way up the thickly carpeted staircase. His knock was answered quickly and a tall, slightly balding man opened the door with a welcoming smile. He reached out a hand which Wilson shook self-consciously as he was ushered into the room.

McCartan escorted him to a large desk and motioned him to a wooden chair, before going behind the desk.

"Well, I see you are no worse for the cowardly punch on the jaw you received the other day," he smiled as he ruffled through a pile of typewritten pages.

Wilson grinned.

"I've bin hit harder."

"Indeed, you have," replied McCartan admiringly. "I hope you don't mind, but I have friends in high places, and I took the liberty of checking you out when the department passed your letter seeking legal advice on to me a few weeks ago."

He looked straight into Wilson's face.

"You have a remarkable war record for the rank of sergeant." His slight grin was tinged with unmistakable admiration. "Most of it's still hush hush, although the war in Europe has been over quite a while. As an ex-second lieutenant who had a quiet war, I'm very impressed, and envious of your decorations and citations."

He could see Wilson was embarrassed, and looked at him.

"Are you ashamed of your war service?" he asked, puzzled.

"No, sor," muttered Wilson. "Over the years of warfare, I began to think that there must be another way of settling arguments an' solvin' disputes without indulgin' in wholesale slaughter. Certainly I'm proud that I was able to do my bit for my country, but on reflection, I'm nat proud at doin' what I was asked to do on certain occasions. That's why I'm here. I've grown to believe the pen is mightier than the sword."

"Quite, quite," said McCartan, somewhat taken aback. He smiled reassuringly and continued, "Forgive me for presuming you would be one of those gung ho wallahs who rejoiced in killing. By the look of this report you did plenty of it."

Wilson shrugged.

"Nat as much as the guys who dropped the bombs on Nagasaki and' Hiroshima, an' if they kin live wid it, so can I. Incidentally, Billy Kelly, a first-preference man was my staff officer for the last three years of the war in Europe. We also served a stint together in Burma. He an' I are the only members of our original platoon to survive."

"An' now you're on opposite sides. That's too bad," replied McCartan soberly. Wilson was silent for a moment.

"Billy Kelly was the man who spoke up for me in the Harbour Police Office. He's on our side," he said guardedly.

"But he wasn't wearing the compulsory badge?"

"He's suspended indefinitely. He hit a ganger for sacking one of his mates, another ex-squaddie who's an Arab."

"An Arab?" echoed McCartan.

Wilson smiled apologetically.

"It's one of the derogatory names we have for the casual workforce. Outsiders, parasites, skulls, Arabs. It's part of the dockside folklore. The thing is the outsiders don't see the term as an insult. They revel in it. Rather like General Montgomery's desert rats."

"Yes," mused the lawyer. "They took that insult from Field Marshal Rommel as a compliment."

He returned to the papers on his desk.

"Would Mr. Kelly testify? I'm afraid we're going to need all the help we can get. I haven't been able to sway anyone involved in this issue," he stated as he looked across at Wilson.

"As you know, I've been making clandestine visits to the schooling pen and have communicated my horror at the treatment of union members such as yourself to the General Secretary in the London office. My letters have been answered, but with negative, stalling replies. The closed shop is a powerful weapon, and most politicians and the judiciary are frightened of it. I gave the union an ultimatum last month when this thing reared its ugly head; it has run out without anything concrete. All we can do now is show them we mean business by taking a court case against them. Did you succeed in persuading anyone other than yourself?" he added softly, his eyes probing the other man's features.

He sighed as Wilson shook his head.

"I have already lodged the papers and the case could be heard in a month."

McCartan continued as he rose and walked around the desk, taking Wilson to the door of the office.

"This could get dirty and dangerous. Your opponents know every move you make. They seem to have an in with the Harbour Police and the RUC. You will really be under the spotlight, and to be honest, even if you win you'll lose. I'm calling in markers from influential friends and hope to raise the public awareness within the next few weeks. It's really a case of natural justice being turned on its head. Newspapers would be an ideal platform, but the union barons could close down the presses with just a slight nod in the right direction." He looked straight at Wilson. "This could be the toughest battle of your career, sergeant."

Wilson donned his cap.

"I'm aware of that, but we've no other option. We are grateful for yewr help in the matter, sor," he said, opening the door. "I've to meet the rest of the seven in the upstairs lounge of Pat's Bar as soon as I leave here. It usually deserted at this time a the day."

"Mr. Wilson, I think if you held your meeting on the Moon, your enemies would be aware of what took place," McCartan replied anxiously. "But as you say, it's either fight or fade."

"That's just about the sum of it. I'm only good at two things: killin' an' countin'," Wilson replied with a wistful smile, "An' now that the war's over, my first trade would be classed illegal."

The lawyer didn't answer, but watched him as he walked stiffly down the stairs and into the street.

He looked at the leafy avenues and wide streets as he walked towards the bus stop. He decided on an impulse to cut through the grounds of the university. There were no gates or railing as these had been taken away to help in the war effort and were never replaced.

He wondered if the day would ever come when someone from York Street would be welcomed in the hallowed halls and educated as a right, on equal terms with the rich and privileged.

Stopping at the war memorial at the front of the building, he took off his cap and stood to attention as he read the names of the fallen. Turning stiffly, he lit a *Park Drive*, walked through the front entrance and crossed University Street. As he waited for a bus to take him to the town centre, he wondered what Monday would bring. He was sure his absence from the quay this morning would be noted. He looked around him as the thought entered his head that he might even have been followed. He smiled and realised he was getting jumpy.

113

The barman nodded tersely in the direction of the ceiling when he eventually entered Pat's Bar on Belfast's dockside. He walked up the narrow staircase and opened a door that led to the lounge bar. Three men were seated in the darkness at a table littered with Guinness bottles. Cigarette smoke wafted over their heads.

"Well, what's the position?" growled a short sallow-faced man with a growth of whiskers, and a full moustache.

Wilson sat down heavily.

"The case is goin' ahead in a month, an yer man is gonna try an' git a bita publicity for it."

"I think we shud git our MP to raise it at Parliament. We shudn't be tryin till do this ourselves."

"That's a good idea, Alex," Wilson said with a large grin. "Yer big man that owns the wee shop in York Street shud be able till raise it at Stormont."

"Stormont's no good. Them fella's up there cudn't give a fiddler's about workin' class people. We need till go till the British House of Commons. Let's contact Harry Diamond the MP fer the Falls Road. He speaks fer the workers."

"Why nat?" mused Wilson. "He has a good track record. We cud spread the word that we're goin' down that road and maybe give Shaw somethin' till think about."

"Did ya hear about oul Charlie Anderson?" asked a grey-haired man with a cigarette hanging from his lower lip. His thin and angular features were covered with acid burns.

"Naw," answered Wilson, with a touch of anxiety.

"He wus foun' lyin' down Quinn's place wid a busted face an' a fractured arm. He's in the Mater. A latta the boys are sayin' it's them bastards gittin' their own back fer the two kids in the White Lion." He paused reflectively, his face strained in the glow of the cigarette. "Oul Charlie cudn't a bate Casey's drum. Probably headin' fer a fish supper when them cowardly bastards jumped him."

Wilson tried to lighten the atmosphere.

"Let's nat leap till conclusions. It cuda bin anyone, Tam. Yew know all the crazies head for the chip shop."

Tam nicked the burning end of the cigarette to the floor and blew on the burnt end before putting the butt behind his ear.

"I still think it was them bastards flexin' their muscles," he growled, "so if yer still lukin' the second man fer the court case, put mi name down. Oul Charlie wudn't a hurt a fly," he added angrily.

Wilson looked at him sternly.

"Are ye sure, Tam? Once in there's no goin' back."

"Yis," came the half-whispered reply. "I'm gonna do it fer oul Charlie. If yew let people walk on yew, then pretty soon they'll shite on yew. An' nobody's gonna shite on me," he finished with a growl.

The other men remained silent, as Wilson pulled a sheet of paper from the inside pocket of his jacket.

"I'll need yer address an' other details, an' yill need till sign yer name at the bottom."

Tam looked at him blankly.

"Yew'd need till do that. I niver learned till write," he said, bowing his head.

"No matter," replied Wilson, "just put yer X on that dotted line."

"Make it two exes," shouted one of the other men.

"What fer?" growled Tam.

"One fer yer name an' one fer the university yew went to," roared the other man, his voice dissolving in a burst of laughter.

The rest joined in as Tam laboriously scratched an X on the dotted line.

Reilly's body arrived at his home in Wensley Street at six o'clock on Friday night. His daughter watched from the sofa as the men carried the coffin in and placed it on trestles under the window that looked out into the narrow street. She was dressed entirely in black and held tightly to the hand of the woman who sat next to her. The men unscrewed the brass fittings and took off the lid. They placed it against the wall beside the coffin before taking their leave. A small woman wearing a dark shawl followed them up the hall and closed the door behind them.

Reilly's daughter rose and walked the short distance across the room to look at her father. Her companion who accompanied her, held her reassuringly.

"Isn't he lovely Sally? He luks twenty years younger."

The other women came to look in the coffin and agreed with Sally's companion. She looked at the remains of her father as tears clouded her eyes.

"He reared me since my mother died of scarlet fever twenty years ago. He was the finest father a girl could have," she said softly. Her voice trembled and she began to sob. "It broke my heart when I left Belfast to go to London, fifteen years ago. But he made me leave. He didn't want me workin' in the Mill or anywhere like that." She turned to the woman beside her. "What am I going do, Belle? I have no one to come home to. I tried for years to get him to have a telephone installed, but he wouldn't hear tell of it."

Belle sniffed.

"Probably knew he'd be tormented by all the neighbours wantin' till use it till ring the doctors or the buroo," she replied.

"But I would have been able to speak to him and find out how he was. You know he wasn't a man for writing letters," Sally replied sadly.

Belle took a box of snuff from her apron pocket.

"Well, yew needn't wurry about his funeral. There was enuff penny policies in the drawer till cover that. Are yew sure he had no savings like a post office account, or a wee tin box somewhere? The oul lads are the hell fer the tin boxes and secret hiding places. When it's all over, go through this oul place with a fine tooth comb."

"He'll get a good send-off. Money's the least of my worries," murmured Sally reflectively as a woman who had been sprinkling perfume around the coffin went to the front door in answer to a polite knock.

Paddy entered the kitchen with a large cardboard box under his arm. He set it down on the sideboard and walked to the woman in black.

"I hope yew don't min', but I brought a few little sundries that might save yew making soup an' such fer all the people that will be comin' till pay their last respects. There's also a few bottles a stout and a bottle a whiskey if yew want till use it. Nat that I'm implyin' that people shud take drink on a sad day like this, but ye cud always keep it till yiv mebbe a bad dose of the coul," he finished courteously.

He took her hand and clasped it tightly. His face was expressionless as she withdrew it quickly, placing the five-pound note in her cardigan pocket.

"Thank yew very much Mr. Conway, for being so kind and thoughtful," she said earnestly, as the big publican moved from her side and over to the coffin. He looked down at Reilly's serene features.

"Do yew know sumpthin'?" he murmured with genuine affection in his voice. "That's the first time I've seen him with his cap off. Such a shame, I've bin servin' him drink fer nigh on thirty years an' I never once saw or heard him being outa order with any other fella human being, or say a bad wurd about anyone."

"That's an epitaph any man wud be proud of, Paddy," she smiled, showing her gratitude in her tear-stained eyes.

The other women were already unloading the box, and taking the contents into the scullery. A large kettle was on the gas stove and a teapot the same size bubbled away beside it. They and other pieces of delft and catering equipment had been hastily borrowed from the Reverend Stitt in the nearby Maguire's Memorial church. Sally had wanted to hire the catering utensils but the neighbours wouldn't hear tell of it.

A few hours later the little house was crowded. The scullery door was opened and some men stood in the small yard. Sandwiches were passed around by the women who walked among them.

Sally Reilly watched from her seat on the sofa as the men, each with his cap in his hand, proceeded to the coffin and looked for a moment or two at the remains. She turned to the woman at her side.

"I didn't know my father was held in such esteem, by so many."

"Aye they're a close-knit crowd, the Dockers, an' they're

every one the same as himself: walkin' time bombs, their lungs filled with the dirt an' stour of every nation under the sun. Same as us, God help us," she said looking at the ceiling. "Every day breathin' in the filth billowin' outa that stinkin' mill chimney across the road."

A tall beefy man with a pencil thin moustache caught Sally's eyes. He was impeccably dressed and stood out from all the other mourners. She took in his grey houndstooth suit, cut to accommodate his bulky figure. His shirt was white and his tie black, as were his brightly-polished brogues. His full head of greying wavy hair was swept back, except for a kiss curl that decorated his unlined forehead.

"Is he a stevedore?" she asked quietly.

Her companion tucked her shawl around her shoulders, as she glanced disapprovingly.

"That's Henry Harvey—Ireland's answer till Clark Gable. Do yew nat know him?"

Sally continued to stare.

"No," she whispered.

"Aye right enuff," conceded her companion, "Yev bin away a brave while."

Sally didn't answer. Henry's eyes continued to search the room until they found hers. He strode towards her and reached for her hand.

"I'm sorry fer yer troubles," he said softly.

She looked into his dark brown eyes as he put a white five pound note unobtrusively into her other hand. He turned quickly on his heels and walked to the coffin, where he stood a few moments in melancholy silence before accepting a cup of tea and a sandwich. He groaned inwardly when the door opened to reveal his brother, Sam, looking slightly the worse for drink. He was covered in fishmeal, and the odour immediately invaded the room.

Henry looked crossly at him.

"Is yewr head coul?" he asked angrily, nodding at Sam's cap.

Dust flew from it as Sam hastily removed it and several of the women began to cough. Sam's face was tight and tense as he glared around the room.

"I'll nat stay long, missus," he called to Sally, "I'm jist here till say goodbye till my old mucker. An' I hope them bastards that killed 'im won't be able till sleep in their lousy beds. Bate intil the groun' he was, jist like all the rest of us."

Henry moved forward to speak to him. "Don't cum any closer," he growled. "Yew might git yer lovely suit covered in the dust of honest toil."

He watched with wry amusement as the women sprayed perfume discreetly to kill the smell which had the same stench as decaying flesh.

"Away home an' git washed an' cum back when yer sober and at yerself and stap lettin' yer family down," muttered Henry.

Sam's face contorted with rage. He was about to attack his brother when he saw the pleading face of Reilly's daughter.

"I'm terrible sorry, missus. Yer da is dead, but he's still the best man in this room an' that's why I cum till pay my respects. An' I'm sorry fer yer troubles," he added as an afterthought, before turning swiftly and leaving the room.

"Wonder why he wus so overcome," whispered one mourner devouring a sandwich. "He wus gonna blatter oul Reilly two weeks ago at a card game."

Henry found himself staring at Sally Reilly. He judged her to be about thirty-five years old, and noticed the mourning clothes hid a trim figure. Her hair was still dark, without any trace of grey. The legs showing beneath her long skirt were shapely and attractive. She caught his glance and for the first time since she'd heard of her father's death, a small smile played across her features. Henry responded in kind as he reached for another sandwich

She was wakened from her reverie by another younger man, in a lounge suit and open-necked shirt. He took her hand and looked down at her. She thought he was impossibly handsome. Tousled black hair fell across his forehead and grey eyes looked at her warmly from an unlined face

"My name's Billy Kelly. I've worked and drank wid yer dad fer quite a while. We were muckers." He smiled sadly. "I'm gonna miss him," he added before turning and walking to Henry Harvey.

"Good turn out," he said.

"Can't bate free sandwiches," countered the ever-cynical Harvey. "I didn't know Reilly was the father of a fine lukin' woman."

"Neither did I. I remember her vaguely before she bailed out," admitted his companion. "Listen, when yer ready till go, give me a shout. I've a wee bita news fer yew."

Henry put down his cup.

"Let's go nigh," he said, smiling briefly at Miss Reilly who watched his departure with more than a passing interest.

"When's the funeral?" he asked one of the women standing in the street.

"Three o'clock Monday. That's ta give the men who wurk at the dock time till git finished," she replied.

"I wurk at the dock too," replied Henry indignantly as they walked away.

"Mebbe she thought yew were a tailor's dummy outa Burton's windy," grinned Kelly. He wrinkled his forehead. "Terrible reek in there. Is he goin' off already?"

"That wus our Sam," scowled Henry. "Typical of him to cum till pay his respects straight from a fishmeal boat."

"I though he worked wid yew at the spuds."

"He does, but there wus little or nobody at the schoolin' pen this mornin', so wee Jim and Sam were shanghaied by Uncle fer a puffer wid about a hunnert ton in it. He wus annoyed wid me sendin' him and made a point of showin' me up at the wake. I don't know what I'm gonna do wid him."

"That's what I want til tell yew," muttered Kelly. "The blues held an emergency meeting this mornin' an' Tasty asked for an' gat a directive. A fortnight from now, no one will git a job on the quay without a current union card."

"Bollocks," snarled Henry, throwing down a *Woodbine* he was just about to light. "That manes all of my potato men. "

"Though yew might like till know," said Kelly

"Fancy a drink?" asked Henry, nodding in the direction of the White Lion. They stood at the corner of Henry Street and watched silently as an old woman walked from her front door to the edge of the kerb and began to throw breadcrumbs onto the middle of the road. A flock of seagulls immediately flew from the roof of the spinning mill.

Kelly shook his head.

"I'm goin' up till Peter's Hill till git a good bath, then home till the house of silence."

"Yer da still fell out wid yew?"

Kelly grinned bitterly.

"Better than that. I heard he proposed they take my button off me fer bringin' the union intil disrepute."

Harvey shook his head in disbelief as Kelly walked towards his home to collect his towel and shaving gear. As he walked past the York Street door of the White Lion, he saw Head Constable McKinstry enter the bar with two constables behind him. On an impulse he followed behind them, moving close enough to hear the conversation as the policeman buttonholed the barman.

"Did Kelly have cross words with the two men whilst he was with them?" asked the senior police officer.

The barman shook his head.

"Naw," he said. "In fact, it wus the opposite. They were very friendly. The big one wus a bit the worse fer the drink an' Kelly advised them to go home because of the tension. He left them an' went till the lounge a full ten minutes before they went to the bogs."

"Yes but Kelly could have come down to the toilets an' you wouldn't have seen him. Isn't that right? So he could have been responsible. We've just been made aware of another old fella, this time a second-preference man, badly beaten, being found on waste ground in Quinn's place. According to witnesses he was along with Kelly a little while before the assault."

The barman laughed derisively.

"Yew mane oul Charlie Anderson? Kelly loved that oul fella. Wudn't harm a hair on his head."

"Well, he was close to the scene before both events, and you must admit he has a hair-trigger temper," McKinstry replied defensively.

The barman leaned over the counter.

"Listen, Head; no disrespect, but I think yer barkin' up the wrong tree. Before they went, the biggest one turned his tumbler upside down, an' yew know what that manes in a dockside pub?"

The head constable pursed his lips, and turned to his colleagues.

"It signifies the guy that turned the tumbler reckons he could beat any man in the house. Another of your stupid Irish customs," added the Scotsman derisively. "Do you think that's why they were filled in?"

"Most guys wuda give them a by-ball because they were drunk, but somebody obviously took umbrage. Those two kids weren't regulars here. So it must a jist been random ... Somebody ... Mebbe a local without the price of another pint gat annoyed at the way they were flashin' their money an' used the glass episode ta follow thim an' give them a blatterin'."

"Was there any strangers in?" continued the police officer.

The barman thought a little.

"Naw, jist the usual punters. There wus a group of sailors sittin' close till the door, but they left jist after the assault. As I tole Kelly, they probably didn't want involved. We don't git many foreigners in here. The sailors wud usually stay on the waterside of the Street. Anyway, they're more interested in wimmin, an' we don't have any of that tomfoolery in here," he added for the benefit of the police officer.

McKinstry scowled at the mention of loose women as he rose from the bar stool.

"Will you call in and make a statement for me? I'd be obliged," he finished with a forced smile.

"No problem," muttered the barman, knowing if he didn't the pub would be subject to a rigorous patrolling every night at closing time.

Grunting approval, McKinstry moved out into the street followed by the two constables. Easing his large frame into the black patrol car, he barked out an order to the driver.

"Up to the Mater, till I meet this other casualty. He might have seen who attacked him. I still think this is connected to the events of the past few days on the Docks."

He turned to the men beside him.

"Keep your eyes and ears open when you go off duty. I want

this case cleared up. I've already got a call from my boss. He wants me to take a squad onto the quay on Monday morning to assist them lazy half-baked bastards who call themselves harbour peelers. I'm not looking forward to that," he finished with a grunt.

He glanced out of the side window at the streets crowded with people on their way to and from the pubs, the picture houses and the dance halls. He wound down the car window as he saw Henry Harvey leave the bar.

"Are yew still behaving yerself, boy?" he shouted patronisingly.

Harvey averted his eyes to the kerbstones.

"Yis, Head," he replied deferentially as the car sped away from the kerb.

Henry returned to Reilly's wake after supper. He scowled and closed his eyes with disapproval when he saw Sam and Jack seated on the sofa beside Sally. The house was packed. He handed over a half-a-dozen bottles of stout to one of the women and looked around for a seat. Sandy Carstairs was in a drunken sleep on a chair close to the scullery door. With a mischievous grin, he motioned one of the men to open the yard door and carried both the chair and its snoring occupant into the yard. Opening the door, he slid Sandy effortlessly onto the top of the box-shaped toilet and walked back into the room. He smirked to himself when he saw Sally looking at him with undisguised admiration.

Taking his hip flask from his jacket pocket he solemnly saluted the occupant of the coffin before taking a swig.

A well-dressed man whom he knew to be a boilermaker in the shipyard moved over beside him, and asked quietly, "How are yew fixed with this problem on the quay, Henry?"

"That bastard Wilson and them other rag tags have fucked up the whole system. It'll niver be the same fer any of us an' we have them till thank fer that!"

"Do yew nat think they'll win their case?" continued the boilermaker.

"I don't," replied Henry authoritatively. "The union's are too powerful. What the fuck does a solicitor or a judge or any a them other parasites know or care about manual work or the men who perform it? Them oily bastards would know more about ordering a four-course dinner washed down with fine wine followed by a few glasses a five-star brandy, after they've done a good day's wurk sending someone down till cells fer hard labour."

Henry's voice was bitter, as he remembered his own trial and imprisonment. He looked squarely at his companion.

"How wud yew take it if the caulkers or the riveters in the yard decided till take up boilermaking?" he asked with a sly grin.

"No way wud we let them do that," snapped the yardman.

"Well, it's the same thing on the quay. Demarcation lines: the closed shop. Jist like in the shipyard. Aye an' jist like judges an' solicitors. Cud yew picture them allowing some court official till take up their duties jist because he spent years workin' in the courts? Nobody wid sense wud expect that. But them bastards, Wilson an' the rest, refused till respect the peckin' order an' that's why we're in the situation we're in. I kin tell yew me an' my squad are backin' the blues up till the hilt. We haven't any delusions of grandeur," he added pompously.

"Hey, Clark Gable!" called his brother Sam with a mocking look on his face. "Stap shoutin' or yill waken the corpse."

Henry threw him a distasteful glance.

"I'm glad till see yiv washed yerself fer the occasion."

Sam growled as the jibe hit home.

"I've already apologised till Miss Reilly. I tole her smell was the product of honest labour. Somethin' yew wud know nuthin' about."

The watchers roared and Henry wisely remained silent. Kelly's information troubled him. He was wondering how he could keep his squad employed without union cards. Deciding to take the bull by the horns, he approached Sally and told her he had an important phone call to make. He assured her he would return as soon as the business was completed. As he left, he was pleased to see she looked suitably impressed.

Collins was entertaining a friend from the legal profession, when he received the call from the phonebox in Great George's Street. He was surprised and amused to hear Henry's voice on the other end of the line. He loved the calculated crawling tone that told him the red-button man was looking a favour and listened intently until he finished.

"You've nothing to worry about," he assured him. "I call the shots in that direction. You and your men provide a good and cheap service, and there's no way I or the other stevedores will accept change in that department. We've already made an agreement for the non-union checkers to be provided with courtesy or affiliated cards. I don't see why the same can't be done with your squad. Call in and see me on Monday."

He put down the phone and lifted his drink. They had taken dinner on the veranda of his spacious home in Whiteabbey, and were enjoying the view of the Belfast Lough. He smiled across the table at the barrister and his wife who had joined them for the weekend. Looking reflectively at the calm peaceful waters he spoke tentatively.

"That was a call from an old friend and employee seeking help on a thorny issue concerning his welfare. Of course I gave it. I grew up with him and owe him a favour. Whilst I've been moderately successful, one should never forget one's roots. This is a far cry from a parlour house in Spencer Street, but one must never overlook one's friends, no matter what their station in life," he repeated condescendingly.

The barrister sipped his wine.

"But of course," he agreed, whilst his wife clucked approvingly.

Collins thought the time appropriate to quiz his learned friend on the ethics of the displacement of the second-preference men. He rose and put his napkin on the table.

"If you ladies will excuse us, we'll retire to the study for brandy and cigars."

The women nodded in agreement and the men walked slowly up the tree-lined path to the house.

"I've just received a case of the most excellent brandy, from a friend in the shipping business. Perhaps you'd do me the honour of taking a few bottles with my compliments when you leave tomorrow," he purred as they entered the house.

"But of course," replied his companion courteously.

Henry smiled smugly as he made his way back to the wake. Pulling a *Woodbine* from his pocket he lit it and continued through Michael Street until he reached Wensley Street. He decided not to tell his brothers and the rest of the squad that their jobs were safe. He chuckled to himself as he saw the wisdom of that decision. It would keep them on the back foot and insecure. That way he could control their behaviour and, in Sam's case, his arrogance.

Entering the house he took off his cap and smiled at Reilly's daughter. He was relieved to see Jack and Sam had gone. He sat in Sam's vacant seat and looked at Sally. He couldn't contain his emotions.

"Yer beautiful in yer grief, girl," he whispered passionately.

Sally recoiled from the blast of alcohol as he moved his face towards hers. She jumped up in indignation.

"Mr. Harvey, remember where you are," she cried. Henry felt a tinge of embarrassment as the room fell quiet. The mood of euphoria deserted him as he looked at Sally's angry features.

"I'm sorry," he replied haltingly. "It's just, yer father wus such a good frien' an' fer a moment or two I felt an overwhelming need to protect yew, now that he's gone."

Sally looked into his embarrassed features, and felt she had overreacted. Smiling gently, she sought to reassure him.

"Please sit down Mr. Harvey. I've heard all you men have been under tremendous pressure over the last few days. So have I: what with the death of my father and the travelling from London." She smiled, and took his hand. "Please accept my apology. This is a trying time for all of us. Please sit down and tell me how long you knew my father."

Henry took a deep breath, and pulled a crumpled handkerchief from his pocket and buried his face in it. She instinctively put her arms around his neck as he bowed his

126

head to her breasts and began to sob. Some mourners watched sympathetically, others were not so moved.

"No wonder they call him Ireland's answer till Clark Gable. He's a better actor than Tom Mix," chortled one of the women washing dishes in the small scullery.

"Aye," answered her companion, with a trace of admiration in her voice. "That singing fella Johnny Ray cudn't turn the tears on any better than Henry when he's lukin' fer sumptin'."

"Aye," replied the other one, smothering a giggle, "an' we all know what sumptin' he's lukin' fer."

Both women burst out laughing and continued with the washing.

After a few moments Henry excused himself and left the house. Sally walked to the door with him under the watchful eye of Belle.

"I'm sorry fer yer troubles," he muttered sadly in the darkness of the narrow street.

She watched as he weaved unsteadily away from the house. He straightened up and stopped sobbing as he turned into Henry Street.

"That wus a narrow escape," he muttered with relief as he entered the warmth of the White Lion. He downed two glasses of whiskey laced with Guinness in quick succession before heading for his home. He pulled his cap across his eyes and hoped there would be no trouble tomorrow. He failed to notice the two men who had followed him when he left the bar. As he turned into the darkness of Earl Lane, one of the men hit him with a savage punch on the back of the head. He turned angrily with a loud roar and felled his attacker with a retaliating right hook that had all the power of his body weight behind it. As he stooped to deliver more punishment, a heavy blow from a wooden cudgel wielded wickedly by his attacker's companion sent him crashing to the pavement.

Jim was wakened by a continual banging on the front door. He looked at the alarm clock and saw it was 7a.m.

"Probably Henry with a change of orders," he muttered in

exasperation as he got out of bed. The cat shook itself and followed him down the stairs. He lit the kitchen light and looked around apprehensively, but the floor was bare. The loud continuous banging had sent the cockroaches scurrying back to their dens. He opened the door to his Uncle Sam who brushed past him and walked to the kitchen.

"Henry's bin attacked. The cops found him in Stable Lane. Somebody knocked him unconscious."

"Is he in hospital?" the boy asked with concern in his voice.

Sam ignored him and spoke to his mother who had just come down the stairs.

"Makus a cupa char, Aggie," he ordered.

He turned to Jim.

"Naw," he replied scornfully, "the stupid bastard wudn't go. He's gat a lump as big as a melon on the back of his nut but other than that, he's his usual girnin' self. Says he doesn't know what happened. One minute he wus walkin' from the wake, next minute somebody attacked him from behin'. He gat one dig in an' remembers nuthin' else. Two night cops foun' him about one o'clock this mornin'."

"It's a wonder nobody foun' him before that," shouted Mrs. Harvey from the kitchen.

"There's no lamps there. The cops stumbled over him," explained Sam. He turned to Jim. "Go yew down till the Spencer Dock and take over Henry's cargo. Explain to the checker what has happened, if he doesn't already know. I'll organise the rest of the men," he continued as his sister-in-law handed him a cup of tea and a slice of toast.

"Do yis know what happened till Henry?" asked Mrs. Harvey.

"According till McKinstry he wus hit wid a blunt instrument from behin'. He wusn't robbed or anythin' like that. It cuda bin a red-button man or a blue-button man not happy wid the way some of their colleagues have bin beaten-up."

"But, surely Uncle Henry wudn't a been party till the like a that," protested Jim.

"Well, him an' Kelly are as close as shite till a blanket, an' a lot of people, includin' the cops, think Kelly's behin' some of

128

the beatin's. But listen kid," he added with a twinkle in his eye. "In Henry's case it cud a bin anybody, for he's tramped on more toes than a learner in John Dossor's school of ballroom dancin'." He finished the tea with a flourish. "I'm away roun' till detail them other lazy bastards. I'm in charge until Henry recovers," he added with a tone of authority and pride in his voice. He disappeared out of the door and down the hall, slamming the front door with a ferocity that woke Lizzie. She staggered down the stairs in a panic.

"What's up, what's wrong?" she cried.

"Yer Uncle Henry's bin beat up," cried her mother.

Lizzie rubbed her eyes.

"I hope whoever dunnit gits a medal," she sniffed before returning to her bedroom to get dressed.

As they sat down to breakfast, Jim looked at his mother.

"Whata yew say we git wee Johnny McMullen till rap us up from nigh on?" he asked.

"Whatever fer?" cried his mother indignantly. "Shure I niver fail till git yis up in the mornin'!"

"I know, mum," he replied softly, "but Sam's heavy bangin' on the dure has sent the clocks back till their dens. If we git wee Johnny till blatter the door knocker every mornin', about half an ire before we git up, mebbe we won't havta fight the bugs for possesion of the kitchen. He does it for other people in the street, before he goes till his job in the shipyard. Mebbe he'll do it fer us."

Mrs. Harvey smiled with pride.

"Yiv gat yer da's brains, there's no doubt about that. I'll call roun' an' see his wife Jinny, an' arrange fer him till start the marra. It'll be grate if it works, son."

Jim blew on his tea to cool it. He looked affectionately at the cat curled around his legs.

"Only thing is, we're gonna have till start buying cat food fer Tibs," he said.

"I won't mind that," answered his mother with a shiver.

A few moments later he was walking through the harbour gates at the bottom of the Duncrue Road, on his way to the Spencer Dock.

Sam called into his mother's house and grinned with amusement as he saw Henry trying to wash himself at the kitchen sink. Mrs. Harvey's face was set in a thunderous frown.

"Don't yew be windin' him up," she warned over the click of her knitting needles.

Sam ignored her and addressed his younger brother.

"An' where do yew think yer goin', boy?" he asked as Henry, stripped to the waist, bellowed and moaned as he washed his face and arms and upper body, sending soapy water cascading over the floor.

"I'm goin' till the schoolin' pen," he answered.

There was a steely tone to his voice and Sam nodded as he continued, "I belted one of them bastards as hard as I cud an' his face must be bearin' the marks."

"It wus Friday night. Fight night in York Street. Shure there'll be many a man bearin' woun's, an' they'll all have an alibi," his brother replied.

Henry grabbed a towel and dried his face.

"There wus at least two of thim," he growled. He held out his right hand and pointed to a large gold sovereign ring on his third finger. "The first one gat the full benefit of that between his jaw an' his temple. I reckon it'll require stitches, so I'm goin' till the pen ta see if anybody has a woun' like that. Then I'll redecorate the rest of his face, an' leave him a shirt-full a broken bones fer good measure," he added viciously.

Sam's features hardened.

"I'm goin' wid yew. The other bastard might be there an' I'll sort him out."

Henry grunted brotherly approval and reached for his Simmit and shirt. When they left, their mother put down her knitting and took a floor cloth to the water that lay on the linoleum.

Turning into Earl Street, they saw Jack standing on his door step.

Not a word was spoken as the three men continued in the direction of the cross-channel schooling pen.

Four

HEAD MCKINSTRY WATCHED AS THE DAY shift officers filed into the station duty room. He'd been up all night and was in a foul mood. Despite his mixture of coaxing and threats, Henry Harvey had refused to make a statement or give a description of the men who had attacked him. He'd solemnly warned the red-button man not to take the law into his own hands. His eyes scanned the bulky occurrence book that recorded the events of each day.

"Typical Friday night," he grunted.

His officers had been kept busy from one end of dockland to the other.

He looked up and saw the men sitting awaiting orders. He nodded to the duty inspector sitting beside him. The inspector rose and addressed the constables.

"Before I detail the rest of yew, I want the officers in the front row to proceed immediately to the dockers' employment area at the bottom of Great George's Street. Sergeant Orr will take command. Mix among the workers, and stay close to the gangers. Make sure your presence is noted and felt. Take no nonsense. Arrest and detain anyone who causes even the slightest problem. The Harbour peelers will be there in force, so they'll back yis up if there's any trouble. Their own station is just across the road from the compound and any prisoners can be held in their cells. Don't be afraid to use force if it's necessary. Away yis go. Yis 'ill need till be there before the schoolin' starts."

He waited until they left the room before speaking to the remaining section.

"The Head wants to address yis re a few issues that happened over the last coupla days," he said before sitting down.

McKinstry rose and looked at the men for a moment before speaking slowly through pursed lips.

"It's been an eventful week. I know we get a lot of assaults in this area. It seems to be the nature of the beasts that inhabit it to find joy and pleasure in rearranging each other's faces. Up until last week that's the way it has always been, and that's the way we've policed it. No malice, not intentional. Nearly always sporadic and random." He paused and rubbed his jutting chin pensively. "We can live with that, and we can control it, but last week's events have taken a sinister turn in the fact that they've all been connected to the labour problems on the Belfast Quay. Five men have been seriously assaulted in tit-for-tat beatings emerging from this feud between the first-preference and second-preference men, who up until last week worked in reasonable harmony.

"A legal wrangle is in the melting pot and meanwhile all hell has broken loose on our patch. After this briefing, I'm getting in touch with the powers that be in the big house up at Stormont to see if someone can move the case forward, and get a decision, one way or the other. I know some of you have a personal interest in what is happening, but whatever the result, we must police it."

He took a deep breath before adding firmly, "And if that means cracking the heads of someone near and dear to us ... then, so be it.

"The latest victim was Henry Harvey: a well-known brawler and agitator who was found unconscious last night by two of my officers. If I know Harvey, he'll be looking for revenge as soon as he's fit enough. So we'll need to watch out for that individual on our travels. There will also be a funeral from Wensley Street on Monday afternoon and, as characters from both camps will feel the need to pay their respects, we'll have to have a strong presence in the area.

"Lastly, some of you are connected to the docker fraternity either by marriage or blood. I'm asking you to keep your ear to the ground and pass on to the station officer responsible any information you may gather. I know it could be seen as informing on your own families, but remember when you took your oath you pledged to do your duty without fear or favour. A good officer would arrest his granda if he had to, and some of you may have to before this mess is sorted out. The duty inspector will detail each of you accordingly, and remember to defend yourselves at all times. Good luck," he finished, adding, "I'm off to a double brandy and a good sleep."

He turned wearily to the inspector as the men filed out and into the Street.

"Put a twenty-four hour watch on Billy Kelly. Second an officer from Greencastle or Musgrave station, who wouldn't be known to the local populace. He can work in plain clothes. Give him the mugshot of Kelly that's in my office from the last time we entertained him overnight. I want his every move to be recorded. He's too close to the people being assaulted for it to be coincidental."

Jim trudged into The Sportsman's Arms and sat down wearily on a bar stool.

"What's it to be, young fella?" came the familiar voice of the owner.

"A pint shandy, Paddy," replied the boy through parched lips. "Nat many in the day?"

"Naw," replied Paddy, "An' there'll be less a fortnight from now if they can't git union cards."

"Any trouble this mornin'?" Jim continued anxiously as the barman set the pint down beside him.

"I believe there was more peelers than workers in the pen," answered Paddy as he took the money. "A sergeant read the riot act before schoolin' began. Yer uncles combed the schools lukin' fer the culprits who downed Henry last night, but without any luck. They spent most of the mornin' in here."

"I know," muttered Jim ruefully, "I got a quare roastin' in the Spencer Dock. I thought the spud lorries were niver gonna stap comin'." He looked at the clock. "It wus about half twelve when the last lorry left. I'm goin' home an' straight till bed." He took a grateful swallow of shandy. "Thank God it wus quiet in the pen," he added as an afterthought.

"Aye," replied Paddy. "Nobody wants this trouble, but it isn't gonna go away." He nodded up the bar. "Wilson's tryin' till sort it the legal way, but he isn't gittin' much backin'. A blue-button man came in here a few minutes ago and threw a pinta beer over him."

Jim looked at the man at the other end of the bar. His head was cradled in one hand and the other hand was cupping a half pint of Guinness. He was staring at the floor.

"Uncle Henry says him an' the secret seven are responsible fer creatin' most of the problems," Jim muttered.

Paddy nodded sagely.

"There's always two sides till every story, son, but Wilson's right about one thing. It should be settled legally in a civilised way. There's no call for all this violence."

Jim nodded wearily in agreement and finished his drink.

"Thanks, Paddy," he said politely, before walking into York Street.

He moved slowly, looking into the shop windows at his reflection as he passed. His cap sat at the back of his head, exposing his long and lank dark hair. He was studying his thin and callow features when he collided with a woman coming out of a shop.

He put out a hand to steady her and murmured a quick apology. She was wearing mourning clothes covered by a long dark coat.

"Aren't you the boy who was with my father when he died?" she asked.

He immediately recognised her as Reilly's daughter.

"Yis," he said, automatically taking off his cap and standing awkwardly in front of her.

"I've been meaning to get in touch with you," she continued. "I've a possession of my father's I would like you to have." She looked enquiringly up into his eyes. "Perhaps you could come with me now and get it?"

He smiled gratefully.

"Yis," he repeated.

She took his arm and turned in the direction of the railway station.

"Aren't yew stayin' in yer dad's house?" he stammered.

"Heavens, no!" she answered with a slight shudder. "I've taken a room in the Midland Hotel until my father is buried and his affairs are put in order. That should take another day or two."

The porter at the entrance to the hotel eyed them curiously as they made their way up the steps and into the foyer, where she requested her room key.

"Were you workin' today?" she asked, wrinkling her nose.

"Yis," he answered quickly, "I wus at the spuds, but that hum yer gettin' from me came from a fishmeal boat I wus at a few days ago. It's a devil of a smell till git rid off. I've myself scrubbed raw," he continued apologetically.

She smiled knowingly.

"I'm Reilly's daughter. I had all that when I was a child growing up in Wensley Street. Flour, cement, maize meal, but as you say the fish meal was the worst. Just standing here with you brings it all back," she added wistfully.

"Yer father was a good man," muttered Jim, not knowing what else to say.

They entered the lift and he closed the gates behind them. As the elevator climbed slowly upward, Jim looked at her guardedly. Her head reached his shoulders and her figure was slight. She had small dainty hands, one of which she held his arm with as they left the elevator and walked along the corridor towards her room.

He watched as she took off her coat and threw it over a chair. She carefully removed her hat and set it in a wardrobe, looking in the mirror as she fluffed her hair. He noted absently that it was long and dark. He was too frightened to look at her closely and cast darting glances when he thought she wasn't aware.

"Have a seat, Jim. Would you like a drink?"

He felt his face blush and his hands grow clammy with sweat.

"Yis," he lied.

She went to the cocktail cabinet and produced two miniatures of whiskey.

"Sorry there's no beer. I can send down for some?"

He shook his head.

"Irish or Scotch, then?"

"Scotch," he replied lamely.

She poured his drink into a crystal glass.

"Aren't you going to sit down?" she repeated with a disarming smile.

"My clothes is covered in spud dust an' I don't wanta dirty the seat," he stammered.

"Okay," she conceded, going to the wardrobe and pulling out a large coloured eiderdown which she flung over the sofa. He sat down gratefully and nursed the whiskey nervously as she opened a drawer and produced a small cardboard box which she reached to him.

"I bought that for my father years ago," she whispered sadly. "When I found it the other night it was still in the paper wrapping. He never took it out of the box. I would like you to have it," she continued, sitting down beside him.

Jim looked at the gold wristwatch with an expanding bracelet. He didn't know what to say and his face burned with an intensity that made him think it would explode.

"I've niver owned a watch. Thank yew," he mumbled, uncomfortably aware of her closeness. The aroma of her perfume and the nearness of her body made him even more nervous.

She took a sip from her glass and looked across its rim at him.

"I'll bet you've plenty of girlfriends," she said with a laugh, emptying her glass with a flourish.

He knew she was teasing him.

"No, not really," he managed to murmur.

"No wonder," she grinned. "That pong must get where you're going ten minutes before you do."

He blushed and rose awkwardly.

"I know. It's terrible. I usually stay in the house until it fades. Maybe I'd better go," he added, putting his glass on the table.

She took his hand and led him back to the couch.

"What you need is a bath. One filled with herbs and sweet smelling salts. That'll chase the fishmeal. I know there are no bathrooms in York Street, but there's a beautiful one here. A long soak and you'll smell good enough to eat."

She entered the bathroom and he heard water running. He sat nervously until she came back and poured him another whiskey.

"In you go when you finish that. There's a robe behind the door. I'll be back in a few minutes."

He watched in a daze as she put on her coat and left.

Jim swallowed the whiskey and walked warily into the bathroom, and undressed, before climbing gingerly into the tub. He hesitated as the sweet smelling fumes filled the room.

"I'll come out smellin' like a pansy," he thought as the effects of the whiskey began to chase his nervousness and loosen his inhibitions. He'd never been in a tub except on the odd occasions he had paid a visit to the public baths in Peter's Hill.

He was washing his hair when the door opened and Sally walked in and put a brown paper parcel on a chair. She had discarded her coat and her mourning clothes and was wearing a long robe tied tightly around her waist. It accentuated her trim figure. She was barefoot and looked even smaller.

"My, you're smelling better already," she said as he looked at her with disbelief. "You'll need a bit of help with your back. Give me the flannel."

She pushed him forward and began to wash his shoulders and lower back. She moved gently and compassionately over the part of his shoulder that was inflamed by the heavy bag carrying. The hand with the flannel drifted down to his buttocks and around to his taut stomach. As she moved her head close to his, he felt her other hand glide between his legs. She fondled him for a brief moment and then kissed his lips. He reached out to embrace her, but she moved away with a smile.

"I just wanted to check if you liked me. I see you do. I'll be waiting for you. There's some new clothes in that bag," she murmured as she closed the door.

His heart was beating so fast and so hard he was sure she could hear it in the other room. After soaping and scrubbing every part of his now sweet smelling body, he climbed out and walked to the towel rail. He turned as the door opened and Sally entered. She was naked. She looked at his slim but muscular body, and smiled as she saw he was more than ready for her.

"I couldn't wait," she murmured breathlessly, as she stood on her toes to kiss him.

He grabbed her hungrily. Lifting her effortlessly, he laid her gently on the bed.

"Have you done this before?" she asked, looking up at him with surprise in her eyes ... He raised his head from her bosom.

"I saw John Wayne doin' it in a pitcher in the Duncairn," he replied shyly and apologetically.

She pulled him closer to hide her smile of amusement, and kissed his ears and his neck and his hairless chest as he lay on top of her. She sensed his inexperience and used her hands to help and guide him.

"Easy, my prince, easy. We've got all the time in the world," she whispered.

Some hours later both lay exhausted and trembling. Jim looked at the sleeping Sally and wondered what age she was. He knew she was much older than him, but wasn't sure how much. His head was still spinning from the swiftness of events since he had bumped into her outside the shop. He studied the fine features of her face and thought with an inward smile that she certainly didn't resemble her father in looks. Her face was pretty, but tired-looking, which was understandable, given the reason for her visit to her home town. Her make-up was smudged and streaked from their hectic lovemaking, and he knew he'd been taught things that he would never forget. Her brown eyes were wide-set and her nose was slightly pointed. There was nothing wrong with her figure though, he thought, feeling his body stiffen. He moved slightly, somewhat embarrassed.

She opened one eye and looked at him coyly.

"I'm going to wrap you up and take you home with me," she said huskily as she moved closer and pulled him on top of her.

He felt her squirm beneath him and heard her moan softly and passionately. She threw her arms around his neck and held on so tightly, he thought he would suffocate. Some moments later they lay still in each other's arms. She knew however that his powers of recovery were incredible and began to extricate herself. He didn't let her go willingly and watched sullenly as she moved towards the bathroom. He was still watching when she emerged some moments later with a bathrobe hanging loosely on her.

"I'm going to ring room service for something to eat," she called. "What would you like? I can get them to send up a menu."

Jim found himself unable to answer. He had no idea what to order. She seemed to read his mind.

"How about a big steak with lashings of potatoes and vegetables, followed by ice cream and coffee?" she asked, lifting the room telephone.

"I've niver tasted coffee," he answered hoarsely with a trace of embarrassment.

Sally smiled.

"That's okay. We'll make it tea for you."

"I'd like coffee," he replied with a shy smile.

She went to the bathroom and came back with a robe which she threw at him.

"Slip that on, whilst I order."

She watched as he self-consciously obeyed her. She motioned him to sit down at the table, and returned to the phone. He listened as she called out her requirements.

"Just leave the trolley at the door, I'll bring it in myself, my colleague and I are in conference and don't want to be disturbed," she instructed before putting the phone down and turning her attention to Jim.

Seeing his complete bewilderment, Sally crossed the room and sat on his lap.

"Relax, Jim," she said soothingly, brushing away the eager hands that grasped her. She held his face and kissed him, before moving around the table and sitting on a chair facing him.

She leaned her elbows on the table and smiled at him. "You know, I'd really like to take you back with me, but I don't think your mother would like that," she said laughingly.

At the mention of his mother Jim rose quickly to his feet.

"I forgat about mi ma!" he cried hoarsely. "She'll be wonderin' where the hell I am. Sally, I'll havta go," he added walking towards the door.

She took his arm.

"Surely you don't have to report to your mum every time you're late?" she asked.

"It's nat that! I toul her I wud go straight home from work an' nat take any drink the day. She knows I wudn't break my word an' she'll be terrified."

"But why?" asked Sally. "You're a grown man—"

He interrupted her.

"Mi da was late cumin' home one night. She roamed the pubs lukin' fer him not knowin' he had dropped dead in the shipyard. Nobody came near her till tell her until ires later. She'll be outa her mind ... "

Sally gently sat him down.

"Is there anyone close to you with a telephone?" she asked quietly.

"Aye," he said blankly, "Mrs. Crooks in the corner shop."

"Have you the number?" she continued patiently.

"Aye. She lets us use it to phone the doctor."

"Let me have it," she continued, lifting the telephone. "Who were you working for today?" she whispered.

"Mr. Collins," he answered limply. Dialling the numbers he gave her, she waited until someone answered.

"Hello. This is the secretary of Mr. Collins the stevedore." She cupped her hand over the speaker and turned frantically to him. "What's your second name?"

"Harvey."

She regained her composure.

"Could you possibly pass on to Mrs. Harvey that her son Jim has volunteered to work late for us and did so only on the condition that we would notify her. You will? Good! That's very kind of you," she added before replacing the phone.

"I'm so sad to hear how your father died. That must have been a terrible time for you." She held him close and pulled his lips down to hers. They were in bed when the doorbell rang announcing the arrival of the dinner trolley.

Five

HELEN WILSON ROSE QUICKLY AS HER husband staggered into the living room and fell to his hands and knees on the floor. Panic gripped her as she rose quickly from her chair by the fire.

"Sammy, what's happened? Have yew bin injured?"

The smell of alcohol filled the room and her tone changed from concern to anger and astonishment.

"Are yew drunk?" she shouted, staring at him as he tried unsuccessfully to rise from the floor.

He looked up at her and she was disgusted to see the front of his jacket and shirt were stained with beer. He was sweating profusely and his face was grey and frightened. The door opened and she saw the concerned features of one of her neighbours.

"Is he alright?" she cried.

Helen stared at him, her face a mask of contempt.

"He's full drunk, Sarah," she answered as tears filled her eyes.

"Indeed he's nat," yelled Sarah defiantly, as she rushed to lift him from the floor. "He passed my window the same as he does every Saturday, straight as a soldier walking at rifle pace," she added breathlessly as Helen helped her to lift her husband. "I turned away till put the kettle on an' I heard a screech of car brakes, an' then a latta shoutin'. When I gat back till the windy, a car was speedin' away an' Sammy was lyin' on the groun'. Them bastards attacked him an' laid him out," she continued as they put the red-button man gently on the settee. "I ran till git help till lift him, but when I gat back, he'd rose and staggered home. Yid better git him till the Mater," she added grimly as they saw blood oozing slowly from the side of his head.

"I'm gittin' the peelers first," cried Helen, as she ran to get the flannel from the kitchen sink, "Sarah, will yew run till the pub an' ask them till phone the barracks?"

She began bathing the wound on her husband's head. Her neighbour nodded vigorously and ran out of the door.

It seemed like only a few minutes had elapsed when two burly policemen burst into the living room. They took off their caps and threw them on the kitchen table. Helen had covered her husband with a blanket. One of the policemen knelt down beside him and began to speak quietly and urgently.

"Sammy. Who did this? Did yew see them?"

As he continued to ask questions, his colleague drew Helen into the scullery.

"We've tasked an ambulance. It'll be here shortly. Now tell me what happened," he said softly and persuasively.

He listened impassively as Helen told of the events leading to their arrival. He wrote the details into his notebook, and looked her squarely in the face.

"There's an awful smell of alcohol comin' from him. Are yew sure he didn't fall under the influence? Yew say Mrs. Sarah Cochrane saw him on the Street after a car passed. Did she see anyone assault him? I'll need till speak till her."

At that moment Helen's neighbour entered the scullery and immediately put her arms around the bewildered woman.

"Yew kin speak till me nigh," she said quietly, as Helen sobbed in her arms. "Sammy Wilson isn't a heavy drinker. I've niver seen him drunk in all the years I've knowed him, and that's a long time. As I tole Helen, he passed my windy at the usual time and gave me a wave ... "

"Did yew see him being attacked?" interrupted the constable, as his colleague joined him.

"No," replied Mrs. Cochrane defensively, "but when that car roared away, he was on the ground ... "

"Did yew git the number of the car?"

Mrs. Cochrane screwed up her face in exasperation, and remained silent.

"Can yew describe the car, or any of the occupants?"

Helen lifted her head from her neighbour's shoulder.

"I tole yew Sarah was fillin' the teapot at the time."

He closed his notebook and looked at his colleague.

"Any joy?"

"He's out of it. Unconscious! Smells like a brewery," he added under his breath.

The sound of the ambulance in the street caused Helen to sob loudly. Sarah held her tightly.

"Where's the childer?" she asked, as the crew burst into the room.

"They're away till the matinee in the Troxy. Thank God they weren't here till see this."

She watched with anguish on her tear stained face as the medics gently laid her husband on a stretcher and carried him to the waiting ambulance. The policemen followed them into the street.

"Go yew wid them, Jimmy, an' see if yew kin learn any more. I saw this guy on the quay this mornin'. He made a speech for tolerance and a peaceful end till the dispute. Seems till be a prominent player in the issue, so there cud be somethin' in what the oul lady says. But by the smell of him, I'm surprised he didn't collapse outside the bar when the air hit him."

"Are yew speakin' from experience?" grinned his colleague.

His partner replied with a wry grin.

"I'm a cop. I can't afford till drink the way them dockers do. Get yew in there an' stay close till Wilson. I'll havta report to the duty officer. The Head'll wanta know about this latest development."

The doors closed and anxious neighbours watched apprehensively as the ambulance sped off in the direction of the Mater hospital.

Kelly had just closed his front door when he heard the ambulance siren wail as it sped along York Street. He tucked his towel under his arm and walked towards North Queen Street. He was approaching Southwell Street when a car stopped beside him. He paid no attention until he heard his name called. He looked around and saw the back door of the car open. A man in the passenger seat spoke through the wound down window.

"Jump in, Billy," he called pleasantly. Billy recognised him as a first-preference docker.

"No thanks, Alec," he replied as he kept on walking.

"Billy, we need to talk."

Kelly stopped and surveyed the occupants. Four men sat in the black Austin Cambridge. All blue-button men. He stopped with a weary smile and moved towards the door which had opened for him.

"What are yew gonna do? Take me on a one-way ride?" he asked wryly.

The car abruptly sped forward.

"Don't be silly. We're yer brothers in union," snapped the driver as he drove into Dale Street and down Little Georges' Street. They stopped at the corner of York Street and when the road was clear, the driver crossed straight into Nile Street, and across Nelson Street.

"Left or right?" said the driver to no one in particular.

"Left," grunted the man beside Kelly. "An' don't stap till yew git till the enda the Stormont Wharf."

"Are yis a man short, Tasty?" asked Kelly wryly, addressing the man who had spoken.

"Aye, we are," replied Tasty. "An' he's a good man, only he hasn't gat the fuckin' sense he was born wid. We thought we'd take him for a drive an' try to instil in him some of the pride that seems to have deserted him."

"An' we also wanta try an' bring him roun' till our way a thinkin'. Git him till stap giving succour till a parcel a thankless bastards that are about till be run off the quay," added the driver, glancing over his shoulder.

"Stap the car," said Kelly, his disgust showing on his face.

"Nat till we explain our side of the story. I know yer a tough guy, but nat even Rocky Marciano cud bate the four of us. An' there's a spud-jammer in the boot, shud we need it," he added coldly.

144

Kelly relaxed and pulled his cap down over his eyes. A few minutes later the car passed the Stormont shed and stopped at the end of the quay.

"Nat a sinner aroun'," murmured Tasty. "A man cud go fer a swim here an' wud niver be seen agin."

"Aye," replied the driver. "Especially at a time like this when the tide's on the ebb."

"Niver min' that," snapped the front seat passenger, "we don't want till be givin' Billy the wrong idea."

He paused.

"Listen Billy, yer breakin' yer oul fella's heart an' there's no need fer it. Why don't yew cum back in the fold? Yill nat even havta apologise till the committee or till the foreman yew struck. Just tell us here an' nigh, yill nat be takin' any further part in the proceedings or goin' witness fer that bastard Wilson."

His voice took a tone of desperation.

"Kin yew nat do that Billy? Kin yew nat support the oul man who's heartbroken by yer stupid an' obstinate actions? The reds have no chance a winnin', in court or outa it, an' there'll be no place on the docks fer anybody that fought their cause. Quit nigh, Billy, an' yill have prosperity fer the rest of yer life. Yill be luked after an' protected by the most powerful union branch in the country." He paused as Kelly remained stone-faced and silent.

Tasty intervened hastily.

"We don't want an answer nigh. Yew've the resta the weekend till think it over. If yew agree till come back intil the section, then don't go near the deep water gangers. Stand oul Ducksy Gorman. He's gat a handy spot fer yew that'll be there till ye die or retire. If yer nat in his school on the day, then the gloves is off. No man is bigger than the system, Billy, nat even yew. A few minits ago yew wanted out. Yew kin git out nigh. The walk back 'ill give yew plenty a time to think over our proposal. An' Billy," he added, as Kelly climbed obediently and silently from the car, "please make the right decision 'cause there's no Plan B. We'll be in the Terminus Bar if yew want till talk."

Kelly watched as the car roared off down the breast of the quay. Shrugging his shoulders, he placed his towel firmly under his arm and began running towards the harbour gates.

He slowed to a walk when he reached the hut that housed the harbour police. He nodded tersely at the officer on the gate and started running again. He didn't stop until he reached Paddy's Bar. Throwing his towel on the counter, he ordered a pint of Guinness and pondered recent events.

He froze when Paddy said, "Have yew heard about Wilson?"

He listened intently. When the barman finished, Kelly took a sip from his pint.

"Nat like Sammy till break the habit of a lifetime an' git drunk."

"He wasn't drunk," retorted Paddy. "He had his usual two halfs. He'd just ordered the second when Bernie Weatherup came in drunk, ordered a pint and then threw the lot into Wilson's face with a force that knocked the cap off his head. I don't know how he kept his temper, but he did. I threw Weatherup out an' tole him nat to come back. Wilson niver said a word. He jist sat there, the beer drippin' from his face and onto his shirt and coat. He tuk his time an' finished his drink as if nathin' had happened, an' there wus no way he was drunk when he left."

Kelly's face hardened.

"I wus with Weatherup a half an ire ago. He's a blue-button man. Him an' a coupla his colleagues tuk me for a drive down the quay, an' there wus no way he was drunk either."

Paddy's normally placid features were angry as he continued harshly, "I went across the road till see Mrs. Wilson when I heard it. He wus already away till the hospital. I tole her the smell of drink came from the pint slung at him. The pore woman's distracted. I'll be callin' intil the barracks the marra till tell the peelers the same thing."

"Good on yer, Paddy," Kelly grunted grimly as he finished his pint. "That's where I'm goin' nigh. This thing has gone far enuff."

"Stap it, Billy," Paddy called anxiously after him. "Stap it before somebody gits killed."

Kelly changed his mind halfway across York Street. He turned abruptly and strode briskly in the opposite direction

146

from the police station. He paused at the Terminus Bar, close to the corner of Whitla Street, and barged through the front door.

He shouldered his way past the drinkers and ordered a pint of Guinness and a glass of Black Bush. He finished the whiskey in one gulp and looked around the drinkers. The men who had taken him for a drive were seated at a window beside the door. They had seen him enter and waved at him. He smiled and, lifting the pint of Guinness, walked towards them.

Tasty rose with his hand outstretched, a wide smile on his face. "Glad to see yew tuk our advice, Billy. Welcome back till the fold."

Kelly brushed past him and walked straight to Bernie Weatherup. He grinned inwardly at the look of panic that filled the man's eyes. Reaching over the table he lashed the pint of Guinness savagely into Weatherup's startled face. As with Wilson, the docker's cap flew off with the force of the liquid.

Tasty reached out to restrain Kelly and found himself thrown over a table and into a corner. Another member of the company rose, snarling oaths and collapsed instantly as Kelly's right elbow crashed into his jaw. The barroom fell silent as Kelly glared at the remaining members of the group.

Tasty had recovered, but made no effort to climb out of the corner. Weatherup cowered in his seat. The rest of the company kept their eyes firmly fixed on the floor, away from the naked anger on Kelly's face. He looked at Weatherup with contempt in his eyes.

"If Sammy Wilson was six months dead, he'd still be a better man than yew. That pint is in return for the one yew slung over him. He's much too civilised to retaliate, so I'm doin' it for him." He stepped back a pace and looked down at the man on the floor. "I'll be outside for the next ten minutes if any a yew tough guys want ta take me on. One till one or all together. I don't care." He looked scornfully at Tasty. "I may nat be Rocky Marciano, but I'm willin' till take that chance. I'll even let yew go fer yer spud-jammer," he snarled before striding forcefully through the pub door into the Street.

Tasty stumbled out of the corner, and helped to lift his fallen colleague onto a chair.

"That man's a raving fuckin' lunatic. He cuda fuckin' killed me!" he yelled.

"You go out that door inside the next ten minutes an' that's precisely wat he will do," came an amused voice from the bar.

Tasty looked angrily at the speaker.

"Stay yew ta fuck outa it, Belshaw!" he snarled.

Belshaw flicked the ash off the end of his cigarette before putting it into his mouth. He looked at Tasty with contempt. "Don't be sounding off at me, fat boy. I don't scrabble at the docks fer a livin', so I'm free till speak me mind. Sammy Wilson's lyin' in the Mater hospital an' most folk reckon youse guys are responsible fer that. Yer lucky Kelly didn't kill all of yis."

He swivelled on his bar stool and put his feet on the foot rail. Turning his head, he grinned mockingly at Tasty, who was still shaking visibly.

"Youse guys 'ill be in the Mater beside Wilson, if yis are daft enuff till go out that door within the next ten minutes. I haven't seen Billy Kelly as angry as that since the night he literally knocked the shite outa Bimbo Jackson. I saw it runnin' down his trouser leg an' onto the Street. Nat a pretty sight. Watchin' a man crap hisself with fear."

He turned back to his drink, before adding mockingly, "An' there's no back door in this pub."

The man who had fallen under Kelly's elbow regained consciousness. He looked around the barroom and then at Tasty.

"What the fuck happened? I wus only tryin' till git outa his way!" he whimpered, rubbing his jaw.

No one noticed a young man dressed in a tweed jacket and brown trousers as he moved silently to the public phone on the wall at the back of the bar. He had come in immediately behind Kelly and witnessed the brawl. He dialled and began whispering into the receiver.

Kelly heard the screech of brakes and turned to watch the police car mount the kerb before pulling to a stop a few feet from where he stood. McKinstry threw himself from the passenger seat before the car stopped moving. He held his blackthorn stick like a weapon in front of him as he

148

approached Kelly slowly. Despite the seriousness of the situation, Kelly grinned.

"Niver in the history of motion pitchers has the seventh cavalry bin late," he said mockingly.

The Head wasn't amused.

"Git in the car, Billy. Don't make it any worse fer yerself."

The crowd had emptied from the pub into the Street and watched with baited breath as Kelly locked eyes with the RUC man and his officers. No one was more surprised than McKinstry when the docker walked to the back of the car where a police officer was holding a door open, and quietly climbed in. The Head turned savagely on the watching crowd.

"Git away back intil yer den of iniquity, yew parcel a wasters, before I arrest the lata yew fer clutterin' up the Street!"

He followed Kelly into the back seat of the police car. The constable closed the door behind him and raced round to the passenger seat as the car sped off towards the police station. Kelly found himself trapped between two large men. "Why'd you throw a pint round that man, Billy? It's not like you to provoke a fight."

Kelly gave him a puzzled look.

"News certainly travels fast. How cud yew have known that when yew weren't in the bar?"

McKinstry continued to look straight in front of him. Kelly shrugged and continued, "He did the same thing to Sammy Wilson, just before a car in which he was a passenger knocked Sammy down and sent him till the Mater. I wus on my way till the barracks till tell yew this but I guess my temper got the better of me."

The Head kept his glance on the road before them.

"Let's hope you haven't broke that other guy's jaw."

Kelly looked at him with surprise.

"News certainly does travel fast," he repeated. "Yew seem to know everything that happened. How cud that be? Mebbe I shud start lukin' behin' me as well as in front."

"Good police work. Nothing else," snapped McKinstry, as the car stopped at the station.

As they left the car, the police officer beside Kelly fumbled in his pocket. McKinstry brushed him aside.

"No need for cuffs."

McKinstry looked at Kelly and was exasperated to see the amused grin still on his features. "Follow me," he said curtly and began climbing the steps to the station door.

Once inside he took off his greatcoat and hung it on a peg. He turned his attention to the car crew.

"Get back on the street, and keep an eye on what's happening. And don't be flying around. Cruise slowly. If I hear you are speeding through the streets, I'll bring you back and send you out on foot."

He turned his attention to Kelly.

"In here, Billy," he ordered pointing to a door. "I don't want to be disturbed," he shouted to the station guard. "I'm interviewing a suspect re: disorderly."

The officer nodded as both men disappeared into McKinstry's office.

He motioned Kelly to a chair and sat down heavily behind his desk. He took a crumpled packet of *Players* and offered it to Kelly. When he declined, McKinstry placed one between his own lips and lit it. He inhaled deeply and watched the smoke climb to the ceiling.

Leaning over the desk he looked at the docker. There was no anger in his voice as he spoke softly.

"What's going on, Billy? You mentioned Sammy Wilson. You say Weatherup was in the car that knocked him down in Earl Lane. Can you prove that, Billy? I've been up to the Mater to see Wilson. The doctors still don't know what caused him to be unconscious. My officers say he was reeking with drink when they tried to interview him. How do you know he didn't fall as the car passed by him? His face was marked but I'm told that was the after effects of working at a boat full of railway sleepers soaked in creosote. The doctors say there was no bruises consistent with being beaten or, indeed, hit by a car. Only a cut on his head, and that could have been caused by the fall to the ground."

He took another draw from his cigarette.

"Billy, there's things happening here that defy logic. This red- and blue-button thing is spiralling out of control. There's been a spate of beatings in the past few weeks. Henry Harvey fell victim and was lucky he wasn't killed. The only connection we have is that you were more than friendly with all the victims. That's the only lead we have. Worse news is that a foreign national, a seaman, has been admitted to the Mater hospital, in what seems to be a random attack.

"But never mind that. I need your help. This has gone beyond a dockside labour squabble. There are powerful forces at work and this thing stretches up to Stormont and maybe beyond. I don't know as yet, but I've four of my best detectives working round the clock, and I don't like what I'm hearing."

He crushed the cigarette into an ashtray and promptly lit another one.

"Do you know a docker called Billy Bradley?"

Kelly nodded immediately.

"What's the connection with Wilson?" continued the Head.

Kelly thought for a moment.

"Bradley's a first-preference man, but he served for a while with Wilson and myself in the rifles."

"Would he be sympathetic to the red-button men?"

"I don't think he'd agree to what's happenin'. Can't see him getting' involved though."

McKinstry shook his head.

"He is involved. The same gab-shites that took you for a ride did the same with him earlier. They roughed him up a little: not too much. Just enough to scare him."

"What did he do to deserve that? An' how did yew know about my tour of the Sinclair Wharf?" asked Kelly, leaning forward in his chair.

The Head lit another cigarette, and ignored the last question.

"Seems he helped Wilson out at the sleeper boat. Made things a bit easier for him. A red-button man whose connections are all first preference reported him to the heavy squad. They took him to the same spot they took you and said he was finished on the quay. Unlike you he immediately came to me. Those mugs were just out of custody when you attacked them. My detectives say they have enough evidence to bring charges against them for physical assault and issuing threats against Bradley."

"That sounds good," replied Kelly.

"It isn't!" roared McKinstry, blowing smoke down his nostrils and slapping the desk top in anger. "As you deducted, news travels fast around here. The representative of the dockers' union phoned me half-an-hour ago to say there was no way Bradley was being blackballed from the quay, or victimised, or physically attacked. He claimed it was just a little horseplay that got out of hand. He was a valued employee and union member and was under no threat, real or imagined from anyone in the Dockers' section of the trade union. Technically, I couldn't do anything about the blackball situation. That's a matter for the union. I could however get them on the aggravated assault charges according to the evidence gleaned by my detectives. A couple of minutes later I got another call from my immediate superior. He told me to release those gentlemen, forthwith, and to drop all further enquiries. Bradley also called in to say it was all a misunderstanding, and he wasn't pressing charges, so I had to release them anyway. With no firm evidence of assault on Wilson, there's no way I can hold them," he finished with an air of resignation. He looked at Kelly. "I'm swearin' yew to confidentiality. There's big stakes being played for here, Billy, and I'm not sure what they are. Something that's above and beyond a petty labour dispute. It seems to be political, and I'm not into politics. I'm a police officer, and as a police officer, I'm warning you now to be careful. I have no evidence to suggest you are in danger. Just be careful when you're working. Stay out of the hatches and keep an eye on any winches and cranes you're working under."

Kelly studied him for a moment.

"Are you sure you're nat exaggerating the situation, Head?"

McKinstry rose and brushed the cigarette ash from his tunic.

"Just be careful until this thing goes to court. I have pulled strings in an effort to get the case tried as soon as possible. Although to be honest, I can't see the court reversing the decision made on the ground. Trade unions are very powerful organisations, and governments tend to give them the benefit of the doubt in issues like these. Incidentally, I'm putting the word round that you will be done for disorderly behaviour. So there's a cell for you here if you'd feel safer."

The docker grinned sardonically and shook his head.

"An' what about the cops who are married to the daughters or sisters of first-preference men? Don't yew think they'll blow the whistle if I stayed here?"

The Head studied him for a moment.

"They're not all bad, Billy. Some of the blue-button men have told me they're ashamed of the situation, but there's not a lot they can do. They have to toe the party line, whether they like it or not. I know for a fact the decision to disown the red-button section has caused great embarrassment to the union hierarchy."

Kelly nodded his head.

"I understand," he said softly, walking towards the door.

"Stay out of trouble, Billy," said the Head, with genuine concern in his voice. "Don't let them goad you into violence. If you do I won't be able to help you. Worse than that: if Tasty and his henchmen prefer charges against you ... then I'll have to bring you in again." The docker nodded understandingly.

He strode quickly from the police station and stopped at his house. He walked up the darkened hall and into the living room. He saw his father in his usual seat with the evening newspaper on his lap. He had company. Kelly smiled grimly as he recognised the five elderly men who filled the room with their presence. The smile left his face when he saw a packed suitcase sitting in the centre of the room.

His father spoke. His voice was torn with emotion.

"I want yew outa here. Either yew go, or I go," he said grimly.

Kelly looked at his father sadly.

"Yew didn't need till bring the Dockers' committee to tell me that."

"The committee's here at my behest. Yew've niver obeyed anyone since yew left the army. My colleagues are here to see yew obey my wishes one way or the other. Don't think they're enjoyin' any a this. They're nat. They've all sons a their own.

Only difference is, they're proud of their lads. Unlike me, they didn't rear corner boys who strike out at those who try to help them. Benny Simpson will be outa work fer a day or two because of yewr cowardly an' unprovoked attack on a man who was only tryin' to make you see sense."

"What about Sammy Wilson?" asked Kelly.

"Wilson doesn't come intil the equation," said one of the onlookers calmly. "He's slabbered enuff about the law decidin' this issue, an' we're quite prepared till face him in court. Don't fergit, Billy; it wasn't blue-button men who attacked the two young lads who are still in the Mater hospital. Wilson's actions in challenging the authority of the union branch that gave him a good living has torn the workforce apart. Nat only the workers, but their families too, have suffered. We had to nip it in the bud. The withdrawal of the red-button paybooks was maybe done in haste, but by Heaven, it'll be them who'll repent in leisure. Yew don't bite the han' that feeds ye. Wilson learnt that when he had to take a turn at a sleeper boat. A pencil pusher's no good in the houl of a sleeper boat, or any other boat fer that matter. It's hard graft. But he's like all the rest of thim, brought it on himself. Anyway ... " He paused and cleared his throat before continuing, "We don't care about Wilson or his likes. We care about yew. Billy Bradley has seen the error of his ways. He's back in the fold and forgiven. He understands yew can't win a fight by embracing yer enemies. Yew still have a last chance to realise that fact. Yer father asked us to be here becos he knows yew won't lissen to him. He thinks maybe yill consider heeding the committee."

Kelly didn't answer. He looked across the room at his father who was trying to ignore the tears in his eyes.

"I have some other personal things in my room. Can I get them before I leave?"

His father tried vainly to stifle a sob as he nodded silently.

Billy lifted the suitcase and left it in the hall. He ran quickly up the stairs, and went to the wardrobe in his room. From under a pile of papers and boxes he lifted a bulky envelope. Ripping it open, he took out a wad of paper money and stuffed it into his trouser pocket. He looked around the room for a moment or two before taking a large picture frame from the wall. There was a hole the size of a man's head in the wall behind the picture. He put his hand in up to his armpit and searched the cavity wall with his fingers until they located a small hook that was secured to the wall with a piece of string attached to it. He tugged the string slowly upwards and put his fingers tightly around the soft package attached to the end of it. He pulled the leather bag gingerly through the hole and untied the straps that bound it. Rolling it onto the bed, he unwrapped a holstered Walther PPK 9-mm pistol from an oily cloth. Pressing a button on the butt of the weapon, he allowed the magazine to fall onto the bed, and placed it beside another that lay in the leather case. Pulling back the slide with a vicious jerk, he deftly caught the round that flew from the breech with his other hand, and thumbed it back into the magazine he had taken from the weapon. He pondered for a moment or two, then replaced the magazine in the pistol, checked the safety catch and tucked the gun between his trouser belt and the small of his back. He put the holster holding the spare magazine into the bag and replaced it in the wall cavity.

Returning to the living room he addressed his father.

"What about Soldier?" Kelly asked.

"The dog is yours. He's on the street most of the day. Yev only to whistle an' he'll follow yew if yew want till walk him. His lead's in yer suitcase."

Kelly nodded tersely and walked out of the door without another word. His father's uncontrolled sobbing stopped him halfway down the hall. He felt his own eyes fill up and almost turned back. Except for his time in the army, this was the only home he'd ever had. Gritting his teeth, he forced himself to ignore his father's grief and walked out into the Street.

He strode across York Street towards the Sportsman's Arms. He knew he would have no problem getting put up for the night, but equally knew whoever took him in would be classed as backing his stand and therefore be subject to intimidation from whichever side felt betrayed. He decided to stay over night in the small hotel a few doors from the bar. He was about to enter the front door when he saw Reilly's daughter and Jim Harvey walking in the opposite direction. Harvey was carrying a large brown paper parcel. He sat his suitcase down and waited until they reached him.

"Could I speak to yew, Miss Reilly?"

Sally stopped beside him.

"Of course," she replied. She looked at Jim Harvey and added, "I'm staying in the hotel and Jim's been kind enough to help me move a few things back and forward from my father's house." She looked pointedly at Kelly's suitcase.

"That's what I wanted to talk to yew about," he said with a wistful smile. "I wus wondering if you'd let me stay in your father's house for a few days. My da and I have had a disagreement an' I'm on the street," he added lamely.

"Yew cud stay wid us, Billy. Mi ma wud be more than glad till keep ye till yew gat a roof over yer head," blurted Jim.

Kelly smiled warmly at him.

"I know I'd be welcome in yewr home, Jim, but my enemies wud then become yewrs, an' yer mum has had enuff grief in her life without invitin' more," he replied, turning his glance to Sally. "I could pay you rent in advance. I reckon it'll be a week or so after the funeral before the people that own the mill houses will be lukin' to put in a new tenant," he added politely.

She smiled at his good manners.

"Perhaps we could discuss this over a drink," she said, canting her head in the direction of the nearby public house. Kelly lifted his suitcase and held open the door for her and Jim.

"Take her an' my case intil the loose box, Jim," he ordered. "I'll get the 'Do Not Disturb' sign." He entered the small snug a few minutes later closely followed by Paddy.

The publican smiled widely at Sally.

"My goodness, Billy, yiv excelled yerself taday. This is the most beautiful woman to enter my premises in a long, long time," he gushed.

Sally laughed, immediately warming to the barman's good-natured banter. He walked over to her and clasped her hands tightly.

"Yer father was a gentleman. He'll be sadly missed. Wud

yew have a wee drink on me in honour of his memory?" Paddy asked respectfully.

"I would love a scotch and ginger," she replied softly. Paddy looked at Kelly and Jim with enquiring eyes.

"The usual for me," said Kelly as Jim ordered a bottle of stout. Paddy glanced at him reprovingly.

"C'mon now, wee Harvey. We can't drink a farewell toast to an oul dear friend wid stout."

"Make it a scotch and ginger," replied the boy, causing Kelly to glance curiously in his direction.

Moments later the barman entered with four glasses of whiskey. He set the tray on the table and reached Sally and Jim a bottle of dry ginger with their drinks.

"There's yer Bush, Billy. I'm havin' one wid yis, if yis don't mind," he said in a voice filled with humility. He looked at each of them as he raised his glass in the air. "May God be wid yew, Sammy Reilly, an' may yew be wid God," he murmured softly.

Kelly took off his cap and raised his glass to Sally.

"Good men are missed," he murmured. He looked pointedly at Jim Harvey. The boy glanced down at Sally.

"I only knowed him a wee while, but he helped me out an' wus good till me," he stammered, close to tears. They drank quickly and sat down.

"I'll go nigh an' leave yis till yer business," said Paddy. He bowed to Sally as he left the snug. His smile quickly turned to a worried frown as he looked around the drinkers in the bar. He'd heard about the ruckus in the Terminus, and knew Kelly's attack on the first-preference men had heightened the tension.

"This is one weekend I'd like ta see over," he muttered softly to one of his barmen.

Back in the snug Jim rose to leave.

"Yew two have business ta conduct, so I'll go," he stammered. Sally grabbed his jacket and gazed at him with warmth that didn't go unnoticed by Kelly.

She looked directly at the older man.

"Have you any objections to this young man staying?"

Kelly grinned.

"I've no secrets from Jim."

"Well," replied Sally, "I think we can do each other a favour. Firstly, the house doesn't belong to the Mill. It belongs to me. I purchased it some years ago. I knew my father was happy there among people he knew. I bought the house without his knowledge, and arranged for the weekly rent to be to be sent to me by the people who collected it. He was a proud man and would not have accepted the gift of a house from a woman," she added with a smile. "So you can move in today, and stay as long as you want."

"I cud bunk in the wee hotel next dour till after the funeral," Kelly suggested helpfully

"I'd like you there as soon as possible. I'd be pleased knowing my father's remains weren't left alone during the night," she added, finishing her drink. "For doing me that favour you can have the first week rent free. Then we'll see. Maybe you and your father will have settled your differences by then. If you want to go over now, I'll follow behind and explain the situation to those neighbours who have been helping out."

Kelly rose and shook her hand.

"Thank yew, Miss Reilly."

She smiled up at him.

"Call me Sally," she murmured.

He looked enquiringly at Jim.

"Where were yew havin' it the day? I didn't see yew at the corner?" he inquired.

"I was at the Spencer Dock replacing Henry before I met Miss Reilly in York Street about one o'clock," Jim replied.

"He's been kind enough to give me some of his time to help me clear stuff from the house and take care of some business before the funeral." She nodded at the brown paper parcel beside him. "That's his last delivery." She switched her glance to the boy. "However, it's a bit late. Maybe you should take that parcel home and deliver it tomorrow."

Jim nodded agreement.

They left the bar a few minutes after Kelly. Jim watched the docker cross York Street, before turning to Sally.

"Thanks fer all yev done," he said haltingly as they parted.

He paused as he saw the puzzled look on her face.

"It's me who should be thanking you," she replied.

"No," he stammered as his face lit up. "I mane about the union card."

She laughed.

"That was no big deal. Union cards can be bought in any high street in England. I can't understand why it's so difficult to obtain one here. I simply phoned a connection in London and arranged for a fully paid up card to be sent to you by air mail. It should arrive on or before Monday. After the story you told me about the current trouble on the docks, I'm only too pleased to be able to help you."

He couldn't hide his delight, and gave her a spontaneous hug of gratitude. She sniffed a little.

"You should have left those old clothes off," she murmured reproachfully.

"I'll do it as soon as I git home. I'll need to think up a story till tell me ma, as to how I gat them," he replied childishly.

She smiled at his immaturity.

"Tell her you got a bet up at the horses," she said helpfully. "Will you be over to the wake tonight?" she added.

"Yis," he replied eagerly.

"Would you go with me and a few others to the White Lion for a drink later on?" she continued softly, adding with a mischievous smile, "for services rendered."

She loved to see him blush and laughed out loud as his face turned crimson.

"And don't forget to wear your new outfit," she added as she pressed a wad of notes into his hand. "That's for helping me get over my grief. Give some of it to your mum. I'm sure she could do with it."

He said nothing as she crossed the main road and walked towards her late father's residence.

Some moments later he opened the kitchen door of his own home and smiled nervously at his mother, who immediately jumped from her rocking chair.

"Son, I'm sure yer tired, I've yer supper on the pot." She spotted the parcel he was carrying. "What's that?" she asked.

"I gat a bet up an' bought some new stuff," he stammered.

"Ach that's grate," she beamed. "What did yew buy?"

He realised he didn't know what was in the package.

"Jist a few things," he mumbled. "I'll tell yew later."

Running up the stairs to his room, he took out the money Sally had given him. He counted twenty pounds in single notes. He slipped ten pounds into the butt pocket of his blue jeans and put the rest in the top pocket of his jacket. Placing the parcel on the bed he tore it open and took out a blue serge single breasted suit. Beneath it was a light blue shirt and a matching neck tie and socks. His head was spinning as he tried to calculate how much the package was worth. He lifted the shirt and found a white Simmit vest and underpants. Tucked neatly in the bottom of the bag was a pair of black brogues. He staggered back down the stairs in a trance, carrying the contents of the package.

"Yew musta won a fortune!" cried his mother as she gazed open mouthed at the clothes. He took the ten pounds from his top pocket and gave it to her. At first she refused to take it, and started to cry.

"Yer good enuff till me as it is," she sobbed. "Yew keep it an' enjoy yerself."

"I won't enjoy it if yew don't help me to spend it," he said putting his arms around her. "Nigh," he added, "I'm gonna git dressed an' let yew see me in my finery!"

"Yill luk like a million dollars," she said, tucking the ten pound notes into her purse.

Some minutes later he emerged from behind the scullery curtain. His mother glanced up from her knitting.

"Luk at ye," she laughed, her eyes filled with tears and laughter. "Yer a picture of yer da," she added wistfully, as she turned her glance to her late husband's photograph on the mantlepiece.

Helen Wilson lifted her eyes from her husband's gaunt features as a shadow fell over his hospital bed. The well-dressed man smiled gently at her before introducing himself.

"Hello. I take it you are Mrs. Wilson. My name is James McCartan. How is Sammy?" he said with concern in his voice.

She looked at her husband's drained features.

"He's sleepin' at the minit, but thank God he's nat in any danger."

"I received a phone call saying he'd been beaten up again by fellow dockers," replied the stranger in a shocked tone.

At that point Wilson groaned and opened his eyes. He stared for a few moments at the stranger before he recognised him. He tried to rise from his pillow, but Helen reached over and spoke tenderly to him.

"Don't Sammy. Yer still too wake till rise," she pleaded. She looked with concern at the visitor. "It seems that was all a mistake. The doctor reckons he took a slight stroke. He is also prone to bouts of malaria, so they're still doing tests till establish what caused him to collapse in the street."

She looked at her husband.

"All he wanted till do was a day's work an' come home till his family. Nigh by the luk of it, he'll niver work again." She began sobbing.

Wilson glared at her.

"Stap that nonsense woman," he snapped. "I'm nat dead yet, an' I'll be outa here in a few days as right as rain." He looked at his visitor. "Git yerself a chair, Mr. McCartan, an' sit down an' tell me what's happenin'."

McCartan did as he was bid. Returning to the bedside he sat down and took off his gloves before pulling a bulky envelope from his inside pocket. He took a pair of half-rimmed glasses from his breast pocket and looked over them at Wilson.

"I was on the quay today. The news hasn't yet reached them that your collapse was accidental and not the result of a beating. Your friend Kelly threw a pint of beer into one man's face and injured two others. I'm told they were in the car that drove by you."

Wilson looked at his wife.

"When I staggered intil the house I tried to tell yew what happened, but I cudn't git the wurds out. Even when them two peelers were swearin' bline I wus drunk, I jist cudn't git my tongue goin' till tell them I wus ill," he scowled. He tried to climb out of the bed. "I need ta git down there an' try till stap this!"

"It's Sarday afternoon, Sammy. There'll be no one on the quay," said Helen softly, as she held his hand and squeezed it gently. McCartan helped the distraught woman comfort him.

"Don't worry, Sammy. The head constable has the situation under control. He's flooding the pen with policemen until this thing blows over. As you know I've been working flat out to try and resolve the situation. I've been corresponding with the union headquarters in London. I'm afraid the deadline I gave them has passed."

He pursed his lips and looked with concern at Wilson.

"We'll have to go through with our threat of court action."

Helen rose to her feet with a steely gleam in her eye.

"There's no way he's goin' till court in the state he's in."

McCartan smiled gently at her.

"I agree with you completely, Mrs. Wilson. I'm afraid the case will have to be dropped." Both stopped speaking and watched as Billy Kelly walked past McCartan and leaned over Wilson, looking intently at the marks on his face.

"Cut meself worse shavin', sergeant," Kelly said with a wry smile.

He looked across at Helen.

"Don't worry. He'll be outa here in no time," he said as he walked around to her side of the bed and gave her an affectionate hug.

A huge smile wreathed Wilson's features as he successfully hauled himself up on one elbow.

"That's what I've bin tryin' till tell her, but she has me dead an' buried."

Kelly released Helen and returned his gaze to Wilson.

"That'll be the day," he grinned. He switched his attention to McCartan. "Are yew havin' any luck on the legal front, sir?" he asked respectfully.

"Call me James," said McCartan as he studied the man who had lifted the spirits of both Wilson and his wife in a few

162

moments. The worried look returned to his features. "I was just telling Mrs. Wilson we may have to drop the proceedings. It wouldn't be fair to subject Sammy to any further pressure and strife."

Kelly looked at the red-button man.

"He's bin under worse pressure," he muttered.

"I take your point. But that was when he was much younger and in different circumstances," replied the lawyer. "I couldn't and wouldn't take the risk of subjecting him to the full rigours of a court trial that could last two weeks. Two weeks in which he would be under the spotlight."

Wilson put a hand on McCartan's arm.

"I want to be there. We're bate if we don't show."

"You could be defeated even if you do put up a show. David doesn't always slay Goliath. In fact the records show it's more the other way around. I'm inclined to agree with Mrs. Wilson. It's too big a risk ... Better you signing on the dole than lying in the graveyard."

Kelly leaned over and ruffled Wilson's sparse hair.

"The man's talkin' sense," he smiled. He looked up at the entrance to the ward and saw a group of men walking slowly by each bed as if they were looking for someone.

He smiled at Wilson.

"Here's yer admiration society comin'.."

He waved his hand in the air and the group moved towards them.

"Who are they?" whispered McCartan.

"Red-button men," he replied, as they both moved back to let the men closer.

The new visitors were dressed in working clothes and each held his cap self-consciously in his hands. Wilson beamed as he lay back in the bed.

"Thanks lads, fer callin' in," he muttered. "Sorry I made a fool a myself," he added, a trifle embarrassed.

They called out a greeting in unison, before one man stepped forward.

"Sammy, the boys held a meetin' in Pat's Bar today. We've gat two men till go forward for the case and a handful of men have agreed till give evidence. We've also agreed till keep goin' till the pen every mornin', even if we don't git selected. We're gonna do this thing yewr way." He turned to the rest of his colleagues. "Isn't that right, boys?"

The resounding cheer was so loud it brought the matron hurrying down to chastise them. The spokesman looked across at Kelly.

"Billy, we appreciate yewr part in this thing, an' we want yew till know we are grateful. However, yew shouldn't jeopardise yer own livelihood."

Kelly said nothing, but put a comforting arm around Helen who looked at the men with gratitude.

The staff nurse furiously ringing the bell signified visiting time was over. Each man said his farewell and the group walked slowly to the door, followed closely by Kelly and McCartan who moved off to allow Helen to have the last few minutes alone with her husband.

As they walked past the rows of beds, Kelly glanced at a man whose right eye and lower right jaw was covered in bandages. He was in pain and mumbling incoherently. He stopped on impulse when the patient cried out for help in German. He looked at the man whose face was completely covered in bandages, except for his mouth and eyes.

"*Keine Sorgen: hier nimmt man sie in pflege.* Don't worry: yewr in good hands," he said comfortingly, before moving to catch up with McCartan.

The lawyer took his arm.

"We need to talk. After I run Mrs. Wilson home, can you and I have a cup of coffee somewhere?" he whispered with a sense of urgency.

"No problem. Only I don't drink coffee. I'll take somethin' stronger," replied the docker. Half-an-hour later, McCartan walked warily into the bar just across the road from where they'd left Helen at her front door. Kelly beckoned him into the snug and waved at the barman. The lawyer looked around his surroundings.

"Is it wise to come here?" he asked quietly.

Kelly smiled coldly.

"As yew tole Sammy Wilson; nowhere's safe. But sometimes yew kin do more under the nose of the enemy."

His companion nodded as Paddy barged in and smiled at both men. He fixed the sign to the front of the door before whispering in Kelly's ear, "Keep it low, Billy. There's a coupla blues with their backs till the wall of the loose box."

A wry smile brightened his features as Kelly ordered. He looked at McCartan.

"First time anyone has ever asked for coffee on its own, sor. Usually it's mixed in with whiskey or brandy or rum."

The lawyer smiled.

"Maybe I'll try one of your cocktails some other time."

This caused both Kelly and the publican to laugh out loud.

"Niver heard them called that before," grinned Paddy as he closed the door.

McCartan produced a large brown envelope and proceeded to take typewritten pages from it.

"Since the red-button men came to me for advice, I've been writing to everyone concerned," he stated as Kelly took the proffered bundle of papers and began to read. "You know this started in 1948 when the blues opened their books for the first time after the war?"

Kelly nodded.

"That's when I came in. My dad coaxed me to come out of the army, an' against my better judgement, I did."

"That wasn't a large intake, and the majority of the men were, like you, ex-service. It was the second batch in 1955 that caused the red-button men to take stock of the situation. The larger intake earlier this year saw the formation of what is known as the secret seven. That's when I got involved, and you know the rest," replied McCartan He stopped when the door knocked and Paddy entered with the drinks.

When the barman left, he looked squarely at Kelly as he added milk and sugar to the steaming coffee.

"Violence won't solve the issue," he said softly as he stirred the drink.

"It solved World War II," muttered Kelly with the ghost of a smile. "The death of Hitler, the Nuremberg hangings. The big bombs on Japan ... "

McCartan shivered as his companion threw the glass of Bush down his throat, and rang the bell on the wall beside him.

Kelly looked across the table and continued, "It seems we haven't learned from the hard lessons of the past. The debacle in Korea where the allies tried to talk and fight at the same time. The uprisings in Kenya, Cyprus. They're all products of weak political decisions." He rose from his chair and shouted over the top of the snug, "Same again, Paddy."

McCartan could see his point, but continued his argument.

"Fair enough, but we need thinking men, not fighting men at this juncture. Sammy Wilson left the war behind, as did most of us. This issue will be fought in the confines of the high court, not in the back streets and alleys of Sailortown. None of the officials of the trade union, nor indeed, the representatives of the red-button section want to see blood on the ground, and neither do I."

He rose and continued with an assurance he didn't feel. "You are a loose cannon, Mr. Kelly, and whilst I appreciate your bravery and dedication to fair play, I have to tell you that you are becoming a liability to this cause. The violence that left men from both sections in hospital must stop. If idealists like Sammy Wilson are to win this case then their credibility must be preserved. To do that you must abide by the rules of civilisation, and not the law of the jungle."

Kelly looked at him for a moment with a slight hint of a childish smile. He touched his cap with his fingers in a mock salute.

"Message received an' understood, sir. I hereby promise I shall not resort to violence, except in self-defence," he replied with a warm grin that immediately set the lawyer at ease.

McCartan fingered through the paperwork.

"The news today that the reds have produced men willing to test the court system and also witnesses is good news. It's a difficult case and by no means a foregone conclusion, but I believe natural justice will prevail, if given half a chance."

Kelly toyed with his drink and nodded sagely, as if his mind were elsewhere. Despite the aura of menace and aggression that seemed to enshroud the lean and muscular docker, McCartan found himself warming to the man.

"Can I ask why you threw your hat into the ring?"

Kelly's features were blank as he struggled for an answer.

"I have my reasons," he said tiredly. "Maybe it's inbred," he laughed. "After all, my dad has been a trade union activist all his life and aren't they supposed to stand up for the underdog?"

McCartan put the letters back into the envelopes.

"Without sounding too patronising, Mr. Kelly, I believe you are a better trade unionist than any man on the quay at this moment. None of them stand to lose more than you, if this all falls apart."

He called the barman and ordered a double Bush.

"Are yew nat havin one yerself, sir?" asked Paddy.

McCartan smiled.

"Maybe another time."

He looked around the bar. "Your public house has an atmosphere and a certain ambience I've never encountered anywhere else in Belfast," he concluded.

As he rose to leave, he offered his hand.

"Mr. Kelly, it's been a pleasure and an experience meeting you."

Paddy watched as the front door closed behind him.

"What the hell's an ambience?" he roared at Kelly as both men shook with laughter. Kelly emptied his drink and rose to leave.

"Be careful, Billy," whispered the barman with genuine affection in his voice. A young man, who had entered the bar a few seconds after Kelly and the lawyer, finished the half pint of Guinness he'd been lingering over. He nodded a terse thank you to the barman and walked slowly to the door that Kelly had left by. Paddy lifted the empty glass with a flourish and put it under the geyser.

"Good luck an' come again," he called.

Six

KELLY WAS ALMOST BOWLED OVER BY Henry Harvey entering the bar. Despite his problems he grinned as he took in the red-button man's attire. His light brown Chelsea boots were polished to a standard that would have passed muster on any parade ground. He was wearing a matching suit adorned in windowpane check. The top button of his cream shirt was opened and a green cravat was tied loosely around his neck. A toggle denoting a horse's head held it tight to his throat and the two ends of the scarf lay across his shirt front.

"I wus comin' intil see yew. I heard yer homeless. Have yew somewhere till stay?" growled Henry, ignoring the amused look on Kelly's face.

"Yeah. I gat fixed up earlier in the day with a temporary abode," replied Kelly as both men moved back into the bar.

Paddy grinned as he saw them.

"Pull them knives outa my back," whispered Kelly as he paid for the drinks.

Henry looked briefly at the first preference seated behind them. He nodded curtly at them, before turning to Kelly.

"How's that bastard Wilson?" he asked, loud enough for the whole bar to hear.

"He's improvin'," replied Kelly.

"That's a bloody pity. He's the instigator of all this nonsense," retorted the red-button man.

His remarks drew a growl of approval from the men at the table. Kelly smiled inwardly and took no offence: as usual,

Henry was playing both ends against the middle and, under the circumstances, he couldn't fault him.

Paddy sidled up beside them.

"Cud I ask yis till change the subject lads?"

"No problem," nodded Henry, knowing he had made his point.

"Are yew for the wake tonight?" asked Kelly as Henry ordered another drink.

"Yis," replied his companion.

He lowered his voice.

"I'm goin' till the hotel for a drink, 'cos I won't git pace in any a these pubs. I had till leave the Stalingrad for the Duchess was lukin' me till accommodate her, an' I've gat too much on my min' fer that nonsense," he growled.

He threw back a glass of whiskey laced with Guinness and put the empty tumbler on the bar. Kelly almost laughed out loud when he pulled a yellow polka dotted handkerchief from his pocket and proceeded to wipe his mouth and pencil thin moustache.

They left together and paid no notice to the young man at the bus stop, who waited until Kelly crossed York Street before sauntering slowly in the same direction.

The porter at the hotel entrance eyed Henry warily as he approached him. His mood changed when he saw Henry was sober.

"Good day, sir," he called, extending his hand, into which Henry discreetly placed a folded pound note.

Reaching the lounge, he pulled a wad of notes from his pocket and placed one on the bar top. He took a *Woodbine* from a battered silver cigarette case and put it between his lips as he eyed the other customers in the lounge.

"Glass a whiskey an' a bottle a stout. An' have one yerself," he said tonelessly to the barman. He continued to look around him as he waited for the drink. His eyes passed and then returned to a man dressed in a dark lounge suit, a white shirt and a monogrammed tie. He was sitting alone, sipping a brandy. A spotless white linen handkerchief hung half in and half out of his top jacket pocket. Henry thought he recognised the man, who seemed to have the worries of the world on his shoulders.

He looked away as his gaze was returned with a smile. His thoughts wandered to Sally Reilly. He knew she was staying in the hotel and had hoped he might have seen her in the bar. His eyes wandered back to the man at the table as he called the waiter, in a strong cultured accent. The voice was familiar: so familiar that Henry recognised it immediately. A vision of the first and only time they had met came instantly. Henry grimaced. The last time he'd heard that voice it was sentencing him to six months' hard labour in the Belfast High Court on the Crumlin Road. Ordering another drink quietly and quickly he prayed the judge wouldn't recognise him.

His mind returned to Sally Reilly. He was taken by her. He took a final sip from his drink and decided to visit the toilet before leaving. He had just undone his fly buttons when he heard the door swish open. He stared down at the urinal as someone sidled up to the one next to him. He froze as the man took a cigarette from his mouth and spoke to him in a casual, civilised tone.

"Excuse me for engaging you in conversation before we've been formally introduced: but I'm sure we've met before. Are you a barrister or a solicitor?" He began to chuckle. "I'm certain you're not one of the hopeless individuals who come before me on a daily basis." He continued to chuckle as he proceeded to answer his own question. "Of course, I'm only joking. You are much too well dressed to be a native of this area." He laughed as he nudged Henry playfully with his shoulder.

Harvey thought quickly as he buttoned up and instantly assumed the identity of a tourist he'd befriended a few months earlier.

"A'm afraid I haven't had the pleasure, sir. A'm from the United States of America. A'v bin lookin' up my family connections."

The judge swished his manhood playfully before putting it back into his trousers.

"I'm quite sure I have seen you before," he persisted. "Are your family connections local?" he continued probingly.

"No. We're originally from the Free State."

"What brings you to Belfast?"

"I was billeted in this hotel during the last war and thought I'd pay it a visit before I went home," Henry replied, almost forgetting to add his American accent.

The judge didn't seem to notice and nodded knowingly as both men washed their hands.

"I'm in the same business as yourself," continued Henry. "I'm a law man in a little ol' place called Texas. I'm sure yew've heard of it."

He nodded soberly as they both moved towards the door. "Are you a Texas ranger?" he asked.

Henry smiled condescendingly.

"I'm an attorney at law in a place called Dallas," he continued, opening his wallet and producing a business card the American visitor had given him.

The judge glanced at it briefly before putting it in his pocket.

"No names, no pack drill," he whispered sternly, before adding sweetly, "But you can call me Honey as I do think we're birds of a feather. Would my learned, colonial friend care for a drink at the bar?"

The pun was completely lost on Henry, who by now had assumed all the mannerisms of a visiting American. He ignored the judge's hand as it hovered fleetingly on his left buttock.

"As long as we don't talk shop, your worship," he drawled.

"So, what has you in this backwater?" continued the judge as they both leaned on the bar top and waited for their drinks. Henry replied word for word what the Yank had told him when he asked a similar question.

"Just tyin' up a few loose ends before I return to Dublin. I'll be back in the Lone Star State, this time next week."

He was in need of a smoke, but didn't want to produce his battered cigarette case. He called the barman who was at his side in an instant.

"Son, let's have one of those King Edwards, and git one for my friend the judge."

They moved to a corner table and the waiter dutifully carried their drinks to them. He lit the judge's cigar and then turned to Henry. The judge took a deep draw and settled in his seat. Henry could feel his free hand cruising up and down his leg. He made no attempt to remove it.

"Tell me," said the judge as he moved his hand further up Harvey's leg, "do they still have executions in Texas?" Henry puffed on his cigar.

"You bet!" he grinned triumphantly.

Some hours later they staggered out into Whitla Street. The judge walked to a Daimler parked outside the Dainty Café on the opposite side of the road. Henry watched as he climbed into it and started the engine, putting the automatic gear of the car into the drive position. He looked into the open window, and the judge smiled with pleasure as Henry placed his hand on his knee. The smile turned to a look of alarm as Henry pushed down heavily and the judge's foot sent the accelerator to the floor. The car flew across the road like a bullet from a gun and ploughed into a telephone box where it came to rest. Henry followed and looked through the shattered windscreen. The judge was snoring soundly, his head resting on the large luxurious head rest. There wasn't a mark on him.

Henry staggered to where the phone and the coin box lay. Reaching through the broken door he lifted the phone. He then moved in further and rang 999. Before leaving the scene, he leaned into the car and patted the judge affectionately.

"Goodbye Honey. I hope you git six months' hard labour."

As he strolled into the nearby Terminus Bar he heard the clang of the fire engines as they raced the few yards from their base at the bottom of Whitla Street. McKinstry was on the spot in minutes. He suppressed a growl of fury as he recognised the driver.

"What's the score?" he asked the senior Fire Officer.

"The phone box is a write-off, but the old guy isn't hurt," came the amused reply.

"Can I move him?" asked the police officer urgently.

"We've tasked an ambulance, but if you can get him to the hospital, well, the sooner the better. He doesn't seem to be seriously injured."

McKinstry nodded tersely to the waiting constables, and they gently lifted the snoring driver into the back of the police car. They drove off quickly. At the police station, the head constable ordered the driver to stop.

"I'll look after this myself. You and your colleagues take a half hour break, and then get back on the Street again."

The men nodded as he climbed into the front of the vehicle and drove off in the direction of the Malone Road. He looked with narrowed eyes at the reflection of his sleeping passenger.

"Thank goodness there wasn't another fruit merchant with him in the car," he thought. He returned his gaze to the road.

Twenty minutes later they were seated in the judge's home. His long suffering wife swore the officer to secrecy, and implied he would benefit from his handling of the incident. McKinstry nodded sagely and helped put the judge to bed. On his return to the station he wrote the incident in the occurrence book, stating the judge had been taken ill at the wheel of his car after having coffee in the Dainty Café. This would be verified by the owner of the café when he interviewed him at a later date. He phoned the Fire Officer on duty and asked if he'd smelt alcohol at the scene.

"Of course not," replied the station officer glibly as McKinstry put the phone down with a satisfied smile. The smile disappeared as he went into his own office and locked the door. Lifting the phone he dialled quickly. As a detached voice said "Yes," the police officer spoke softly into the mouthpiece.

"The grey fox was at his old waterhole today and up to his old tricks. His means of transport has been written off. Thankfully, there were no passengers. He's back in his lair and the tracks have been covered up."

The line was silent for a moment, then a relieved voice said quietly, "Message received and understood. Your vigilance and loyalty will not be forgotten." There was a slight pause, as if the speaker were conversing with someone else. "What about the car?" he asked.

"It's already in the police car pound at Musgrave Street. The engineers there are examining it at this moment. I wouldn't be surprised if they find a brake pipe has been cut. The judge has put quite a few of the local natives away, and someone could have taken advantage of his visit to the Dainty Café to even an old score," he replied. The line clicked dead as the self-satisfied smile returned to McKinstry's face. It was replaced by a thoughtful expression as he looked at the visiting card the judge's wife had taken from her husband's pocket. He read the black text. HIRAM T. AHERN, ATTORNEY AT LAW. The address was in Dallas, Texas. He turned the card absently and saw some handwriting in a thin pencil scrawl on the back. A humorous but icy smile flickered across his features as he read the words. He placed the card in his tunic pocket. The smile remained as he buttoned the flap.

It quickly faded when his office door opened and a constable informed him that a man had been found injured in a toilet cubicle in the Stalingrad Bar. He grabbed his blackthorn and put on his cap.

"Let's go!" he roared.

The barman directed him to the scene.

"I've already called for an ambulance," he said.

The man was slumped on the bowl, his trousers were at his ankles and his face was a mass of bruises. He was semi-conscious. A curious crowd had followed them to the small room. McKinstry turned and slammed the door shut.

"The cubicle door's been forced open," said the constable.

"Best method of attack," mused the Head. "Get your opponent when he's at his most vulnerable."

He turned to the barman.

"Who is he, Crozier?" he asked as the constable knelt beside the injured man and spoke to him.

The barman spread his hands.

"Don't know, Head. He was talkin' to Henry Harvey for a while. Harvey left an' yer man went till the toilet. It was one of the girls found him."

"The girls?" queried the Head incredulously. "In the men's toilet?" he added.

"Yew know how it is in here," replied the barman apologetically. "Any port in a storm."

"Any strangers in?" snarled McKinstry, changing the subject.

"This place is buzzin' wid strangers. Black men, brown men, Yanks, Gerries, Dutch ... It's a dockside bar. Naturally a lot of them bailed out when this happened."

"His wallet's still here, and there's money in it. So it wasn't motivated by robbery," called the constable who was trying unsuccessfully to revive the injured man. McKinstry reached for the wallet, as two ambulancemen carrying a stretcher came through the door. He pulled out a few cards and studied them before putting the wallet into his tunic pocket.

"Where are yew taking him?" he barked at the ambulance men.

"The Mater," answered the oldest, a fat man who was having difficulties moving in the small confines of the cubicle.

"We'll be up behind yew," he replied. He turned to the policeman who was still on his knees. "Have you checked the place out in case there's anything left around? Maybe a button or something pulled off during the struggle? Did you check his hands?"

The constable rose.

"Doesn't seem to have been a struggle. This guy was literally caught with his trousers down."

"Call scenes of crime to this location on the car handset, and stay here until they arrive." He turned to the barman. "Keep those rubbernecks out there, Crozier. I don't want them tramping all over a crime scene."

"What if they need to use the toilet?" asked the barman.

"Let them use the Ladies. After all it's 'any port in a storm', isn't it?" he mimicked sarcastically. "And if I catch any of them pishing in the lane, they'll be up in front of the beak the marra," he snarled as he brushed past the barman and into the street.

He gunned the car engine and stopped a few streets away at Henry Harvey's home. He pushed past the old woman who answered the door to his hammering.

"Where is he?" he said bluntly as he strode up the long hall.

"He's in bed, Head," whimpered the old woman, frightened out of her wits. McKinstry climbed the stairs two at a time and saw Harvey seated on the side of the bed trying to put on his slippers. Striding forward he grabbed the bewildered man by his hands and forcibly opened both of them. He then turned

175

them to look at the knuckles. He quickly released them when he saw they were unmarked.

Harvey sat back on the bed and eyed the policeman frostily.

"What's this all about, Head?" he asked quietly with the air of an innocent man.

The cop ignored the question.

"Were you drinking in the Stalingrad with a newspaper reporter?" he barked.

Henry's face turned white.

"He tole me I wouldn't be identified!"

"Did you beat him up?" roared McKinstry.

Henry rose from the bed.

"No way. He was askin' me about the trouble on the quay. Said he was writing an article about it ... "

"How did he know to get in touch with you?" interrupted the policeman.

"He jist walked inta the bar an' sat down beside me, an' started askin' questions. I didn't tell him anything. I have enuff problems without gittin' involved wid reporters."

"You sure have, Henry—or is it Hiram?" answered the policeman with a sneer. "Hiram T. Ahern, from Dallas, Texas. Attorney at law."

He enjoyed watching the red-button man squirm. Henry was dressed in spotless white long johns and rose to put on his trousers.

"I kin explain that, Head," he replied lamely. "How did yew find that out? Did the head porter squeal on me?"

McKinstry exploded.

"You wrote your name on the back of the card, you dozy ballocks."

Henry rose and looked pleadingly at him.

"Head, I had nuthin' till do wid the car crashin' ... "

The head constable grabbed him forcefully by the throat and threw him down on the bed. His knee was jammed against Henry's testicles.

"What crash?" McKinstry snarled.

Henry said nothing as the white spittle flecks hit his face, causing him to grimace.

"There was no crash. It didn't happen. Yew imagined it all. Yew weren't there, and yew won't ever grace the Midland with your poxy presence ever again. And if you ever see a certain judge you'll run a mile to get out of his sight. Is that right, Hiram?"

Henry nodded agreement.

"Whatever yew say, Head," he answered in a puzzled tone.

McKinstry released him and straightened up.

"It might interest you to know that your friend Hiram T. Ahern has never been to Texas in his life. He's a con man from Ballymena whom we've been after for a long time. If you ever see him again, ring me immediately. I'd love to talk to that individual."

He lifted his blackthorn from the floor.

"I'm going to interview this reporter when he comes round. Let's hope he corroborates your story, or you'll sleep in a different bed tonight," he snarled before racing down the stairs and out of the door. The old woman curtsied with genuine respect as he stormed past her.

He was about to enter the barracks when a tall man with a mop of unruly black hair called to him from the house next door. He wore a striped suit, a white shirt and a maroon tie. His shoes were brown, and a cigarette dangled from his lips.

"Any word on any arrests re these beatings, Head?"

McKinstry shook his head.

"Nothing yet, Doctor Calder. We just can't seem to get a breakthrough. None of those attacked recollect anything. They seem to have been hit from behind, by people who knew what they were doing. Only big Henry Harvey was able to fight back. He shook off an initial attack and returned fire. He told me he left one of his assailants with a busted cheek. Henry hits hard so the guy could possibly have a broken jaw. However he was hit, again from behind by a second man and that put him out of the game. So we know on that occasion there were at least two attackers."

Calder nodded.

"I know Harvey, although he's not one of my patients. It's a bad business. The area has a name for rowdiness, but I can't remember a time when so many of my patients have been affected. Previous brawls didn't produce the serious injuries we've been seeing over the past few days. I've given out more prescriptions for tranquilisers since the fighting in the schooling pen. Virtually every household in the district has been affected. Some men are feigning sickness, because they don't want to go back to the quay until this business is settled. Families concerned are in turmoil, with the menfolk in some homes openly hostile to each other."

McKinstry nodded in baffled agreement.

"I'm going up to the Mater now. We just found another victim in the Stalingrad. By the way, have you treated or heard of anyone with the injuries handed out by Harvey?" he asked quietly.

"Not off-hand," replied the doctor. "I'll check up, and let you know."

"Thanks, Doc," replied the police officer.

He watched as Calder climbed into a long black saloon car that was known all over the district, and drove off. He waved and climbed the steps into the barrack.

"Visitor for yew, Head," called the station guard as he walked towards his office. He turned to the man sitting nervously on the chair outside his office and beckoned him to follow. Inside his office he lifted a sheaf of paper messages and studied them as the man entered behind him. "Sit down, Mr. ... "

"Hamill," replied the well-dressed man. "Todd Hamill."

McKinstry put the papers back on the desk and pulled out a twenty packet of *Players* cigarettes.

"What can I do for yew?" he asked quietly as he lit the cigarette and took a deep grateful draw of tobacco smoke into his lungs.

"I'm a full time officer for the trade union concerned in the recent problems on Belfast Docks. I've been pushing my superiors to sort this issue out in the name of socialism."

He stopped as the police officer grunted and moved on the chair. He pulled the holster of the large Webley revolver to the front of his body and settled back further.

"Bloody nuisance, these things," he muttered apologetically as he nodded Hamill to continue.

"I must report that the majority of the officers abhor the descent into criminality by some of our members. However, we believe this is the product of hopelessness and helplessness that stems from non-representation. At a meeting of officers a few days ago we agreed that the red-button men had a genuine case that must be addressed. It was proposed by me and seconded by another officer that we call on the powers that be to subsume the red-button workforce with the blue-button workforce as soon as humanly possible. We sent a letter to that effect to the secretary of our union. It came back a few days later. We were told the matter was *sub judice* and therefore the secretary or the union was unable to act or comment on it."

McKinstry interrupted again, this time impatiently, but politely.

"That's very commendable, but I don't see that it is a concern of the RUC. I have a man lying seriously injured in hospital and I need to get up and interview him. Do you think what you've told me is the concern of the police?" he added.

"Not necessarily," replied Hamill. "But I think this is."

He reached into his jacket pocket and produced a piece of paper which he handed to the police officer.

McKinstry read the large handwritten words out loud:

You would be well advised to discontinue your attempt to have the reds amalgamated with the blues. It will never work and won't be tolerated. We have your home address, your phone number, and your car licence number. We know what school you deliver your children to every morning before you go to work. We know all about you, and will not hesitate to use any means available to stop your nefarious plan. Heed this warning. There won't be another.

McKinstry turned the letter over and saw the reverse side was blank.

"Did you receive this through the post?"

"It was in my pigeonhole this morning. There was no stamp," Hamill replied impassively.

"Internal mail from some of your colleagues?" continued the police officer.

"Could be," Hamill admitted, "but it could just as easily have been brought into the office. That happens regularly. The girl in reception would put it in my pigeonhole and let me know via the phone. At an appropriate time I'd go down and collect the mail."

"Was it the only letter today?"

"No, I run a large branch and I get quite a lot of mail."

McKinstry looked him in the eyes.

"Are you going to do what they ask?"

Hamill rose and smiled tightly.

"Of course not."

"I can't protect you," warned the policeman. "You know the term *sub judice* will be used until this case comes to court. In other words this situation could run a lot longer than we expect it to."

"I came to report the threat, not to lie down under it," replied Hamill moving towards the door. "For better or for worse, most of the second-preference men are my constituents, although none of them has ever worked for the provender mills they claim membership of. However, it is my job to get the best deal possible for them."

"Are you telling me these guys are members of a branch they've never worked for?" asked the police officer, looking thoroughly bewildered.

Hamill nodded grimly and rose from his seat.

"One more thing ... " called McKinstry.

Hamill stopped at the door.

"Have any of your colleagues received similar threats, either verbally or in writing?"

"None that I'm aware of."

"Should I send an officer to check on Monday morning?"

Hamill again smiled tightly.

"Do you think that is the concern of the trade union?"

McKinstry returned his smile.

"Point taken."

He stubbed out his cigarette and lifted his hat and blackthorn stick. He strode out behind Hamill and into the guardroom.

"Joe, get me a driver on the double. I'm going up to the Mater to check on the latest casualty."

He looked up at the station clock and shuddered.

"The night is young," he muttered glumly to himself as he walked down the steps and into the back seat of the patrol car.

Seven

MINNIE KNEW WHO WAS AT THE door before she opened it. However, the freshly washed and shaved face of Kelly caused her to panic. She looked up and down the street in consternation, much to the amusement of her visitor. She stood aside to let him enter.

"Git in quick! If any a the neighbours see yew I'll git the business end of my da's cattle stick across my backside," she whispered frantically. Kelly moved up the hall and into the kitchen and sat down. She noted he was dressed immaculately. His hair was neatly combed, as if he were going somewhere special.

He crossed his legs and lay back on the settee.

"I called to see if you'll go with me to the Plaza tonight. Yer da's spies 'ill nat see us there." He was unable to hide his amusement at her fear, and this added to her annoyance.

She put her hands on her hips and glared at him.

"Can't yew understand it when people say no? My da has left hard an' fast orders that I have nuthin' till do wid yew. He doesn't want a drunken whoremaster fer a son-in-law," she stated through tear-filled eyes.

"That kinda narrows the field fer yew in this district."

She sprang forward and slapped his face.

"How dare yew say the men of York Street are drunken whoremasters?"

He grabbed her by the arms and pulled her down beside him.

"I didn't say that: yew did," he replied with an infuriating grin that caused her to struggle wildly in an effort to free herself. Suddenly her face was close to his and he kissed her. It was a slow tender kiss. He laid her gently back onto the settee and her arms flew around his neck. When he released her, she smiled sadly.

"Billy, I dursen't. I dursen't," she whimpered. His eyes hardened, but his voice was soft as he spoke.

"I want yew to go wid me tonight. I don't want to be out drinkin'. I'm livin' in a house wid a corpse fer company, an' I'd like fer a change till talk till someone who'll answer me back. I want ta be wid yew, girl. Even if only fer a coupla ires. Remember the night we went till the Silver Slipper? Well, I haven't had a dance since then." He stood up and looked at her. "I'll be over in Barney's fer the next ire. That shud give yew time till git changed. If yer nat there, I'll know I'm wastin' my time." He turned and walked out of the room. Minnie continued sobbing into her handkerchief as her father's austere features glared down at her from a photograph on the fireplace.

Kelly walked slowly down Henry Street. Except for an old woman feeding pigeons and seabirds, and some children swinging on a nearby lamp post, it was deserted. Sticking his hands into the trouser pockets of his brown serge suit, he walked aimlessly past the White Lion and into York Street. He hoped she would come to him. The events of the past few days were weighing heavily on his mind.

He saw Jim Harvey on the other side of the road and crossed over. The lad was attired in a two-piece suit complete with dress shoes and a shirt and tie. As he got closer he noted a piece of dark cloth, cut in the shape of a diamond, sewed onto the left sleeve of his jacket.

"Reilly?" he asked nodding at the mark of remembrance and respect. Jim nodded shyly. Kelly slapped him affectionately on the shoulder.

"Yer a good kid," he said earnestly. "Have yew time ta have a pint wid me?"

Paddy was absent and the drinks were set up by his brother who also worked in the bar. He was not as vocal as the owner and the payment was accepted in silence as the two men climbed onto barstools. The public house was almost deserted, except for a few men scattered at different tables.

The door flew open and a bedraggled figure lurched into the bar. He paused unsteadily as if trying to find his bearings, before shaking his head and staggering to the pub.

"Givus a Johnny Walker," he slurred as the barman approached him nervously. He put his hands on the bar top and laid his head down, as if he were about to sleep. The barman eyed him sternly.

"I think yew have had enuff!" he said frostily.

Jim watched as Kelly left his stool and walked towards the man.

"Alfie. How'd yew git intil such a state?" he asked, genuinely concerned. The drunk raised his head and gazed at Kelly for a moment or two before a light of recognition shone in his eyes and caused him to laugh cynically.

"I'm celebratin' losin' a job I've had for thirty years. The only job I know an' the only job I've ever had." He began to chuckle to himself. "Billy," he laughed, "I've bin up an' down York Street an' Sailortown. I've had at least two drinks in each one, an' I gat them all on the slate."

He glared at the barman.

"This is the only place I've bin knocked back," he snarled.

Kelly straightened him up. The man's clothes were caked with dust and gave off an aroma of many cargoes. His once black boots were stained with a coating of grey powder.

"Why don't yew go home an' sleep it off, Alfie," he coaxed as Alfie lay like a limp doll in his arms.

"Can't go home, Billy! I've bin drinkin' since Thursday when them bastards tuk our paybooks. I drunk the lot. I went home last night and wrecked the house. The neighbours called McKinstry an' his henchmen give me a diggin' an' threw me intil the street."

He straightened up and released himself.

"I spent last night in a cell. God knows where I'll spend this night," he added before dropping to the floor like a limp rag.

"I'll call the peelers," cried the frightened barman.

"No, yew won't," answered Kelly with a trace of steel in his tone that caused the barman to stop in his tracks. Kelly knelt down and threw the man over his shoulder. Rising effortlessly he gazed at Jim. "If Minnie comes in, tell her I'll be back in a minute. Alfie kin sleep it off in my house."

Jim nodded dumbly as the docker opened the front door and walked out into the street with Alfie hanging over his shoulder.

"What will happen to Alfie when he isn't able to pay the money for all that drink?" asked Jim when Kelly returned a few minutes later.

Kelly shrugged.

"He'll nat be able to go back into the pubs he swindled until he cleans his slate. Yew only pull a trick like that once. I'm more worried about his run in wid the cops. Those guys aren't a bit fussy where they blatter yew wid their batons."

"Cud he be hurt?" asked Jim

Kelly lowered the empty pint tumbler and ordered two more drinks.

"He'll know the marra when the drink wears off," he replied grimly. The bleak look disappeared as he saw Minnie walk nervously into the snug.

The taxi crawled slowly up Chichester Street towards the queue that had formed outside the Plaza.

"Quare crowd the night," muttered Kelly, to no one in particular.

"Aye," drawled the driver as he rolled down the window and threw a cigarette butt into the street. "There's a load a German navy men docked in Belfast. I've bin kept quite busy haulin' the sailors up from the Pollock. Most of 'em's comin' here."

Kelly's face clouded for a moment. He noted Minnie's concerned glance and smiled as he paid the fare.

"Well, it's a free country. Are they uniformed sailors?" he continued as he waited on his change.

"Yes. They're from West Germany. I believe they're here fer a few days to take part in a ceremony to honour the dead of two world wars."

"Good fer them," muttered the docker without any enthusiasm, as he and Minnie climbed out of the car.

The driver grinned impishly.

"Only one problem: There's a Canadian aircraft carrier in fer repairs, an' a latta them are also in the queue. So don't be surprised if World War Three breaks out." He laughed at the prospect as he gunned the taxi away from the kerb.

Kelly took Minnie's arm and noted the different uniforms in the long line that was slowly moving towards the door. There was also a smattering of khaki among the naval blue. As they walked past the brightly-lit entrance towards the end of the queue, one of the smartly dressed stewards supervising the crowd called his name. Kelly recognised him and stopped. The young man, dressed in a red jacket, navy trousers and a black bow tie, waved him over.

"Here's a pass for tonight, Mr. Kelly. Compliments of the house. Go on in, and please Mr. Kelly, no trouble. We're gonna have our hands full wid this mixture an' wudn't want an input from the current feud ragin' on the quay."

Kelly took the tickets gratefully.

"Yew have my word, Patrick," he said with a wry grin as he and Minnie moved towards the foyer that led to the ballroom.

"Who's he?" she asked as she held his arm tightly.

Kelly smiled. She loved his smile and snuggled closer to him.

"That's Patsy Mooney's son. His da's a red-button man, an' a close friend of Sammy Wilson."

"The guy in hospital?" asked Minnie, adding, "How is he?"

"Doin' alright," grunted Kelly. "He might git out tomorra. He wants till attend the funeral."

The dimly-lit ballroom was almost empty. They moved straight onto the dance floor and Minnie clung to him as Kelly whirled her gracefully to the music of the eight-piece band.

"It must be great till have friends in high places," she muttered coyly as he stooped a little to lean his cheek against hers.

"Yeah. Let's make the most of it. When that crowd gets in, there'll be scarcely room to breathe, niver mind dance."

186

She nodded and marvelled at how light he was on his feet, as he swept her through the intricate steps of a foxtrot.

When the set finished, he led her to the plush seats at the edge of the dance floor.

"Yew mustn't a spent all yer time killin' people or beatin' them up: or drinkin' the peace out," she remarked teasingly. He adjusted the crease on his trousers and loosened the middle button of his jacket. He was glad to see the tension had left her face, and smiled as she moved closer to him.

"We taught each other to dance to kill time in the barrack room," he explained. "One of my corporals ran a dancing school in Ballymacarrett. He taught us the finer points of terpsicory. The barrack room floor was covered with chalk footprints."

Minnie smiled in disbelief.

"I can't believe it. Big tough soldier men dancin' wid each other."

The band struck up a new tune and his reply was lost. He rose and took her hand, and pulled her to him. She began to laugh and he looked down at her.

"What's so amusin'?" he asked as the floor began to fill with dancers.

"I hope yew weren't this close when yew were dancin' wid the corporal," she giggled.

She looked up to see his reaction and found he wasn't looking at her. His eyes were fixed on the features of a man dancing beside them. She shivered. They had a look of anger that frightened her as he glided closer to the other dancer. She noticed the man had a facial wound just below his right eye. The scar tissue seemed fresh. He locked eyes with Kelly and his blank stare turned to fear.

She almost fell over when Kelly spoke to him in what she thought was gibberish. When the other man recovered, he replied in the same way. His teeth were tightly clenched as he answered, and a closer look showed his jaws were wired together.

The music stopped and the man left his partner on the floor pushing his way roughly past couples who were waiting for the next dance. Minnie rolled her eyes sympathetically as the girl who had been dancing with the German angrily made her way back to her seat. Kelly moved to follow the injured man, but she restrained him. The anger left his face as he looked at her frightened features.

"Yew promised the boy at the door," she said anxiously.

Kelly gave her a reassuring hug as the music began.

"Don't worry," he muttered quietly. "I wus jist sayin' hello to an old German buddy. I thought he was miles away from here."

"Did yew do that till his face?" she whispered fearfully.

"No. But I think I know who did," he replied thoughtfully.

He moved her in the direction in which the German had left the floor. Holding her closely, he looked over her head and saw the seaman in conversation with four other men whom he immediately recognised from the altercation in the supper saloon.

He nodded respectfully when the man known to him as Karl raised his coffee cup and smiled challengingly. He remembered his promise to the doorman, sighed, and swiftly wheeled Minnie to the other side of the room. When the dance ended, they walked silently in the direction of the coffee bar. She watched him for a moment or two. His grey eyes were clouded and thoughtful as he sipped at the drink. She didn't ask for an explanation and wasn't surprised when he didn't offer one.

Her thoughts on the matter were interrupted by raised voices at the other side of the ballroom. She watched fearfully as two men in different uniforms exchanged blows. As their terrified partners and other dancers rushed for safety, two of the doormen patrolling the floor raced to quell the disturbance.

They were quickly overpowered by shipmates of both combatants as the fistfight developed into a full blown brawl. Kelly grabbed Minnie protectively as women screamed and tables and chairs were hurled onto the dance floor.

"C'mon. This is where we bail out," he said tersely.

Minnie followed as he guided her through the thick struggling mass of humanity. Some were rushing to be involved in the fighting whilst others were scrambling to reach the safety of the seating area.

The steward who had given Kelly the passes was on the floor and being severely beaten by two sailors in the uniform of the German navy. Minnie looked at him.

"Aren't yew goin' till help him?" she cried.

He nodded grimly and ran to the rescue. Instead of raining punches, he stopped and yelled at the seamen in what she took to be their own language. The men immediately straightened up and stood to attention. Kelly continued to shout at them and pointed to the door. They saluted, and instantly left the scene. Kelly picked the grateful and embarrassed doorman from the floor.

"Yewr in the wrong line a work, son," he said dryly.

Turning to Minnie he saw panic in her eyes as she looked behind him. Sensing danger he turned quickly and saw the bald-headed seaman about to swing a fist, wearing a silver knuckleduster, at the back of his head. He dropped quickly to his knees and as his attacker flew over his head, Kelly's left hand clamped on his throat and his right gripped his testicles. Karl screamed in agony as Kelly tightened his grip. He rose without effort, and held the unfortunate man across his shoulders for a few seconds before raising him above his head and hurling him into the dense knot of brawlers. Minnie watched open-mouthed as he disappeared in a sea of legs and arms. At that moment a posse of police officers arrived at the front door with drawn batons.

Kelly steered her towards the emergency exit, and a few minutes later they were walking towards the taxi rank outside the city hall.

"What did yew say to those navy men?" she enquired

Kelly grinned.

"I told them I was an officer from their ship and asked for names, numbers and rank. That sent them scarpering double quick."

"That wus quick thinkin'," she replied.

He laughed mockingly.

"Don't fergit, I used till be an officer and a gentleman till the docks corrupted me."

"Why did yew learn to speak German?" she asked with childlike curiosity as the taxi sped along Corporation Street.

His face clouded and hardened as he looked straight ahead.

"I wanted to say sorry to the soldiers on sentry duty, before I broke their necks or cut their throats," he muttered grimly.

The rest of the journey was spent in silence.

She waited in the shadows as he paid the taxi man, lowering her head as neighbours passed on their way home. Kelly's good humour had returned.

"Yewr place or mine?" he said flippantly. He looked at his watch. "Yer da's well on his way an' won't be back till the marra night," he said wickedly.

"I ain't sittin' in no house wid a corpse in it!" she cried with a shiver.

"That's it then," he replied.

He watched patiently as she fumbled with the key before opening the door. She stamped her feet and banged the side of the door in an effort to chase any vermin that might have been in the room. Walking gingerly across the darkened room she fumbled with a match and lit the mantle. He sat down as she took off her coat and walked into the scullery.

"Why doesn't yewr da git the electric in?"

"Doesn't trust it. Says it's nat natural, an' as long as the shops sell mantles we'll be usin' gas for lightin' as well as cookin'." She turned to him and did an imitation of her father speaking. "Why pay fer two servants when one kin do both jobs," she growled.

"Fair play till him. Reilly was the same. I'll have till git a supply a mantles in," he shouted as she continued into the scullery.

"There's a coupla pig's feet here if yew want them," she called.

"I told yew what I want," he replied, walking in to join her. She had her back to him and he put his hands on her shoulders and kissed her lightly on the neck. She turned to him.

"Did yew really kill Germans?"

Kelly shrugged.

"Everybody did."

"Would yew kill my da, if he crossed yew?" she asked with genuine fear in her voice. He pulled her closer and looked deep into her eyes.

"I'm nat allowed till kill people any more since the war ended," he replied with an amused smile.

She didn't resist as he took her away from the stove and led her gently up the stairs. In the darkness of her bedroom, she allowed him to undress her and found herself opening his shirt buttons and loosening his trouser belt.

He kissed her face and neck and she knew she was lost. The man who held her had come to mean everything to her. She knew she would always be putty in his hands, and the fear of her father's wrath faded as he laid her gently on the bed and entered her welcoming body with a tenderness that caused her to sob. He leaned over her face and gently kissed her tears until her weeping subsided. Her body began to respond to his thrusting and probing and her sobs turned to cries of pleasure and delight.

Neither of them heard the key turn in the front door. Both froze at the sound of heavy footsteps on the stairs: seconds later her father's voice broke the strained silence as he knocked on her bedroom door.

"Minnie. Are yew sleepin'?" he whispered softly.

She sat bolt upright almost throwing Kelly out of the bed.

"No, da!" she yelled. "What has yew back?"

"Engine trouble. The ship hadda return. Will yew cum down an' make me a bite till eat? There's a good girl."

Kelly lifted his head and stared into Minnie's terrified features. She put her finger to her lips and climbed out of the bed. He heard her fumbling around and then the scratching of a match on the box as she lit the gas mantle. She took a rumpled dressing gown from the back of the door and hastily put it on. As she opened the door to go down the stairs, she again cautioned quietness with her finger over her lips.

He didn't know how long he had slept when he was awakened by a hand on his throat. He saw the glint of the silver plated Walther pistol heading for the base of his neck, just below his left ear. He heard the harsh and heavy breathing and smelt the rancid breath of the man on top of him. His left hand shot out and grabbed the gun. Sliding his little finger quickly along the barrel he jammed it between the hammer and the firing pin. He ignored the pain as the hammer fell repeatedly against flesh and bone. His other hand reached for his attacker's face. The would-be assassin screamed as Kelly's thumb searched for and gouged out his left eye. He dropped the weapon which remained attached to Kelly's finger. Quickly releasing his finger, he fired point blank. The round plunged into the side of his attacker's astonished face and blew half of it away. In the split second of light caused by the ignition of the bullet, he saw the unseeing one eye of the dead German officer staring up at him before the black curtain of the night fell again.

He awoke with a start and gazed at his surroundings. The dark German forest had vanished, but the face of the man he had killed remained. Gradually it faded and the familiar surroundings of Minnie's room made him realise he was having a bad dream.

He lay and gazed at the flickering mantle until his heart began to beat normally. He had not experienced that dream in a long time and shuddered at the memory of the long-ago encounter that had cost a German officer his life. He had retained the soldier's personal side arm and holster as a trophy and smuggled it home. He secreted it in the wall cavity of his room where it had lain until a few nights ago. He realised he had resurrected the nightmare as well as the weapon.

Looking at his watch he saw it was two a.m. Minnie had been gone over an hour. The bad dream was quickly forgotten as he felt an urgent need to empty his bladder. Searching the room with his eyes he sought out a utensil that would ease his problem. Using all his wartime skills he moved slowly and silently to the nearest side of the bed. Putting a hand lightly on the floor, he looked under the bed and was relieved to see a white chamber pot glistening at the other side. Scarcely three feet away, it could have been ten miles. He clenched his teeth and moved inch by tortured inch as his swollen bladder threatened to burst. Fifteen minutes later, he reached out and slowly picked up the pot. Throwing back the bedclothes he put it between his legs. His sigh of relief was cut short as he heard someone climbing the stairs. He quickly pulled the blankets over the receptacle as the urine flooded into it. Seconds later the door opened and Minnie appeared with one hand indicating silence and the other with five fingers outstretched. She closed the door quietly and returned to the kitchen.

Kelly waited until he could no longer hear her footsteps before throwing back the blankets and lowering the chamber pot back to where he found it.

Moving slowly and as quietly as he could, he began to gather his discarded clothing, thankful he had left none downstairs. He dressed himself in the mantle light and sat on the bed to figure out his next move. Stepping cautiously towards the window he froze as a board beneath his feet creaked with a sound that would be heard in the room below. The window was half-open and he pushed it up further to allow him to climb through. Clambering silently onto the apex of the scullery roof he gently closed the window. As he braced himself against the wall of the house, he heard the heavy measured footsteps climbing the stairs.

"I toul yew there was no one here," Minnie said angrily. "Who'd want till brake intil these hovels? It musta bin the mice that flutter about the floorboards and the ceilings now and again." Her voice rose to an indignant shout. "What are yew lukin' under the bed for? Do yew think I sneaked somebody in?"

He grinned despite his precarious position as her father retorted, "I'm lukin fer a rat."

"Well, yill nat fine it now. It'll have scarpered," she cried.

"Aye," replied her father grimly, adding, "We'll need ta set a trap."

Kelly looked at the back windows of the house next door and decided to make a move. The blinds were drawn and the home was silent. The small mill houses had no back entries, and each butted on to the other. He knew he couldn't climb his way out, so he decided to drop into the backyard next door. He got onto his backside and slid down the roof to the guttering. Peering through the twilight he estimated the tiled floor of the backyard to be six feet below him. He prayed the occupants were asleep and hoped the ground was clear of obstacles as he leapt from the roof. He didn't see the three strands of thin rope that stretched across the yard and served as a clothes line. The first rope caught him under the chin and the second lapped around the back of his neck, forcing the breath from his throat and leaving him hanging suspended two feet from the ground. He almost blacked out as the ropes tightened around his windpipe. He reached up and tried to untangle them but his weight held them tight against his throat. He was losing consciousness when the ropes broke and he fell to the ground winded and breathless.

Tugging gently at the back door he was relieved to find it wasn't barred. He crept tentatively into the house as Minnie's father pulled up the bedroom window and looked out into the gloom.

"What ta hell was that?" he heard him yell.

He didn't hear Minnie's reply as he concentrated on silently working his way through the darkness to the front door of the house. Lifting the latch quietly he eased the door open.

Reaching Reilly's house he fumbled for his key and then looked at his watch. The luminous dial told him it was twenty past four. Closing the door he felt his way into the darkened kitchen. He groped around the wall until he reached the settee and threw himself down on it. He loosened his tie and top shirt button. Within minutes he was sound asleep.

He was awakened by an anguished scream that echoed all through the house. Daylight lit up the edges of the window blind that had remained down since the day Reilly had died. As he sat up on the settee and tried to gauge his bearing in the darkness, he heard frantic footsteps on the stairs. He jumped to his feet and ran to the bottom of the stairs. As the shadowy screaming figure approached him he leapt forward and caught him in a necklock forcing him to the ground.

"What the fuck are yew doin' here?" he shouted harshly, as the fully clothed man struggled to escape from his grip.

"It's me, Billy—Alfie. Let me go. I'm goin' home," he pleaded.

Kelly released him instantly and lifted him to his feet.

"Yer alright," he whispered reassuringly. "Yew've bin havin' a nightmare." He carried the man into the room and placed him on the settee. His visitor continued to whimper as Kelly lit the mantle.

Alfie looked around him fearfully.

"How did I get here? Where am I? Where am I?" he asked in a frightened tone.

A strong smell of urine filled the room and Kelly could see his companion had wet his trousers.

Kelly sat down beside him.

"Yew collapsed in Paddy's. I brought yew over here 'cause yid nowhere else till go. Other events caused me to forget yew were here."

He looked at the man who was still cowering with fright.

"Yew scared the shit outa me. Yew musta had a bad dream," he added.

Alfie started to shiver and rolled his eyes.

"No bad dream, Billy. It wus a lovely dream; I wus back in the good books wid the wife. I wus kissin' an' cuddlin' her. When I woke, I wus cheek till cheek wid somebody. But it wusn't my wife. The room was as black as the ace a spades." His voice took on a note of hysteria. "There was a bloody man in bed wid me an' he wus as cold as a corpse!" he cried, covering his face with his hands.

Kelly rose and ran quickly up the stairs. He took the matches from his pocket and quickly lit one. He looked at the bed and the unseeing eyes of Reilly looked back at him. Alfie had pulled the sheets from the bed in his terror stricken haste, and Reilly's naked body lay uncovered and glistening in the early morning light that was filtering through the room's solitary window.

Kelly grinned and threw the bedclothes over the naked body before going back downstairs. He sat down beside the sobbing man and held him close.

"It's Reilly."

Alfie looked at him with frozen eyes and began to sob uncontrollably.

Kelly grinned despite the seriousness of the situation.

I'm sorry, Alfie. I brought yew over an' jist threw yew in the bed. I niver lit the light. The ould dolls musta decided till give Reilly a good clean-up before his final journey. They probably washed him in the bed because they didn't want to stain the coffin. Sam Harvey was in earlier an' stunk the place wid the smell of fishmeal an' yew know how long that stench stays in a room."

Alfie continued to shudder. He looked up at Kelly with shame-filled eyes.

"I wus kissin' him, Billy. Honest. I thought it was the wife. Goodness knows what wuda happened had I nat woke up," he sobbed.

Kelly nursed him like a frightened child.

"That's alright, Alfie. Let that be our secret," he whispered softly, trying hard not to laugh at his stricken companion. He released him gently and rose from the settee. "I'm gonna git us a cuppa. We've both had a hard day."

As he took the packet of Lyons Green Label tea from the cupboard, he looked at his reflection in the mirror over the sink. A red mark from the pressure of the clothes line circled his neck like a bad burn. He knew he'd had a lucky escape. Had the ropes not been rotten, Minnie would have had some explaining to do the next day.

The front door closed with a bang and brought him back to the present. He wasn't surprised when he looked into the kitchen and found Alfie had disappeared. As he waited for the tea brewing, he went out into the yard and opened the toilet door. He stepped onto the square box that served as a seat and felt around the back of the cistern. His hand closed on the familiar shape of the Walther PPK. The face of the dead German appeared briefly in his mind but he cast it away quickly.

Putting the weapon into his jacket pocket, he returned to the scullery and poured out a cup of tea. He shivered as he thought of what might have happened to Alfie had the pistol been in its usual place underneath his pillow on the settee. He kept it there when he was sleeping. He looked at the settee. "Too late to lie down now," he thought. He grinned as he imagined Alfie tearing across York Street like a bullet. He hoped his wife would let him in. The thought of Alfie kissing and hugging Reilly's corpse sent him into convulsions of laughter as he lifted his cup. His mind returned to the lucky escape from Minnie's house. He sipped pensively at his tea and hoped she realised he was safe.

He was awakened by the sound of church bells. He lay for a moment before rising. Taking the gun from behind the cushion at his head he returned it to the back of the cistern. Stripping, he filled the sink with cold water and sluiced his body from head to toe before walking up the stairs and taking clean underwear from a cabinet drawer. Dressing quickly, he tidied up the scullery and the kitchen before going to the bedroom. He threw the bedclothes onto the floor and placed Reilly's rigid body gently on the floor beside them. He turned the mattress to hide the stain of Alfie's urine and placed a sheet over it, before putting the bedclothes on top. He ran down to the scullery and returned with a floorcloth. Climbing under the bed, he wiped dry the telltale signs of Alfie's terror. He made the return journey to the sink and rinsed out the floorcloth before leaving it where he found it.

Walking out into the bleak sunlight he saw his dog rush towards him. He knelt and patted the animal affectionately with one hand as he took the chain from his pocket and clicked it on to its collar with the other. Straightening up, he allowed the animal to pull him in the direction of North Queen Street.

"Okay Soldier," he murmured warmly, "next stop, Napoleon's nose."

As they passed in the shadow of the giant flax spinning mill, he thought about his encounter with the German merchant men in the dance hall. Had Minnie not been with him he would certainly have checked out if the man's injuries had been caused by a blow from a hand wearing a large ring. He remembered the patient he'd passed in the hospital ward when he had visited Wilson. It could have been the same man, with injuries caused by Henry Harvey, and not an indiscriminate attack on the streets of Sailortown. He thought of Karl flying through the air and hoped he hadn't broken any bones.

Passing a public phone box at the corner of Brougham Street he pondered a few minutes before deciding to ring McKinstry.

Tying the dog to a nearby lamp post he made the call.

"Head Constable McKinstry is off-duty. He returns tonight. Can anyone else help?" said the voice from the phone.

Hanging up, he stepped outside and untied the dog, allowing it to pull him in the direction of the Limestone Road.

McKinstry was on duty and feeling pleased with himself. He'd entered the station after being phoned at home by the night sergeant, and arrived to find one of the plainclothes officers detailed to watch Kelly waiting for him in the interrogation office with four prisoners. The desk sergeant was told he was not to be interrupted under any circumstances. The suspects were German nationals, and one bore the marks of a recent assault. Another had his teeth clamped together from a previous encounter. The Head listened impassively as the plainclothes officer told how the men had left the Plaza ballroom behind Kelly and Minnie after the Docker had defended himself against a cowardly attack from one of the men armed with a knuckleduster. Rescuing their fallen colleague they had raced out after Kelly and saw his taxi leaving. They followed and the officer went after them. They got out of the taxi at the same street as Kelly and his female companion. The police officer realised they were stalking Kelly. He held them at gunpoint and marched them to the nearby station. They were arrested after a variety of weapons was found on their persons.

"Can any of you speak English?" growled McKinstry.

The tallest one glared back at him.

"We want to go to our ship," he hissed.

McKinstry jumped up and smashed the top of the table with his open palm.

"Not until yew give me some explanation as to why yew were carrying offensive weapons. Why would peace-loving sailors have marlin spikes and knuckledusters?" he snarled lifting a foot long marlin spike that looked uncannily like a police baton. "What was this for? To beat up the wimmin if they didn't oblige? Or mebbe to blatter the man who bate yew up an' humiliated yew in the chippie? You are not leavin' here until I get some answers."

He walked around the table to the man with the injured face. "You didn't get those injuries by accident, so yew'd better settle down and give me some answers." As he walked back to his seat he saw one of the men grinning defiantly at him. Turning quickly he grabbed him savagely by the hair and hauled him from the chair. He crashed him against the room wall and tightened his grip. "What do you find so funny, Gerry?" he snarled, digging him viciously in the ribs. His second punch sent the man to the floor.

He turned to the constable beside him.

"Take those three to different rooms and get the boys to check their stories."

He nodded at the man writhing on the floor.

"Leave this one with me. Send someone in to take notes," he added grimly. The German's eyes filled with fear and the head constable knew he understood what was said.

Two hours later four signed confessions were on his desk. All the serious assaults of the last few days were admitted to by the men. Further questioning showed they were really after Billy Kelly. They had assaulted the men they saw with the docker, assuming them to be his friends. The chance meeting in the dancehall provided an opportunity to exact the final revenge. McKinstry's eyes were hostile as he watched them being herded to different cells. He cast a grateful glance at the plainclothes officer.

"Thanks Sergeant. If yew hadn't apprehended them, Kelly wuda probably wiped them all out," he said with a grin.

He threw the written confessions to the desk sergeant.

"Notify their captain they're in custody pending trial for assault with deadly weapons."

Outside the station, he smiled and broke into a jaunty step as he walked to his car and began the drive back to his home in Greenisland.

He was in the midst of a contented doze when the harsh

jangling tones of the telephone awoke him with a start. He lifted the receiver.

"What is it?" he snarled bad-temperedly, assuming it was the station guard at York Street station. His head cleared quickly when he heard the clipped tones of one of his superiors.

"My phone hasn't stopped ringing for the last two hours. My superior; the representative for the seamen's union; the German ambassador; the Minister of Home Affairs; and the big man himself all want to know what you are playing at?" came the sarcastic reply. McKinstry was dumbfounded.

"What's this all about, sir?" he asked uncomfortably.

"Call your station. Tell them to release the German nationals immediately and take them to their ship. Tear up the forced confessions, and just pray that you won't be losing your rank," replied the cold informal voice.

"They weren't forced confessions, sir. We got them dead to rights. There are men lying in hospital seriously injured by these thugs," stammered the police officer.

"Release them, David."

The voice was a little softer, a little more understanding, but still firm.

"Let them go and forget the incident. I'm advising you as a friend. You are stepping on the toes of people in high places by continuing to investigate petty incidents seemingly linked to the Docks dispute. They want the matter to die a natural death. It won't if you keep raising issues. Those confessions, whether forced or otherwise, have established there is no local input in this business. In other words, the situation would be perfectly normal if the sailors hadn't been attacked first. The reprisals and following bloodshed is down to that and has nothing to do with the trade union policies on the Belfast Dock. Apparently it all started over the men jumping a queue in a fish and chip shop." The voice hardened again. "Is that something to lose your rank over? Do as I say, whilst I'm still able to help you."

The phone went dead. McKinstry placed it on the cradle and then lifted it again.

"Release the Germans, and take the tail off Kelly," he said quietly. "Just do what I say," he said tiredly and put the phone down.

"Trouble?" his wife asked, as she looked up from the Sunday papers.

"Could be," he grunted. "Someone's markin' my card. I think it's political."

"After what you did for that pansy judge, they should be promoting you," she sniffed.

He wasn't listening. He was curious as to whom were the people in high places he kept hearing about, and just how high they went. He suddenly remembered the journalist who'd been injured in the Stalingrad Bar. The freelance writer wouldn't make a statement. He claimed he'd had too much to drink and had fallen in the toilet. He refused to co-operate, and McKinstry reluctantly left the ward. He checked the files in the station and found the man had been caught more than once in the company of local prostitutes. No charges had ever been brought against him. Two of the German sailors confirmed beating a man fitting the journalist's description in the toilet of the bar. He'd been assaulted because of a brief association with Henry Harvey earlier in the day.

Another piece in a puzzling jigsaw, he thought as he settled back in his chair.

Jim Harvey opened his eyes as his mother shook him gently.

"There's yer porridge an' toast," she said softly, nodding at a tray on the table beside him.

He rolled over and sat up.

"Thanks, mum," he said sleepily.

She sat on the side of the bed and watched as he lifted the bowl of porridge.

"I didn't hear yew cum in last night. Was the wake on till late?" she inquired softly.

"Aye," he replied. "It was a private affair an' Miss Reilly got them to stay open until midnight. It wus more like a party than a wake."

His mother rose wearily.

"That's the way it is round here. Give thim a good send off an' fergit about them an' theirs," she muttered sadly.

Jim watched as she left the room. He was glad she hadn't heard him sneaking Sally into the parlour. Or when they'd quietly left a few hours later, after making love on the settee. York Street was deserted as they walked arm in arm to the hotel. She had certainly taught him much about life and love in the few days they had been together. They walked up the steps and she rang the night bell. A few seconds later the door was opened by a sleepy eyed porter.

"Mr. Harvey has been decent enough to walk me from my father's wake. Would it be in order for us to have a nightcap before he leaves?" she asked sweetly as she pressed a note into his hand.

"Of course, ma'am," smiled the porter. They ordered two whiskies and Jim followed Sally to a table in the deserted, darkened bar room. As they sat down he studied her features in the half-light. It was a soft and attractive face, especially when she smiled at him. He had given up trying to gauge her age, but thought her to be in her early thirties. He smiled at the recollection as he munched his breakfast cereal. After the drink he had solemnly bid her good night, in a respectful tone, loud enough for the porter to hear, and left. Finishing his breakfast, he looked at the clock and saw it was 10.45 a.m. He pulled the bed clothes over his head in an effort to shut out the church bells that were ringing since early morning.

During their moments of passion Sally had repeatedly asked him to go with her to London. She had begged him to consider it, saying there was a bright future for him. He hadn't answered. As he lay astride her, she kissed his face and waited for the answer that never came. She sighed and snuggled closer to him.

"At least I had you for a little while," she whispered.

He closed his eyes and was about to snuggle under the bed clothes when he heard his mother's footsteps on the stairs.

A few moments later she entered the room and lifted the tray. She was fully dressed and wearing her favourite camel hair coat. Perched on her head was a hat of the same colour with a large feather protruding from it.

He sat up.

"Yew'll be late fer church, ma," he said with concern in his voice. "Leave thim an' I'll take thim down later."

She lifted the dishes and smiled at him without speaking. He watched as she left the room and heard the front door close as she walked out into the street. She almost collided with two nuns, hurrying down to St. Joseph's Chapel.

"Good morning sisters," she said politely.

"Good morning," they chorused in unison as they sped past, quickly leaving her behind. She turned into Earl Lane and walked along towards North Thomas Street. She could see her sister-in-law, Florrie, standing at the corner of the street. They both moved into Dock Street, and along Nelson Street. Some moments later they climbed the stairs of Mariners' Church at the corner of Marine Street and sat in their usual seats. The church was crowded with the district's members of the Church of Ireland. They took their hymn books from their handbags and waited for the service to begin.

After the first hymn, the minister approached the pulpit and addressed the congregation. He was a small man with a shock of white hair and silver-rimmed glasses.

"I want to speak firstly about the trouble now ensuing on Belfast Docks which has complications for all of us in this Parish." His voice was harsh, clipped and cultured. He put both his hands on the rail of the pulpit and looked down at the worshippers. "As you know, men have resorted to violence in an effort to sort out a situation that should be left to the trade unions concerned. Men from the district have been set upon and beaten by fellow workers who believe might is right. I have been to the hospital and spoke to these unfortunate individuals, some of whom have been severely injured. Some of their wives are sitting among you today and I pray that you will all offer comfort and sympathy to these ladies.

"Life in Dockland is hard enough, and for men to fall upon

and prey upon each other in this way is an affront to the God who made us. I have spoken to the police officer responsible for the area and he tells me he will leave no stone unturned in his efforts to bring the culprits to justice."

He allowed a tight smile to cross his features.

"I have ministered in this community for more years than I care to remember." He gazed with fondness at his silent audience. "I have baptised many of you. Married many of you! Not literally, of course, but you know what I mean," he added with a ghost of a smile on his gaunt features.

He paused for a moment, and ran his fingers through his hair. His tone became sombre.

"I have also had the sad duty of burying your family members. So I am not only part of this community; in a way I am part of you; an extension of each family that comes here to worship. I know the hardships that every day brings. Some of you are widows of the last great conflict, and others, industrial widows whose husbands died from accidents on the work front caused in most cases by employer negligence, or the stress that comes from trying to feed and clothe a family in these hard and unrelenting days." He bowed his head for a moment, as if choosing his words carefully. Leaning on the pulpit, he surveyed the congregation.

"This dispute is a cancer that will spread if we don't get to the cause of it. Mr. Burgess, the Headmaster of the Public Elementary school that also functions in this building, tells me it has infiltrated the classes. Yes," he continued grimly, "Some of the children are bringing the problems of the dockside into the classrooms. Mr. Burgess has also spoken over the telephone to the head constable and other responsible parties. Like me, he has appealed for a speedy and just end to this explosive situation."

He gazed with affection at the worshippers.

"I have also spoken to my fellow ministers of the faith, Father Mullen in St. Joseph's and the Reverend Stutt in Maguire's Memorial and the minister at Sinclair Seamen's Church. We are working closely together to end this issue as there are members from all our congregations involved.

"I'm told there are three camps and three schools of thought in this complicated conundrum. We have in our holy places, wives and relatives of the men who are giving the beatings, and also wives and relatives of the innocent men on the receiving end. I know you are all at your wits' end, as this issue seems to be getting worse instead of better. Some men are trying to resolve the situation through the courts and I would pray that it goes that way instead of the senseless and shameful practice of hospitalising those who do not agree with you."

He smiled sadly.

"I know the area is renowned for men settling their differences physically, in man to man confrontations that are deemed honourable and ethical, but this current situation, if it is not resolved, could result in the loss of life, and I think the men, women and children of this parish have suffered enough over the last few decades. We must not let the situation tear the community apart. I know there are other people involved who do not come from this district.

"I also know there are rich people, powerful people, who are interested only in furthering their own causes. Therefore, I would again beg you to follow the counsel of those who say the only way is the legal way. The men who collected the two shilling pieces from their fellow workers believe they suffered a wrong that needs to be righted. The men who committed the act that inflamed their fellow workers and trade unionists are also of the opinion that they are right and are not technically against putting their beliefs in front of a judge and jury. Then there's the third element. The men called the Arabs, skulls or scavengers, or that most dreadful of words, outsiders. They are non-union men who also try to eke out a living on Belfast Docks. Sadly they are not wanted by either the red-button or blue-button men. But they too, have families that need to be sheltered and fed and clothed. Families that worship in seats next to those with the privilege and power of the trade union behind them. The trade union gives them some muscle with regards to labour laws and natural justice. The non-union man has none of these admittedly limited rights, and most of the work he gets is what the others don't want. I'm told these men are treated like dirt."

"Not anymore they're not. They're parasites, steppin' intil our men's shoes an' wid great delight, I might add," cried the bitter voice of a woman sitting close to Jim's mother. The minister quickly overcame the shock of being interrupted in mid sentence and looked in the direction of the speaker.

He recognised the woman and answered softly.

"I understand your grief and pain, Mrs. Wilson. I was in the Mater Hospital today visiting your husband, Sammy. He is, I'm glad to say, leaving hospital tomorrow. He tells me he will try to be at the funeral of Mr. Reilly, who was an outsider for many years. This is a selfless gesture and should be commended. Your husband is at the forefront of the fight for justice and you should be proud of him."

"My husband has been told categorically by people concerned that no matter how the court case goes, he will never work as a checker on Belfast Docks—" replied Helen Wilson.

She stopped in mid-sentence as another woman interrupted heatedly, "But he's a union man an' will still git work of some description. Our men have bin told they will nat be schooled if they don't have a card. An' how kin ye git a card for the right to work, if yew haven't gat a job? There are some in this room whose husbands an' sons are all first-preference dockers, bringin' in good—aye, very good—money every week an' yet they begrudge a livin' till men who have followed the docks all their lives ... Where's the milk of human kindness there?" she added bitterly.

This caused another woman close to Aggie Harvey and her sister to address the speaker angrily.

"Our men and their fathers before them made the docks what it is, and they're entitled to bring their sons and other blood relations intil the union before scavengers who come till the docks because they can't git work anywhere else."

She turned her venom on Helen Wilson.

"Where wus yewr husband during the early forties when there was tons of work an' our men had till work all the ires God sent, to help the war effort? After the war he showed up at the docks an' gat a red button an' a handy number. But that wusn't good enuff fer him. He wanted a blue button. It wus him who wrongly advised the others till git legal help an' it is him who is responsible fer them being forced off the quay. Him an' them other slabbers called the secret seven."

"My husband was at the sharp end of the war effort fightin' the Germans," Helen replied calmly and quietly. "Whilst yewr's hid below the bed durin' the air raids, my man wus wallowing through mud an' blood fer King an' country. Six years he wus gone. Six years of my life I lay in bed at nights wondering where he wus an' if he'd ever cum back till us, whilst yours wus lyin' snug as a bug beside yew, wondering how much money he wus gonna earn the next day ... "

The minister waved his arms for silence as the two women glared angrily at each other. He looked down at the tired, angry faces.

"As I said, we have all sides of the problem worshipping here today. All with their own fears for the future of their families. We must not let the hatred that is ripping the outside community apart find its insidious way into our morning worship. All we can do is to pray that God will enter the hearts and minds of those who pursue their policies with physical violence, and show them their way is wrong. I would ask you to bow your heads with me as we beseech Our Heavenly Father to take a hand in the proceedings and bring them to a swift and just closure. And that the end result will be seen as good to all concerned. Let us pray."

He looked down at the women, some of whom were sobbing quietly as he closed his eyes and spoke passionately; asking God to provide some sort of miracle; for nothing short of a miracle would do.

Eight

SAMMY WILSON WOKE FROM A NAP to see two well dressed men standing at his bed. He looked at the ward clock and saw it was nowhere near visiting time. As he eyed the men warily, two nurses appeared with chairs and his visitors sat down on each side of him. Other nurses appeared as if out of nowhere and placed screens around his bed. The men wore black, tailored Crombie overcoats over pinstriped jackets. He couldn't see their trousers or shoes but noted their starched collars and dark blue ties. Both men wore grey chamois dress gloves. One had a white carnation in the buttonhole of his top coat.

He looked at the man nearest him.

"Are yis undertakers?" he said sarcastically.

Neither man replied. The one closest to him slowly peeled off his gloves.

"Yer nat gonna work me over, are yew?" muttered Wilson with a wry grin.

The second man smiled benignly down at him.

"On the contrary, Mr. Wilson, we want nothing more than to put a serious proposal to you."

His voice was a guarded whisper.

"What sorta proposal?" asked Wilson suspiciously.

"Security for life and a chance to educate your children to the highest degree, if that is what you wish, and lastly a chance to give your long suffering wife the kind of life she longs for," replied the second man, slowly and deliberately.

"An' who do I have till kill to git those things?"

Both men laughed mirthlessly, as one delved into the

inside pocket of his jacket and produced a piece of foolscap which he handed to Wilson. The red-button man gazed at the page with a puzzled expression, before turning it over. He looked at his visitors.

"It's blank."

"Precisely," whispered the man closest to him. "It's a bribe, Mr. Wilson; a full blooded bribe by the people we represent to get you out of their hair and the process that is disrupting the dock labour force and causing awkward questions to be asked in very high places."

Wilson gazed at the inscrutable faces.

"How kin it be a bribe when there's nothin' on it?"

The apprehension he felt had evaporated and had been replaced with curiosity.

"If you sign your name at the bottom and add today's date, everything we told you will be yours. If you don't there'll be no physical evidence to suggest the offer was made," came the guarded reply.

"Why go through all this, when you are so sure of winnin' the legal argument: and why me? I won't be testifying. I'm tole I'm nat up till the strain."

The man nearest him patted his arm warmly, and continued in a voice that was cold and devoid of emotion.

"You are a war hero. A sincere family man, oozing intellect and honour. The kind that can raise the passions, and sway juries. You don't need to testify. You scared the pants off a lot of highly influential people when you threatened to start another union branch. The fact that you've been hospitalised by the strain and pressure of trying to guide your comrades gives your campaign a certain edge that makes our clients nervous. We want to remove that edge. According to the doctors you'll never be capable of hard physical work again, anyway. So no matter what develops you'll still be the loser, and you'll hardly be able to send your children to Queen's University on your army pension. You've really nothing to gain going down that road."

He smiled as he saw the confusion in Wilson's eyes.

"How cud I face my comrades, if I backed out?" he asked wearily.

"You don't have to face anyone. We can give you a new life and a job that will pay well and won't tax your health. We can even move you to the mainland if you so wish. The choice is yours."

He rose slowly from the chair and his companion did the same. He pulled on the chamois gloves.

"You've given plenty to the system, Mr. Wilson, and it continues to kick you in the teeth. Sign that form and add the date and your life and the lives of those you love will transform dramatically. There are highly powerful and influential people, far beyond the dockers' union and your local members of parliament who want to see this protest die a quiet and ignominious death. We can't stop it going to court, but we can try by legal means to weaken its case."

He pointed at the blank sheet.

"Either way, put that sheet in your locker drawer: it will be returned to us. Think over carefully what we've said. It could be akin to a reasonable win on the football pools and we all know how hard that is to come by," he added softly, allowing a warm smile to flood his sallow features.

It quickly faded.

"Good day to you, Mr. Wilson. I do hope you do the right thing for yourself and your family," he added as both men opened the screens and discreetly disappeared from his view.

"What do you think?" muttered the man who had done most of the talking, as they walked slowly to the Ward exit. His companion smiled with a look of relief on his face.

"It's in the bag. Every man has a price, and he knows he's fighting a lost cause."

McCartan found Wilson to be unusually quiet when he entered the ward with Helen a few hours later at visiting time. Helen stroked her husband's hand tenderly and put the faraway look in his eyes down to fatigue. Even a visit from the ebullient Billy Kelly did nothing to raise his spirits.

McKinstry observed with a baleful eye the hundreds of workers trudging sullenly into the schooling pen at the side of the harbour office. He had men positioned discreetly at the various entrances in what was a joint operation with the Head Constable of the harbour police. Both senior police officers had agreed that the RUC should be in uniform and the harbour police in plain clothes. They would infiltrate the schools and help prevent any problems. The dockers knew the harbour officers and were well aware of their presence among them. They knew the dockside police force had the same powers on the quay as McKinstry's men had in the streets. Both senior officers believed and hoped this operation would constrain any trouble.

Rain was falling and he could feel it working its way down past the storm collar of his heavy overcoat. Now and then he wiped the drizzle from the visor of his peaked cap, but otherwise stood rock still, providing a picture of the unmoving, unbending symbol of the law.

He watched as the men, all wearing flat caps and top coats, formed into semi-circles around each ganger. The wail of the muted horn of the nearby tobacco factory had just faded into the misty air when the harbour office clock began to chime. As he watched, the semi-circles became like living things: moving, pushing, shoving, swelling and diminishing. Some of the men uttered little cries of despair as they tried to catch the eye of the ganger, others glared stonily at the man who held the power of employment in the palm of his hand. Within minutes it was all over. The gangers barked orders at the selected men and pushed their way roughly through the remainder. Some foremen climbed into cars, others made their way over the foot bridge that led to the dock sheds.

The head constable of the harbour police, who, like himself, was in full uniform, joined him.

"A lot quieter today, David," said the officer.

McKinstry didn't answer. He was watching the remaining men as they turned to leave the compound.

"It's like a cattle mart," he muttered wearily.

"More like a slave market," answered the harbour officer. "Men come from all over Belfast and beyond. No matter how many times they're rejected and humiliated by the gangers, they still come back. Today, above all days, is a bad day to be left. They won't be able to get their insurance cards stamped, and that means those not taken today will have little or no chance for work the rest of the week."

"Can you tell if there's many second-preference men left, Alan?" asked McKinstry as they both walked towards the main entrance to the compound.

"Quite a few as far as I can see."

They watched as some of the remaining men began to run quickly in the direction of the footbridge.

"What's happening?" the RUC man muttered nervously.

His companion grinned.

"Nothing to worry about: they're racing round to the Irish Transport compound in Dock Street to see if they can get a lie-on."

"What's the situation there?" asked McKinstry curiously.

"Much better than here! They don't have any second-preference and once the registered dockers are schooled then it's open to everyone else. A shrine to socialism, compared to this place. They still have their moments of nepotism though."

He looked at the retreating men who were now specks in the distance.

"I think it's the nature of the beast we call dock labour," he added softly and philosophically.

The schooling pen, which had been heaving with humanity a few moments earlier, was deserted except for the officers and their constables.

"Would you like to come over to the station for a cup of tea or coffee? I'll know the situation better when my men report back," Alan said helpfully.

McKinstry nodded curtly and beckoned a uniformed sergeant to him. "Dismiss the men and detail them to ordinary duties. Make sure there's a pointsman controlling the traffic at the corner of York Street and Whitla Street. There's been a spate of accidents there recently, involving horses and carts. Tell him to take no nonsense from carters, who think they have precedence over everything else that moves. And make sure the officer wears his long white armbands. We don't want him being knocked down," he added sarcastically. The sergeant touched his hat briefly in a form of salute and hurried away.

The coffee was warm and welcome. McKinstry sipped pensively in the quietness of the cosy and comfortable office of his counterpart on the Belfast harbour. He was not a fan of the harbour police and saw them as amateurs. He regarded their little courthouse where they tried and sentenced people found guilty of offences on harbour property, as something out of a music hall sketch. Alan entered the room and sat down beside him.

He was a heavy, well-proportioned man aged about forty-five. Twenty years in the armed services as a military police officer gave him the credentials to join the harbour force when he left the army. In a few swift years he had climbed the ranks to his current position. As friendly and outgoing as McKinstry was guarded and private, he was nevertheless a good officer and the only man in the force the RUC man respected. To him, the rest of the rank and file were akin to the Keystone cops.

Alan set his coffee cup on the desk and lowered himself into a chair.

"My sergeant reports the majority of men left today were red-button men. The guy from Queen's University who claimed to be an industrial lawyer was going among them, making notes and taking names. Otherwise there was no trouble. Ironically, the reds are directing their venom, not against the first-preference men who created this fuck-up, but the outsiders who are gleefully exploiting the situation and filling the gaps."

"Aye," agreed McKinstry wearily, pushing his cap to the back of his head. "Christmas has come early for the Arabs."

The men detailed to the hold of the potato boat at the nearby Chapel Sheds had the same feeling, but for a different reason. They noticed one half of the hatch was already filled to the coamings with unmarked cardboard boxes. Further investigation proved the cartons contained bottles of Black Bush Irish whiskey. Their joy was short lived when a member of the ship's crew climbed down the ladder and positioned

213

himself where he could keep a weather eye on the cargo and the holdsmen.

They watched him closely as he sat down beside the cardboard boxes. Uncle, the ship's foreman, was bellowing orders at the deckmen. A few seconds later the winch roared into life.

"Luks like we're bate, Davy," muttered one of the hatchmen to his companion as they waited for the first heave.

"Mebbe nat," answered Davy. "What are these sailors, Jojo?" he yelled above the roar of the winch.

"Whaddya mean? They're sailors, aren't they?" replied his companion with a baffled expression on his face.

Davy turned from him with a look of contempt and called to another holdsman.

"What nationality are these guys, Arthur?"

"Russians," came the quick reply.

"Thought so," yelled Davy.

He was a thin but wiry outsider with a reputation of a tough guy from the nearby Tigers' Bay area. He didn't wear a cap like most of the other men and his dark hair was soaked with the still falling rain that was holding back the first heave of the seed potatoes destined for Egypt. Only a few hatchboards had been stripped from the beams in an effort to keep the floor of the hold dry.

Uncle leaned over the hatch and Davy called to him.

"This guy's wearin' a gun an' we're nat gonna wurk till he's removed."

The ganger looked in the direction of the sailor and saw he was wearing a revolver on a belt strapped around his waist. He grabbed hold of the deckhand who was helping to raise the derricks, and by gestures and pidgin English made him understand the problem. He sped to the Captain's cabin and a few minutes later the armed man was removed, and a youth put in his place. The holdsmen played cards as they waited for the rain to stop when the hatchboards and beams would be lifted. As they sat in a small tight group, the boy, aged about fifteen, watched their every move with the frightened eyes of a child.

Davy whispered to the men beside him.

"I'm gonna make a play till get that kid outa the hatch. When I do, yew guys git over there and release some of that Irish from Russian custody. Catch my drift?"

The men nodded and watched as he rose and stretched his legs and arms in exaggerated movements.

The galley boy watched nervously as he moved towards him. When he was a few yards from the lad, Davy unbuckled his belt and pulled his trousers and underpants down. Grabbing his penis, he waved it at the young crewman as he galloped towards him.

"Here boy, I've gat something for yew," he shouted harshly.

The lad didn't understand the words, but knew the body language. With a frightened yelp he rose and ran to the ladder. As soon as his back was turned, Jojo scaled the side of the cardboard boxes like a spider. Within seconds he had two cartons lowered to his companions who buried them under dunnage and a huge tarpaulin on the other side of the hatch.

Davy was dealing the cards when the steerman glared into the hatch. The men ignored him. A few seconds later a muscular seaman climbed down the ladder and took over the position abandoned by the cabin boy. Jojo had taken the two boxes from an inside tier and the outside row of the cargo was undisturbed. The seaman ran his eyes over the unbroken stack and seemed contented. He turned his attention to the card players and scowled at them.

The crack of hatchboards being thrown to the deck caused the card school to break up. The rain had ceased. They moved from the centre of the hold to the shelter of the between deck as the sailors began to lift off the hatch beams with the winch. Uncle called to them.

"Blind off that section beside the other cargo first. The skipper wants it secured," he shouted over the roar of the winch.

The holdsmen nodded obediently as the first heave dropped into the hatch and stopped two feet from the floor. Two men ran forward and pushed the ropeful of potato bags into the corner of the hatch close to the whiskey. They yelled to the winchdriver to lower and quickly threw the sacks onto the floor. The hook flew shorewards and returned quickly with another heave. Within minutes, half of the floor was covered with a carpet of potato sacks. The men continued to pile layer upon layer until the winch ground to a halt and the driver shouted, "Tea break."

"What if they find the boxes?" asked Jojo as he and Davy headed towards Susan's Café, just outside the Dock gates.

"They won't. Pretty soon we'll have that end blocked off and there'll be no need for the guard. As soon as he goes we'll havta figure a way till git them ashore."

"Nigh yer talkin'," growled Jojo gloomily, as they joined the long line.

They managed to find a table and the other holdsmen squeezed in beside them. As they chewed on their egg baps, Davy put his head down and whispered hoarsely, "Take off yer socks." Their jaws stopped working as they stared at him. "Do what I say," he added, as he began removing his boots. The men stared for a second or two and then followed suit. After they'd stuffed their socks into their pockets and replaced their boots, Davy grinned across the table.

"If this works out, oul Reilly's send-off is gonna be remembered as the best ever in Dock Ward."

They finished their break and returned to the boat. The sailor was already in position, nursing a cup of steaming coffee. After the second heave, Jojo asked the inevitable question.

"How are we gonna git thim off the ship?" he whispered to Davy as he picked up the rope sling, folded it, and hurled it unerringly onto the hatch coaming. The hatchman lifted it and deftly tossed it ashore. The winchman could see the holdsmen and he lowered the heave without aid from the hatchman. Davy quickly stripped the rope and both men threw the ten sacks into the narrow space between decks.

"I'm thinking about it," he answered over the noise of the ship's winch. At ten-thirty they had blocked off access to the whiskey. The sailor smiled and climbed over the hatch coaming and disappeared onto the deck. There was a short break in the proceedings as the deck men loosened the guy ropes and topped the derrick. A wooden ladder was handed over to the holdsmen. Dropping one end of it to the floor, they climbed down to fill the remaining half of the hatch. They moved the dunnage containing the two cartons into the nose of the hold and started to uncover their prize, unobserved.

Breaking open the boxes they saw the contents were half bottles, twenty-four to a box.

"That makes it easier," grinned Davy joyfully. "They're nat as bulky as a ten glass bottle an' easier till carry. Now lissen in while we've gat the chance till talk. If we fill every pocket of our overcoats and jackets, and squeeze a coupla inta our trouser pockets, I reckon we'll be able till carry eight apiece ashore. That shud clear both boxes."

"What about our socks?" asked Jojo.

Davy grimaced.

"I thought they'da bin ten glass bottles. I planned till put one in each sock and tie em round our necks." He brightened visibly. "But this is better. Nigh when yis are leavin' the shed, don't go out by the peeler at the gate. Go through one of the side gates that'll be open till let the lorries in. Head through Clow's Flour Mill an' that'll take yew intil Pilot Street. Then it's every man fer himself. When the first heave comes in, we'll take it in turns till fill our pockets ... OK?"

The men nodded in agreement and walked out to meet the first heave.

"Kin we put our socks back on?" asked Jojo.

Davy looked at him with undisguised scorn.

"Nigh yiv gat thim off, keep thim in yer pocket, an' give yer a ma a chance till wash them. Yew musta a had thim on fer a fortnight, by the smell a thim."

"They were fresh when I put them on a month ago," protested Jojo, without a trace of shame in his voice.

Davy shook his head and returned to the task ahead.

"Every man knows what till do? When there's a break in proceedin's or a lull in the speed, one of yis jump down and fill yer coats. Don't lave it too late, cause we'll be outa here shortly if we continue at this speed."

The men nodded obediently as the roar of the winch heralded the arrival of another heave.

When the last sling was emptied, they walked stiffly down

the gangplank and squeezed past a cart that was lodged in an open gateway. They paid no attention to Henry Harvey as he placed a large box beside the carter.

"There's two dozen ten glass bottles a poteen there, Danny. Sell them for a poun' apiece. The boys goin' till Reilly's funeral will be gatherin' at the Stalingrad and Paddy's. They'll want it till drown their sorrows on such a sad day."

The thin-faced driver covered the box with a rug and nodded tersely.

"Take a coupla bottles yerself, for services rendered. I'll git the dough aff yew later."

The carter spat a mouthful of tobacco juice onto the floor of the shed before asking, "Where's it from?"

"Portglenone," replied Harvey. "It comes highly recommended."

The driver shook the reins and the horse moved into Prince's Dock Street. At the junction of Pilot and Garmoyle Street he decided to sample the drink as he waited for a break in the traffic. Unscrewing the cap of one of the bottles containing the white liquid, he took a deep drink before replacing the cap.

He smiled with contentment as the raw poteen seared its way to his stomach. He burped contentedly.

"Highly recommended," he sniggered, before cracking his whip and causing the horse to leap across the junction and several lorries to swerve to avoid a collision.

Todd Hamill was finishing his lunch in the canteen of Transport House when Edward Kyle entered the small room. His angry eyes searched for and found Hamill.

"My office," he barked curtly, before turning on his heels.

The other men who were seated with Hamill kept their heads down during the brief conversation.

"Luks like somebody's about till git a ballockin'," said one man sombrely as he bit into a sandwich.

Hamill didn't reply. He pushed his plate away and rose from the table.

"Good luck," whispered another officer as he left the room.

Kyle answered the knock on his office door with a scowl. Hamill entered timidly.

"Sit down," snarled his superior.

His desk was littered with papers and letters. He leaned on them as he glared at the officer.

"Have yew bin voted onto the Executive or Regional committee, without my knowledge?" he snapped, his voice heavy with sarcasm.

Hamill shook his head.

"Then what the fuck are yew doin', callin'a meeting till sort out issues that don't concern yew?" Kyle thundered, his face a mask of anger.

"If yew mean the issue of the red-button men ... "

Kyle interrupted him savagely.

"I mean an unlawful, unconstituted, unsanctioned, illegal meeting in this very building to usurp the efforts of a fellow officer, namely Brother Shaw to handle a situation that is fraught with danger for the good and welfare of this union an' its members."

"But the reds are members ... "

"Nat yewr fuckin'members! They're the headache of Shaw and he's dealin' effectively wid them."

He took a deep breath before continuing.

"If yew like yer job, take this advice. Burn that threatenin' note, an' go till the barracks an' tell the peelers yer takin' this thing no further."

"But it's a personal threat ... "

Again he didn't get finishing the sentence, as Kyle angrily opened a drawer in his desk.

"An' what do yew think they are—Scotch mist?" he bellowed as he hurled a sheaf of letters over the desk top.

The full-time officer didn't answer as his superior retrieved the bundle and put them back in the drawer before speaking slowly and evenly.

"The Dockers' union is the strongest in Britain. Having such a powerful branch as part of our membership can mean the difference between a prolonged strike, or an almost instant settlement." He paused for breath. "An' if yew think I'm goin' to jeopardise a weapon such as that for a coupla hundred men, then yew shudn't be an officer. Anyway," he continued wearily, "They've lost nothin' other than a status they thought they had. According to Shaw it will soon blow over if bleedin' hearts like yew an' the other misguided reps who attended that illegal meetin' git off yore high horses an' mind yer own business. It's a matter for Shaw to sort ... "

"But I was ordered down to see them at a meeting hall in York Street," protested Hamill.

That made Kyle more abusive.

"That was an error by some fool in administration. When Shaw heard it he went down and tuk over. That wus yewr cue to back off and leave well enough alone. The reds collectively sent in a letter of complaint addressed to me. I forwarded it to the officer concerned, namely Shaw. It had nothing to do wid me, or yew. So keep yer nose outa other officers' affairs. Do I haveta draw yew a map? Maybe yew wud rather work voluntarily for some charity like Doctor Barnardo's or the Sally-Ann. I kin arrange that, 'cause they're always cryin' out fer volunteers, but they're nat as well paid as yew." He stopped for breath before adding, "Git back till lukin' after yer members in the Provender section and keep yer nose outa other branch affairs. Let the dockers settle the unrest. They know what to do and won't hesitate till do it. Anyway the reds 'ill be history as an organisation in a few weeks time: so stay outa Shaw's way."

Hamill rose slowly and nodded dumbly. The ferocity of the senior officer's attack had drained him. He looked at Kyle who had literally dismissed him and was writing with a fountain pen on a blank piece of paper. Hamill cleared his throat and Kyle looked up impatiently.

"Yew still here?" he growled.

The officer stuttered as he struggled for words. He quickly sat down and looked across the desk with beseeching eyes.

"Well, actually, sir ... Brother: I was hopin' to speak to yew about another issue. As yew know my wife and I live wid our three children in rented dwellings. I've heard about the union supplying mortgage loans an' thought I cud make a request for one. We'd like a wee house in the suburbs. Maybe I shud approach yew another time," he stammered as Kyle lifted his eyes from the paper.

He was amazed to see the anger disappear and a wide smile cover Kyle's features.

"Of course, Brother Hamill. The union provides such loans with reasonable interest. All the officers take advantage of the scheme, an' why nat? Yewr as entitled as anybody else in the building to that privilege. Yew cud drive till yer wee house in the country using the car provided by the union. So yew'd be savin' on that wouldn't yew?"

Hamill noted the sarcasm, but paid no heed to it, as his boss continued, "Call in an' see my secretary as soon as yew've torn up the note and cancelled yer request for police action. I'd also expect yew to take no further interest in the aforementioned red-button saga."

He put down his pen, and his eyes were friendly.

"Yill find we are quite good in lukin' after the interests of loyal and responsible employees. Perhaps yew could also find time to attend the funeral of the outsider who is being buried. He wasn't one of our members, but it'll do no harm to show the caring side of our union. Don't, however, talk about the present situation or git involved in any dialogue wid any of the sea-lawyers who may try to trick a statement outa yew." He smiled coldly. "Hide behind our old friend, *Sub Judice*. That covers a multitude of sins." His tone softened. "Please see yerself out as I've gat quite a lat to contend with. An' good luck wid the loan. I can't see yew havin' any problems."

Hamill nodded dumbly and backed out into the corridor. He walked down the staircase to his own office and sat down. After a few minutes wrestling with his socialist conscience, he took the threatening letter from his pocket and tore it to shreds.

"If yew can't bate 'em, join 'em," he whispered despondently to himself, as he lifted the phone book. Ringing the number, he waited until the desk sergeant answered.

"My name is Todd Hamill. Cud yew let Head McKinstry know I've decided nat to proceed wid the issue I called into see him about. Tell him it's been settled by my superior, an' I'm happy to leave it there," he added before putting down the

221

phone. He lifted his overcoat from the peg behind the door and made his way downstairs to the foyer.

"Make a note of all calls till I return, sweetheart," he said to the receptionist who answered with a nod.

He parked his car outside a newsagent's on York Street and walked the short distance into Henry Street. Men were already gathering at the corner of Wensley Street, and strolled self-consciously toward them. He became acutely aware that his soft grey hat and Crombie overcoat made him look conspicuous. There were four black limousines and a funeral car lined up the small street. He checked his pocket watch and saw it was a few minutes before half past two. He hoped it wouldn't be long before he was back in his office.

One of the mourners sidled close to him, staring at him through bleary narrowed eyes. He was a small man wearing a bulging brown overcoat that was buttoned tightly around an ample waist. A grimy cap was pulled low across gaunt features that studied the stranger. His breath smelt of stale whiskey.

"Aren't yew the union fella we saw in the hall the other day?" growled the man, moving even closer to Hamill.

"I am," Hamill replied. "I've cum here till pay our respects to the dead man on behalf of the trade union," he added with a wide smile.

"But he wasn't in the union. Said it wus only fer glipes who cudn't luk after themselves," countered the other, narrowing his eyes as he continued. "Do yew nat think yew shud be out werkin' fer the likes a me, who is a union man instead a cumin' here an' wastin' yer time at the funeral of a man who doesn't contribute till the scheme?" he added aggressively as he pushed his face closer to Hamill's.

"Just a little Christian courtesy," retorted the union man, moving away until his back was against the wall of the public house. Another group who was listening to the exchange moved closer.

"Niver min' that shit. Any wurd about us gittin' our books back?" one man yelled.

Hamill looked at the speaker, who was approaching him menacingly.

"It's *sub judice*, at the moment, so I'm afraid I can't talk about it, Brother," he replied limply.

"What's the fuck's *sub judice*?" replied the man with a blank look on his face, as he and his companions closed dangerously on Hamill.

Before he could reply, a petite woman with her grey hair tied in a bun and wearing a black woollen shawl over her shoulders, turned viciously on the speaker, and slapped him on the back of the head.

"Don't yew dare swear at the funeral of a dacent man, Sharkey, or I'll take off my boot an' give yew such a blatter on yer big ugly gub."

The man immediately moved away, and the others followed. Hamill flashed the woman a look of gratitude that went unheeded.

He watched as the coffin, carried by four men, emerged from the house into the Street, and was placed on two stools. Women and children gazed over the half-doors of the little houses as glass-covered wreaths were carried out and put on top of the coffin. The women scattered around began wailing and weeping as the cortège wended its way slowly into Henry Street. Hamill noticed a few of the men were wearing the blue lapel buttons and others the red of the second-preference. Some wore dress suits and overcoats whilst others were wearing the clothes they worked in. Their features were lined and grey with anxiety.

A wizened man with a weather-beaten face like a wrinkled plum sidled up to him. His mouth was toothless and his chin almost touched his nose. His eyes were red-rimmed and blank.

"Wanna buy a five naggin bottle a Black Bush, mister? It'll help the sore head yer gonna have before this dispute is settled."

Hamill looked at the hand grasping his coat lapel. It was covered in a filthy ragged glove with the fingers all cut off.

"Five shillin's, mister. Chape at half the price."

The union man smelt the stench of urine and cigarette smoke on the man's grimy clothes. But the overpowering smell was that of whiskey. Every time the man addressed him, the alcohol hit his face like a slap. He reached into his pocket and skilfully separated two half crowns from the coinage and reached it over. The bottle was placed dexterously in his overcoat pocket by the man who grasped the money and disappeared into the crowd.

As the cortège was about to turn into York Street it was approached by a horse-drawn four-wheeled cart. The vehicle was piled high with bales for the nearby spinning mill. The carter was lying prone across the front of the cart and the reins were trailing on the ground. As the horse continued to bear down on the hearse, the driver panicked. He sounded the horn and the animal leapt onto its hind legs and whinnied in fright, before depositing its two front hooves onto the bonnet of the car.

The women watching screamed, and the car accelerated clear. The horse closed on the men carrying the coffin. They stood, rooted with fear to the spot, as the wild-eyed animal trotted blindly towards them. Henry Harvey recognised the carter and realised what was happening. He raced from the cortège and ran straight at the animal as it bore down on the men and the coffin. From a distance of about three feet, he hurled himself at the horse's head and wrapped his arms around its neck. Turning in mid-air, he propelled himself onto its back and pulled viciously at the bridle strap holding the long silver-plated bit in the animal's mouth. The horse screamed with pain as the bit tore the side of its mouth wide open. Blood gushed over Henry's jacket and trousers as he forced the animal's head sideways. He continued to pull upwards until the beast collapsed in a heap at the feet of the mourners. Henry sat on its neck until the coffin and the shocked cortège passed.

The horse's weight pulled the cart onto its side, dislodging its cargo and the carter onto the kerb. Women who had been watching the procession fled in panic as the bales of tow bounced all around them. Three lemonade bottles slid from under the bag of straw and smashed on the pavement.

Two policemen lifted the carter and laid him with his head resting on the mill wall. Angry women attacked the senseless man and had to be physically restrained by the lawmen. Henry climbed from the horse's back and raised it gently to its feet. He took the feed bucket from a hook on the side of the cart and put the strap over its ears. As it gulped hungrily at the oats he walked to the policemen who were putting the broken bottles into a paper bag. One bottle broken at the neck held a quantity of white liquid.

The constable sniffed.

"Poteen."

He nodded at the carter as Henry gazed quizzically at him.

"He's as drunk as a coot."

"So's the horse. Somebody spiked its feed bag," replied Henry wearily. He sighed with dismay as the other constable took a small wad of pound notes from the carter's jacket pocket.

"Probably sellin' the stuff, an' samplin' it at the same time," he commented dryly.

He reached the money to his colleague who was putting the bottles into a bag.

"Better keep that as evidence as well," he added.

Henry cursed under his breath and rushed after the funeral. He joined Kelly and Jim at the front of the procession. They halted outside the Bowling Green pub for a few moments as a mark of respect, before continuing to walk past Sussex Street.

They stopped facing the Sportsman's Arms and the coffin was put into the damaged hearse. The mourners followed on foot as far as the Edinburgh Castle pub, before climbing into the three sedans. A lorry driver pulled in behind the cars and other men climbed onto the back of the vehicle. Henry purposefully walked to Sally as she stood at the hearse. He scowled as he saw Jim beside her.

"I thought yew were goin' back till werk," he growled.

Jim lowered his head.

"I have asked Jim to accompany my father's remains to the graveyard. He has been of immense help to me over the past few days," murmured Sally with a smile that melted his heart.

Henry returned the smile.

"I'm sure his colleagues can manage without him for the next few hours," he replied, climbing into a black limousine behind the hearse.

Henry's smile turned to a worried frown as the car passed

Sam and Jack and the other carriers. Sam grinned smugly as he looked at Henry. The grin said none of them would be returning to work. He settled back in the seat.

"When the cat's away, the mice 'ill play," he muttered to himself.

"Did you say something?" asked the driver.

"Jist thinkin' out loud," replied Henry wearily as the car began its journey to Carnmoney. He had resigned himself to the loss of the profits from the poteen and hoped the carter would not implicate him.

Todd Hamill stood among the mourners who were left. He waited for a respectable moment or two before moving off in the direction of Transport House.

A drunk collided with him as he stepped from the pavement.

"Wanta buy a drap a Black Bush, chape?" he slurred as he grabbed the union man's arm in a vice-like grip.

Hamill recognised him.

"I've already bought one from yew," he replied fearfully, showing him the half bottle from his overcoat pocket.

Hamill was about to place it back when a strong hand came from behind him and clasped the half bottle in a firm grip.

He looked over his shoulder and grimaced when he saw the stern features of the head constable. McKinstry's other hand stretched to grab the drunk, but he was too fast for him. He watched as the man sped over the road, before returning his gaze to Hamill.

"Don't worry. We know where he lives. He'll be in the petty sessions the marra. There's no doubt a that. So will yew. Did yew know that in the eyes of the law, the receiver of stolen goods is looked upon as an abomination? If there were no receivers, there'd be no profit in thievin'," he added as he took Hamill's arm firmly and walked him in the direction of the police station.

Nine

THE REVEREND STUTT'S FACE WAS CREASED in a worried frown as he walked from his car. The coffin lay at the side of the open grave. Two gravediggers leaned on their shovels and tried to hide their bored expressions with a look of forced humility. There was a stench of whiskey in the air. He had smelt it when he had conducted the brief service in the little kitchen house, but didn't expect to encounter it in the sanctity of a burial site. He took closer examination of the men around him and saw their glazed eyes. He was horrified when he saw the passengers on the back of the lorry drinking freely from whiskey bottles and other bottles containing a clear liquid which he assumed was just as lethal. Shuddering, he opened his Bible and began to read.

One of the mourners shuffled closer with blank eyes. He slipped on a wet sod and fell across the coffin. The mound it sat on was drenched and greasy with overnight rain. The Reverend Stutt stopped speaking and watched with horror as the coffin slid precariously towards the open grave. The two diggers tried to grab it, but the smooth wood rolled from their grasping hands and fell with a dull thud to the bottom of the grave. The mourner scrambled to his feet with alarmed features and frightened eyes, holding his hands out in a plea for forgiveness. There was an unnatural silence that lasted a few seconds, as the shocked gathering came to terms with what had happened. It was broken by the sharp brittle crack of knuckles hitting flesh as Henry struck the man responsible.

The drunk quickly followed the coffin into the open grave,

taking mounds of clay with him. The gravediggers grabbed hold of Henry who roared in anger as another man took advantage of his position and punched him on the jaw. He easily broke free from the half-hearted grip and slapped his would-be captors viciously on the side of their heads, causing both to scream out loud and drop their shovels as they raced from his anger. The man who had originally attacked him was making a quick getaway. Henry began to pursue him but tripped over the shovels and fell headlong into a group of mourners which included the Reverend Stutt who became trapped at the bottom of a pile of heaving bodies as the men wrestled and fought in the freshly turned mud.

Jim looked across at Kelly who returned his worried glance with a cynical grin. He motioned for the lad to stay where he was and moved to the graveside He looked down at the unfortunate man lying prone on top of the coffin, before running to the heaving mass of bodies and extricating the Reverend who had adopted a foetal position whilst clinging to his open Bible. Kelly lifted him to his feet and walked him away from the men who were screaming vile obscenities at each other whilst struggling to stand upright. Henry eventually made it to his feet and was examining the muck that covered the horse's blood on his suit when a blow from behind felled him. He rose to his feet with a roar that would have awakened the dead. He didn't seek out his attacker. Instead he lashed out at the man closest to him, sending him spinning over the top of an adjacent gravestone.

"Red-button bastard," snarled another as he jumped onto Henry's unprotected back.

Harvey plucked him from his shoulders and threw him in the direction of the freshly dug grave. He collided with two mourners who were assisting the drunk from the open grave. The impact sent all three hurtling into the open hole.

The gravediggers had reached the sanctuary of the small administration building. After hearing their breathless story, the enraged clerk hastily lifted the telephone. He waited until an enquiring voice spoke on the other end.

"Can yew come quickly till Carnmoney?" he yelled harshly. "There's a riot in the graveyard."

McKinstry glared at the bottle he had taken from Hamill's overcoat pocket. His eyes left the object and stared coldly at the union rep.

"'For export only', it says on this bottle—which means yew are guilty of buyin' contraband goods, mister."

The luckless Hamill had nothing to say. He was picturing the greeting he would get at Transport House when this story unfolded. His stomach turned as he saw himself standing in the dock of the petty sessions. He eyed the police officer.

"What happens now?" he asked in a resigned voice.

The officer stared at him for a long moment, before speaking in a low, comforting whisper.

"Nigh, that's up till yew, son. A court case cud maybe end yer career as a union official. Youse fellas are supposed till be like Caesar's wife. Whiter than white and beyond reproach."

Hamill gulped and nodded. It was a favourite saying of his boss. He remained silent as the policeman continued.

"Will yew play ball wid me if I get yew outa this?" he asked softly.

"Yes!" Hamill blurted, trying unsuccessfully to hide his relief.

McKinstry rose and walked round the desk. He straightened his gun holster and moved it further around his waist.

"There's somethin' fishy about this whole business. Yisterday, yew asked me to investigate threats agin yew. Today yew phoned my sergeant to say it's all sorted, an'yer happy."

He rose and banged the desk with his fist.

"Well, I'm nat happy! An' I won't be until I git till the bottom of it!"

He lifted a chair and sat down beside Hamill.

"I'm outa my depth in this one. It's politically driven. Politics make strange bedfellows they say, an' it seems as if them cute hoors up in Stormont have jumped inta bed with the trade unions. The result is lawlessness in my patch." He paused for breath. "I want yew to keep me informed of all that's happening in Transport House with regard to the current problem. I need to know what's at stake an' what's the price to be paid for whatever's in the meltin pot."

He smiled gently when he saw the look of panic cross Hamill's face.

"Don't worry," he added, touching the man's shoulder reassuringly. "I just want till know who them slimy bastards up there are gonna pish on next."

His voice hardened.

"But I want till know it before they take their dicks out. Will yew help me? I give yew my word yew won't be incriminated in any way. Yew cud phone me from a call box if yew hear anything that might interest me, an' I'd only require yer services until this bloody court case is settled."

He stuck out his hand.

"Is it a deal?"

Hamill shook his hand gratefully, and nodded vigorously.

"Can I go?" he asked nervously.

"Shure an' why nat? For I have nuthin' against an upright an' solid citizen. Git away back till yer warm work an' don't let me see yew on the streets a Sailortown unless it's on official business."

Hamill couldn't hide his pleasure.

"Does this mean there won't be a court case?" he asked as he opened the door.

McKinstry smiled.

"We are nat in the habit of prosecuting innocent men. By the way! Don't yew want yer whiskey?"

"No thanks. Drink it yerself, sor. When yer off-duty of course," he added quickly.

McKinstry smiled mirthlessly.

"I'm afraid it's nat my brand."

"I know yer a Scotsman, but it's Black Bush," stammered Hamill. "Isn't that the best?"

McKinstry lifted the bottle from the table and reached it to him.

"The seal's broken, an' the bottle doesn't contain Black Bush. It's filled with about ten per cent whiskey till give it a colour an' the other ninety per cent is urine. Probably still warm when yew bought it."

He grinned as Hamill's face changed colours.

"Next time yer offered somethin' at a low price, I mightn't be around to put yew wise ... Only a fool buys a bottle wid a broken seal ... "

The phone rang and he lifted it.

"I knew it wus too good till last," he roared into the mouthpiece.

He turned to Hamill.

"I'll have ta leave yew," he snarled. "There's bin a riot in Carnmoney an' the police at Glengormley are bringin' the culprits back here." He rolled his eyes to the ceiling. "They shuda shot the bastards! Imagine disturbin' the sanctity of a graveyard." McKinstry paused. "Don't fergit till keep in touch," he warned, turning his back to illustrate the conversation was finished.

Hamill rushed from the building and made his way though Great Patrick Street to the union rooms. His fear had transformed into cunning. Had the policeman not been busy, he would have taken great delight in passing on the information there and then. He couldn't wait to tell him about the talks and meetings between government and trade unions in an effort to have the Irish Congress of Trade Unions set up a Northern Ireland committee, on which his boss was planning to gain a senior position. Negotiations were at a delicate point and there was a possibility the Committee wouldn't be formed if the red-button episode brought the trade union and, inadvertently, the government into disrepute. A threatened dockers' strike in Britain was already causing problems and the closed shop principles of the Belfast Dockers, relayed by letter and telephone to the head of the union in London by the university agitator called McCartan, were causing more headaches than the local enforcer Shaw had imagined when he had disbanded the entire red-button workforce in a fit of bad temper.

He nodded to himself resolutely as he trudged past Simon Murphy's public house. He would take great delight in passing on all the information he could on the matter. He could also use the position to undermine a superior sadly lacking in socialist values, and through time have him replaced by a true socialist: someone like himself. That thought made him smile as he entered his place of work.

Climbing the stairs to his office on the second floor, he became aware of raised voices. He opened the door that led into the corridor and proceeded warily. It wasn't unusual for union members to differ with their representatives, and sometimes it got out of hand. He recognised the voice of Shaw, who was addressing a small group of men outside his office.

"I'm tellin' yew it's a good deal, and we should accept it," he said convincingly.

"It's a cut in the workforce, so it's a non-runner as far as the men are concerned," replied a tall fresh-faced docker with a pencil moustache. His voice was level and controlled, but his features were angry.

"The addition of a forklift truck 'ill cut down the workforce by two men per gang. Nat all of our lads can drive a forklift, so if we have till use an outsider that means a three man cut," shouted another man.

Shaw turned to him with a knowing smile.

"But it will cut down the work fer the rest of the gang. No more runnin' the length of the shed, pulling a truck with a ton a cement begs on it. An' if we don't have a driver, we'll make the stevedore pay extra for one of youse till stand scratchin' yer balls whilst an outsider drives the truck," he argued.

"But what about the men displaced?" asked the docker with the moustache who seemed to be the spokesman of the group.

Shaw slapped his back in a friendly gesture.

"They kin go down the quay, Sid," he laughed. "Take away the few handy jobs that some of the reds and Arabs are still doin."

Sid was unimpressed.

"But it's a cut in the workforce. A fut in the door. If they kin do it at the cement, what's till stop them doin' it at the other boats? The general cargo boats, and the other beg boats."

His dark unbelieving eyes bored into Shaw's face and made the latter feel uncomfortable. He stared at the men seriously.

"It's progress," he muttered, "an' we've gat till address progress. There's a row goin' on at the moment in Britain re the introduction of freight containers ... "

He was interrupted by another member of the group who snarled angrily, "If that's accepted, then there'll be none of us here in a year's time!"

"Of course there will," laughed Shaw putting an arm around the man's wide shoulders. "Containers are a non-runner. They're the brainchild of some idjit who doesn't know there's water at the bottom of Pilot Street. There's only so much yew kin put in a container. They're only twenty fut long, eight fut high and eight fut wide. How the hell's gate are yew gonna stuff forty fut lengths a timber or sixty fut lengths a reinforcin' bars in a box twenty fut long? Another thing: they're made a wood an' are nearly always damaged in transit."

There was silence and he knew he'd won that round and continued confidently, "We're always afeared of the unknown, and that's natural."

He was now preaching to the converted, and he knew it.

"But lissen! Even if containers do take off in a limited way: who's gonna suffer? Nat us. Along wid our colleagues on the mainland, we'll negotiate a deal that will ensure work, an' easy work at that, fer us an' those who cum behin' us. We'll make sure the amount of labour left will be tailored to suit the needs of our present workforce, an' our workforce only. That means there'll be nuthin' fer the parasites that have followed the quay fer years an' lived off our leavin's. Men like the reds who were constantly a pain in the arse until we lowered the boom. The Arabs 'ill be next. We'll close it down an' sew it up fer ourselves an' guarantee easy, well-paid work for those who cum behin' us. It's about time we left our mark on all labour in the port. Consolidate it for our own people and cut out the reds an' Arabs like the cancer they are."

The men were silent as they digested the logic of his statement. Only Sid seemed uncertain.

"But what if the labour needs of the port after all these progressive inclusions is smaller than the present workforce? That would mean there wudn't be employment fer all of us."

The other men growled at his logic. Shaw held up his hand.

"What did I jist tell yew?" he chided gently. "We'll take over the surplus work the Arabs are doin' at the minit ... "

"But that's heavy an' hard work. None of us wants till do that," replied one of the men.

Shaw smiled again.

233

"It won't be heavy and hard fer much longer. That's the area we're gonna experiment in wid the containers. Instead a the potatoes being physically loaded onto lorries on the farms, and then offloaded by han' in the sheds, the haulage firms will send out containers. They'll be stuffed with about twenty tons of spuds per box. Fork trucks or shed cranes will offload them an' all yew will have till do is stan' wid yer han's in yer pockets an' watch."

"Will the stevedores allow that?" asked Sid.

Shaw narrowed his eyes.

"It's already arranged. One man per cargo to assist in the off-loadin' an' a checker to keep tally. A welcome change in the workload, but no change in the workforce. Twenty tons a spuds from the lorry till the shed floor, an' yis won't have till carry a bag. Are yis gonna let a crowd of Arabs do that job?"

He smiled at the grinning faces.

"No! I thought nat! Nigh git back till yer werk. There's loose ends till tie up ta make shure it all goes to our advantage."

The men turned and walked to the door at the end of the corridor. Shaw's eyes caught sight of Hamill.

"Learnin' where the loyalties of a real union rep lie?" he asked scornfully before closing the door in his colleague's face.

Hamill's smug and complacent grin was not shifted by the display of bad manners.

Entering his own office, he threw off his coat. Pulling a piece of blank paper from a drawer in his desk, he took a fountain pen from his jacket pocket and began writing furiously. Half-an-hour later, he put four handwritten pages into a manilla envelope. Sealing it, he addressed it to Mr. McCartan, University lecturer at law, Queen's University, Belfast. He took a stamp from below a paperweight, licked it and stuck it to the top of the envelope.

"The Underdog strikes back," he muttered triumphantly as he placed the envelope in his overcoat pocket. He would call the head constable later on.

"This way I can serve both myself an' socialism," he said to himself.

Wilson watched as Kelly climbed quickly and effortlessly over the closed gate of the Transport House car park. He stood until the docker disappeared into the darkness before walking towards Waring Street as arranged. He turned lazily to observe the face of the Albert Clock that glowed like a full moon in the darkness. It was precisely 5.30 a.m. He looked at the luminous hands of his wristwatch and saw it said 5.32. Reaching Waring Street, he walked quickly until he came to Skipper Street on his left. Turning sharply, he moved the short distance that took him into High Street. Another left turn saw him heading towards the front entrance of the union building which he prayed would be open when he reached it.

He walked up the small flight of steps and turned the handle. The door glided open effortlessly. Kelly nodded from the bottom of the stairs. He waved to him and both men climbed the stairs to the second floor. They moved slowly and quietly through the darkness, using the wall and counting each door they passed until they came to the office entrance they were looking for. Kelly opened the unlocked door and both entered quietly. The room was small, measuring ten feet square. It was filled with office furniture and a desk. Wilson watched as his companion moved to the large window that looked out into Victoria Street. He pulled the blind the officer used to block out the sun when it shone directly through the window. Wilson searched the wall for the power switch. As the room flooded with light, the men looked at each other.

Kelly saw a flicker of doubt in his comrade's eyes. He patted his shoulder reassuringly.

"It's the only way, Sergeant. Kill the head an' the body will die," he whispered. "Shaw comes in earlier than any of the others. We'll be able to do the job an' git out the way I came in."

Wilson nodded and pulled a piece of charcoal from his pocket and began to rub it over his gloved hands before rubbing the gloves over his taut strained face. He threw the lump of charcoal to Kelly who did the same. He watched as Kelly took a length of thin rope from his trouser pocket and wound the two ends around his hands. Nodding grimly to

Wilson, he moved backwards until his shoulders touched the wall directly behind the room door. Wilson turned off the light before removing the sunshade from the window. He pulled the chair from the aperture in the desk that sat beneath the window. Before lowering himself into that space he took a last glance at his comrade's face and shuddered a little. Kelly had the look of a man completely at ease.

Under the desk, Wilson moved his left arm slowly and checked his watch. The hands showed it was 6.45 a.m. Not long now, he reflected grimly. He cast a quick glance at Kelly who was standing as still and as silent as a statue. His hands were closed into fists and raised chest high in a fighting position. The slender rope between them hung in a slight loop. His face was like a mask set in granite. Wilson shivered a little and wondered why he'd allowed himself to be talked into the scheme to kill Shaw.

He was almost asleep when he heard the door open and close quickly. He rose from his hiding place as Kelly draped the rope quickly around the victim's throat and pulled it sharply.

As he rushed forward to stop the victim from struggling or raising the alarm, his stomach turned as he saw Kelly was strangling the wrong person. The person in his grip was a woman. He almost fainted when he recognised Helen. He yelled furiously at Kelly, but the words wouldn't come. He lunged at her assailant in an effort to stop him. He saw Helen's bulging eyes as she recognised him despite his blackened features. As she put her hands on her husband's shoulders and spoke his name, Kelly drew a knife from his belt and cut her throat. As she fell to the floor Wilson screamed in anger and lunged at her killer. He was astonished to see Shaw standing where Kelly had been a few seconds before. He looked to the floor and saw the docker lying open eyed in a bloodstained heap as Shaw advanced with a triumphant grin. The knife glinted in the light of the room as it ripped across Wilson's neck. Again he heard his wife scream.

"Sammy! Sammy!"

The shock caused his eyes to open and he saw with relief Helen's concerned face.

"Sammy! Sammy!" she repeated loudly, her face a few inches from his. "Are yew alright?"

He tried to speak, but the words wouldn't come. His eyes were moist with tears of relief as grasped her hands and kissed them. He looked at her concerned features.

"Bad nightmare."

But the words didn't come out. Helen only heard a desperate croaking sound coming from the back of his throat.

"He's tryin' ta say somethin', Billy."

He saw Kelly standing behind his wife and tried to rise, but succumbed to the pressure of his wife's arms and lay back on the pillow.

"Probably havin' a bad dream," said Kelly.

Wilson nodded his head, as he again grabbed his wife and held her to him.

"Mebbe I shud call the nurse. It's a long time since he's bin this attentive," said Helen with a wry smile.

Wilson shook his head vigorously. He grinned broadly and pointed to his temple with a forefinger which he twirled briskly in small circles.

"He's tryin' ta say he's all mixed up," ventured Kelly, laughing as Wilson again nodded his head in agreement. Helen tried to move back from his embrace, but he wouldn't let go. He held her cheek to his and she felt his warm tears on her face. He motioned to the bedside table.

"Mebbe he wants a drink a water," suggested Kelly.

He poured some into a glass and reached it to him.

Wilson took the tumbler in shaking hands and emptied it. After a moment or two surveying his surroundings, he found his voice.

"Thanks, staff," he muttered gratefully.

"Nigh. Nigh. Didn't I tell yew the war's over, Sergeant," replied Kelly mockingly, as he ruffled Wilson's sparse hair.

Helen gently prised herself free from his arms.

"For a moment there I thought yew were takin' another stroke," she cried tearfully.

He looked up at her. His eyes were clear and bright.

"As Billy says: a terrible nightmare, an' a wake-up call rolled

237

inta one. Lissen love," he added, "there's a piece a blank paper in the drawer. Check if it's still there."

Helen rummaged for a moment or two.

"Is this it?"

He nodded happily.

"Yis," he replied. "Write my name an' the day's date on the bottom of the page: fold it an' put it back."

She exchanged baffled glances with Kelly, but did as she was told.

Wilson grabbed her hands again and squeezed them affectionately as he gazed at Kelly.

"Nigh! Tell me how the funeral went? They wudn't let me out fer it."

The look of anger on his face turned to disgust when Kelly finished.

"How the hell did they git all that drink?" he asked.

"Some guys pilfered it from the boat at the Chapel Shed and Henry's regular assignment of poteen was on sale at the same time. He was arrested wid about half-a-dozen others. They were charged wid disorderly behaviour in the graveyard— physically assaultin' two gravediggers, and causing grievous bodily harm to a man of the cloth. The carter whose horse damaged the hearse was charged wid drunkin' drivin', drivin' recklessly, an' feedin' alcohol to a dumb animal."

Wilson looked at him quizzically.

"How cum yew didn't git charged?" he asked suspiciously.

Kelly didn't speak. Helen looked at him admiringly.

"Billy promised Mr. McCartan he wud stay outa trouble until the court case was over. It wus him saved the minister from being suffocated at the bottom of a pile of them roughnecks. Bloody disgrace the whole lotta them," she sniffed huffily.

"Who was the idjit that fell over the coffin?" asked Wilson.

"Gibby Murdock," replied Kelly.

"Aye. I know him," frowned Wilson. "He's the kinda fella who wud trip over a chalk line. Did they lift the coffin out again?"

"Naw," replied Kelly. "While the peelers were wrestlin' till arrest big Henry an' the others, the gravediggers filled the grave in, so we don't know if Reilly's buried face upwards or face down."

Both men stared blankly at each other for a few moments before bursting into uncontrollable laughter. Helen scowled at both of them.

"Is nuthin' sacred till youse heathens?" she cried, failing to stop the grin that made its way slowly onto her happy, but tired, face.

Jim's mother watched from her front door as he walked towards the lane that led to Henry Street boxing club, carrying a small battered attaché case that held his training clothes. She returned to her rocking chair and heaved a sigh of relief as she sat down. He had told her of the disgraceful behaviour of some of the mourners. She was overjoyed that he had not been involved, and had come straight home. She knew many of them would be in the pub giving Reilly a good send off.

"Plenty a money fer drink, but niver enuff fer housekeeping," she growled to herself as she rose and put the teapot on.

She was toasting a piece of bread when the front door was knocked. The clock on the mantlepiece chimed seven times as she walked into the long hall. The front door was open and she was puzzled that her visitor had not simply walked into the kitchen. She turned on the hall light and recognised Reilly's daughter.

"Come in," she called, and walked back into the heat of the kitchen. Sally entered the room timidly and hesitated a moment before sitting down on the settee. She looked around the room as Aggie Harvey studied her closely.

"Can I get yew a cuppa tea an' a bit a toast?" she asked.

"I would love that," Sally smiled.

She continued to look around the room as Mrs. Harvey busied herself in the scullery.

"I'm sorry fer yer troubles. Yer father wus a good man," she said softly to the young woman as she returned from the kitchen and reached her a cup and saucer.

"Thank you for those kind words. My father's death shocked me, but not as much as the despicable drunken behaviour in the graveyard. I paid for extra cars so they could all go and pay their respects. I should have known better."

Aggie Harvey sniffed.

"I wudn't put anythin' past those louts. Some of them hold nuthin' sacred, except pourin' drink down their rotten gullets," she scowled, handing Sally a piece of buttered toast on a plate matching her cup and saucer.

Sitting on her rocking chair, she looked over at her visitor.

"Is there a reason for this visit?" she asked anxiously.

Sally sipped her tea.

"When my mother died nearly twenty years ago, my father packed me off to relatives in London. I attended night classes after school hours until I graduated in business studies. I now run a thriving concern in the heart of London and employ a good-sized workforce."

"Are yew married?" Mrs. Harvey asked softly.

"No. I never found time or felt the need. When I was lonely, I took a boat home and stayed with my father for a few days."

She grimaced at the thought.

"I loved my father dearly and tried hard to get him to come and live with me, which he flatly refused to do. I hated that little house in Southwell Street. Hated the fact that the sun never shone through its windows because they were always covered with pouse and dust from the Mill, no matter how many times you cleaned them. Hated the fact that no matter how hard you scrubbed the kitchen floor you could never get the grime and dirt off the cracked and broken tiles or get rid of the little insects that were everywhere."

She shuddered visibly at the recollection.

"It didn't annoy my father as he'd never seen anything different. His life was all about second-hand and soiled belongings.

"No work, except dirty, hard, badly paid work, which he had to grovel for, with kindness shown by none, because no one had anything to give him, or those like him."

Mrs. Harvey sipped her tea.

"That kinda thing is life till the like a us. The wee house was home till yer da an' the work was the only way of life he knew," she replied philosophically. She put her teacup on the hearth and leaned forward to put her hand on Sally's.

"Why are yew here?" she asked earnestly. "Is it about my Jim?"

Sally gazed at her for a long moment before she spoke.

"Jim has been kindness itself to me since we met in York Street the day after my father's death. There is something different about him. He's thoughtful, decent and considerate, and these aren't traits you'll find in the men of the district."

"His father wus like that. He wudn't a drunk more nor two or three bottles a stout, an' he only did that till pass himself," recalled Mrs. Harvey with a look of fond remembrance in her eyes. She heaved a long hard sigh. "But his brothers, that Jim's mixed up wid on the docks, wud drink it outa a shitty nappie," she added disapprovingly. Lifting her cup she looked over its rim at Sally. "What do you want with my Jim?" she added.

"I want to give him the chance my father refused. I want to show him there is more to life than being used, degraded and walked on for the privilege of working at cargoes filled with lethal dust that will pollute his lungs and destroy his health. Then in a few short years, when he hasn't the breath or strength to perform the hard physical work, he'll be tossed aside without pension or any other provision to help him. He'll finish up on the dole cadging drink. Is that the life you want for him?"

Mrs. Harvey wiped a tear from her eye.

"God knows—indeed I don't," she sobbed. "But does he have till go away?" she continued, wiping her eyes with her apron hem. "He's the man a this house nigh an' he's all Lizzie an' I have."

Sally squeezed her hand comfortingly.

"He wouldn't be gone forever. He could earn enough to come home to see you every now and again, and also send you something for yourself. I have the means and the money to change his life, and yours. I will send you a written contract with words to that effect. I will protect him and provide for him until he's able to look after himself. London is booming and with my connections, Jim could become very successful."

"Are yew in love wid him?" enquired Aggie softly.

Sally didn't need to answer. It was written all over her face.

"Yewr quite a bit older than my Jim," Mrs. Harvey continued, in a sad, but understanding voice.

Sally lowered her head in defeat.

"Nat to worry," continued her companion. "His granny on my side was twenty years ouler than his granda, an' they were happy enuff until she died during a diphtheria outbreak. An' what did the oul rapscallion do a few years later? He married a woman twenty years younger than himself."

Sally, relieved, joined in her infectious laughter.

"Besides, yew'r very pretty an' yew don't luk yer age," Aggie finished with a melancholy smile.

Sally smiled as if a great burden had been lifted from her shoulders.

"Now I know where Jim gets his charm," she said.

Mrs. Harvey lifted the teacups and dishes.

"I have prayed every night for something that wud take my Jim away from the Docks."

She nodded at the framed photo of his father in naval uniform.

"If his daddy had lived, he'd have followed him intil the shipyard and learned a trade. He hadda go on the quay 'cause we couldn't make do on the wages he'd a gat elsewhere."

She stopped for a moment.

"Do yew know he gives me every penny he gits?" she said with a smile of incredulity that warmed Sally's heart. "Every Thursday, he cums in the door, covered in whatever cargo he's bin wurkin' at an' throws his unopened pay packet on that table there. He takes what I give him outta it, without a wurd. Nat many young fellas wud do that!" she added in a self satisfied tone.

"He has a good heart," agreed Sally, as she rose to leave.

His mother laughed.

"He certainly has. He had a win on the horses the other day an' went out an' bought a new rig out till wear at yer father's funeral: an' he give me ten poun'. Ten poun'!" she repeated, as if she herself found it hard to believe. "What other boy wud do that?"

"I'm very glad he shared his good fortune with you," smiled Sally

The old woman glanced at her with tired weary eyes.

"You're very pretty," she repeated. "I've niver seen clothes like those yew are wearin' except in the big shops in the town centre. Shops they wudn't let the like a me intil."

Sally smiled at the compliment.

"Next time I'm in Belfast, I'll take you into all those shops," she promised, and grinned at the genuine delight in the old woman's eyes.

As they walked to the front door, Sally turned to her.

"Your home is lovely and I'd like to visit you before I leave."

"My door is always open," Mrs. Harvey replied. "Have yew spoken to Jim about yewr intentions?"

Sally clasped her hands warmly.

"Not yet. I wanted to get your consent first."

On an impulse she put her arms around the older woman.

"I promise you, you will not regret this decision. I will only do what is good for Jim's long term future. Let's hope Jim is as sensible as you are."

"I pray till God he is," murmured Mrs. Harvey.

Sally smiled brightly.

"Jim is having supper with me tonight in the Midland Hotel as a token of my appreciation. I would be very pleased if you and his sister, whom he talks so much about, would come and join us?"

Mrs. Harvey hesitated a moment before nodding consent.

As Sally made to move away, Aggie took her hand.

"Are yew sleepin' wid Jim?"

Sally thought for a moment, and decided to be honest.

"Yes! When we get the chance," she admitted in a whisper.

"Are yew nat frightened of gittin' pregnant?" murmured the old woman with a twinkle in her eye.

Sally smiled reassuringly.

"There's a new thing called the pill, Mrs. Harvey. It allows women to have the same enjoyment as the men without being left holding the baby, if you get my meaning."

Aggie grinned broadly and winked.

243

"Cud yew send me over a couple, jist in case?" she replied with a loud cackle that caused Sally to give her an affectionate hug.

Mrs. Harvey watched as her visitor walked into York Street and turned in the direction of the Midland Hotel. Returning to her rocking chair, she pulled it a little closer to the fire and gazed at her husband's photograph. She glanced over at Jim's empty chair in the corner beside the wall cupboard.

"He won't be gone forever," she whispered with emotion. "An' he'll make somethin' of hisself an' make us proud of him, so he will," she promised as her tear-filled eyes returned to the photograph.

Kelly was surprised to see McCartan push through the front door of the Sportsman's Arms. He took off his brown chamois gloves and slipped them into his overcoat pocket. He proffered his right hand to the docker, who shook it warmly.

"What kin I get yew an' what kin I do for yew?" asked Kelly aware that the entrance of McCartan had caught the attention of everyone in the crowded bar. The owner was also a little worried. The bar was packed with mourners, and most of them had been drunk before they arrived. It wasn't a time to greet strangers, especially well-dressed strangers who had a vested interest in depriving some of his customers of their livelihood. He sighed wearily and prayed there would be no confrontations.

Billy noted the owner's concern.

"Let's go somewhere else," he suggested, nodding towards the door.

As they walked into the street McCartan gulped in the fresh air gratefully.

"Have you been to see Mr. Wilson?" he asked as they walked in the direction of the railway station.

"Yis," answered Kelly, pulling the collar of his navy blue reefer jacket up and the peak of his eight-piece cap down, before sinking his hands into the deep slit pockets.

"How did you find him?" continued McCartan softly.

Kelly looked up at him.

"He's a baten docket. Jist like all the rest of thim," he answered tonelessly.

His companion shrugged his shoulders.

"I'm beginning to think you're right. It was a different man I was speaking to a while ago. Preoccupied and vague. Much of the fire has gone out of him. He's certainly in no shape to give evidence, and to be honest, his mind seemed to be on other things. He's not his usual self."

The docker nodded in agreement.

"It's the system, Mr. McCartan. Men like us can never bate it. The docks can't be scrutinised like a courtroom or a well run factory. There are no rules, except the rules of strength an' force, an' they eventually become law."

He smiled again, this time mirthlessly, as he gazed at McCartan.

"The same rules we talked about in the bar the other day. Strength an' force. The guidelines of war. Subterfuge, dishonesty, treachery, deceit, propaganda. Tried and tested tricks of conflict employed by intellectual and educated people with empires to build an' nations to create. Ready an' willin' to ride roughshod over a group of men who are already in retreat an' self-destructin' wid every day that goes by ... "

His voice tailed off as they reached the corner of Whitla Street.

"We kin go inta the Dainty Café for a soft refreshment to please yew, or we kin go intil the hotel an' git a drink that'll suit us both," he grinned.

"All I want is justice for the displaced men," whispered McCartan sincerely as they sat down at a table in the corner of the hotel's lounge bar. Kelly toyed with his drink.

"They know an' appreciate that," Kelly said. "But they also realise that yew an' the secret seven are nat winnin'. Your idea that no one should be employed unless they produce an up to date union card has backfired. Bogus cards are being handed to key Arabs. This is being done to ensure these people remain in their jobs. An' I agree wid that."

He smiled gently at McCartan's look of concern.

"Let me explain," he continued hastily. "Most of these men work at the potato cargoes. They are checkers an' carriers. The carriers are family orientated and pass on their knowledge to their own. Henry Harvey controls an' runs the section like a sergeant major. He gits the job done, widout any fuss. An' it's cheaper. He runs a first-class service on a shoestring. The stevedores know this an', more importantly, so do the union controllers. In the scheme of things, the carriers are employed for their strength, but they also possess a certain amount of knowledge garnered from the checkers over the years. Like the blues, they are family orientated. All blood related; they jealously guard their right to work wid their relatives. The powers that be have tholed this on the principle that if it isn't broke, don't fix it. They also know the potato export industry is one of the biggest earners in Northern Ireland, an' the agents who hand out the wurk wudn't hesitate in passing it onto the Irish Transport Dockers, whose potato men have much the same expertise as our Arabs, but wud constitute a larger pay-out bill as they wudn't tolerate the wages and conditions Harvey's men work under. Neither wud my colleagues in the first-preference section at the cross channel. It's all down till money, Mr. McCartan."

McCartan sipped at his coffee.

"You don't paint a very pretty picture."

"I paint a true picture," Kelly replied stoically. "Technically, your plea for all men to carry cards has actually strengthened the Union's hand an' filled their coffers to a certain extent, as the outsiders will be only too glad to receive them. It also takes away the pressure you put on Transport House in London. Cards have been issued to key outsiders. Others will get them by fair means or foul, an' a blind eye will be turned until they're all covered. There's a guy who drinks in one of the local bars handin' out false cards to anyone who'll buy them. Card carrying men, such as lorry drivers in constant employment in other areas, are beginning to flood the place each weekend. The reds whose faces don't fit are no further on. Soon they'll all be history."

He lowered the glass of Black Bush and gazed wearily across the table at the worried features of the university lawyer.

"That's why Sammy Wilson's down in the mouth. The system has beaten him ... an' he knows it. It's the classic shot in the fut job. He's a soldier in retreat, an' like all soldiers, he's lukin' till save his own skin, and negotiate a surrender he kin live wid. An' who kin blame him?"

"Are you ready to surrender?" asked his companion.

Kelly's grin was cynical.

"All I have till do is stan' a certain foreman, an' all will be forgiven," he answered wearily.

"Will you?"

Kelly thought for a long moment.

"I don't know," he answered truthfully. "One half of me, like Wilson, wud feel it's justified self-survival. The other half wud see it as a rat deserting a sinkin' ship."

"The court case may be in the balance, but it's not a lost cause ... "

Kelly gazed at him, and his voice was warm.

"No one is blaming yew, sir. Yew're seen as a well-intentioned observer doin' his best. But they'll say it isn't yewr fight. The anger raised over the tit-for-tat beatings evaporated when sailors were arrested for the offences. McKinstry said he hadn't enuff to charge them, but was fairly certain they were responsible. Their ship, which was in the wee yard gittin' minor repairs, has sailed, and they're outa the picture now. It seems as if the reds have been badly advised. The secret seven will bear the brunt of the failure. Wilson, especially, will be hounded by all concerned, fer givin' the second-preference men ideas above their station. Others will blame no one, an' simply disappear from the quay. Those who live close will continue to stand the gangers in the hope that they'll be forgiven in time. Others who live in places like Ballyclare, Carrick and Lisburn or further afield simply won't find it feasible to pay return bus fares to Belfast for nuthin' ... Naw," he concluded, "it's finished."

He leaned across the table and stared into McCartan's eyes.

"It's time to make an honourable withdrawal from the field sir. We're bate. In the words of a famous Belfast Dockside philosopher, we've bin fatally shot by a ball of our own shit."

"Wilson is a man of integrity—"

Kelly interrupted angrily.

"Integrity? What's integrity? Kin yew eat it? Kin yew shite it? Kin yew put it on the fire like a shovelful of coal when there's snow on the groun'? Kin yew take it outa the wardrobe an' throw it on the childer's bed, like an extra blanket, when they complain about the coul in the night? Kin yew dander intil the Sportsman's Arms, toss it on the bar an' git a couple a drinks in exchange? Kin yew stroll intil the wife the way them guys have bin doin' fer the last two weeks an' say, 'Nuthin' fer me the day again luv, but don't worry: my pockets are fulla integrity'?"

He paused, and nodded tiredly at McCartan. The lawyer could see the hurt and anger etched in his features as he swallowed the last of the Black Bush.

He rose and spoke quietly.

"I agree with you, Mr. Kelly. Integrity can never be measured as a currency, and that's sad: because if it were, men like you would be millionaires. I appreciate your help in the recent weeks and I will continue to visit the schooling pen and monitor the situation until the court case comes up. My future involvement will be decided when there is a legal verdict. Technically, I'm hoping for the court to order the dockers' branch to subsume the reds into their ranks."

Kelly rose and shook his hand.

"Sorry I blew up. Yewr a champion of the underdog, an' as we say in York Street, yewr heart's in the right place. An' as fer integrity ... If it wus alcohol, yew'd be so drunk yew wudn't be able to git outa yer bed of a mornin'."

He waved his glass in the manner of a toast.

"Good luck," he muttered as McCartan buttoned his overcoat and walked from the room. He peered at his watch in the darkness of the lounge. It was almost six o'clock. He decided to walk to Gallaher's tobacco factory and see if he could meet Minnie. He rose abruptly and within minutes was standing outside the main gates. They were open and the smell of tobacco filled the air. A klaxon horn on the top of the building wailed forlornly and soon the workers filed out.

He moved to the corner of Earl Street, knowing Minnie would pass him on her way home. He watched as the workers poured through the gates in their hundreds. The women and girls were all dressed in emerald green smocks and the smattering of men wore sand-coloured overalls. Minnie didn't speak or acknowledge him as he fell in beside her. Her companions dropped back obligingly to let him walk by her side. Grabbing her arm he pulled her into one of the doorways at the corner of Henry Street. She was about to scold him, but stopped when she saw the strain in his face and the pain in his eyes.

"I'm sorry I haven't got in touch since I had to leave yewr house in a hurry the other night," he whispered.

Her anger returned swiftly.

"I wudn't a knew what happened till ye, only I saw yew at the funeral. Yew're lucky yew gat outa that room before my da came in, or we'd a had a double funeral. Anyway," she continued tearfully, "he's signed off the cattle boat fer a week or two till sort yew out. He suspects yew were in the house, but he can't prove it ... So jist ignore him if he gits at yew, an' Billy, please don't hurt him."

He was about to reply when she was torn from his grip by an angry middle-aged man with a mop of white hair. He was wearing a waistcoat over a thick tartan shirt with rolled up sleeves. Minnie cowered in the corner of the doorway as he advanced on Kelly.

"I tole yew till stay away from my girl, an yewr own da tole yew as well! Mebbe yewr hearin's bad!"

As he finished the sentence, he slapped Kelly savagely on both ears, with his open hands. Kelly's head moved from side to side with the force of the blows. He placed his own hands in his pockets signifying no retaliation. Minnie's father looked at him with contempt.

"Maybe them coupla slaps 'ill move the wax in yewr ears, an' yill hear what I'm sayin'. Stay away from my Minnie. If yew want a tramp till fornicate wid, go over till the Stalingrad. If I see yew wid my girl again, I'll stick a cargo hook in yewr throat."

Turning to his daughter, he grabbed her by the neck with

one hand and unbuckled a broad leather belt with his other. It fell from his waist and he used it to lash her around the legs. She tried to break free, but he released her neck and held one of her arms in a vice-like grip as he continued to hit out with the strap. He dragged her into Henry Street and towards their home. Kelly moved quickly through the crowd that had gathered. Tearing the belt from her father he grabbed him savagely by the throat and pulled his head down until their faces were inches apart.

"She's nat a fuckin' dog, Geordie. Don't be beatin' her like she wus!" he snarled through clenched teeth.

Geordie moved quickly for an old man. This time Kelly dodged the punches effortlessly.

"Don't hurt him, Billy! Please don't hurt him!" Minnie screamed. She raced forward between them, fearful of the anger in Kelly's eyes. A crowd of her fellow workers had gathered and watched in silence as he released the older man.

"Hurt her again an' I'll cum fer yew."

Minnie cried with relief as her father turned and walked towards their home without a word.

Kelly watched as she ran after him. He sighed heavily and was about to move off when a tall freckle faced man with short dark hair stepped into his path.

"Yer good at beatin' oul lads, mate," he said scornfully.

Kelly ignored the taunt and was walking away when the man grabbed him savagely.

"I'm talkin' till yew."

Kelly looked coldly at the hand on his shoulder for a few seconds before smashing his knee savagely into the man's groin. The latter fell with a cry of pain that echoed all over the street.

"Min' yewr own business," snarled Kelly as the man writhed in agony on the ground. Turning to the crowd behind him, he cocked his fists and dropped into a fighting position.

"Any more for any more?" he grinned wickedly.

The men dispersed quickly as some of the women ran to aid the injured man. Kelly turned his attention to Minnie and her father and watched as both of them entered their home and closed the door with a bang. He cast an indifferent glance at the injured man before crossing the road and walking towards the Sportsman's.

The next morning Jim took his place in Ned's school beside him. The older man said nothing, but smiled as Jim held his new union card where it could be seen by the ganger. He noticed few reds in the school. Many had taken out their distinctive red lapel badges in an effort not to antagonise the ganger. The anger and fury of last week had disappeared. The pen was still being monitored by the police, but in smaller numbers. Ned looked at them with a mixture of hatred and contempt.

"Six hunnert ton a salt! Three hunnert ton a hatch! An' I want outa her the day! So don't stan' me if yer nat able fer it!"

He nodded towards three of his fellow blues.

"Winch, hatch, bullrope, number two houl," he muttered as the men nodded quietly and obediently.

The others waited as he looked closely for the holdsmen. Jim was pleasantly surprised as he received the third check after Kelly and a long serving outsider who was rumoured to be decorating the foreman's bungalow.

He fell in step with Kelly.

"Yew an' me, Billy?" he said hopefully.

The older man grinned at him.

"Why nat?" he replied. "Yer getting till be a top man. Ned even called yew by yer right name instead a yer mother's. That means yiv graduated till the hard school of houlsman. Yill be puttin' in fer a blue button shortly," he continued with a mocking grin.

Jim's chest swelled visibly as they made the short journey to the Pollock Basin where the ship was berthed.

The salt was in paper bags each weighing a hundredweight. His cockiness began to evaporate when Ned came over the hatch and separated them, teaming Jim with a short, slim-built, red-faced middle-aged man wearing a tweed jacket and cap. He'd removed the jacket and rolled up his sleeves.

Ned's tone was brutal as he yelled over the roar of the winch.

"Jackie Shannon's one a the secret seven, Harvey! Don't be carryin' him. If he's nat able, give me a shout an' I'll replace him. He's bin a checker fer twenty years an' his han's mightn't be up till hard wurk."

Jim nodded dumbly as the other man walked to Kelly's side. The red-button man moved quickly to reassure him.

"Don't worry. I know the procedure. But it's bin twenty years since I was in the bowels of a boat," he whispered nervously.

Jim lifted a rope sling and Shannon picked up a strip of canvas. They loaded the sling from a pile stacked in the between decks as Kelly and his companion made the first sink to open up the cargo. The twenty sacks were put into the sling quickly and without any problems. Jim heaved a sigh of relief.

Some of the bags had burst during loading, and loose salt lay on every sack they lifted. The bags had hard sharp corners that were sealed with large metal staples. There was no waiting as the hook swept deftly in and out, each heave carrying twenty bags to the shore gang who trucked it into the nearby transit shed. Only Kelly's head and shoulders were visible as he threw the sacks out of the narrow opening he had dug and into the sling. His eyebrows and eyelashes were caked with salt, making him look like an old man. Jim glanced up and saw the ganger watching. He recognised Shannon as the one who had felled him from behind during the fight in the pen. He was surprised to find he felt no animosity. He was just grateful that the older man was pulling his weight, despite being out of condition.

They broke for tea and climbed ashore. Jim sought out Kelly and sat beside him, sipping gratefully at the tepid brew.

"What are yew doin' here anyway?" asked Kelly. "I thought yew were dug in at the spuds?"

Jim's face coloured and he looked around him before whispering, "Henry cum till the house this mornin' an' tole me till go to the corner and stan' Ned."

Kelly grinned.

"An' yew split yer spell with the others?"

Jim nodded.

"Trust Henry till turn somebody's problem intil his opportunity."

Kelly rose and headed back to the ship as Jim walked obediently behind him. After the first two or three heaves he noticed Shannon was slowing down and gritting his teeth with every bag they lifted. He didn't worry too much as they were still ready when the hook descended on them. He studied the cargo for another heave as Shannon walked out to the hook.

"Nat as handy as pushin' a pencil," laughed the docker on the bullrope. "Yew shud give that wee buck half a yer spell fer carryin' yew," he added with a scowl. The holdsman ignored him and pulled the hook to the heave.

Jim watched with silent gratitude as the other pair made the second sink. He knew he and Shannon would have to make the third and final sink early in the afternoon and hoped his companion would be up to it. During a rare break he went to the water bucket and lifted the cup attached to its handle. He took a mouthful and spat it out.

"It's fulla salt," he called to Kelly.

"What did yew expect. Sugar?" came the amused reply.

The rest of the men laughed in unison and Jim grinned with embarrassment.

"What about a fresh bucket a water when yew git time, Freddy?" called another holdsman.

"Why don't yew ask Shannon? He's good at organising things. He'll lift a collection an' git a solicitor till bring it till yew," came the scornful reply from the hatchman.

The bullrope man joined in the laughter as the ganger watched. Jim's companion said nothing as he concentrated on keeping up with the young lad.

They broke for lunch at noon. Jim climbed up the hatch ladder behind his workmate. The man's ascent was slow and tortuous and he was relieved but surprised when Kelly looked into the hatch and, after a moment's hesitation, helped him off the ladder and onto the deck. As Shannon moved away Kelly stopped him and lifted his hands. Jim gasped in horror as he saw the large white blisters. Some were broken and filled with a mixture of salt, blood and pus. For the first time he saw the naked pain on Shannon's face. He also saw the compassion in Kelly's eyes as he spoke gently.

"Jackie. Yew can't go on. Tell Ned. He wudn't expect yew till continue under the circumstances."

Shannon shook his head.

"The big bastard wud take delight in sackin' me an' makin' sure I wus left in the schoolin' pen forever."

He turned his glance to Jim.

"If this young cub tells me till quit, I will. I wudn't want him sufferin'," he muttered through dry lips.

Kelly looked at Jim who shook his head vigorously.

"OK," he answered reluctantly. "Yew know what the cure is?"

Jackie nodded with a whisper of a smile.

"Learned it long ago. Niver thought I'd be usin' it at this stage of the game," he answered wryly.

Jim was thinking about his workmate as he sipped from a bottle of milk. He was too exhausted to eat solid food and slumped gratefully in his chair by the fire as his mother fussed over him. She set down a bowl of cornflakes and clucked disapprovingly.

"There's nat much substance in that," she growled as he poured milk from the bottle into the bowl.

"I know, ma," he agreed, "but I cudn't face solids. I'll make up fer it tonight."

She sat down in her rocking chair and lifted her knitting. Music floated from the radio in the corner.

"That wus a nice meal we had in the Midland last night, wasn't it?" she said.

"Aye," he replied, tucking into his cornflakes.

"Lizzie says Sally Reilly is a rale lady," she continued as the needles clicked loudly. She chuckled to herself. "I wus a wee bit embarrassed at all them different knives an' forks, but I noticed yew knew what yew were doin'... "

"Aye," he repeated absently, "Sally showed me the first time we had a meal together. It's no big deal."

He laid down his spoon and looked across the room at her.

"Mum, Sally has offered me a job in London. She has guaranteed me a good future if I lave Belfast."

The needles stopped clicking as his mother gazed intently at him.

"Are yew goin' till do it?" she asked anxiously.

Jim misread her reaction. He rose from the table and put on his coat.

"Don't worry, mum. There's no chance of me laving yew an' our Lizzie. See yew later," he said gently as he walked out of the door.

She sat down slowly and took a pinch from a box of Carroll's Peppermint Snuff in her apron pocket to clear her head. She lifted the knitting and after a few moments began sobbing. She wasn't sure if they were tears of regret or relief.

Hearing Lizzie coming up the hall she hastily dried her eyes before moving to the scullery and lighting the gas beneath the frying pan. Her daughter lifted the curtain that served as a door.

"Don't make me too much, ma. I'm still full up from that meal we had last night. Sally Reilly knows all the fine points of livin'. I wus tellin' the girls in work about all the delicious things that were on the menu."

She stopped for a breath before continuing, "An' did yew see our Jim ordering the wine for the meal? I wus dead impressed. Do yew think is him an' Sally doin' a line? I noticed she cudn't take her eyes off him," she finished coyly.

Her mother clucked disapprovingly.

"Away an' sit down an' give my head pace. I'll bring yer dinner in when it's ready."

Shannon was already there when Kelly and Jim climbed into the hatch. He had built the first heave himself and was laying the rope and sheet for a second, as Jim joined him. Kelly nodded approvingly.

"How's the han's, Jackie?"

Shannon smiled grimly.

"I'd cut them off an' shove them up my arse before I'd let them slabbers git the better of me."

The winch roared and the hook swung into the centre of the hatch. Shannon's pain was obvious to everyone except himself. Jim noticed he was using his wrists and inner arms to lift the bags into the sling. Blistered skin hung from his palms and fingers, and every time he lifted a bag the pressure forced the loose salt into his wounds. Jim's respect for the man's tenacity and courage grew with every heave. He saw Kelly approach through the cloud of salt that hung over the cargo.

"Jim an' me'll do the final sink, Jackie. Yew tie up wid Hartley, an' lift them handy heaves from the 'tween deck. Wid a bita a luck, another ire 'ill see us out of her."

Shannon shook his head. Kelly looked over at Jim.

"Are yew alright?" he asked with concern in his voice.

Harvey took a deep breath: he smiled at Shannon.

"I've no complaints."

Kelly nodded admiringly.

"Git to it; the both of yew," he shouted as the winch dragged another heave from the hatch.

Jim and Shannon walked to the centre of the cargo. They placed the rope and sheet in silence and Harvey lifted the bag nearest him and threw it into the sling. Shannon watched as his companion cut his way down through the paper sacks. As Jim threw them towards him, Shannon caught them on his forearms and tossed them onto the sling. Harvey jumped from the shallow hole he'd dug in the cargo and lifted the back end of the rope as Shannon picked up the front. Both men grinned tightly at each other. He positioned a sling and sheet as Shannon waited on the hook, and dropped back into the hole. He threw eight bags in the sling before the other heave left. He found the effort hard but not exhausting. Shannon helped him and another heave was ready. Ten minutes later there was room for Shannon. As they widened the sink and cleared more space, Kelly and Hartley dropped in beside them leaving the other pair of holdsmen to clear the remaining layers of the second sink.

As Kelly finished his own heave, he turned and lifted sacks

by himself, throwing them onto the heave Jim and Shannon were building. Hartley made no effort to help, and wasn't asked to. He was a taciturn casual with ten years experience and no love for either first or second preference. Ned purposely teamed him with Kelly, knowing the suspended docker was the best worker in the hatch. Ned also had a vested interest in keeping Hartley fit enough to finish the decorating work on his bungalow.

Shannon was working on instinct alone and was glad of the brief respite Kelly's unselfish action brought. As the floor space grew wider, the heaves were built more quickly and Kelly found more and more time to take the pressure off Jim and his mate. No one spoke as they worked relentlessly in the haze of a swirling mist of loose salt. The thud of the bags hitting the floor was drowned by the roar and whine of the steam winch, as the shore men got closer to the front of the shed and the hook descended faster with every minute that passed. The salt clung to the exposed parts of the men's bodies. It mixed with their perspiration and seeped through their eyebrows and into their eyes. Tears rolled down their faces as their eyes constantly lubricated to clear the stinging powder. Jim felt good within himself, but was pleased with Kelly's welcome intervention. He continued to marvel at Shannon's doggedness. Looking at his own unmarked hands guardedly, he wondered if he would have had the same determination. Shannon looked like a man who had crossed the threshold of his inner pain barrier and was now surviving on strength of mind alone. Hatred of the ganger and the system that had forced him into this predicament kept him going when all else failed.

When the last heave, comprising the sweepings from the hatch floor, was slung to the shore, Shannon walked aft and, hidden from the eyes of the shore men, began to urinate on his hands. He left his fly unbuttoned and walked to the ship's ladder in a trance. He gazed fleetingly at Harvey.

"Thanks lad," he mumbled before making the painful and tortuous climb to the ship's deck.

Ned sipped a mug of hot coffee and watched as he made his way ashore.

"It's nat easy, when yew haveta work fer yer money, shure it isn't, Clegg?" he called to the hatchman.

"Aye, it's easy till deal wid hunnertweight bags when the only effort required is till write their number on a page. I'd a counted mi blessin's if I wus a red-button man wid a handy number like that," replied the hatchman.

Shannon ignored the men.

"Stan' me the marra," shouted the ganger, "I'll have something similar for ye."

They both watched as he staggered towards the dockgate at Whitla Street.

The ganger looked at Clegg with naked triumph in his eyes.

"That's another one who'll nat be back," he laughed.

The hatchman unbuttoned his overcoat and prepared to step ashore.

"I think yer right there, Ned. Shure, yer killin' them pore devils wid kindness."

The hatchman continued to laugh uproariously as he walked down the gangplank onto the quay. He waited until the weary truckers, moving in the direction of the stevedore's store, made their way past him, before crossing to an Austin A40 five-door saloon car. He threw his discarded overcoat into the spacious boot before climbing behind the wheel. The other gang was still working and he had to pick his way through the fast moving trucks. He rolled down the window and felt as if he was going to be sick.

"See you tomorrow, yew hateful bastard," he whispered silently through his teeth as he waved at the ganger.

Ned returned the wave with a cheery smile before turning his gaze to the retreating Shannon.

His eyes narrowed and he turned his attention to the winch driver at the number one hatch.

"Git a move on, Stanley. I want outa her the day," he snarled.

Ten

MCKINSTRY STUDIED THE LETTER THAT HAD arrived with the morning post. It was a long and detailed account of government efforts to have the Irish Congress of Trade Unions form in Northern Ireland. It was unsigned, but he knew where it came from. The writer alleged a conspiracy that led from the Belfast docks to the Prime Minister's inner sanctum at Stormont. Negotiations were at a delicate stage, and police investigations into the recent beatings in and around the area had seriously jeopardised efforts to form the Northern Ireland Committee. For the trade unions operating on an all-Ireland basis, this would mean *de facto* recognition of Stormont rule. The head constable folded the letter and locked it in a private drawer in his desk. He sat back on his chair and lit a cigarette.

He opened another drawer and withdrew the statements concerning the Germans' confession. The detectives investigating the case were puzzled when he allowed the sailors to return to their ship. The captain had guaranteed they would stay out of the dockland public houses if and when they returned to the port of Belfast. He knew the seamen were laughing at him, but he was too long in the tooth to go against the authority that paid his wages. The contents of the letter confirmed what he had suspected. Although he was a police officer from the toe of his boot to the peak of his cap, he wasn't about to endanger his career for the riff-raff of Sailortown.

Besides, he had caught the criminals: it wasn't his problem that the system had set them free. He lifted the statements and pushed them into the heart of the fire that warmed his office.

He watched as they burned to embers before raking the coal vigorously with a poker and placing a shovelful of slack that doused the flame. After a moment or two of self deliberation, he unlocked the private drawer and lifted the letter from the renegade union representative. He placed it in the inside pocket of his tunic. It would be more secure in the safe at home, he thought. There were many sides to this conundrum, and some of his officers came from the area. Although there was a stout lock on the drawer, he had learned long ago that locks only kept honest men out.

He had earlier checked the occurrence book and found the schooling pen had returned to normal. Opening the door of his office he called the station sergeant.

"Tell the duty inspector to call off the dock patrol. Detail two plain clothes detectives to give it passing attention along with their other duties. I'll review the situation in a day or two, but it looks as if the revolution is over," he said. The sergeant touched his cap respectfully and returned to his duties.

Shaw was of the same opinion as he briefed a gathering of stevedores in Collins' office.

"There is nothing now, but small pockets of resistance and we feel the light that sustains them will be extinguished shortly," he said with a confidence that set them at their ease. There was one question from the floor.

"What about the court case?"

Shaw's brow wrinkled momentarily with exasperation, but he answered with a confident smile.

"It's still ongoing," he admitted. "It's a matter for the sovereign union and doesn't concern yew."

Collins looked around the table at the contented faces.

"Can I congratulate you on a job well done, Mr. Shaw. Our figures and the reports from our gangers show the work has been progressing as if there were no dispute. The police presence is almost nil, and the press have no interest. Just one problem," he added cautiously, "McCartan is still monitoring the fact that non-union men are being schooled in front of reds ... "

Shaw interrupted angrily.

"As I've said, that is no concern of yours. McCartan's actions are being observed. Most of the essential Arabs have been issued with cards that give them the same rights to a job as anyone else except the first-preference men. As for the legality of this action, we'll leave that to the men with wigs to decide. We have union lawyers every bit as smart as Mr. McCartan thinks he is," he concluded scornfully.

"How are you selling the containers and flatracks?" continued Collins.

The stevedores watched as Shaw hesitated for a moment before speaking. They noted there was less confidence in his voice when he answered.

"We're gittin' there. It's difficult. A lot of the men are against it. The forklift trucks at the cement boat have shown that the cuttin' edge of technology usually leaves them men down. They don't like change an' it's gonna be hard to sell it to them."

"What about the idea of the roll-on roll-off flatracks?"

Shaw rolled his eyes.

"I haven't even mentioned those."

Collins could see he was getting impatient and wisely remained silent.

Another stevedore at the top of the table continued, "Flat racks are a coming thing in Britain and their usefulness is catching on. This method of loading means a lorry can carry its load directly to the buyer in specially designed ships. This cuts back the expense and damage and waiting when the load is handled in the conventional way. It's a coming system and I can't see it being delayed any longer."

Shaw burst in angrily.

"It's also a system that will cut to the bone the number of men employed on the quay. I have tried to explain to our people that the only ones who will suffer are the outsiders, but they're suspicious an' nat buyin' that argument at the moment. It's gonna be a long hard fight," he finished wearily.

A stevedore wearing a brown tweed jacket and smoking a briar pipe put his hand in the air.

"Can I say something?" he said through clenched teeth that were holding firmly to the pipe.

"The floor's yours," answered Collins politely.

"I think, and it's just a thought, mind you: if Mr. Shaw can't carry his members on these all important issues, then I believe we should consider our options with the cross channel labour force and open up discussions with the Irish Transport Dockers. There's also the potential of Larne as a port to equal, if not surpass, Belfast ... "

Shaw's features were livid with rage as he interrupted the speaker.

"An' I think on the basis of that conjecture I will advise my members that the stevedores have adopted a threatenin' posture wid regards to moving our work to another location. A few lightning strikes followed by a long term walk-out cud mebbe stop some of yew struttin' peacocks talkin' a lotta shite, an' enflaming what is already a dangerous situation," he snarled.

The stevedore was clearly taken aback by his anger.

"It was only a suggestion ... " he began.

Shaw stopped pushing papers into his briefcase and glared at the speaker with undisguised disgust.

"It wus more than a suggestion," he retorted angrily. "It wus an ultimatum! A gun to my head!"

He rounded angrily on Collins.

"I am a senior representative of the most powerful union branch in the country. I cud walk onto the Belfast cross-channel an' paralyse the port, just like that," he growled, contemptuously snapping his fingers. "I will nat be subject to threats from anyone."

Collins had never seen him so angry and turned desperately to the stevedores at the table, specifically addressing the man who had incurred Shaw's wrath.

"I'm sure our colleague was only speaking hypothetically. There is no way we would endanger the relationship between us and the dockers' union."

His eyes locked with the pipe smoker, who hastily agreed.

Shaw regained his composure.

"We know for a fact that the Irish transport union is having the same problems as us with regards to the acceptance of container and roll on/roll off traffic as it's come to be known. It's not beyond the realms of possibility that a merger between the two unions could scupper everybody's plans." He paused for effect and looked squarely into the faces that were gazing intently at him. "We're playin' fer high stakes here, gentlemen, an' I don't want to get mortally fucked in the process."

"Quite. Quite," Collins agreed nervously.

He turned again to the gathering who echoed his words.

Shaw smiled grimly and placed both hands on the top of the mahogany table as he continued to gaze at the men assembled around it.

"There are hard decisions to be taken, an' the red-button saga may pale into insignificance beside these new problems. I will do my best; but remember: the rights and privileges of my members will always be paramount," he finished grimly.

Collins nodded hastily as the union representative turned on his heel and walked angrily from the room.

As the office door slammed behind him, the pipe smoking stevedore looked around his colleagues.

"Arrrogant bastard, isn't he?"

The rest of the men agreed angrily.

"Aren't they all?" another mumbled.

Collins added a note of caution.

"That may be so, but we need that arrogant bastard and his members to get us through this awkward phase, so I would ask in future that you treat him as befits a man in his position. Leave the thought of Larne as a working port to another day. Okay?"

The men agreed without rancour.

Shaw leaned heavily against the bus stop. He hadn't anticipated the veiled threat from the stevedores and didn't regret his outburst. He was glad he had marked their cards.

"It's dog eat dog, an' nobody's gonna eat me," he muttered grimly to himself, causing a middle-aged woman also waiting for a trolley bus to stare at him.

Sammy Wilson woke to find his bed being wheeled from the ward by two nurses.

"Where are yew takin' me?" he asked uneasily.

The nurses smiled comfortingly.

"Yew are goin' to see Doctor Wassel."

Wilson lay back on the bed and closed his eyes. Moments later he felt himself being lifted from the bed and onto an operating table. He was surrounded by men and women wearing surgical robes and masks.

"There must be some mistake!" he cried. "I'm supposed to go home today."

"There is a tumour growing within you that has to be removed immediately," a tall and thinly built white haired man wearing half-moon spectacles replied, as he selected a surgical knife from a heap of shining implements.

Sammy tried to rise as the doctor held the knife above his head.

"Aren't yew goin' to knock me out first?" he yelled.

"No need to," the surgeon replied casually, as the point of the instrument hovered over the patient's heart. "We are going to slaughter you, because that's the only way to cure you. You have murdered and killed and killed and murdered, and now you are going to feel the pain and anguish of death."

"Why do yew want me dead?" Wilson screamed.

The surgeon threw off his white smock to reveal the uniform of a Nazi officer. The officer pulled away the face mask and exposed a blood-soaked throat that was ripped from ear to ear.

"You murdered me," snarled the surgeon.

Wilson fell back paralysed with fright. He saw the knife flash across his throat and watched his blood splash onto the doctor's face. He felt no pain or anger as everything went black.

"It was my job," he whispered fretfully. He was ashamed to find himself sobbing bitterly. "It wus my job an' I hadda do it," he cried defensively.

The surgeon's mouth worked silently, spewing live worms and maggots onto Wilson's chest and face. His features became a mass of festering putrid flesh as his body fell across Wilson's and his arms locked around him in a grotesque embrace. A large black battlefield rat emerged from his skull and proceeded to gnaw at Wilson's bloodied throat. As he tried to push the creature away, he awoke suddenly and found himself looking into Helen's frightened eyes. She held onto him tightly and kissed his bewildered face, as he tried forcefully to push her away from him.

"Another bad one?" she asked softly.

Wilson nodded mutely, and looked gratefully around him, as he tried to stop his body from trembling.

He lay still for a moment, glad to be safe in her arms and in his own bed. His heart pounded violently, and tears filled his eyes.

"They're getting' more frequent, aren't they?" she whispered sadly.

He nodded silently, unable to speak without sobbing.

"I thought yew'd layed all them ghosts. Now they seem to be back with a vengeance."

She looked into his glazed eyes with warmth and affection.

"Dreams can't kill yew, Sammy, neither can ghosts. Only pressure an' stress kin kill yew, an' at this moment in time they're yewr rale enemies, love."

As he lay in the comfort and protection of her arms, her words registered. He rose on one elbow and looked at her.

"When yew brought my bits an' pieces home from the hospital, was there a piece of blank paper wid my name on it?" he asked quietly.

She thought for a moment.

"Was that the piece of paper yew gat me to sign yewr name on?"

"Yis," he replied wearily. "Did yew bring it home?"

"No, it wusn't there. Was it important?"

He smiled mysteriously.

"It wus important yew didn't bring it home." He lay back on his pillow and smiled up at her.

"Y'know; yew're a wise oul girl," he grinned. "Yew hit the nail on the head. If they cudn't kill me on the battlefield, they won't kill me in a dream."

His pyjama top was unbuttoned and she gazed at the rake of

healed up bullet holes that stretched across his upper chest from one shoulder to the other. The sight never failed to cause her to shiver at how close she had come to losing him. He sensed her concern and covered up before pulling her playfully down beside him. As they lay face to face on the pillow, he gave her an affectionate hug.

"Anyway, I've sumpthin till tell yew about a couple a visitors I had last week when I wus in the hospital ... "

Jim Harvey sipped a glass of red wine as he watched Sally pack her suitcase. He had washed the salt dust from his body and dressed in his best clothes. He remembered with a wry smile how he had liberally splashed his face with the contents of a bottle of aftershave she had given him, and caused his mother and sister great amusement when he ran screaming to the sink as the burning liquid almost set his face on fire. He washed it off completely, not happy with the aroma that invaded his nostrils.

"Will you miss me?" asked Sally as she sat down beside him.

"Yis," he muttered sheepishly. As she moved closer to him he could see the dark shadows under her eyes, and knew she was still grieving for the loss of her father. He fingered the watch on his wrist. "Thank yew for everything. You've been very kind."

She reached out and held his hand.

"Jim: would you not reconsider? You have made me so very happy over this last week, and I want so much to repay you for your kindness and consideration. I have so much to give you."

He lowered his eyes.

"It's mum an' Lizzie ... I don't want a lave thim," he mumbled in the little boy voice she loved.

She threw her arms around him impulsively.

"But you won't be leaving them forever. You told me a few days ago you were considering joining the army. Wouldn't that be leaving them?"

He didn't reply as she held him possessively.

"Your mother wants you to go," she continued doggedly.

"She wants you away from the docks. She gave my idea her blessing the first time I met her."

Jim looked surprised.

"She seemed so concerned when I mentioned yewr offer," he answered in a confused tone.

"She wanted you to make up your own mind," Sally murmured. She kissed him lightly on the lips. "Give it some more thought. I'm arranging to have a telephone line put into your mother's house so I can call you and her on a daily basis. I'll also be returning as I want to know her better. That's if you don't mind ... "

Jim smiled gratefully. Sally rose and offered him another glass of wine which he declined.

"What wud I be doin' anyway?" he asked.

"Nothing elaborate or fancy," she replied. "I own a string of shops selling baby-wear. Six to be precise. I have staff to run them, as I do the book-keeping and buying. At the moment I use an outside firm to bring the merchandise, do deliveries and the like. I plan to buy a van, have you trained to drive it. Cut out the middle-man. I'll teach you the rudiments of the business and you can also do other bits and pieces, leaving me free to see the big picture."

She returned to her seat beside him.

"You'll be able to send your mum money every week. You won't be going home every night hurt and sore and wondering if there'll be a job tomorrow. You'll be able to speak to her on the telephone, whenever you feel like it, and you'll be able to give your boss all the comfort and love she needs, if you still find her attractive," she finished with an impish smile.

His answer was to cradle her gently in his arms and kiss her.

As she returned his caress, she knew she was deeply in love with him and prayed silently that he would take up her proposal.

She felt his hands begin to unbutton her blouse, and stopped him.

"Not here," she whispered, rising and leading him to the bedroom. "Let's make a night of it."

"What about your plane?" he muttered, concerned.

"I'll cancel the flight until tomorrow. What about your mother?" she countered with a slight smile.

He grinned cheekily.

"I think she'll know where I am, if I don't show up tonight," he laughed, as he felt her fingers undoing the buckle of his belt.

Sammy Wilson entered Pat's Bar cautiously. This was the first meeting to be called at night and he was concerned that some first-preference dockers would be still drinking in the quayside bar. He was relieved to see the bar was empty. He looked at his watch and saw it was seven-thirty. Seamus the barman turned his head in the direction of the upstairs lounge. Wilson ordered a half-pint of Guinness and nodded. He still felt weak from his hospital stay and hoped he'd be able to climb the steep stairs.

He was disappointed, but not surprised, to see only two men in the room. He sat down wearily.

"Where's the rest, Michael?" he muttered with a sigh.

"Josh didn't cum up from Ballyclare. Sees no point. He's tryin' fer a job on the council down there," replied a tall rangy man wearing a faded blue pair of bib and brace overalls over a washed-out woollen shirt with a frayed collar. "Shannon's nursin' a pair of badly lacerated han's thanks till a spell at the salt, an' Devlin's wife has tuk a heart attack. The rest have not made contact."

"Great," laughed Wilson mirthlessly, cradling his head in his hands.

"I think we shud make this the last meetin'," whispered the man in a checked shirt. "Everybody's watchin us, an' we can't trust anybody nigh."

"I agree," said his companion. "Anybody cud walk up them stairs ... " he added ominously.

Wilson rose.

"Follow me," he said tersely.

They left the bar and walked down Prince's Dock Street and stopped at St Joseph's.

"I can't go in there!" Michael gasped. "It's a chapel an' I'm an Orangeman!"

Wilson's laugh had a hollow ring to it.

"I'm an atheist. So if yew don't tell anyone, neither will I."

He smiled inwardly as Michael gulped and followed him into the darkness of the dockside church.

They sat down in a row of seats at the rear.

"We can't call a meetin' anyway. We haven't a quorum," Wilson said quietly.

Both men stared at him blankly. He began to explain, but was cut short.

"We know what a quorum is," Michael snarled. "We wanna know what yewr next move is. How do we git outa this?"

Wilson swallowed heavily. He addressed the tall man.

"The legality of what the Blues did is questionable and must be tested in the court of law—"

"But when?" broke in Michael impatiently. "We were of the opinion that this wud go to court quickly. We didn't anticipate the Blues puttin' the screws on us by leavin' us in the pen!"

"Mr. McCartan is explorin' every avenue an' attending the schoolin' pen every morning to monitor the bad practice, which is in breach of the union's policies ... "

"Tell that till the blues!" hissed Tam. "They're hangin' us out till dry! I haven't had a wage in a fortnight, even though I've attended the schoolin' pen twice a day, an' bin treated like I wus the invisible man."

"Aye, so wus the rest of us, except when it came till a murder picture like the salt or the rosey snatter boat," Michael sighed.

"Calm down, Tam," replied Wilson. "We don't want Father Mullen ejectin' us for disorderly behaviour," he laughed, trying to inject some humour into the situation.

It didn't work and he looked with concern at his comrades.

"We knew this wudn't be easy ... " he began.

Michael rose from his seat.

"I'm finished with it," he muttered in a defeated tone, before walking out into the street.

Wilson looked anxiously at the other man.

"Tam, yew an' Michael were the men who kept this runnin'. Yew tortured me to collect the money an' then seek legal advice. I've only dun what youse asked me to do, an' I'll be fucked if I accept all the blame."

He rose and glared angrily at the other man who refused to meet his gaze.

"This committee was prescribed by the majority of the reds. Officers like yew and I were duly and officially sworn in. They financed it weekly an' backed every move we made. Nobody said it wus goin' till be easy.

"Don't fergit the two lads who are takin' them till court are still in the ring. So are the various witnesses. We should salute their bravery and back them to the hilt. If we stop now, we'll have betrayed them an' Shaw will have bate us."

Tam raised his eyes.

"We're already bate. It cud take years till bring this case till court," he muttered resignedly.

Wilson could see the anguish in his eyes.

"I wish we'd niver went down that road," Tam added softly, before rising and leaving.

Wilson sat awhile on the bench looking at the spiritual icons of the Catholic faith. He resisted the temptation to mutter a prayer for deliverance and rose wearily from the bench and walked to the public phone boxes in the LMS railway station.

McCartan couldn't enlighten him on when the case would come up, only that it would eventually.

The lawyer could sense the despondency in the red-button man's voice.

"Look, Sam, I'm not going to lie to you. The law of the land has a mind of its own and doesn't work to suit anyone except those who administer it. The Bible says the mills of God grind slow, but I can tell you the mills of justice grind even slower. I will continue to monitor the schooling process until we do get a date for a hearing. I can't do any more," he finished apologetically.

Wilson thanked him and hung up.

"Neither can I. Mark up a victory for Shaw," he muttered sadly to the mute telephone and made his way home.

Shaw was also attending a meeting. A hastily convened general meeting in the function room of Transport House, and for once it wasn't going his way. The large room was packed. Many of the men had just come from their work and were in an angry mood. The worried faces at the committee table didn't boost his confidence.

They listened to the problems raised by Sid Maxwell, the man he had dealt with in his office a few days earlier. Sid's anger was unconcealed, as he addressed the meeting.

"Mr. Chairman, we arrived for work this mornin' at the cement boat in its new berth at Pollock six. We were tole a harbour crane would be dischargin' the cargo instead of the usual ship's winch. We were also tole," he continued as his voice rose in wrath, "that in the future there wud be no need for a hatchman, a winchman an' a bullrope man, an' that these men wud cease to be members of the traditional gang in two weeks' time when it was cleared with the branch. Add to that the fact that we will nat be needin' back-jaggers, an' any fool will see that the gang has been cut by five men. Also add to that fact that the six houlsmen are always outsiders. It seems the only ones being taken for a ride with these new rules is the genuine card-paying regulars. What's yer answer till that, Mr. Chairman?" he snarled before sitting down like a crouching tiger about to pounce again.

Shaw rose to reply. He looked directly at the last speaker.

"Where did yew hear this, Brother Maxwell?" he enquired.

"From the harbour crane driver who took great delight in tellin' us that pretty soon all cargo would be discharged by harbour authority cranes."

The body of the room growled disapproval. Shaw turned his gaze to the crowd.

"None of these contentious issues have been agreed," he said. "We are in the process of negotiating the situation, but as for here and now, nothing has been decided. I know the crane man concerned. He's a slabber. Always windin' our men up."

"Are yew sayin' he's talkin' shit?" Maxwell asked.

"I'm sayin' because a ship is in a crane berth doesn't mean it has till be serviced by a harbour crane, but in this instance, the breast of the quay is much broader than the old berth at the Gotto wharf. The shed is wider an' it's further for the men to run with the trucks. The crane can land the heave right at the door of the shed thus saving the shoremen from wheelin' trucks over crane cables and railway lines ... "

"But we won't be wheelin' trucks!" shouted Maxwell. "The forklift truck will be movin' the heaves."

"That's nat settled yet, an' yewr outa order," Shaw protested.

"Why can't our men drive the crane?" shouted a man from the back of the hall.

"The harbour allows only their own personnel in the cranes," Shaw retorted.

"How much an ire does the harbour office git fer dischargin' the ships?" called another man directly in front of him.

Shaw looked appealingly at the occupants of the packed room.

"I don't see how that matters," he said with exasperation in his voice.

Maxwell stood up.

"It matters immensely," he retorted; adding coldly, "That money will be taken from the price agreed to pay for the discharging of the ship. The cutback in our labour force flows from that. It's a case of simple arithmetic. The extra cost of the harbour crane and its operator is offset by the cutbacks just mentioned. We don't need a bullrope man, or hatchman or winch driver because the crane-driver can do all these things. Therefore they become surplus to requirements."

Shaw's arrogance returned with a vengeance.

"I tole yew we're in a fight till the death wid progress. We, as the elected representatives, are at the sharp end of this battle. This struggle is takin' place all over Britain, an' we can't be left behin'. It's a take and give tussle, an' I believe yew men should leave the committee to continue that fight."

Maxwell again rose to his great height.

"I agree wid the take an' the give bit. We do all the givin' an' they do all the takin'!" he snarled.

The crowd roared in agreement.

"Maybe yew kin do better?" replied Shaw sarcastically.

"Maybe," replied Maxwell calmly. He looked straight at Shaw. "Mr. Chairman, I propose a vote of no confidence in this committee, its secretary, and you."

"I second that proposal," came a dozen voices from the crowd.

Maxwell turned like a true leader and faced the men.

"Just one seconder, lads."

Charlie Goodall stood up on the chair.

"I second the proposal," he shouted above the noise.

"Any amendment to the proposal on the floor?" shouted Shaw as he felt the reins of authority slip from his grasp.

Billy Kelly's father raised himself slowly to his feet. He looked at Goodall with undisguised contempt.

"Mr. Chairman, old scores are being settled here for personal reasons and that doesn't augur well for the branch."

He turned a frosty gaze to Maxwell.

"I niver thought I'd see the day yew'd turn on yer own. Brother Shaw is in the process of negotiatin' more money for the men who work the cement. Okay, it's a smaller gang, but it's more money for less work for those who man it. That seems like nat a bad deal till me." He turned stiffly to the chairman. "I propose an amendment. That the committee ignore this spur of the moment nonsense an' git on wid negotiating a full and final settlement that will be to the good of all."

"I second that!" shouted a man beside him.

Shaw looked at the crowd on the floor with a sinking feeling.

"Okay," he said grimly. "A show of hands for the amendment."

He counted silently and was relieved that all the men didn't think like Maxwell.

"One hundred and fifty five for the amendment," he called after a detailed count. "For the proposal?" he muttered.

He gazed blankly at the sea of hands. Some minutes later he called, "Three hundred and twenty two votes."

"I propose Brother Maxwell for chairman," yelled Goodall.

His two sons nodded gleefully.

"Nigh all we need to do is git da back ontil the new committee," whispered the oldest brother.

"I take great pleasure in seconding that," called another docker dressed in a bib and brace set of overalls.

"Seconded by Brother Lowery. Any other nominations?"

The sea of faces was silent.

"All in favour?" asked Shaw in a muted tone. The crack of his gavel was drowned out by the roar of approval that echoed around the building.

The room became silent as he offered the gavel to Maxwell.

"Will yew step forward and elect yewr committee, Mr. Chairman?"

Maxwell moved to the table and addressed the crowd.

"Can I say before we go any further—any man who is nat a member of a trade union will not be given a job on Belfast cross channel docks. An' any ganger who gives a job till an outsider before the first-preference men have been accommodated will be up in fronta the green table the next day, an' fined or disciplined accordingly."

The crowd roared its approval. He waved the gavel for silence.

"After thankin' the previous chairman an' committee for his sterling service to this branch, I now declare all offices open."

Shaw sat in dumbfounded silence, completely ignored, as the new committee was voted in, man by man. He failed to see Todd Hamill, who had infiltrated the proceedings, leaving the room with a smug, satisfied grin

Wilson entered the Sportsman's Arms slowly and quietly. Paddy looked up from the pint barrels and smiled in his direction.

"Welcome stranger. I though yew'd emigrated!" he called loudly.

Wilson grinned embarrassedly and climbed onto a bar stool.

"Money's tight," he muttered almost apologetically.

"Nat fer some people," muttered the barman as he nodded in the direction of a group of first-preference men.

Wilson didn't look round.

"Aye, it's bin three weeks since the new committee wus

voted in. Hasn't made much difference till our lot," he muttered as Paddy sat a half of Guinness in front of him. "I still go down on a point a principle, but my services are nat required. I think a pregnant old age pensioner with an artifical leg an' no arms wud git a check in fronta me."

"What about Kelly?" asked Paddy, quickly changing the subject.

Wilson took a grateful sip of his Guinness.

"He called into see me a few times when I was ill, but since his father was put off the committee I haven't seen hide or hair of him. He hasn't bin the same man since Minnie's da slapped his jaws."

"He wus a lucky man till git away wid that," replied Paddy.

Wilson grimaced. "If he hadn't bin Minnie's da, he'd be lying in the hospital, or the morgue," he replied grimly.

Paddy nodded in agreement, but brightened considerably as he continued, "Wee Harvey has landed on his feet. Apparently Reiley's daughter's a high falutin' businesswoman in London an' she wants till take him on in her firm across the water ... "

"Is he goin'?" queried Wilson.

"Don't know," replied the barman. "He's kinda worried about lavin' his ma. He wus in the other day, an' tole me all about it. Sally's away back a fortnight ago. Apparently, she gat a telephone put in his house an' she phones him every day."

Wilson smiled into his glass as he lifted it to his lips.

"He's fell lucky," he murmured without malice.

Paddy nodded.

"I felt like grabbin' him by the throat an' tellin' him till git over there pronto. It's nat every day somethin' like that lands in yer lap."

Wilson grinned at the unwitting pun despite his problems.

"Aye. Yew'r right there."

He fell silent as a first-preference docker walked to the bar and stood beside him. The man's face was gaunt and tired. A grey cap was pulled down over his forehead and a heavy black donkey jacket covered a thick army surplus shirt. He leaned on the bar beside Wilson.

"Can I buy yew a drink?" he asked sincerely

He reacted to the surprised look on Wilson's face by continuing, "We're nat all against yis. Every man at my table has nuthin' but admiration fer yis. Especially yew. Yis are experienced dockers an' shuda gat in before some a them wee arrogant gabshites who tuk yewr places."

"Why don't yis do somethin' till help us?" replied the red-button man.

His companion shrugged his shoulders.

"We can't. We've sounded out a few other groups, but we're very much in the minority. We thought things wud change wid Shaw outa the drivin' seat, but it's much the same. The new committee all have sons who are reds, an' they'll surely git in in the next bunch. Goodall has already proposed his remaining two lads. Nat much chance for anyone that's nat family. Yew know how it is."

Wilson smiled sadly.

"Yis," he concurred, without rancour. "Thanks, anyway."

"Will yew have that drink?" repeated the docker.

"Yis," replied Wilson, not wanting to offend the man. He shrugged his shoulders at Paddy's curious stare. He drank it quickly and left for home.

Helen watched as he walked into the kitchen and sat down on his chair. She moved to switch off the radio, but he grabbed her hand as she passed.

"Let it stay," he whispered. "I like that song. It reminds me of our courtin' days."

She moved to the fireplace and lifted a letter from behind the clock.

"That came for yew in the second post."

He stared at the letter, noting his address was typewritten on the front. Helen sat down beside him.

"Aren't yew goin' till open it?" she asked.

"It's awful official lukin'," he stammered.

She took the envelope from him and tore it open before handing it back.

"It's probably a bill," she exclaimed.

He drew out one neat typewritten page.

"It's from a grammar school in a place called Garston, in Liverpool," he said vaguely as he read the contents. She watched his eyes narrow and his brows knit as he read the contents. She rose and walked behind his chair and began reading over his shoulder.

Dear Mr. Wilson,

On behalf of the Board of Governors, I am pleased to inform you that your application for the post as full-time live-in janitor at Craigborough Grammar School has been successful.

We would normally recruit locally, but in view of your excellent references and the fact that you are a decorated veteran of the recent war, the board are in no doubt that you are the man for the job.

It is a permanent post with a non-contributory pension scheme.

In view of your wounds, I can assure you your duties will not be arduous. Any heavy labouring work will be the responsibility of two assistant handymen.

We are, furthermore, delighted to offer a position in our school canteen for your wife if she is agreeable.

As you are aware, the position also includes a four bedroom fully-furnished house in the school grounds.

A small donation will be deducted from your salary each week and will be added to a larger remuneration from the school to provide a home of your own when you reach retirement age. This can be purchased in any part of Britain or in your home town of Belfast should you wish to return there to enjoy your remaining years.

With regard to your children, I wish to assure you that they will be adequately provided for at nearby primary schools.

There will be a small motor van at your disposal, which you can use for your own purposes when it is not needed for school business.

The Board of Governors will, of course, reimburse you all

reasonable relocation expenses for you and your family to move to Garston should you accept the position.

Please reply in writing or by telephone as soon as possible and I will draw up the necessary contract for you to sign.

I remain,
Yours truly
Thomas Calvin Cantrell
Chairman of the Board of Governors
Craigborough Grammar School
Garston, Liverpool.

Helen looked at him in disbelief.

"When did yew apply for that?" she asked.

"I didn't!" he whispered as he continued to stare impassively at the letter.

Helen put her hand over her mouth.

"The men in the hospital?" she cried. "The blank page?"

"They filled it in, an' provided the references," he said quietly, glad he had told her the full story. "It's a letter from Daddy Christmas."

She looked into his face.

"Are yew goin' to take it?"

He stared into the fire.

"I would feel like I've let the squad down."

She sat on his lap and took his hand.

"The squad are not yewr responsibility."

She reached up and took the children's photograph from the mantelpiece.

"They are," she added softly. "Get yewr priorities right."

He raised his troubled glance from the fireplace and looked into her eyes.

"No contest," he replied grimly. "Git packin' whilst I git a pen an' some paper."

The feelings of guilt evaporated as he strode to the cupboard on the wall.

Eleven

HENRY SHOWED THE SUMMONS TO THE police officer on the door of Glengormley courthouse. He followed the constable's directions and found himself in a courtroom crowded with relatives and friends, including his mother. They cheered as he entered, causing the usher to call for quiet.

"How did yew know I was cumin' here the day?" he growled as he sat down beside his mother.

"Wasn't I in the house two weeks ago when the constable left the summons in?"

"An' yew read it when I was out an' wired off all these head-the-balls. Luk, ma," he muttered seriously, "I'll jist git a small fine, so keep them-ins quiet, or I'll git six months."

"Yill git what yew deserve," replied his mother primly.

The resident magistrate entered and Henry almost fainted when he saw it was the judge from the Midland Hotel. After three or four legally represented cases, his name was called and he walked to the dock.

The magistrate lifted his head from his paperwork and their eyes met. He nodded Henry to him.

"Have we met before?" asked the magistrate in a nervous voice. Henry smiled demurely as if he had nothing to lose.

"Yis, sor. The last time we were together yew tole me to call yew Honey. But yewr secret is safe wid me, sor, no matter what transpires today," he added with a wink.

The judge grimaced and returned quickly to his papers.

Henry walked to the dock whilst the clerk of the court read out the charges. The magistrate listened intently whilst

279

studying the figure in the box. He was concentrating so hard he failed to hear a female voice call to him from the body of the court. He grew angry when he saw the usher take hold of an elderly woman.

"What are you doing, man?" he called.

"They won't let me give evidence, sor," cried the woman.

"That's me mother, sor," whispered Henry.

"Bring the lady to the front of the court and don't manhandle her. If she wishes to give evidence, no one should stop her."

"But you haven't heard all the charges, your worship," whispered the court clerk.

The judge beckoned the official to him.

"You know I am standing in for the Right Honourable Hector Hemingway who suffered a fall whilst riding to hounds yesterday?"

The clerk nodded dumbly.

"Then let me conduct the court," hissed the magistrate through clenched teeth.

The official moved backwards silently, nodding his head.

The judge turned his glance to Harvey's mother.

"Swear the lady in," he ordered curtly.

After the clerk had done so, the magistrate continued, "Now madam, tell us your name and let us hear your evidence."

Mrs. Harvey curtsied.

"Thank yew, kind sor. I'm called Mary Harvey an' I jist wanted till tell yew that my son is a hero, nat a criminal. When the funeral was movin' outa Henry Street, a wild horse pullin' a cart full a bales of tow an' driven by a carter fulla poteen an' whiskey, stampeded intil the funeral an' wuda killed some a the mourners, only fer my Henry. Without regard fer his own safety, he leaped ontil the horse's neck and pulled it till the groun' an' held it there till the coffin and the mourners gat by. He's a hero, sor, an' he's being treated as a criminal. The peelers arrested the carter, but they didn't even thank my Henry."

The judge glared at the police officer who was presenting the case.

"Is this true?" he asked.

The officer looked worriedly at his notes.

"I'm not aware of it sor. It happened outside my jurisdiction ... "

Pushing his half-moon glasses further up his nose, the judge beckoned him with his forefinger.

"And where is the drunken carter?" he asked belligerently.

"The horse was drunk as well," ventured Mary Harvey helpfully.

"Was the horse also under the influence, as this lady says?" continued the judge with disbelief in his voice.

"That incident didn't happen in this jurisdiction, therefore I can't answer the question," stammered the officer.

"And who can answer the question? Whose jurisdiction did it happen in?" asked the judge patiently, with an angry scowl on his features. He and the occupants of the courtroom watched as the prosecutor flicked through his notes.

"We're waiting," hissed the judge ominously.

"I believe the incident happened in the York Street area policed by Head Constable McKinstry, and it is as the lady described."

"And this man, this brave man, is being prosecuted?"

"Not for that, your worship. He was arrested for disorderly behaviour in Carnmoney cemetery."

The judge looked at the speaker in disbelief.

"Are my ears deceiving me?" he snarled. "How can one be disorderly in a graveyard?"

"He assaulted two gravediggers, your worship."

The judge smiled grimly.

"Now we're getting somewhere. Where are the gravediggers?"

The prosecutor grinned nervously.

"They sent in sicklines. Apparently their nerves have been affected by the ordeal ... "

"Were they physically hurt?" the magistrate interrupted.

"Not really, your honour."

"They hit my Henry wid their shovels," broke in Mary Harvey, rather demurely.

"Is this true?" asked the judge.

"The men dropped their shovels as they ran from Harvey's onslaught," replied the police officer.

The judge wasn't listening. He was consulting his notes on the case. He raised his head and peered over his spectacles at the prosecutor.

"From what I read, they attacked Mr. Harvey first," he scowled.

Mrs. Harvey started to cry.

"My Henry tried till stap a man kickin' the coffin intil the grave and the gravediggers attacked him, sor."

"They were only tryin' to restrain him. His clothes were covered in blood," retorted the constable.

"It wus blood from the dumb animal, yer worship. My Henry had till hurt it till subdue it!" wailed the old woman.

"I've heard enough. This man has obviously saved lives by his quick and courageous action. It's a disgrace that he finds himself facing a charge of disorderly behaviour," the judge said, as he took a pen from a waistcoat pocket on his tweed suit.

He looked at the body of the court.

"I find the defendant not guilty of all charges."

The court erupted as the onlookers clapped and cheered. The judge waited patiently until the room fell silent before continuing.

"The cost of the court shall be paid by the prosecution, and they shall also take five guineas from their resources and pay it to Mr. Harvey as a token of gratitude toward his act of bravery which should be rewarded and not punished."

He smashed the gavel on the bench.

"Case dismissed," he called, with an admiring side glance at the grinning Henry.

McKinstry received the news with a furious scowl. He never expected to see a High Court judge sit in for a resident magistrate.

"They must be in the same Masonic Lodge," he scowled to the policeman on the phone. His anger turned to amusement as the constable related the proceedings.

"Don't worry," he muttered soothingly. "That big bastard Harvey'll think he's above the law now. But he's gonna slip up sooner or later and when he does ... I'll have him."

He put the phone down and lit a cigarette. It rang again. He recognised the soft voice of his superior.

"Congratulations seem to be in order, David. It's been five weeks from the original fracas on the docks, and three weeks without any shape or form of trouble. Am I right?"

The Head complied with a grunt. The voice on the other end of the phone continued.

"McCartan persists in making a nuisance of himself and continues to bombard the head of the union concerned with letters that threaten legal action. He has had local members of Parliament table questions to the Minister at Stormont. Craig, the minister of labour, successfully batted these into touch by refusing to comment on what is technically a labour dispute. And as the case is heading for court, he is quite within his rights to make no comment on it. Trouble like this is rearing its head all over Britain and the trade union involved is big enough to take care of itself."

"Precisely," agreed McKinstry.

"We are told the Prime Minister is happy with the new agreement re the ICTU. He believes the new Northern Ireland Committee of Trade Unions will keep Eire from poking its unwelcome nose into our affairs this side of the border, and that can't be bad. Can it David? Your efforts in keeping the trouble to a minimum, especially the quick release without charges, of the German sailors, ensured the so-called labour revolt received little attention in the newspapers. Therefore those who opposed the trade union alliance with the government of Northern Ireland, on political grounds, have no axe to grind. That also can't be bad, can it, David?

"Incidentally, the West German ambassador in London took a very dim view of the merchant sailors' behaviour in Belfast: especially on the week their navy was in the port to honour the dead of both world wars. He sends his deepest gratitude for our decision not to prosecute and thus embarrass his divided country. The seamen concerned have been sent home in disgrace. They will be dismissed from merchant service and will no longer be a threat to innocent civilians here, or anywhere else in the world."

McKinstry's smile was genuine.

"That's good news, sir."

"Your part in stopping it going pear-shaped won't be forgotten. Look forward to some welcome news in the coming post. Goodbye."

"Thank you," replied the head constable, softly and politely as a large self satisfied smirk crept across his face.

Kelly left the American Bar and began to walk toward Tommy Allen's barber shop in Dock Street. He felt like a relaxing shave and no one could perform that task better than Tommy. On a sudden impulse he looked backwards and his glance took in the grey coloured transit sheds behind him. He turned and began walking towards them. Crossing over to the gates that marked the entrance to the York dock, he nodded at the harbour police officer on duty close by. The memory of his first job as a docker had rekindled, and he decided to take a few moments to replenish it. The shave could come later.

Walking through the huge wooden doors he was taken back in time. It was 1948 and he had received his first check. The job was a minor one: loading empty beer bottles from the shed into the hatch of a boat lying against the breast of the jetty. His father had taken leave of absence from his permanent job at the Clyde boat in order to instruct his son on the basic tenets of dock labour. Both men went behind a truck and loaded the crates into a rope sling lying across its base. Each truck was worked by a trio of men. His father had introduced him to the man whose job was to pull the truck, after they had loaded it, across the cobbled floor to the narrow breast where the ship's hook would lift the heave of crates and lower it into the ship's hold.

There were many other first time blue-button men, being blooded by their fathers in the two gangs, and an atmosphere of family and comradeship evolved. The camaraderie reminded him of the army life he had reluctantly left to please his father.

During the first few hours the men found time to laugh and talk to each other. He remembered his father pointing out the local characters, and smiled as visions floated around his head. Jimmy Engine: a trucker so called because of the perspiration that floated from his body on the cold air like the steam from the funnel of a train when he pulled the truck back and forth from the pile. Apple Johnny: an outsider who ended every sentence with the adage 'wee apples grow big'. Onion Melvin, who was caught with four Spanish onions on his person. The arresting constable had locked him in the hut to go for another officer to escort Melvin to the station. When he returned, Melvin had eaten the evidence, skins and all, and gained a nickname that stayed with him all his life.

The bottle boat had moved elsewhere and the shed was now filled with sacks of potatoes. He breathed in the earthy smell as he moved slowly up the waterside of the shed. He paused at an open door and stood for a moment on the narrow breast before sitting on top of an adjacent bollard. He eyed the ships from various nations loading or discharging cargo all along the narrow basin.

He had joined an exclusive money-making club that day and hated every moment of it. He had tried hard to fit in because he loved his father and desperately wanted to please him. He glanced down the basin and saw the ship his father would be working at. Although over seventy, the old man had no thoughts of retirement. The dock was not only his work; it was his social life and the only reason for his continued existence.

Kelly grinned in bittersweet recollection of the time he had asked his father to quit. His reaction had been one of astonishment. He well remembered his words.

"Retire? Why shud I retire. Shure I'm only a nipper compared till some of my mates. Bouncer Withers is pushing seventy-five and kin still pull a loaded truck faster than some a the young 'uns, an' wud knock you on yewr arse if yew spoke outa line. Ivan Foster 'ill be ninety in a few weeks time an' he kin work wid the best of them!"

He felt a tap on his shoulder and turned to see Jim Harvey, whose face was covered in potato dust and concern.

"Are yew alright, Billy?" he asked haltingly. "One a the boys saw yew sittin' on the boll and ... "

285

Kelly cut him short with a grin.

"Don't worry. I ain't gonna jump in. I'm reminiscing. This is where I gat my first job on the quay. Johnny Robinson's bottle boat."

He looked at Jim quizzically.

"Do yew know Ivan Foster's over ninety and still pullin' a truck at the Clyde boat?" Kelly asked.

Jim shook his head.

"I thought ye had till retire at sixty-five."

Kelly looked at the ships lined against the harbour walls.

"Nat on Belfast docks, yew don't. Oul dockers don't retire. They keep goin' till they run outa steam or seize up. That's what's gonna happen till my da, nigh that he's bin voted off the committee," he added bitterly.

Harvey could see the alcohol was making him melancholy. He changed the subject.

"A lat a the boys haven't seen much of yew this last few weeks."

"I've bin keepin' myself till myself. Gat some thinkin' till do," Kelly replied wearily. He rose from the bollard. "Y'know I wus jist headin home from the Yankee when all these memories started floodin' back." He rose and smiled at the youngster. "What's this I hear about yew goin' till London till be a big tycoon?"

He laughed at the flush of embarrassment that filled Jim's face. His own face tightened as he continued, "Go boy. In five or ten years' time dockwork is goin' to be hauled into the twentieth century an' there's gonna be little work here for the dockers—let alone anyone else. Git out while yew can. Shure yew kin always come back if yew don't like it."

He prodded Jim playfully.

"Go an' ask Henry till let yew away for a few minits. I want ta buy yew a drink."

"Henry's at Glengormley court. I'll ask the checker if he kin do widout me for a wee while."

Kelly nodded.

"Tell him yer doin' me a turn. He'll nat refuse yew."

Seamus nodded a greeting and moved to serve them as

they entered Pat's Bar. As they sat down with their drinks, Jim spoke.

"What did yew mean when yew say there'll be no work?"

"It's simple logic, son. The war's bin over about fifteen years now. Wars are fought to make rich men richer an' ta cull the manhood of the human race. The last war was fought wid weapons more superior than the ones my dad and your granda had in the previous conflict. The boffins who were building the weapons and armaments have now turned their talents to cutting back on the expense of manual labour. Instead of making machines that kill, they're now producing industrial equipment that will do manual work in a faster an' chaper way. Like the forklift trucks that are now creepin' ontil the quay. Add to that the cargoes being shipped in containers. Nat a lot at the moment, I grant yew. But there's new overhead cranes being built at the Herdman channel an' it doesn't take a fortune teller to forecast that in a few years' time this place will be hummin' wid the roar of machinery doin' our work.

"London and Liverpool dockers resisted this technology as long as they cud, knowin' it would sound the death knell of labour as we know it. Now it's spreadin' like a disease all over Britain and the rest of the world."

"Can't the union do anything about it?"

Kelly smiled grimly.

"The union 'ill be too busy lukin' after its own to have any concerns about anyone else. The outgoin' chairman an' his committee cudn't stap it. Neither will the new lot. Deals will be made an' the Arabs 'ill be the first casualties. They'll be chased from the quay in the name of economy an' progress, an' their jobs will be taken by first-preference men, who'll proceed to change the direction of labour to suit themselves. Any work they don't fancy, they'll refuse to do, or ask for exorbitant wages till do it, an' the shippin' agents will transfer it to the Irish Transport dockers who'll be only too glad to take it. That way the first-preference men will be in control of events. They'll be a workforce that is entirely subservient an' loyal to the branch first an' the trade union second. Naw," he concluded wearily, "Git out boy! Git out while the goin's good.

Take up Sally's generous offer. She's made sumptin' of herself an' she wants till make sumpthin' of yew. Don't let her down. Yewr only a number here son, an' a very low number at that."

Jim digested his words as he rose to order another drink. They were chilling in their context, and slightly unbelievable. He didn't think a machine could do the work of a man, but he didn't venture an opinion as he sat down with the drinks. Kelly tossed the whiskey down his throat and rose to leave. He pushed his cap to the back of his head and looked squarely into Jim's face. His grey eyes were expressionless, but his voice held a quiet menace as he muttered, "Take Sally's offer. If yew don't; I'll cum lookin' fer yew to bate sixteen different colours a shit outa yewr stupid carcass. Heed what I say," he said, as he angrily rose to leave the bar.

"If my father was alive today, I wud do anything fer him."

Kelly stopped in mid-stride as Jim's softly spoken words hit him like a punch in the mouth. He turned angrily.

"What are yew gittin' at, kid?"

Jim's voice trembled as he continued, "If my father was not lying in a grave in Carmoney, but wurkin' yards away at the Clyde boat I wud run down that road an' greet him wid tears in my eyes, an' I wud do anything he asked of me, widout question."

Kelly grabbed him savagely by the shirt front and smashed him against the barroom wall. Seamus stopped drying a pint tumbler and watched silently, as did the smattering of men in the pub.

Jim trembled but continued to stare back defiantly at Kelly's enraged stare. He saw what looked like tears in his bewildered eyes. The grip on his shirtfront relaxed. Kelly continued to look at him for what seemed like an eternity, before he completely released his grip.

"Why don't yew go an' talk till him, Billy? He needs yew more than ever nigh that the rest of his world's fell apart," Jim pleaded softly.

Kelly closed his eyes and shook his head violently from side to side.

"He won't talk till me," he muttered.

"He will, if yew do the right thing. He loves yew and no cause or principle shud separate a man from those he loves," Harvey whispered.

Kelly lowered his head and walked slowly into the street. The drinkers continued to watch as Jim finished his drink with shaking hands and rose to leave. Seamus eyed him as he walked past.

"Yew've gat balls to burn, boy," he said admiringly.

Kelly continued through the harbour gates and into the ITL café just past the Ministry of Agriculture's potato examining depot. He walked through the tables filled with dockers, carters and harbour employees, and joined a queue at the counter.

"Egg soda an' a mug a tea," he muttered tersely to the girl who moved to serve him.

He saw a vacant seat and nodded at the other occupants of the table.

"Where are yew the day, Billy?" one said conversationally.

He waited until he swallowed a mouthful of soda before answering tonelessly, "Nowhere, Tony. I'm takin' a couple a days off till sort a few things out."

"How's yewr da feelin' now he's off the committee?" asked another. Kelly paused in mid-bite and gazed coldly at the speaker. "How wud yew feel if everythin' yew valued in life was taken from yew? He's gutted, but he's still out there. He's a man a principle. A better man than yew an' I will ever be, an' they can't take that away from him."

The men at the table judged his mood and wisely left him to eat the rest of his meal in silence. He moved from the table with an acknowledging grunt and walked into Pilot Street. A ship's winch roared and he watched a single derrick swing shorewards and land a heave of flour onto a waiting truck about fifty yards from where he was standing. He stood for a moment or two before walking into the Rotterdam public house next door to the café.

Apart from a couple of men playing darts at the other end of the room, the bar was deserted. He waited until the balding and bespectacled middle-aged owner looked in his direction.

"Givus a Black Bush, Joe," he said courteously, despite the anger within him.

The barman, wearing a white shirt with a blue necktie, and a black apron tied around his waist, smiled warmly.

"Comin' up, Billy."

Joe Donnelly kept a strict house and only those who obeyed his rules were allowed to drink in his bar.

"How's yewr father?" he said conversationally as he sat the drink down.

Kelly smiled, knowing his concern was genuine.

"He's bearin' up, considerin'," he replied softly.

Donnelly returned the smile.

"That goes widout sayin'. Once a gentleman, always a gentleman! It's their loss. Yer dad shud put his feet up an' enjoy life nigh that he's nat spoon-feedin' an' wet nursin' them load a hallions."

Kelly nodded thankful agreement as the barman moved off and left him to his thoughts. He hadn't the heart nor the inclination to mention that his father and he were not on speaking terms.

Harvey's words had cut him deeply. He realised how his father was held in high esteem even by those who disagreed with his principles. He knew the old man needed his support during this period in his life and wondered why he had allowed their relationship to drift. Both were guilty of care and concern for their fellow human beings, but in different ways. The branch meetings were the only functions his father attended. He dressed in his best suit, brushed his shoes till they shone and wore a collar and tie each time he went there.

Kelly looked around the low-ceilinged bar room with its darkened exterior. A little snug just beside the main door was used by people who wanted to drink in private. Billy Kelly senior favoured this pub when he was drinking. He remembered his first drink with his father had been in this very bar. Joe had fixed him with a quizzical yet amused stare as he set up the pint shandy.

"Yewr father's a true gentleman. Drunk or sober. I hope yew'll be the same."

Billy knew his cards were being marked in the time honoured tradition of the dockside community. Like father, like son! He nodded vigorously at the time. Now he wasn't so sure.

The bar was spotlessly clean, and the red and black tiled floor would soon be covered by the feet of the men from the flour boat who chose to slake their thirst with beer instead of tea. Taking a crumpled envelope from his pocket he withdrew a typewritten letter he had found in the hall of Reilly's house when he rose that morning. It bore his own address and he knew his father had thrown it through the letter box on his way to work. Taking a swallow from his whiskey, he read it for the second time. It was headed TRANSPORT HOUSE, HIGH STREET, BELFAST.

Dear Sir and Brother,

You have been summoned before this committee to answer to disciplinary charges brought against you by the dock foreman whom you viciously assaulted some time ago. This is a serious charge and could warrant the loss of your membership of this branch and all the benefits that go with it.

The previous committee has bent over backwards in an effort to appease you because of the high esteem in which your father, William Kelly senior, is held. However, there is no room in this branch for undisciplined members who bring it and the broader trade union movement into general disrepute.

As I'm sure you are aware there are many men who would willingly adhere to the principal tenets as laid down by the branch with regards to the behaviour of its members, in exchange for the high quality of work and earnings this membership brings to those who earnestly and conscientiously strive to work within its parameters.

Your assault on a brother carrying out his duties, and your recent support for those who would destroy the very fabric of our branch cannot be tolerated any further. However, because of the tremendous respect in which this branch holds your father, I've been instructed to tell you that:

—A verbal apology to the Brother you assaulted is requested and will be accepted.

—A formal and written assurance that you will desist in the future from assisting or associating with those who would destroy the branch and all it stands for by legal or any other means is requested and will be accepted.

Adherence to these requests will allow you to resume your privileges and responsibilities as a member of this branch. This letter, if tendered to the chairman of the branch committee within three days of this date, will cancel the disciplinary hearing and allow you to retain your status as a card carrying member with all the benefits it brings to you and those who come behind you.

Failure to comply will result in a date being set for a disciplinary hearing that, under the circumstances, will undoubtedly result in you being dismissed from the branch and barred from working on Belfast Docks. You will also be denied membership of any other section of this great and sovereign trade union.

I am

Yours etc.

Brother Sid Maxwell

Chairman

"Nat an unreasonable request, under the circumstances," he thought solemnly as he folded the letter and he finished his drink. It would also perhaps mend his relationship with Minnie's father. Shrugging his shoulders wearily in confusion, he left with Joe's warm words of farewell being cut short as the bar room door closed. He smiled tightly as he realised how much moral fibre Jim Harvey had to say the things he did.

"Maybe it wasn't courage," he thought as he walked aimlessly down Pilot Street. "Maybe they are the words of a friend trying to steer someone he cares for in the right direction." He felt shame at his reaction to Jim's courageous outburst. He stopped at Tommy Allen's barber shop. When his turn came he settled wearily into the chair. As the elderly proprietor wound a white sheet around him, he gazed at his reflection in the mirror.

"Just a shave, Tommy," he muttered tonelessly. He continued to look at his reflection as Tommy skilfully soaped his stubble.

There was little talk as the barber sensed his mood.

Kelly opened the door of his newly acquired home. Entering the small kitchen he lit the mantle before wearily falling onto the sofa. He looked around the room and realised how much he missed his own home. A piece of paper protruding from beneath one of the frayed cushions caught his eye. He absently pulled it free and began to read the handwritten message:

Deepest sympathy on the sudden and untimely death of your beloved father. We know how much you loved and cared for him. How he idolised you. And how proud he was of you. No words from us can describe the pain you must be feeling at this sad time being parted from each other. You are in our thoughts and prayers. May God bless and comfort you, through this time of grief.

He knew the letter was meant for Sally Reilly, but it suddenly and forcefully brought home to him the depth of his deepening feud with the father he loved and idolised. Jim Harvey's words came back to him.

"If my father was not lying in a grave in Carmoney, but wurkin' yards away at the Clyde boat I wud run down that road an' greet him wid hugs an' tears in my eyes, an' I wud do anything he asked of me, widout question. He loves yew and no cause or principle should separate a man from those he loves."

He put the card on the table, and tried to muffle with his hands the deep sobs that seemed to come from his heart and filled his eyes with tears that streamed down his cheeks. He walked slowly to the outside toilet and brought the Walther pistol back in with him. He laid it in the palm of his outstretched hand and looked coldly at it. He saw for a split second the blown away face of the Nazi soldier. With a sudden movement, he grabbed the slide and pulled it back savagely to put a round into the chamber. He slid the safety catch forward and pulled back the hammer. Almost nonchalantly, he placed the barrel of the weapon below his right ear, and took his index finger from the side of the weapon, onto the trigger.

As his finger slowly tightened, he heard a knock on the front door. The noise brought him back to reality. Taking his finger from the trigger he pushed the hammer forward gently. He engaged the safety catch and placed the gun beneath the cushion on the sofa, before rising to open the door.

Sammy Wilson gazed at him with concern. He walked silently up the hall as Kelly closed the door behind him.

"I'm gittin' out," said Wilson tersely, as they sat down facing each other.

Kelly said nothing, as his visitor continued.

"Young Harvey called to see me. He's worried about yew."

Kelly rose and walked to the scullery, emerging a few minutes later with two glasses of whiskey.

"A farewell drink?" he muttered dryly, as Wilson at first refused and then changed his mind.

"I don't drink spirits, but today I'll make an exception," he said lamely.

"Where are yew goin'?" Kelly asked as he swirled the whiskey in the glass before taking a mouthful.

"Garston, in Liverpool," he replied quietly.

"Did they git to yew?"

"Yis," he said simply and sadly.

He looked at his companion defensively and eyed the drink warily before taking a sip that caused him to screw up his face.

"Yew understand, don't yew?" he asked anxiously. "I had to weigh up the situation, an' think of my own family. Helen read the letter the same time I did, so I had no choice. I wudn't have run otherwise."

Kelly rose and emptied his glass. He crossed the room and sat down beside his friend.

"Yew niver ran away in yewr life; jist moved to a better

foxhole!" he replied with a warm grin. "No one can fault yew for that."

Wilson smiled gratefully.

"Remember the time we landed in Normandy in a glider that left us miles away from our estimated drop zone?" he asked as Kelly looked at him blankly. "We came upon a French farm and stole a coupla chickens to cook an' eat as we were starvin'."

Kelly recollected the occasion and smiled broadly.

"Aye; the farmer's wife came out an' ate the balls of us. She said the Germans had been there for years an' niver once stole from them. We were only there ten minutes an' we were neckin' her livestock. She then proceeded till chase us outa the farmyard: an'our platoon, armed till the teeth, ran like greyhoun's till get away from her."

Wilson laughed.

"We used the manual. When faced wid a superior enemy, there's a time till fight an' a time till run."

Both lapsed into silence savouring the memory of a far away day.

"I brought that incident up because I think it's time fer yew till run, Billy. This isn't yewr fight. Under the circumstances, it shudn't have bin anybody's fight. A lot of the reds who were in good jobs before this dispute are now openly questioning the validity of our action. McCartan's heart's in the right place, but he doesn't understand the nature of the monster he's tryin' to subdue. It has tentacles that stretches aroun' the wurld. We cud niver bate it. Wound it slightly mebbe: but it'll eat us before it's through. To be fair till him, though: we brought him intil it and he certainly hasn't let us down. He's bin chasin' everybody from union bosses till members of Parliament. An' it's nat as if we give him a whole latta money till begin with."

Kelly nodded agreement.

"Maybe it wudn't a started if Shaw hadn't bin so quick to take the paybook in the first place," he murmured.

"We'll niver know, nigh," replied Wilson sadly.

Kelly didn't answer. Both men enjoyed the silence as Wilson chose his moment.

"There's another reason I decided to git out, an' it concerns yew," he murmured.

"Go on," replied Kelly tersely, staring at his whiskey glass.

"Yewr puttin' yewr job on the line to protect me. I'm the only survivor from the platoon. An' that's the reason yew signed up for a grievance that shudn't concern yew. I certainly appreciate yewr concern, but cannot allow yew to wreck yewr own life. It also makes me feel responsible for the rift between yew an' yewr father."

Kelly rose and filled the two glasses. Wilson had no hesitation in accepting his. He felt he might need it as he continued, "Remember, towards the end of the war when the lads ran into a minefield that killed a few of them and wounded the rest ... "

"How cud I fergit?" whispered Kelly sadly. "I see their faces every day."

"But yew did the right thing," persisted Wilson.

"Left them to be burnt alive?"

Wilson grabbed him roughly by the shoulders.

"Yew left them in a field ambulance. The Gerries were hard on our tails an' the lads were in no condition to move. Yew did the right thing. Yew weren't to know the battalion on our tails consisted of Nazi stormtroopers."

"Dirty bastards torched the ambulance," remembered Kelly. "I hear them screamin' every night."

"Yew've gat till forget it, Billy," shouted Wilson with more conviction than he felt. "The war's bin over for years."

Kelly looked at him sadly.

"Nat in my head it's nat."

His eyes locked with his companion.

"Don't tell me it doesn't affect yew?"

"It does," agreed Wilson. "The sheer horror of it won't go away overnight. We did some terrible things in order to stop the Nazi war machine."

Kelly held his head in his hands. "I kin agree till that up to a point. I didn't like killin' the Gerries, especially up close when yew cud see the horror in their eyes. But that doesn't annoy me. It's the thought of our lads roasting like them chickens we stole off the oul girl. Only the chickens were dead when we roasted them."

Wilson sighed.

"They were my comrades too," he murmured, lowering his head.

Kelly nodded sadly. Both men had tears in their eyes.

"How are yew gonna explain yewr absence?" asked Kelly after a long silence.

"I'm nat," replied Wilson. "We're packed an' ready for tomorrow's Liverpool steamer."

Kelly dug into his trouser pocket and brought out a crumpled piece of paper.

"I gat a letter too," he whispered wryly, handing it to his friend.

After reading it, Wilson turned to him.

"Do it, Billy," he cried earnestly. "They're givin' yew a chance to return with honour. They're only defendin' what they believe in. It isn't a crime to fight for what yew believe. Write the letter an' end it fer yewrself an' yewr da. Let whatever reds are left take care of themselves. Anymore a that whiskey goin'?" he added with a smile and a friendly nudge that caused Kelly to lean over and embrace him warmly.

An hour later he rose from his chair and staggered across the room. Kelly grabbed him before he fell.

"C'mon an' I'll git yew home," he grinned as Wilson's eyes danced in his head.

"I fergat till give yew a message from wee Harvey. He said till tell yew if yew do what he says, he'll do what yew say." Wilson cocked his head and stared blankly. "Does that make any sense till yew?" he croaked before collapsing in Kelly's arms.

Stooping, his companion hoisted him onto his shoulders and walked down the hall and into the street, ignoring the curious looks of passers-by as he carried his friend to his home in Spenser Street.

Helen Wilson looked on in disbelief as Kelly laid her ashen faced husband gently on the sofa. He grinned apologetically at her.

"Don't be too hard on him, Helen. He's fulla whiskey. He tole me a few home truths an' brought me outa the wilderness of depression, an' I'm a better man for it."

She moved forward and embraced him.

"Thank God, Billy. He wanted yewr blessin' before he did anything. I hope fer the sake of me and the children yew gave it," she added anxiously.

"Absolutely," replied Kelly, as he made for the door.

"Well, in that case," smiled Helen, steering him towards a seat, "wud yew join me in a wee celebration before yew go? I've a bottle a whiskey that's bin lyin' in that cupboard since the pope wus an altar boy. Would yew have a wee glass wid me?"

"Wud a cat lick milk?" replied her visitor with a disarming grin.

Helen Wilson looked curiously at the man opposite her. She could see why Minnie was crazy about him. The ravages of alcohol didn't seem to affect him. She looked at her sleeping husband and compared him mentally with her visitor. Sammy's hair was grey and thin. Kelly's was black and bushy and lay lank across his forehead. His grey eyes were alive and active whereas Sammy's were tired and washed out blue. Both men were around the same age, yet her husband's skin was pale and chalky, whilst Kelly's was blooming with health and vitality. His shoulders were wide ... She stopped the comparison. She loved her husband for his kindness, his thoughtfulness, his generosity. And as for drinking, Kelly probably spilt more alcohol in a day than Sammy would drink in a month. He interrupted her thoughts.

"That's the last a my squad lyin' there, Helen," he muttered affectionately. "I wud give him my last breath, an' that's a fact."

His words weren't slurred, but she knew he was drunk.

She studied him for a moment.

"How did he get that rake a bullet holes across his chest, Billy?" she asked purposefully.

Kelly thought for a moment or two.

"Funny yew shud ask that. What did he tell yew?" he asked.

Helen shrugged and smiled.

"I stapped askin' long ago, but the other day the kids walked intil the scullery an' he was stripped till the waist washin' himself. They asked him the same question an' he tole them he fell over the straw an' the hen kicked him. He niver talks about the war, Billy, but his bad dreams are comin' back agin," she said sadly.

"It'll all be history when yis git till Garston, Helen, so don't worry," he smiled bitterly as he continued, "He gat those wounds in the latter part a the war. The Normandy landin's. We went in with the first battalion till a place called Ranville. It wus quiet. We expected a welcomin' committee, but the Gerries were obviously elsewhere, thanks till our intelligence forces. We made our way to our next objective, a place called Longueval. It wasn't a doddle, but it wasn't hard. I only remember the name of the place because I should have died an' bin buried there, except for the selfless intervention of yewr husband."

He looked at Wilson with affection as he continued.

"I wus map readin' till pinpoint our location when Sammy saw a hedgerow sniper drawin' a bead. He jumped in front of me an' took the tommy gun rounds from shoulder till shoulder. Thankfully they missed his spine. His return fire killed the sniper before he hit any more of us. I'd be rottin' away under a headstone somewhere in France, had he nat put himself in harm's way.

"He returned to us when his wounds were healed an' we fought on till the war ended. Only he an' I survived from the original platoon. That's the bond, Helen. That's why I'd do anything fer him."

He smiled at her solemn face.

"Don't tell him I tole yew or he'll kill me an' there'll only be him left."

Rising, he reached her his glass.

"I've talked more about the war in the last few hours than I have in the last ten years. Why is that, Helen?" he asked tiredly.

She could see tears in his eyes, and longed to hold him and comfort him, but knew he would be shocked at such a reaction.

"I don't know, Billy. There's thousands like yew. Poor

bewildered souls. Givin' up part of yewr lives till fight for yewr country an' then cum back an' have till fight fer yewr jobs.

"My Sammy wusn't the only red-button man till fight the Germans. An' what do they git? Tossed out on their arses, wid nat a penny till their name. Jist because some a them questioned a system that is putrid and corrupt. I've had till pawn a few things till see us through these last coupla weeks."

She looked at him with panic in her eyes.

"Billy, don't tell him or he'll skin me. The only things left of value in the house are his campaign medals an' God forgive me, I came close till pawnin' them last week."

The outburst caused her to sob bitterly. Kelly put his arms around her as she fumbled for a handkerchief. He brought a wad of pound notes from his pocket and placed them in her hand. He fought her silently as she tried to return the money.

"That'll let yis arrive in style. Shure yew kin pay me back when yis are on yewr feet."

He moved towards the door.

"Y'know," he said pensively, "A lat a the blues fought in the same conflict, Helen, an' they think their rights are in peril. Besides a latta them are nat happy that the reds have been black-balled."

Helen dried her eyes.

"It's a bloody shame when men lose the right till fend for their families, an' nobody gives a damn," she continued angrily. "I'm glad yew sided wid Sammy. That means we'll be goin' where a man's talent will guarantee his job an' nat the colour of a badge in his lapel."

Wilson rolled on the sofa and began snoring loudly. They both smiled as Kelly released her gently. She looked at her husband and Kelly could see the love and affection in her eyes.

"Do yew remember that wee song he used till sing in Paddy's lounge on the odd Sarday night we'd go out together?" she whispered. Kelly looked at the floor and nodded reflectively as she began to sing softly:

They used to tell me I wus buildin' a dream,
An' so I followed the mob ...

When there wus buds to bloom, or guns to bear ...
I wus always there ... Right on the job ...
They used to tell me I wus buildin' a dream
Wid peace an' glory ahead ...
Why shud I be standin' in line
Just waitin' fer bread?

She stopped and sat on the end of the settee, smiling with affection at her sleeping husband and running her fingers through his hair.

"Keep in touch, Helen, please. I'll expect a letter as soon as youse settle in," he murmured warmly as he kissed her gently on the cheek.

"What about Minnie?" she asked as he walked down the darkened hall.

"Minnie doesn't want a drunken troublemaker," he answered sadly as he opened the door and walked out into the darkness. He was gone before she could reply.

Reaching home he sat down with a writing pad and a pen. He knew if he didn't write the letter there and then, he wouldn't do it later. He examined it thoroughly. The writing was a tifle shaky, but readable. He left it on the mantelpiece and went wearily to bed.

The next morning Jim Harvey watched as Kelly entered the schooling pen and walked slowly by the deep water gangers. Many eyes were on him as he stopped beside Sid Maxwell. They exchanged good-natured pleasantries as Kelly reached him a white envelope. They shook hands and Kelly walked up to Capper Quinn and apologised. Quinn embraced him warmly. Joining with a group of first-preference dockers in front of the foreman known as Ducksy Doyle, he smiled with embarrassment as Tasty gave him a friendly wave.

Harvey felt a surge of emotion he found hard to hide. He saw McCartan watching the proceedings with more than a little interest. Jim would miss Kelly's strong reassuring presence at his side, but knew their paths would continue to cross until he fulfilled his part of the unwritten agreement to join Sally in London. His train of thought was broken as Uncle addressed the men around him.

"Welcome till the rosy snatters boat," he growled. "Two hunnert ton at the Milewater shed an' I want outa her today: so if yew haven't the heart or the inclination fer a hard but profitable days work, fuck aff. Otherwise, c'mon ahead."

Jim was about to move out for a check when Reilly's gaunt and pain-filled features floated into his vision. He thought of the last time he'd worked at the chemical boat, and remembered how much the spell had taken out of him. He looked at the other tired and hungry faces surging forward to take job checks from the foreman's open hand, and stepped back resolutely.

Kelly had already been schooled to a soft job on the ship's deck. He smiled as Harvey walked out of the compound. The lad made his way to the chapel shed and sought out Henry. He and his brothers were standing at the checker's desk as Jim approached.

"I thought I tole yew till stan' Uncle the day. Are yew fuckin' stupid or sumptin'?"

"Mebbe he gat squeezed out," his brother Sam suggested in the lad's defence. Jim smiled shyly.

"I didn't git squeezed out. I decided I'm nat gonna kill myself like Reilly did for three poun' one an' eightpence divided five ways."

"Good on yew boy," roared Sam, flashing a defiant glance at his enraged brother.

"Yill do what I tell yew or yill nat be here," snarled Henry closing in on the lad with threatening gestures.

"That's wut I cum till tell yew. I'm finished wid the docks: I'm goin' till London," replied Jim, as the nerves in his stomach twitched.

"Is that right?" snarled Henry. "Well, away yew go! An' when yew cum back a few days later, don't be cumin' till me lukin' fer a job, and don't send yewr ma roun' till torture my ma, because yewr nat wurkin'. Yew kin go till the mill as a doffer. Yill nat be back here."

"What's takin' yew till London, son?" enquired Jack.

Jim smiled at the friendly tone of the question.

"Sally Reilly has offered me a job."

Henry felt a pang of jealousy.

"Yewr dick must be bigger than yewr brain," he snarled.

The pent-up anger in his nephew exploded at the insult. Jim clenched his right fist and it flew like a rocket to the base of Henry's jaw, sending him sprawling to the straw-covered cobbles. The onlookers waited for him to rise and tear the upstart apart. After a few seconds they realised he was out cold. Sam was overjoyed.

"I've waited a long time till see that big bastard git his come-uppance," he roared, adding for the benefit of the astonished watchers, "By one of his own like, nat by any strangers." He approached Jim with awe in his eyes. "That wus some punch kid. Yew caught him cold, but yewd best git outa here before he comes roun'."

His nephew nodded dumbly. He had thrown the punch in anger and was frightened of the consequences.

Sam seemed to read his mind.

"Go on, kid. He won't come near yew. Me an' Jack 'ill convince him he wus outa order."

His eyes danced with enjoyment as he continued, "The big bastard fancied Sally himself an' that's why he's annoyed." He put a comforting arm around the bewildered lad. "Go on home boy, an' good luck till yew. Yiv made the right decision till git outa this game. It's the road till an early arrival at the graveyard."

Jim took his advice and walked stiffly out of the potato shed. His mother hugged him tightly when he told her his plans. She watched proudly as he lifted the telephone in the hall and rang Sally Reilly. Raising her eyes to the photograph of her husband, she smiled broadly and gave a thumbs-up sign before returning happily to her knitting. When he came back to the kitchen she stared at him intently.

"Well?" she enquired.

"Sally's all delighted," he replied shyly. "She's sendin' the plane tickets the marra."

His mother smiled coyly at him.

"Plane indeed! She must be missin' yew very much," she purred, grinning at the blush on his features.

He walked into the hall to close the front door, and froze when Henry's shadow fell on him. He stepped back defensively.

"Don't worry," said the older man tersely. "I haven't cum fer a return bout. I was outa order an' yew did what any man a honour wuda did under the circumstances. I deserved it, but don't ever try it again."

Jim remained silent as he continued.

"Here's yewr pay fer last week an' a couple a poun' extra. Give yewr ma her share, an' don't fergit till send her money from London. If yew don't I'll come over there an' bate yew good-lukin'," he grinned with the attempt at humour.

Jim gasped when he promply grabbed him in a bear hug and burst into tears.

"I toul yewr ma I wud luk after yew when yewr da died," he sobbed.

Jim returned his embrace.

"Yew did, Uncle Henry," he replied not too convincingly.

Henry let him go and pulled a huge handkerchief from his pocket.

"Don't fergit what I said about yewr ma," he sobbed as he wiped the tears from his eyes and walked into the street. "One less mouth to worry about," he growled as he took a kick at a stray cat that had foolishly crossed his path.

Maxwell's glance was openly hostile as he looked around the group of stevedores gathered in Collins' office. When the door closed and the room quietened, he rose to his great height and scrutinised each face before speaking. His voice was level and controlled.

"Gentlemen: some time ago I was voted in as the chairman of the branch that services this assembly. I am now the man you have to deal with to ensure the smooth running of cargo to and from Belfast." He paused for a moment. "I'm nat gonna be like

Shaw and dazzle yew wid paperwork an' figures. All I need to tell yew is what's in here." He pointed to his head. "The past coupla months have been occupied with the so-called red-button episode. I can assure yew now, that episode has been dumped in the history bin, no matter which way the law decides. The fallout has allowed us to forget about other more important issues, such as containerisation and mechanical technology. These twin evils, an' yew would say necessary evils, are poised to tear the heart an' soul out of an industry that has remained unchanged for decades.

"We can fight progress or we can accept it. But we can't ignore it if the rest of the world chooses to use it. Therefore the answer lies in compromise."

He paused for a moment, and took a sip from a glass of water beside him. He could see he had their undivided attention, and continued.

"We are happy wid the fact that the new technology takes a lot of the hard work away. We are nat happy that it will cause redundancies among our members. The new committee has asked that any redundancies be voluntary. We would also ask that our oldest members are given an attractive package that would encourage them to leave the quay."

He paused as Collins indicated that he wanted to speak, and nodded consent.

"Providing we receive guarantees to move forward, I have no objection to our group looking into this proposal. How many men are we talking about?"

"There are precisely forty men over sixty five," replied Maxwell. "The rest of the redundancies would need to be voluntary, and carry a big enticement."

"Over sixty-five?" gasped a dark-suited grey-haired stevedore. "Surely they should be already retired?"

Maxwell looked at him with undisguised contempt.

"Our oldest member is almost ninety and he'd work yew intill the groun'," he scowled.

"Let's not git personal," intervened Collins quickly as both men glared at each other. "There are moves afoot to introduce decasualisation to Northern Ireland and I'm sure the business of arranging severance packages will be dealt with by the government of the day," he added reassuringly.

"I don't care who pays the bill as long as it's done," growled Maxwell. "New rates wud have to be struck an' new manning quotas agreed. Remember; mechanisation could treble the tonnage in an' outa the port and we want our share of the profit that will bring," he added

"That's understandable," muttered a small cloth-capped stevedore wearing a tweed jacket and smoking a pipe. "As long as your demands are reasonable."

Collins nodded.

"We are entering into a new grey area in stevedoring, which will be rewarding to all concerned. If we work together we can strike a deal that will be beneficial to all."

Maxwell nodded approvingly.

"One more thing. This upheaval will mean loss of jobs for some of our members. We propose to move into all areas of dockwork. It may take a few months or even a year. But it will happen. Therefore, any outsider or Arab or whatever you propose to call them will nat be employed in what we would term our work. They, of course, have no right to redundancy or any other monetary payments that would constitute a drain on yewr resources. We will fill the void an' no one, except those wid a vested interest in gittin' chape labour, will notice."

He paused for argument.

Collins looked at him.

"Some of those men have spent a lifetime on the quay."

"Nat my problem. If the reds kin go, so can they," replied Maxwell dismissively. "There is no outside labour directly involved with decasualisation in Britain. If yew want the scheme, yew must take the whole package. Anyway: it's no skin off yewr collective noses. The changeover will be seamless. Yew'll nat notice."

"Most of my work is done by outsiders. They've been with me for years. How can I tell them they are going to be replaced?" asked a small man, with a large carnation in his jacket lapel.

"That's your problem. Replaced they will be. As I said, the

days of chape labour on the cross channel docks are gone," replied Maxwell dismissively.

The little man rose angrily to his feet.

"They are nat chape labour. They get the goin' rate an' are the best workers on the quay, bar none. They do hard an' dirty work that yewr men will nat entertain. The end result will be the bulk of my stevedoring work going to the Irish Transport, an' that'll be me outa business." Other men around the table growled approval. Maxwell was unmoved.

He looked at Collins, and spoke to him directly, ignoring the others.

"There are far-reaching decisions to be made, an' I'm here to speak on behalf of registered dockers only. There's bound to be casualties. Yew can't cook an omelette widout breakin' the egg shells. Some of our men may have to face redundancies. I'll accept that on their behalf. But I can assure yew when that time comes there won't be an Arab wurkin' in Belfast docks. I will ignore the slur that outsiders can work better than our members an' treat it wid the contempt it deserves.

"Wid regards to the rumoured development of the port of Larne, if any of our traffic is diverted, we will be expecting our dockers to be taken there at the expense of the stevedores to service those ships. There will be no half measures on that."

He looked around the faces at the table.

"This meeting will show yew where I'm cumin' from. Meet us halfway an' we kin do business. I don't see any other alternative, because there isn't one. Double-cross us in Belfast an' our cross channel colleagues on the mainland will paralyse all shipping until the *status quo* is returned. Thank yew, gentlemen."

The response was muted but respectful. He left the room quickly and unaccompanied.

Collins looked at his colleagues with some concern.

"The king is dead. Long live the king," he muttered sarcastically. "Hard days ahead, gentlemen. It looks like both sides will need to adapt to survive," he added cheerlessly as he thought of Henry Harvey and wondered how he could break the bad news.

Kelly walked across the deck of the ship he was working on and was pleasantly surprised to see his father at the bottom of the gangplank. Both men eyed each other as he reached the shore.

"Long time since you bought me a pint, whippersnapper," his father growled with a grin on his face. They hugged each other warmly to the delight of the watching dockers.

A few moments later they were standing in the Rotterdam Bar. Joe had grinned with pleasure when the men walked in together and insisited on buying the first drink himself. Kelly senior was surprised when his son ordered a pint shandy. As the drinks were placed on the bar top his father lifted his and looked at his offspring.

"As the governor of North Carolina said to the governor of South Carolina ... "

It was a toast his father used many times and Billy joined him in the punchline.

"It's bin a long time between drinks."

They laughed happily as they moved to a table.

"Are yew gonna stay in Reilly's?" asked his father, after a few moments silence. He answered the question himself, before his son could reply.

"I think yew shud. Yew need a place of yewr own. Yew kin always call intil me for yer food, cos I generally make enuff fer two anyway."

Kelly smiled.

"That wud be good, dad."

"Yew cud also take Soldier if yew want. Or he kin stay wid me.Whatever suits yew."

Kelly looked over the pint tumbler.

"Thanks fer keeping him. He showed more gratitude than I did."

The old man waved his hand disparagingly.

"That's water below the bridge, an' we'll talk no more about it. It took a lotta guts to do what yew did, an' I won't be stintin' in my admiration fer yew. There were times when I despaired for yew: but nigh yewr back in the fold an' I hope yew stray no more."

Kelly thought of Wilson, bags packed and ready for a new life away from the docks.

"I won't, dad. And that's a promise. I've no reason till," he muttered.

His father threw back his drink and yelled with delight at the barman.

"Joe, the prodigal son has returned! Kill the fatted calf! An' if that's outa order, give everybody a drink, an' heat up two meat pies fer me an' my lad."

"Praise be to God," whispered the bar owner, crossing himself in deference.

Kelly watched as his father collected the two meat pies. He was pouring sauce onto his when the old man spoke.

"By the way, Minnie's da came roun' from the boat he wus workin' on. He says yew kin call till see her any time. She's bin brakin' her heart over yew. Said she wus goin' till run away if he didn't let her see yew. He's goin' back on the cattle run next week. He's sorry fer the altercation between yew an' him. I tole him it was as well yew respected old people, or he'd be a corpse nigh."

He fingered his pint tumbler reflectively.

"What are yew gonna do about yewr wife an' my only grandson?" he asked softly.

Kelly sighed heavily.

"I've bin givin' that more than a little thought these last few months. I'm goin' to git in touch wid a solicitor and the Rifles' Association." He looked at his wristwatch. "Minnie shud be leavin' the factory for lunch in about ten minutes. I'm headin' down till meet her ... "

The old man waved his arms.

"That's alright son. I don't wanta hear no more. I know yew'll do what's best."

Kelly's eyes filled.

"I will, dad. I will. Minnie means everythin' to me, an' I want to end my days wid her," he replied.

His father rose quickly.

"I'm away till the toilet," he scowled, moving quickly to hide the tears of joy that cascaded down his cheeks.

They saw McCartan returning to his car after a visit to a lunchtime schooling pen as they walked into Pilot Street. He reached his hand in friendship to Kelly's father, but the gesture was declined, as the old man walked on.

"I'm glad you've settled your personal differences," he said with warmth, "But the fight goes on. Nothing has changed. Justice is being turned on its head."

Kelly nodded sympathetically and patted him reassuringly on the shoulder.

"I'm outa it nigh, sir. Good luck wid yewr fight," he whispered firmly before moving swiftly in the direction of the tobacco factory.

McCartan turned up his overcoat collar and walked swiftly towards the Inside Inn. He studied the legend printed above the public house door, as he unlocked his car.

'I often wonder what the vintner buys

Half as precious as the goods he sells.'

The maxim was attributed to the Persian poet Omar Khayyam. The law lecturer shook his head wearily and wished the answer to his problem was as simple, as he drove to his office at Queen's University. Another quotation from Khayyam came to his tired mind. He pursed his lips as he silently mouthed the words ...

The moving finger writes; and, having writ,
Moves on: nor all your piety nor wit
Shall lure it back to cancel half a line,
Nor all your tears wash out a word of it.

Sighing heavily, he accelerated and passed a group of men walking listlessly from the schooling pen. The stoop of their shoulders and downcast eyes only made him more determined to see justice done.

Kelly studied the sea of emerald green smocks and tan overalls as the Gallaher workers rushed home for their midday break.

He quickly positioned himself at the corner of Henry Street. Minnie emerged from the crowd and rushed towards him, arms outstretched. Her eyes were filled with tears of joy as he grabbed her and held her tightly. He couldn't resist the impulse to kiss her, and the passing girls roared their approval.

"I'm gonna set the wheels in motion," he whispered gently, "an' yewr gonna be the next an' last Mrs. William Kelly ... "

He hesitated, before adding, "That's if yew'll have me."

She looked at his mischievous grin, and sobbing with delight, nodded agreement.

He returned to the ship ahead of the rest of the gang. Leaning on the waterside rail he gazed into the dark murky waters for a long moment or two before pulling the loaded Walther pistol from his inside jacket pocket. The weapon fitted snugly into his outstretched palm, where it lay hidden from intrusive eyes. As always, when he handled the gun, a vision of the mutilated features of the German soldier he took it from floated across his mind. This time he didn't dismiss the image and studied it astutely, as if trying to absolve himself and free the anguished soul of the long dead officer whose reflection now stared up at him from the glassy surface of the lough. Leaning over the ship's side, he dropped the weapon. The torn and tortured face of the dead warrior rippled to nothingness as the pistol sunk slowly to the bottom of the Clarendon Dock.

"My war's over, so is yewrs," he muttered softly and sadly, as he watched the waves lap lazily against the hull of the ship.

Epilogue

The following is a brief account of the court case which began in the Belfast High Court in February 1962. It is gleaned from the daily reports in the Belfast Telegraph. The full story of the court case can be found in the Belfast morning and evening papers dated from 20th February to the 3rd March 1962.

Mr. McGonigal who represented the defendants told the jury that they should not consider whether the system on Belfast Docks was just or unjust. The union could not hope to control itself centrally and the branch system was introduced to look after the trade and industry its members were engaged in. Therefore, the branch was responsible for the control and discipline of its members.

Summing up for the plaintiffs, Mr. Harrison said it was the 11/10 docks branch that operated and controlled the recruitment of labour. There was always anger and disquiet among second-preference dockers when sons and relatives of the first-preference became dockers.

In his summing up of the case on Friday, 2nd March 1962, Mr. Justice Sheil repeated the evidence previously given. He stated: 'The truth from the evidence is that the organisation of the system was something entirely outside the union. The branch was eager to help in the war effort, but cautious of overflowing its labour force. The recruitment of second preference was a good idea that sorted out many problems. One thing it did not address was the fact that the red-button section had no input to the senior branch and was out on a limb as far as the affairs of the branch was concerned. This would come to a head when the rules of the union were breached or broken.'

After an absence of some two hour the jury found in favour of two red-button men and the two union officials were guilty of conspiring to injure the plaintiffs in denying and hampering their efforts to seek work on the Cross Channel Docks. They also found that the AT&GWU had no case to answer.

It was stressed that there was very little chance of the two red-button men ever becoming first-preference-dockers as they were not the sons or near relatives of dockers. There was also little chance of getting their paybooks back.

A few days later, on the 25th March 1962, the second-preference system was abolished. From that day onwards there would be only one preference on the Cross Channel Docks.